ALL MEN
ARE CREATED
... AN AMERICAN STORY

Sparta Territory: The Beginning

CHRISTOPHER "CHRIS" NUELS

ARCHWAY
PUBLISHING

Archway Publishing books may be ordered through booksellers or by contacting:

Archway Publishing
1663 Liberty Drive
Bloomington, IN 47403
www.archwaypublishing.com
844-669-3957

ISBN: 978-1-6657-1095-4 (sc)
ISBN: 978-1-6657-1093-0 (hc)
ISBN: 978-1-6657-1094-7 (e)

Library of Congress Control Number: 2021916451

Print information available on the last page.

Archway Publishing rev. date: 08/30/2021

CONTENTS

PART ONE

For my late grandmother and mother, my heart and soul.

PART ONE

PART ONE

ONE

The Battle

CAPTAIN ROBERT VETTER lay in silence on the cold, wet ground. He made sure to keep his silhouette low so he wouldn't highlight himself in the predawn light. An early-morning mist lay heavy above the leafless trees and obscured the Confederate camp below. The upcoming sunrise made the valley glow with a mystical light created by the mist and sun fighting for supremacy. The battle between the mist and sun was a precursor to the violence planned on this mystical morning.

He peered out over the valley below and could barely discern faint, flickering gray bodies moving through the sparsely grown forest. Farther ahead from the gray wraiths, a few dim campfire lights could barely be discerned. Captain Vetter knew the lights were from the remaining camp fires from the previous night's meals.

Based on his reconnaissance of the camp from the previous day, he knew the Confederate camp slept under very light security measures. They believed the closest Union troops were two-hundred-plus miles away. They were correct in believing the closest Union troops were some distance away; their comfort in that fact had been the exact reason his special unit was created—to sow fear and discord among the Confederate troops in an effort to dissuade them from fighting the Union troops. For this purpose, they were unlike any force ever created. However, he knew that regardless of how special a unit was, the difference between success and failure often had nothing to do with anything they had been trained to do. For this mission, he knew real success depended on complete secrecy and surprise before the attack.

His orders were to find targets of opportunity and create as much fear and turmoil in the Confederate ranks as possible. He knew there would probably be a major battle in the area, but he wasn't privy to any such plans. The early-morning attack had been planned well, and he knew that in a very short time, the mystical quality of the valley would be violated by very stealthy, focused, and otherworldly violence. He knew this because he was the coordinator of the unfolding plans and that his unique crew of men provided the executioners.

The war had to end; so many people had died, and the Union was in jeopardy of breaking up. General Lee was on the run and needed to get back to his supply base. With the losses in Atlanta by General Sherman and victories in the Shenandoah Valley, the mood in the Union army was that the Confederates were ready to give up. His small unit was already a year in operation, and the new tactics it utilized had been devised to try to speed up the war's end. He would make sure he did his part to save the Union.

TWO

Amra

AMRA PEEKED OUT of the branches and tree limbs he used as cover. He squinted so the whites of his eyeballs wouldn't give away his position. Earlier reconnaissance had identified a token security picket of four Confederate soldiers in the area, and he was about to enter the camp. Sloping down about fifty feet in from his position, he could see and smell the tobacco smoke that emanated from two of the guards. The other two were leaning against a tree, not moving, possibly asleep. The scrub would cover him all the way to the soldiers. It didn't matter to Amra. Life would quickly be over for them.

Over his issued uniform of wool trousers and blue shirt, he had draped burlap bags to distort his image. He had learned this tactic as a boy when hunting kob antelope in southwest Africa, and he had incorporated it as a tactic. The use of cover and concealment by any soldier in this war was considered cowardly and dishonorable. Men walked into battle shoulder to shoulder and died honorably.

His unit of irregulars—or the "freedom unit," as they called themselves—was far from a group of ordinary soldiers. The majority were former slaves intermixed with Southern white men. Most of the white men had been prisoners of the Confederate army and released by Union troops. Instead of choosing freedom, a few had asked to fight with the Union army to get revenge against the Confederacy.

———

Union soldiers had freed Amra almost two years ago. He had volunteered to join the army because he was a warrior and didn't like working the land. Before being captured, he had been the prince of his village, and he had four brothers. His village had been known for its hunting prowess. They had grown powerful by trading the meat they hunted with other tribes throughout the land. He relished the idea of fighting back against the people who had brought Amra to this country in chains. Also, the opportunity to learn more about the new land where he lived was overwhelming.

Amra's six-foot, six-inch frame and muscular features made him an anomaly among slaves. His back was straight, his gaze true, and he had to look down on most people. When he had been a slave, he had always been heavily chained and repeatedly beaten. White men didn't like any slave looking them in the eye without fear. Because of his size, his former masters used him as a stud to impregnate female slaves. Just like breeding horses and cows for superior stock, they wanted to breed Amra to get a superior stock of slaves to work the fields.

The first time he was given to a woman to breed with, he refused. As a result, the owner whipped him until the blood from his back soaked the ground. It took him nearly two months to recover from the beating and be able to stand again. The next time he was given to a woman to breed with, he refused again;

this time the owner beat the woman in front of him and afterward cauterized her wounds with hot irons for his disobedience. To Amra, this kind of cruelty to women was unheard of.

He didn't understand what the woman was saying during the beatings and subsequent burnings, but he promised he wouldn't be the cause of more of that type of anguish again. He could still remember her screams and the blood coming out of her eyes from the brutal beating.

He spent six years as a stud and had over thirty-five children. He kept track of all the women he impregnated and the children they birthed. A few weeks after the birth of the child, both the mother and the child were sold. He knew this only because the new owners would come and inspect him to see what kind of investment they were making. He wasn't able to see any of his children. The owner didn't want him to develop any fatherly connection with the children. In his home country, Kushite warriors honored their children and family above anything else. No physical pain compared to the loss of his progeny. It was the greatest disgrace for a child to grow up and not know his or her ancestry. He was a Kushite warrior from a noble family and could trace his lineage all the way back to the rulers of Egypt.

When the Union army attacked the plantation where he lived, Amra quickly realized he had an opportunity to get back at the master who had cost him his freedom. When the Union soldiers walked into the master's house, they found Amra with the lifeless master in his hands, the master's head completely turned around and his eyes looking back over his backside. Amra had snapped the master's neck with his bare hands. Amra expected to die, and he was prepared to die for killing his former master. Instead of death, the Union soldiers offered him a chance to get revenge on the Southerners who had perpetuated slavery and the men who had fought to preserve it.

At first, Amra was a little reluctant; he just wanted to go

home. However, his warrior blood demanded that he learn the enemy's way of fighting. If he was ever to be free, he would take the lessons he had learned back home and ensure that the white man would never subjugate his people again. His early attempts at being a normal soldier and walking into battle side by side didn't fit well with him. He didn't understand why the soldiers walked blindly into enemy fire. He knew that by using the techniques of war he had been taught in Africa, he could destroy more of the enemy and risk fewer Union lives.

His superiors quickly noticed his refusal to fight like a normal soldier and his late-night and early-morning forays into enemy camps. Instead of punishing him for his disobedience, they moved him to a different unit. His new unit was very interested in learning his way of fighting. How to use stealth and the land to defeat the enemy was the Kushite way of war. However, the way they applied his techniques wasn't honorable; their missions were violent, horrible, and meant to put fear in the Confederate soldiers. They dismembered and desecrated the bodies of Confederates in hopes of destroying their morale. The methods were totally deplorable to his Kushite sense of honor, but the choice was either them or him. He wanted to live, return home, and maybe even find some of his children and teach them the Kushite way.

All this passed through Amra's mind as he crawled toward the encampment below. He had strapped his bayonet knife to his side and his khopesh to his back. He'd had the unit armorer create the khopesh. It was a great weapon for the slaughter he was about to inflict. With his eyes focused on the four sentries immediately in front of him and violence on his mind, Amra unstrapped the khopesh and pulled his bayonet free. With the silence of a large predator about to kill, four men would soon become none.

THREE

Fieldhand

FIELDHAND OBSERVED THE ambush site with anticipation. Some people called him a crazy man and a murderer. He relished the blood of the Confederate soldiers and the Negroes who had helped them. They were all his enemy. Every throat he cut, arm he chopped off, and manhood he dismembered was another swipe at the evil men who had destroyed his life and the people he loved. He would go to whatever depths of depravity his leader wanted. He was usually the one who killed the kids and wives, butchered the dogs, or slit an old woman's throat. If there was grisly work to be done, Fieldhand would get it done. Who better to do an honest day's work than a "field hand"?

He had been born a slave, and the story goes that when the master realized he was a baby boy, he called him Fieldhand. His mother, fifteen months off the boat and still speaking mostly African dialect, didn't understand what the master meant and took to calling the boy Fieldhand. The name stuck with him his whole life, and everybody seemed comfortable with it. His father, whom he had known until he was about six years old, had gotten sold off; his name was Luke. In secret he called himself Little Luke; the only people who knew or called him by that name were all dead in one night of blood and fire.

At fifteen he was allowed to get married to another slave named Wanda. She was older than him by ten years but still considered old enough to bear children. By the time Fieldhand was married to Wanda, she had already birthed four children, and all them except her youngest daughter were sold into slavery to other plantations. Wanda was a good woman resigned to her fate and didn't have much to say about being married to a younger man. Over time they became close, and he came to love the little daughter, Cassia, as if she were his own. They had another daughter, Tarrie, three years into their marriage, whom they were allowed to keep.

Life was hard for slaves; they woke up before dawn to work in the fields and didn't stop until right after sunset. He was a hard worker, a good provider for his little family, and he was basically content. The master usually left alone slaves who worked hard, followed the rules, and didn't make a fuss.

After the summer crops were harvested, the slaves were allowed to have a fall festival celebration to recognize the hard work they had put into the season. This was probably the only time that offered slaves a little chance at happiness; it was also a time when slaves were allowed to marry. Fieldhand's youngest daughter, Tarrie, was ten years old, and she was excited about this year's celebration. This was the last year she would be considered a child, and she would be forced to work in the fields with her parents. She would start to be considered a young woman. She already showed the promise of being as beautiful as her older sister, Cassia.

Her mother had gotten scraps of fabric from a house slave and had made Tarrie a beautiful dress. Even though it was made out of rags, the dress was hers, and it was the most wonderful thing she had ever seen. Fieldhand remembered seeing Tarrie that morning in her dress. He had never felt proud about anything before, but seeing his and Wanda's creation, he thought she was the most beautiful thing in the world. When you were a slave, your family members could be sold off at any time. He felt a sense of pride in his young daughter; he loved her older sister, Cassia, but this was his true-blooded daughter. The sun was shining, and she seemed to glow in the sunlight as she twirled around in her dress. Fieldhand always tried to keep this image of her in his mind, but it would always be smothered by the other images of the fateful night when she died.

On the day of the fall festival, celebrations started right after noon. The slaves were allowed to come out of the field early after being in the fields since before dawn. Most of the cooking had been completed the night before, so the food was laid out: pies, meats, vegetables, and cakes. All the food they would see in a year's time was accumulated in a single day. It was a wondrous occasion, and all the slaves were excited. The music started, and all of them danced a jig, displaying their skills at keeping pace with the music. The strong African heritage was evident in the music and dancing. This was also the time when slaves who had received permission could marry; weddings were performed en masse and concluded with a mass jumping of the broom.

Fieldhand could play the bongos but played only during special occasions. He had learned when he was a child that most white people became a little afraid when slaves played the bongos. One master even believed the slaves were trying to have some special talk through bongos. His mother had taught him the special talk of bongos; if the master had known the truth, he would have destroyed all the drums. When he played the bongos during special occasions, he told those who understood to be strong, to love their family; one day they would have freedom. He tried to put hope into his drums.

At night when all the festivities were complete, the new couples retired to their new places as husbands and wives. The unmarried young ladies and men were ushered away and closely watched, but of course there were always a few who went unnoticed.

The master's young son, Jeremiah, and his friends joined the party tonight. This was the first time young Jeremiah had been allowed out as a man. Jeremiah had just celebrated his fourteenth birthday; being a man, in his eyes, was already a foregone conclusion. He had all the confidence and arrogance of a Southern aristocrat and a little size to help support his claim. He had always been an ornery kid, finding pleasure in the abuse of others.

Fieldhand was a little concerned to see young Jeremiah; he was near the same age as Cassia. Everyone knew that when he decided, he wanted to have Cassia; the only thing that could keep him away was his father. Though Cassia was only thirteen, she was well developed because of the hard work in the fields; she seemed a lot older than her young age. Her African heritage was evident in her jet-black skin, and her body had the curves of a young woman. She would be a very beautiful woman, and the master already had plans to sell her. Fieldhand had hoped the master's desire to sell her would keep her safe until she was sold.

Fieldhand didn't know Cassia and been flirting with young Master Jeremiah for a while. He had noticed her when came to the house to deliver a message for one of the overseers. After that, young Jeremiah had brought young Cassia a few sweets and mentioned to her that she was too pretty to be in the fields and should work at the big house. Cassia was a very simple but lovely girl, and all this seemed big in her life. Working at the big house in clean clothes with access to food all the time seemed like a great idea compared to working in the fields.

Unbeknownst to Fieldhand, young Jeremiah had enticed

Cassia to meet him by the creek on the night of the festival. Young Jeremiah told Cassia he wanted to talk about her working at the house and give her a gift. Of course, Cassia couldn't keep any secrets from her little sister, Tarrie, and she didn't know Tarrie had followed her into the night to meet Jeremiah.

After the celebrations, Fieldhand played the bongos for a few more hours for some of the remaining revelers. Finally, after the remaining musicians retired, Fieldhand went home. Wanda asked him where Cassia and Tarrie were, and he told her he had thought they were already home. It was then that he realized that both of his daughters were still out.

Fieldhand felt a cold wave of panic take over him. The fact that his two girls were missing couldn't bode well for either. It was late, and he knew nothing good could come of two young slave women being out at night by themselves.

Fieldhand went from cabin to cabin, asking about the whereabouts of his daughters. Nobody had seen them together, but one woman had seen little Tarrie headed toward the creek area. Fieldhand immediately took off toward the creek, heart beating, a dread coming over him. Tarrie couldn't swim, so if she fell into the water, she would drown. There were also wild animals in the forest, and they would see young Tarrie as a small animal and a possible meal. Fieldhand hurried to save his daughter; he would have to find Cassia later. After coming out of the woods and entering the clearing near the creek, Fieldhand felt like he had just entered the gates of hell.

They had set up a large bonfire by the creek, and there was a group of young whites with Master Jeremiah. Along with the whites, there were two slave hands, who were overseers for the master. They were all gathered in front of the bonfire. Fieldhand could see bottles of wine in a few members' hands. Whatever they were doing, they were packed around, and Fieldhand could get a good glance at what had their attention.

Fieldhand moved silently through the forest to get a better look. His dread for his missing daughters became a physical pressure in his chest.

He worked his way around, almost near the water's edge, but a little farther down from the group.

Fieldhand was finally able to get a good glimpse of what had the men so mesmerized and excited. He zeroed in and was witness to the most horrendous and shocking scenes in his life. He could see the edges of a torn cloth or blanket laid out on the ground. He caught a quick glimpse of what appeared to be his daughter Cassia lying on the ground. The boys were surrounding her, hooting and hollering in their drunken revelry, preventing Fieldhand from seeing what they were doing. She screamed her voice raw due to some unimaginable pain he couldn't see. The noise pierced him to his heart and soul at the same time.

There was a slight pause in all the noise the boys were making, and Fieldhand hoped that whatever cruel game they were playing on his daughter had stopped. His hopes were dashed by Cassia's next scream of agony, which seemed to ignite the excitement of the boys, because they grew louder in their celebrations.

Fieldhand had enough and burst on the scene, screaming for them to get off his daughter. The second overseer saw Fieldhand come out of the wood line; he aimed his rifle at Fieldhand and told him to stop. Fieldhand stopped about ten paces from the group of men, and everything got quiet. He still couldn't see his daughter, but she had stopped screaming when her father jumped out of the woods toward the young men. Young master Jeremiah stepped forth and drunkenly said, "Hold up right there, nigger. We are celebrating the harvest. Why do you want to interrupt us?"

The other boys laughed at his joke. He continued, "Just gone off now. We will be done celebrating. Yer youngins will be turned back to you when we are done. Hell, a father should be proud that a white man is blessing his daughter with this special attention."

To emphasize his point, he looked around at his small group of friends and asked, "Who's next?"

A young man, a little older than the others, stepped up and walked toward the group of boys. Fieldhand still couldn't see what was going on but knew his daughter was being hurt. It wasn't long before another loud scream from her ignited the excitement of the boys, because they started hooting and hollering again.

Fieldhand couldn't stand anymore; he lunged for the boy, but another boy got in his way. Fieldhand hit him with a meaty right hook on the side of the head.

All the years of working in the fields had made Fieldhand strong, and the hit was infused with all the fury only a father could possess upon seeing someone trying to abuse his daughter. The punch connected to the back of the boy's head; there was an "oof" sound, and he fell over, his legs twitching. Before Fieldhand could get any closer to Cassia, he felt pain explode in his head.

When Fieldhand came to, he sat on the ground with his back against a tree. He was tied up around the waist and around his feet. He felt bruises on his face and was having issues breathing; he could have broken a rib. One of the black overseers stood next to him with a gun at the ready. All the boys were standing around the boy Fieldhand had hit; the boy still lay on the ground, unmoving.

Young Master Jeremiah was on his knees next to the young man and had his hand over the boy's face, checking for breathing. He stood up and looked at Fieldhand. "Nigger, you will hang for killing this man."

Fieldhand noted that Cassia was sitting up while restrained by two boys; her dress was tattered and worn, but at least she wasn't screaming anymore. Master Jeremiah, his golden-blond hair highlighted by the fire, had a sneer on his face. He walked over to Cassia and pulled a knife out from his belt. He looked at Fieldhand and said, "Before you die, you and all niggers will know that if you kill a white person, your whole family will suffer." He pulled his knife out and cut across Cassia's throat; hot blood spurted on Fieldhand's face and body. Fieldhand watched his daughter's life leave her eyes and slumped to his knees in pain.

Almost forgotten in all the drama was young Tarrie, whom one of the overseers still held. The overseer asked Master Jeremiah what he should do with her. Master Jeremiah told one of the other white boys to move Cassia's dead body out of the way and to bring Tarrie over.

Fieldhand grabbed Jeremiah's legs and started begging the master not to do anything to Tarrie. Master Jeremiah looked down at Fieldhand and said, "What do you think I am? Some sort of monster." He looked at Tarrie, then beckoned one of his friends over and said, "As a celebratory gift for harvest, I am giving you this young nigger slave girl for your own. When you leave here tonight, I don't ever want to see here again."

Watching his older daughter get murdered in front of him and his little Tarrie being given away as punishment must have snapped something inside Fieldhand; his whole world went red.

When Fieldhand came to, he could see the sun peeking through the branches of the trees above him. He was on his back, and his whole body ached. He suddenly remembered the events from last night and immediately sat up. The scene that met him was something he had seen only before in a butcher's shop.

There was blood everywhere, on the plants and in the dirt. Body parts were strewn all over the area where Cassia had been beaten and abused. Some of the bodies were just torsos with limbs, no heads. Master Jeremiah's body, or what was left of it, lay face up in the early-morning sun. His face was frozen in a horrible look of agony. A black arm from one of the overseers protruded from his stomach. Fieldhand counted the torsos and body parts of the six white men and two black guards involved in last night's terror.

Fieldhand noticed that Cassia's body had been clothed and placed on her back with her hands folded. Her look was serene, if not for the gash under her chin where Master Jeremiah had cut her throat.

He heard a whimper over by the tree where he had been tied up and immediately thought of young Tarrie. He jumped up and ran over to the tree. The ropes used to hold Fieldhand looked as if they had been ripped apart, not cut. Young Tarrie was lying down and had gathered her torn dress over her. She moved a little stiffly, and Fieldhand felt an enormous joy that at least one of his daughters was alive. He reached over to shake her awake, and she opened her eyes. When she looked at him, she let out a wail, like someone had poured hot water on her. She immediately started to scoot away from him. Fieldhand started to speak soothing words to her to let her know it was okay.

Tarrie started whimpering, "Devil" and "Demon."

It was then that Fieldhand looked down at himself and realized he was completely covered in blood. There wasn't a place on him that didn't have dark spots of dried-up blood. He could only imagine what his face and hair must look like with all the blood on him. He told Tarrie it was okay and that he was going to the river to wash the blood off.

He walked over to the river, stepped in up to his waist, and started washing the blood from him. He was at it for about five minutes before he thought he had done enough to seem presentable to Tarrie. He stepped out of the water and walked over to where he had left her. To his utter horror, she was gone. Fieldhand looked around and could only guess that she had gone back home. Fieldhand set off after her.

It was the day after the celebration; the slaves had the day off, and nobody was up when little Tarrie ran through the dirt road back to her slave shack. Fieldhand had almost caught up to her before she hit the open area where the slaves lived. Instead of following her into the open, he decided to use the woods and make his way to the back of his house. The fact that there were six dead young white men wouldn't go unnoticed very long, and the first people to blame would be the slaves.

Fieldhand quietly made it to the house, and he could hear Tarrie inside crying and telling her mom that the devil had taken over her daddy, who had killed Master Jeremiah and his friends for what they had done to Cassia. She said her daddy had turned red like the real devil and had taken apart the young boys.

As Tarrie explained the events of the night, Fieldhand couldn't help but listen to the monstrous acts he had committed after seeing his youngest daughter being violated. He started to wonder whether he had really been possessed because he couldn't remember any of it. He told himself he could have never in his right mind done the things Tarrie explained to her mother. Fieldhand was brought out of his thoughts by what his daughter said he had done to Master Jeremiah. She said the "devil" had taken time to kill Master Jeremiah and that she had never heard a white man scream and cry so loud in her whole life. She said the devil kept saying over and over again, "What do you think I am? Some sort of monster?"

She said the devil had cut off the man parts of the slave overseer who had hurt her and stuck them in Master Jeremiah's mouth to keep him quiet. Tarrie went on to describe how the devil had gone to each body and cut it apart. Tarrie said she had never seen so much blood in her young life. At that moment, Fieldhand opened the door and let himself into the house. His daughter immediately grabbed her mother; his wife looked at him with a little apprehension and relief at the same time. The events from the previous night and the sight of his family again overwhelmed Fieldhand, and he started crying as he explained to his wife everything that had happened.

Those harrowing events were a little over five years in the past. Since then Fieldhand had become a fugitive and eventually a soldier in the Union army. He had run away that same morning and had had no contact with his wife or Tarrie since then. He prayed every night that they were safe.

Since becoming a soldier and fighting in the war, he had witnessed deeds more horrific than the one that had set him off. Some of the acts had been done for the good of the country, and a lot had been done against the people of the country. He didn't relish the opportunity to do horrific deeds on young white and black men who fought for the Confederates. However, he knew everyone he killed would be one less rapist and abuser who could visit the same atrocities on other children, black or white. The blood was shed in honor of his dead daughter and all daughters brutalized by slave masters and their ilk. He would continue to collect the blood debt due to him and his family until he died! The unsuspecting rebel soldiers in the valley below would suit his needs well.

FOUR

Fessa

FESSA WASN'T PART of the upcoming attack on the Confederate camp below. He was lying next to Captain Vetter and knew the plan of battle as intimately as the captain. He could read and write and was very adept at handling all the duties associated with an aide de camp for a general officer. He handled everything for Captain Vetter and knew the plane of attack more intimately than any other soldier. His ability to read and his education made him perfect for the messenger's corps. His extensive historical background gave him unique insight into the war being fought for the soul of America, which most black men didn't understand. His fascination with war throughout the ages and the changes war had brought on the world made him wonder how this guerilla warfare would be perceived in the history books at a time when fighting out of the shadows was considered cowardly.

As Captain Vetter's aide, Fieldhand was privy to all the planning sessions and talks of tactic and politics. Captain Vetter had told him he was unlike any other Negro he had met; he was educated. He was probably more educated than the man he was following, but the true depth of his knowledge had to be a secret; otherwise, it could become a problem. To most of the other senior military leaders, he was like a fly on the wall—of no value and tolerated as long as it didn't make any noise. Even though he was on the side fighting to end slavery, he was still considered the lowest form of a man by his so-called saviors. His feigned ignorance gave the white men free rein to discuss anything and everything—from politics and weaponry to the plight of the Negro after the war. He learned that the leadership really didn't care whether slaves were free; most could never see them as equals. They were concerned only with saving the Union and ending the rebellion. If they could stop the rebellion and keep slaves, they would do so. Fessa listened, learned, and absorbed everything said. He couldn't speak to anyone about what he had learned, not even fellow Negro soldiers. He had learned a long time ago that both white men and black men feared his education and knowledge, and those had gotten him into the situation he was in now. He remembered well.

The angry storm outside the eastern part of Pittsburgh was a sign that the world wasn't happy in the place where it found itself. Professor Ian B. Phoenix pondered this as he studied the earliest documentation of the American settlers. He was attempting to consolidate the few writings by the original American settlers and give an accurate account of their experiences. Good or bad, he wanted to portray what it had really been like for the original Americans, the Indians. The thunder and lightning in the background were a fair representation of his feelings on the whole subject. His portrayal of the pre-American Indians would go against the current belief that early Americans were peace-loving and God-fearing people. The actual truth was bloody and sometimes cruel in the name of survival.

The "gong!" of the recently installed doorbell in the old building woke the professor from his contemplations. He was the only one in the building, and he immediately rose to find out who would be attempting to enter the library this late in the evening. He looked at the clock on the wall; it was 3:16 a.m. Where had the time gone?

Opening one of the ancient doors to the old library building required a little bit of effort from the aging educator. Once the door was open, he realized there was no one at the door. He walked out the door to see whether there was anyone who could have possibly stepped back after ringing the doorbell. To his dismay, there was no one around.

He didn't stay long because of the hard-falling rain. He turned around to walk back inside and noticed the basket in front of the unopened door. He reached down, looked inside, and noticed there was a baby inside. A quick inspection revealed a small black child. Professor Phoenix picked up the basket and looked around one last time to see whether the owner of the basket was still around. There was no one to be seen. His first concern was to get the child out of the wet and stormy weather.

Fessor had always heard this story of his beginnings. Professor Phoenix had taken him, named him Plato, and raised him as his son—not as a slave but as a free child and the only "living son" the professor ever knew. He was raised with an education that far exceeded any black man and most white children of the time. He excelled at all subjects and even showed signs of genius. He had an exceptional natural capacity for intellect. Young Plato was an avid learner and had even challenged the professor's knowledge of world history. Evidence of Plato's intelligence was put on display when the professor told Plato that one day he would be a free man just like him. Due to the professor's teachings, Plato had a very good understanding of the plight of the African American and, more importantly, how different he was compared to the norm.

Young Plato responded, "If all men were created equal, then why am I not born to freedom like the white man is? Why do I have to wait to be free one day?"

The day after his fifteenth birthday, Professor Phoenix informed Plato that they would host a very prominent senator from the Southern delegation of the proposed Confederacy. Plato was told he was to be on his best behavior and answer all the senator's questions honestly. At the time, Plato didn't understand why this was so important to the professor, but he would comply because he loved the old man like the father he never had.

Plato was upstairs in his room, reading the last pages on the history of the Spartan race. He was totally impressed by the Spartan society and that such a small country had survived in some very tumultuous times. Dame Angela came to his door and said Professor Phoenix was ready for him to come downstairs and meet Senator Clement Jackall of South Carolina, a prominent Southern politician and slave owner.

Tonight Professor Phoenix would prove to Senator Jackall that Negros could be equal citizens with the right education and opportunity. Plato would show this senator that any man with an education could rise and become a contributing citizen and didn't need to be treated as chattel or livestock. In Plato he would show an educated and cultured Negro was equal to any educated white man.

The professor watched Plato walk down the stairs and was very proud of his adopted son. Plato personified education, intelligence, and culture. His clothes were simple but elegantly cut. He walked down the stairs with an air of confidence and arrogance not seen by the Negro race. In all aspects, save his color, he was a gentleman and the definition of a man.

It was hard to discern Senator Jackall's reaction to Plato

walking down the stairs. He watched him with a stare of aloofness, but at the same time, he was alert like a predator in waiting. Plato was introduced to Senator Jackall as Professor Phoenix's adopted son. Plato put his hand out for a handshake, and Senator Jackall firmly grasped his hand and let go.

After introductions they sat down to eat a delicious dinner of large lobster tails, shrimp, and various other seafood selections, Plato's favorite foods. Senator Jackall asked for a wet towel to wash his hands. He stated that where he was from, it was good practice to wash one's hands after touching niggers; they carried some of the worst afflictions, he said. Plato was immediately taken aback by this statement; he had never been called a nigger in his whole life and looked at his adoptive father for guidance. Professor Phoenix just looked at Plato with a knowing smile that told him, "It's okay. Just words." After wiping his hands clean, Senator Jackall started the conversation by asking Plato whether he thought he was better or equal to a white man.

Plato had often thought about this same question, because he knew he was smarter than most men, including whites, simply because of his education. But he had always come back to the simple reality that without his education, he wasn't much of a man. The education Professor Phoenix exposed him to made him a worldly man; he knew the politics of great nations in detail, including the reasons for wars and the inherent nature of man to conquer and want to be in control of all his surroundings, including anyone he felt was inferior.

Drawing up his courage with the comfort of his adoptive father beside him, Plato told Senator Jackall he was neither equal nor better than a white man but that he was a man. He further explained this by stating he knew that in comparison to his brothers and sisters in bondage in the South who hadn't had the introduction to education and the ways of the world, he had extensive knowledge of both, and his skin tone didn't make a difference in his capacity to learn. Through his knowledge of history, he had learned that a man should be judged by his actions, or lack of them, as they relate to his contributions to society. Plato finished his statement by saying that to judge a man simply by his color was a conservative view of the human race as a whole.

Senator Jackall gave a small smile and told Plato that was well said, that he had never heard a nigger talk the way he did. He complimented Professor Phoenix on his education of Plato and told the professor he had also witnessed a circus, in which they had taught the little chimpanzees how to respond to sign language. He also stated that Plato was a good representation of his race and that maybe in two or three hundred years, all niggers would be able to learn the way Plato had. Based on his observations in the South, he truly believed Plato was the exception, not the norm. He even offered the professor an opportunity to bring Plato to the South so he could further the cause of the Negroes by showing Southerners that niggers could be educated.

That dinner seemed like a lifetime ago for Plato, now called Fessa. After Senator Jackall's invitation, Professor Phoenix had gone south with Plato to the senator's plantation to show Southerners that Negroes could learn and be citizens. Senator Jackall was the personification of a gentleman and informed the professor that Plato would be taken care of. About two miles from the professor's house, the carriage was stopped, and two men pulled Plato from the carriage. A hood was put over Plato's head, and his arms were tied behind him. He was hit over the head, and all was blackness after that.

When Plato opened his eyes, he was greeted by the light of five lit torches; his hood had been removed. He knew he was in a barn based on the smell of hay and animals. Plato was chained with his arms up in the air, and next to him the professor was also shackled with his hands above his head. Senator Jackall was talking to him. Senator Jackall told the professor that what he had created in Plato was a contradiction to God and his plan. Niggers were meant to serve, not think; regardless of education, they would never be equal to white men. He thanked the professor for inviting him to his house and said he was glad to have the opportunity to get rid of this travesty of nature before the abolitionists got ahold of him. He promised the professor that from this day forward, Plato would cease to be, and only a slave would remain.

In front of the professor, Plato was beaten long into the night. The pain from the whip was unlike any experience he had ever had in his life. His fifteen-year-old body rebelled from the abuse, and he vomited, pissed, and defecated on himself before the night was over. He wanted to die before he ever felt another lash on his skin. He had lost sight of the professor in his pain, and after that act was done, he could see tears running down the professor's face.

It was then that he noticed Senator Jackall pull out a revolver and put it to the professor's head. The senator stated that any white man who felt that niggers were equal or better didn't deserve to live. The sound of the gunshot was worse than any lash Plato had received that night. In a loud bang, the only man he had ever known as a father was gone. Plato truly felt alone and lost.

The days and years that followed after the professor's death were a blur to him. Eventually, he became known as Fessa; most of the slaves knew him only as the former slave of the professor who had tried to train niggers. So instead of "professor," his name was abbreviated to Fessa. He learned early in his captivity not to say much, if anything, even to slaves. The slave state of mind was truly a phenomenon to Fessa. They didn't have anything of their own; they lived simply by the whim of the master and were degraded worse than animals, but they constantly vied for notice by the master, hoping to increase their stations by extra clothing or food. They reminded Fessa of a pack of wild dogs who used to be behind the library. He would go out, throw them scraps every day, and watch the interaction of the dogs and how they expected his arrival and acted; his captivity was similar.

The horrific rapes of men, women, and children by the master, the drunk whippings in which slaves were forced to have sex with animals, and countless other heinous acts were the staples of slave life. Kept in a constant state of fear through their ignorance, terror tactics, and just plain brutality, slaves never learned or even comprehended any sort of freedom or unity; those were only injurious or deathly to them. Even someone as well educated as Fessa couldn't see past his current state; he was too fearful of the unexpected.

Fessa was often brought into the main house and told to read in front of white guests of the senator; after reading, he was taken outside and strapped to a pole for his crime of being able to read. If he didn't read, he was strapped to the pole for disobeying his master. Either way, he got beat. The beatings or whippings were moments of pleasure when compared to being given to one of the master's more deviant guests. Fessa refused to remember the nights and days when he was gang-raped and subjected to things no civilized man should be witness to. In his mind, this was some of the worst humiliation imaginable. The masters felt like if they could think or feel something, then they could do it.

Eventually, as the rhetoric for secession started to grow, the commonplace activities of beatings and rapes subsided. The South started to focus its efforts on the preservation of its way of life through slavery. The South was gearing for war, a war it felt was righteous and true. Banners were raised, and lines were drawn. The act of Northern aggression would stop, and the Southern way of life that allowed for ownership of slaves would be retained at all costs.

Fessa remembered the day he finally got his chance for revenge on Master Jackall and his chance at freedom. Master Jackall was hosting a party for some Southern officers, whose sexual taste was a little bit more exotic than the norm. They were scheduled to depart for the war and wanted one more night of decadence before they left. Their taste was primarily for younger boys and girls, but Fessa didn't escape unscathed. He did, however, escape being the main attraction at the party. The men weren't interested in the humiliation of another uppity nigger; they wanted to satisfy their carnal urges.

Some of the men brought in a new drug, opium. Some of the more traveled men had learned that opium was used to control Asian sex slaves by getting them addicted. All the slaves at Master Jackall's parties were made to smoke it. They thought it made the slaves more malleable and even appreciative of their sexual abuse. A lot of the sex slaves had started to become addicted and would be in a comatose state or pass out.

Fessa feigned to pass out, and someone attempted to wake him by kicking him a few times, but he was eventually dragged out and left outside near the pigsty. This was what they had done to every slave who passed out in the last two parties; Fessa had depended on this. He immediately left the outside area of the pigsty and entered one of the large barn buildings, where the horses for the guest were kept. Most, if not all, of the guests stayed the night, too drunk and exhausted to depart after all the debauchery. He had written a note that would identify him as a trusted messenger for his master. One of the gentlemen's horses and the fact that he could read and write would support his story. He had taken the clothes of one of the guests and was starting to put the outfit on when he heard voices coming toward the barn. He immediately knew that it was Master Jackall.

He opened the barn door and could see Master Jackall leading a slave girl into the barn. Fessa knew her as Saree, a deaf and mute slave girl the master had recently purchased. She was in her mid-twenties and didn't have any children. She had never been given any education and was trained only on household tasks like cleaning and dishes. She couldn't do anything else and often stood in one spot for long periods when she was outside the house. Most white men considered it taboo to mess with the mentally unstable, and she had been sold cheaply from household to household. Since Master Jackall had bought her, Fessa hadn't known anybody to be abusing her, at least until now. Fessa followed and found a spot above where he could watch. He needed to get inside and get a horse.

Master Jackall closed the door and immediately slapped the girl across the face. The impact of a grown man hitting such a small-statured girl hurled her across the barn floor like a rag doll. She ended up directly under where Fessa was hiding. Fessa knew what the master was about to do; he had been the victim on numerous occasions. The master didn't care whether the slave was a man or woman, boy or girl; he wanted only to cause pain. But this went beyond mean; she couldn't even speak or scream.

Fessa noticed two cotton hooks behind the master. The master couldn't hear Fessa move from his location; his undivided attention was given completely to the grunts of pain from the helpless girl. Fessa slowly crawled from his hidden location and slid down from the loft on a hanging rope. Fessa heard the woman's piercing scream as the master started to abuse her.

So intent was he on the ruin of the woman that he didn't hear Fessa come up behind, now with two cotton hooks in hand. The master was bent over because of the small stature of the woman, so his naked white ass was highlighted in the lantern light.

Master Jackall was deep into his gratification when the sharp, piercing pain of the first hook lanced his anal cavity. Master Jackal screamed a loud high pitched "Aieeeeee!" All thoughts of the woman beneath him burned away due to the molten hot pain in his back.

He turned around to see Fessa staring at him, the remaining hook being switched from his left hand to his right. Master Jackall had just enough time to witness the exchange from hand to hand before Fessa swung the cotton hook with all his might. The meaty impact of the cotton hook hit the side of his face, the sharp end entering the ear and settling in the brain. Once the hook was embedded, Fessa pulled the master forward and slammed his head into the wooden post the woman was leaning against. His head hit with a jarring thud, and he started sliding down the pole.

Fessa pulled the woman from under the dying man and settled her to the side, her eyes wide with fear. Fessa immediately grabbed the other cotton hook, still protruding from Master Jackall's anus, and yanked with all his strength. The rip opened him up from the back, and his intestines started to slide out. The last noise Master Jackall would ever make was a guttural and hoarse moan.

Just like that, Fessa's nightmare was over. He took a few minutes to check on the girl, but she was dead from the abuse. Fessa finished changing clothes, mounted his horse, and left.

That had been almost five years ago. He had become a soldier to save his life and join the fight for freedom. His upbringing as the adopted son of a professor of history had enabled him to get a keen grasp on historical events. He had always been fascinated by the great battles in history—from the Spartan wars with Lionites and the 300 to the great exploits of Alexander the Great and the recent American Revolutionary War. He used to sit in on his adopted father's history lessons to the children of America's nobility and understood that war was the harbinger of change.

When he first joined the army, he had always placed his tent near the commander's tent and would always hide outside and listen to the battle plans being drawn out and the conversations of the white officers. Captain Vetter said General Lee was taking a big chance by putting all his forces in play in the upcoming battle. Last night he had heard that General Lee was on the run and needed to get to his logistical lines of support. Northern troops were tired, and the Union was weary of the war for slaves. If the South won this next battle, it could influence Northern politicians to concede to some of the Confederacy's demands in hopes of ending the bloodshed.

Fessa knew more than any other black man that the upcoming battle would be a decisive point in this long, drawn-out war of brother against brother, master against slave. The attack they were involved in this morning held great significance in the upcoming battle because they were attacking a cavalry element reputed to be led by General Fitzhugh Lee. Similar to armies in the past, the cavalry still had a strong reputation as a game-changer in a war. They could provide ground reconnaissance on a huge scale and were the ultimate shock troops, especially with the introduction of pistols and rifles. Fessa understood that by disrupting the cavalry's moves, they would put limitations on General Lee's ability to see the battlefield. The brutal attack by the "ghost" unit this morning had been just a precursor to the larger attack by regulars expected to come.

Fessa understood the purpose of the special unit to which he had been assigned. He understood that in war, extreme methods were required to get desired effects. The mental state of a soldier could be a deciding factor in a battle. His "ghost" unit, mostly composed of former black slaves and white prisoners, was a Southerner's worst nightmares come to life, with armed black men killing white people in the most horrible ways imaginable. This either angered Confederate soldiers beyond sanity or scared them away from battle forever. Either way, his mind was taken out of the fight. In his education, Fessa had learned that throughout history, guerilla tactics had been both successful and disastrous. War was a game of chances, and the man who took the most tactically sound chances increased his chances of winning.

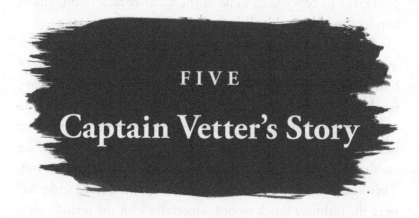

FIVE

Captain Vetter's Story

CAPTAIN ROBERT VETTER felt that the upcoming battle this morning would finally be the end of his tour of duty as a leader of his mixed band of former Negro slaves and white prisoners. It seemed like yesterday that he had been in the halls of the academy at West Point, learning the ways of war and how to be a future leader in a new country. At the academy, the strong feeling of comradeship, stronger than that in most college fraternities, had previously overcome nearly all social, religious, and political differences except for the War of Secession. Overnight all that changed when Southern cadets started resigning to join the forces of their native states. Cadet Vetter, born in Georgia, loved life as a cadet and as a future member of the US Army. Even his father told him he was better served fighting in the Army of Georgia and needed to return home; Cadet Vetter maintained his hope of becoming a leader in the US Army, not in the Army of Georgia. He strongly believed the old adage "United we stand, divided we fall." When he was required to have an additional oath-signing ceremony to confirm his commitment to the Union, he didn't have any reservations—to the dismay of his family. Once they found out about the additional oath signing, he was disinherited from the noble Vetter name and told never to come to Georgia again.

He had thought his loyalty to the Union would give him some credibility as a stalwart advocate of the United States, but the situation seemed to work in the reverse. The Union leadership always looked at him with a disdainful eye because they felt he was either a spy in their midst or a traitor to his family. Either way, he didn't get the credit he felt he deserved, and it would continue to play a part in his military career.

His current assignment was the result of the distrust his leadership had in him by giving him an assignment over regular Union soldiers. His group of seventy-plus men was primarily made up of former slaves and former white prisoners of the South. A little over a year ago, he had been so embarrassed to take over the unit; he couldn't believe that a man from West Point would be so depreciated as to be given command over a bunch of men, who in most people's eyes were little more than savages. He was initially going to resign immediately after finding out his command was going to be over Negroes. However, a quote by Patrick Henry always reverberated in his thoughts after he read it. "The battle, Sir, is not to the strong alone; it is to the vigilant, the active, the brave. Besides, Sir, we have no election. If we were base enough to desire it, it is now too late to retire from the contest. There is no retreat but in submission and slavery! Our chains are forged! Their clanking may be heard on the plains of Boston! The war is inevitable; and let it come! I repeat, Sir, let it come!"

He considered himself both vigilant and brave, and he understood there was no retreat from the course the country had set itself on. One side would be the loser, and the other the winner, but the country overall would be scarred. He knew in his heart that war wasn't a glorious adventure and that there would be great battles and heroes. His first encounters with war as a lieutenant at the Battle of Carthage had introduced him to the real horrors of war.

The memories of the battle were forever etched into his young mind. Before the battle, he had felt that he possessed the courage and fortitude to stand through anything war could bring his way. What the best formal education couldn't teach him, the war of life would help finish his education, and the realities were harsh.

Neither nobleman nor commoner is given any distinction on the battlefield. Bodies blown to pieces from cannon fire are indiscriminately placed together after the battle, and pieces of one man may intermingle with pieces of another man and be sent home in boxes. At least the officers were sent home in boxes; the enlisted men were placed in a hole in the ground and buried without much reverence. The stench of dead and burned bodies, coupled with the images of grossly dismembered and disfigured soldiers, would always remain as vivid pictures in his mind.

He survived the almost day-long battle, too concerned during the battle to focus on the individual dramas going on around him. He learned he did have the focus to stay in battle, something he quickly learned; after the first gunfire and cannon fire went off, fortitude was lacking in a lot of men. He was horrified by the number of men who, upon hearing the first roars of the cannon and seeing the destruction around them, decided to turn around and run. Many men died with their backs to the battle, easy targets for the rebel shooters.

After the battle, he checked on his men and met a lot who had either an arm or leg amputated, sometimes both. No amount of good would ever erase the horrors he had witnessed. A man wasn't designed to witness so much horror and pain, but maybe that was the way it was supposed to be for it to never happen again.

They did, however, prepare himself for the mission to which he had been assigned.

The guerrilla warfare his little band of men waged was meant to dishearten Confederate soldiers and cause fear among their ranks. Most men were superstitious, and Captain Vetter and his men played on their superstitious fears. They came in at dawn or late at night like wraiths, and where they passed, men died in horrible ways. Some of the Southerners were already starting to say the killers were the souls of slaves trying to help the Union win the war on slavery. After one battle, when the wolves were on the bodies almost immediately after the fight, Confederates started to whisper that there were ghouls devouring men in battle.

All the superstitious fear played well into Captain Vetter's efforts to cause mayhem and uncertainty in the Confederate ranks. It was vital that his little contingent of men remain clothed in mystery. After almost two years in his current command, he came to realize he was part of something unique in US history. His band of Negroes and former white slaves was probably the first of its kind in the United States. This was one of the few times Negroes were given the opportunity to be something other than be house servants or field slaves; they could serve side by side with white men. They took to their training with a zeal he didn't understand at first, but he understood now. They were working hard because they were working for themselves, and they knew they now had a play in how their future turned out. If they didn't fight, there was a good chance they would go back to the life they had been freed from. They would do whatever it took to make sure that would never happen again.

He knew that if the Confederates found out the Union army was using Negroes to kill white men in a horrific manner, it would cause an outrage throughout the South and could possibly provide new motivation and energy in their ranks. All this went through

Captain Vetter's mind as they got ready to initiate their attack on the unsuspecting Confederate soldiers in the small valley below.

For Captain Vetter, the battle went exactly as planned. Two of his most lethal soldiers, Privates Fieldhand and Amra, initiated the first phase of the attack on two fronts. They were responsible for eliminating the minimal security pickets the Confederates had placed out front. Once the pickets were eliminated, phase two commenced, in which the other men infiltrated the openings Fieldhand and Amra had created. The men quietly went through the sleeping camp they had been observing for the last two days and indiscriminately killed in silence. They had orders to eliminate as much of the leadership as possible. No guns would be fired; the deaths of the soldiers would be by sharp or blunt instrument. They didn't need to kill all of them, just enough to cause terror and confusion.

The two openings Fieldhand and Amra created were near the tents where the Confederate leadership slept. They snuck through the camp, moving from one end of the camp to the other, indiscriminately killing the sleeping men. They moved almost at a trot, stopping only to end a rebel's life, then not stopping until they reached the other side of the camp. If the alarm was raised before they reached the other side, the men were told to retreat into the woods and not put up a fight.

The final phase of the attack was for men located at various points around the camp to start shoot kerosene-filled arrows into camp, immediately followed by arrows strapped with sticks of dynamite. They started with the cavalry horse enclosure. Captain Vetter didn't believe his men could kill the horses quietly, so he resorted to fire and dynamite as a way to diminish the Confederate capability and continue to cause as much chaos as possible. He knew he took a chance by waking the camp, but he believed in their initial shock and chaos, coupled with his retreat plan, and that his unit would be safe.

The fight was quickly over. The sun was still rising when the fires and explosions started to go off.

The unit retreated about ten miles from the actual battle to a well-hidden valley to regroup. After the initial head count, Captain Vetter had lost two men, both bodies in tow. Initial estimates from his men were that the Confederates had lost over eighty men during the silent killings and the dynamite bombings. At least ten officers and/or enlisted men had been part of the deaths. Due to the close proximity of the animals penned up, the Confederates had lost more than half of the cavalry horses. False trails had been laid in case anyone wanted to follow his unit, but Captain Vetter doubted the unit they had just attacked would have any stomach for another fight. It was always good to be safe. His scouts reported that no one was following. His unit would spend the night here and then move farther north to safer lands just in case the Confederates got lucky and found their trail. The men were on high alert, and pickets were posted far out to give early warning of any followers.

SIX

New Orders

ABOUT TWO MONTHS after the battle, Captain Vetter called all the men together to inform them that he had a big speech to give. When all the men were gathered, Captain Vetter said, "Men, I have just learned that General Robert E. Lee has surrendered to Ulysses S. Grant on April 9, 1865, formerly ending the rebellion against the US."

There was a loud "Yeeeeaaaaah!" as all the men, black and white, jumped up in celebrations, foregoing their normal rules of silence to let everyone who could hear know that the war was over.

Captain Vetter let them have their moment of joy at the war's end. Most of the men were former slaves, and the ending of the war had meant so much more to them. This meant they were free and wouldn't need to worry about going back into slavery. They wouldn't need to fear being sold, beaten, raped, or treated like animals ever again. They were men now, their freedom bought in the blood of the country.

Captain Vetter raised his hand to let his men know he had more to say. Slowly the noise subsided, and he continued. "I also regret to inform you that on April 16, 1865, just seven days later, President Abraham Lincoln was assassinated at Ford's Theater. His attacker, John Wilkes Booth, a rebel sympathizer, was caught and killed."

The men didn't know how to take this; one man yelled, "Lawd, lawd, lawd, the devils have gotten to our angel."

All the men took off their hats as one of the black soldiers, known as Preacher, yelled to say a prayer. "Dear Lord, we humbly beseech you on behalf of a great and noble man taken away from us way too soon. We ask you to watch over our brother and savior, to let him know that his time on this earth is done, and thy will be done. He will forever be known as the liberator, a good man, an American. Thank you, Lord, for sharing another of your sons with us. Forgive us, O Lord, for your children still have to learn. Amen!"

All the men sounded out in a resounding "Amen."

The initial hooting and hollering at the news of the war ending were tempered by the loss of their favorite son, President Lincoln. Overall, the men were happy that they had taken part in the demise of what many considered the evil rebellion. They had all shared in some way the atrocities of the rebellion and knew its demise was better for the country.

Most of the white soldiers started talking about heading home, trying to pick up their lives, and seeing whether they still had wives, children, and family members who were still alive.

For the black men, they didn't completely understand what the end of the war meant for them. Were they now considered citizens and free? Could they now raise their heads and look white men in the eyes as equals, without fear of being beaten or hanged? Would they be provided the education given to white men and be allowed to own their own land without fear of angry white men slaughtering them? So many questions.

Before the war, they had been considered livestock and property. They had originally fought out of revenge and the need to do something to put food in their mouths. What better way to get back at white men for all the atrocities they had witnessed throughout their lives? However, in the backs of their minds, they also wanted to prove they were just as capable of doing everything the white man could do. More than just proving this to the white man, deep down they needed to prove to themselves they were equal. The war had given them the opportunity to become men, something they would never lose again. After being free for so long during the war and now faced with the uncertainty of their status, the former slaves knew there was no way they would go back to being slaves again. They would die and die as men now if they had to.

SEVEN

After the War

AFTER THE WAR, there was a lot of speculation about what to do with a unit of mostly Negro soldiers. The recent death of President Lincoln had left the country in a lot of turmoil. The whole country was in a state of shock at the loss of its president. There were no definitive plans established on what to do with all the recently freed Negroes throughout the United States. All hopes of reconstruction had died with President Lincoln.

Soldiers were given the opportunity to stay in the army. The soldiers in the unit were told they were free and could leave whenever they wanted. The soldiers who decided to leave were given the possessions they owned, thirty dollars, and the option to buy a horse for five dollars for their service.

Most of the soldiers were smart enough to understand there was nothing to go back to. At least in the military, they could have a decent living and food on their plates. Those who wanted to stay were told that a request for them to stay on as soldiers in the

US military had been sent up the chain of command, and they needed to be patient. He also told them that if they had things or business they wanted to take care of, they were free to do so, but they couldn't wear anything that distinguished them as Union soldiers. He also told them he would stay in the current location for about three weeks in case the men found nothing to go back to and wanted to return.

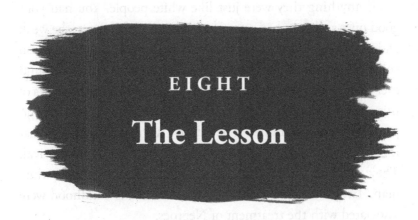

EIGHT

The Lesson

NOW THAT THE war was over, Captain Vetter felt a big weight come off his shoulders. If the South had won, he would have been considered a traitor and possibly hung for it, along with all the men who served under him. Now that the war was over, he felt he had proved his loyalty to the Union, even if it was commanding Negro troops. He didn't want recognition for the job, just trust from his leadership. This was the first time he had to sit down and put his thoughts about the war on paper. He had kept a journal since he was a cadet.

For Captain Vetter, the war had provided him with some enlightenment and a few fears. His "forced exile" as commander of Negro troops had revealed that his education about the Negro had been very inaccurate and extremely limited. He had been taught that the Negro was closer to an ape than a man, that Negroes were minutely elevated a little more than common service beast and could be trained to do only childlike tasks. He had visited the zoo as a child and had seen the apes; the Negroes under his command had been nothing like the apes he had witnessed that day at the zoo.

If anything they were just like white people. You had your good ones and your bad ones, the leaders and followers, the weak and the strong. Hard workers and lazy workers. Even with the iron collar of slavery constricting their every breath, they had found every opportunity to celebrate and laugh. Just like the founders of this great country, they had the same desires to live a good life and provide for their families. They didn't worry much about what they are missing; they were too focused on day-to-day survival. They could die at the whim of even the most disreputable white man. Two of the most scalding memories of his childhood were associated with the treatment of Negroes.

To this day, he could still hear the inhuman wail of a Negro mother as she watched her one-year-old son being sold off to another plantation. Based on a recommendation from his father's headmaster, the little boy was sold to make sure the mother would shortly be ready to breed another. Besides, the boy was from very good stock. The offer of $800 for a baby was unheard of. He could distinctly remember his father's headmaster claiming the girl was young and could always have another. The slave had to be restrained for almost two weeks to keep her from running away or killing herself because of the loss. The headmaster also recommended that, since the girl was so distraught, she should move in and become his maid. His solution was to impregnate her as soon as possible to get her over her distress, the logic being that if she had a half-white baby, the master would be less inclined to sell it and keep it in his household, since it was also the headmaster's. Once she had the new child, she would be okay. The girl, once allowed in the master's house, killed herself by slamming her mouth on a butcher knife within the first week.

The other incident happened when he was barely eight years old and playing with a bunch of Negro children. He had brought a few of his toys to play with the kids. Like most children do, one of the Negro children picked up one of his toys and said, "Mine." This infuriated him so much that he began to cry. When his mother ran into the room to ask what was wrong, he informed her that the Negro girl had stolen his toy and didn't want to give it back. The little girl, who couldn't have been older than five years old at the time, was taken outside and beaten with a switch until she passed out. Some of the welts on her legs were so deep that in about a week, her right leg became so infected that it had to be amputated below the knee. Her name was Velma, and years later, she wished Vetter well on his departure. Even though she had only one leg, she had given birth to four girls and two boys by the time she was twenty years old. All but one was sold to other families. Vetter always carried the guilt of her losing her leg and the misfortune that had befallen her.

He even began to liken his situation in the Union army to that of the Negro in America. Just like being a Southerner serving in the Union army with distrust from his superiors because of his upbringing, the Negro was also alienated in America simply because of his or her color. He remembered a quote. "War makes for strange bedfellows." Never more was this truer.

Being that he was the only white officer in his unit, he could pretty much do what he wanted with his men and their training. One thing he definitely would never do again, was walk shoulder to shoulder in battle and wait to get shot. His unique mission allowed him to train his Negro soldiers on all aspects of being a soldier. He put them through an intense training program, which included horsemanship, map reading, weapons training, and all the other tasks he expected from soldiers. His soldiers also got a lot of education in woodcraft and hunting from the two Indian guides assigned to the unit. They were a self-sufficient unit and foraged for their food. They were also trained in the use of cover and concealment, silence, and patience in battle. Regardless of what race his soldiers were, he would train them to the best of his abilities.

With the end of the war, there also came the flow of normal communications. During the entire war, Captain Vetter wasn't allowed to communicate with his family, because the details of his mission were never to come to light. It was one thing to lead Negroes in traditional warfare like other white men, but to lead them around in the dark to kill men in their sleep wasn't considered very honorable. He had backdated letters from a few of his friends from West Point, who were serving in other parts of the Union army and weren't aware of his assignment. There were also two letters from Fleur, his former childhood sweetheart from back home.

He had decided to stay in the military and continue his service to the reformed US government. When the message came from his leadership on his new orders, the orders were both a blessing and a curse. The blessing was, for his efforts with the irregular unit, he was promoted to major. This was an accomplishment he felt he would never have accomplished if he had been assigned to a regular unit, because of the shadow of doubt the Union leadership had about him. The black soldiers in his unit were given the option to remain in the army and receive thirteen dollars a month, far more than they could have earned as slaves. This was great for the black soldiers because it allowed them to still serve in the army. The curse of the order was that black regiments could serve only west of the Mississippi River because of the prevailing attitudes following the Civil War. His new order had him and the men who had decided to stay on reporting to Port Hudson, Louisiana. They were creating the Tenth Cavalry, which was being established for black enlisted men. He wouldn't be going back East and serving with regular troops; his time and success with the black troops had identified him as a capable white officer when dealing with blacks. Even with his success among the white officers, this wasn't considered much of an accomplishment. He had even heard one of his superiors once say, "Hell, how hard was it to work with animals?"

NINE

Conversation with Fessa "Lieutenant Phoenix"

MAJOR VETTER HAD some decisions to make regarding the future of the men. A lot of the white soldiers had chosen to leave the unit and go back home or go to a regular unit. Captain Vetter needed to reestablish leadership among his small unit. He decided to make Private Fessa an officer and promote him to lieutenant. His leadership had approved after he explained that all his white soldiers had left and that it would be a good sign for the men to see one of their own leading. He also added that if they were going to be assigned to the frontier, there would be minimal interaction with other white troops. The command agreed with the stipulation that the black officer could *never* lead white troops. Major

Vetter smiled at the emphasis of the word *never* but was happy he would be able to promote Fessa.

Fessa was now in front of him, standing at attention; Vetter had just informed him of the pending promotion. Fessa responded, "Sir, thank you for the promotion and the trust in my abilities. This is not the path I had dreamed of for myself, just like I had never dreamed of being a slave. I was raised by a scholar, and being a soldier in armed conflict was the last thing I ever wanted to be. I understand that you think my education and understanding of the military may give me a better chance over my peers, but I humbly think there are better soldiers who would fit this position more than me."

Major Vetter was definitely taken aback by the refusal but gathered himself and responded, "You are definitely right on the point. Your education is definitely one reason you were promoted. But I have also watched you under stress and how you have used your knowledge to guide you to the best decision. You don't fall into your passion like so many other Negro soldiers I have seen. I need someone who will be calm under pressure and able to see the bigger picture. At West Point, I was taught that officers plan and the enlisted execute. Don't think I haven't noticed you observing my maps, listening in on my tactics lessons, and volunteering to assist me when I build our attack models. You have learned a lot about how I am employing guerrilla tactics on the rebellion. I will tell you a little secret. Once I found out I was going to be commanding Negro troops, I did some research. The majority of white men want everyone to believe Negroes are just like monkeys but less hairy. They want everyone to see you as something that is incapable of thought and rationale, lazy and useless, if not guided by a firm 'master.' My findings were quite eye-opening, and I think my conclusion would startle you. I know for a fact that there aren't too many other white men who would agree with me."

Fessa responded, "Sir, what were your findings?"

Major Vetter had planned this conversation and followed by saying, "In science I learned that some animals evolved out of the water to walk on land. Initially, when the fish first came out of the water, it couldn't survive very long, because it wasn't suited to breathe air. Over time, thousands of years, the ability to breathe on land became longer and longer. At the same time, the fish's body started to change to make moving on land easier. As the fish's need to breathe fresh air became stronger than its need to breathe water, its body adjusted to make it so.

"I liken the black man to the fish. His environment prior to coming to the United States was the jungle or his water. He had to survive within that ecosystem, and his intelligence or knowledge was based on that survival. Negroes aren't animals like cattle or dogs but humans just like us, and they can adapt to their new environment in America (their air). When taking him out of that environment and not giving him an identity within the new environment, in his disorientation and unfamiliarity he would be unsure and may seem animal like to the natural inhabitants who normally breathe the air. 'Like a fish out of water,' as the old adage goes. Over time, if given the assistance or tools to educate himself in the new environment, he will eventually evolve and be incorporated. I also believe the United States will gain something of what they are as they assimilate free Negroes into their system. All my education has led me to believe it is the natural course of things.

"You are a testament to what educating a black man can do if provided the knowledge and assistance. According to your story, it is that exact knowledge that made you so dangerous to the Southern whites. You really are lucky to be alive. Since given this command, I have been told on every single request that any support or money to assist in making the Negro a smarter soldier is denied. Any request to make Negroes better soldiers by asking for spare equipment (leftover equipment from dead or captured soldiers that had already been looted) is denied. To add insult to injury, the leadership firmly believes there is only so far you can train black men before they become overwhelmed.

"Since I've been in the military, everything I've been taught about the Negro is contrary to what I have actually witnessed. I honestly believe the perpetual negative portrayal of the Negro has created terrible conditions for both blacks and whites. For the whites, it's not hard to believe the Negroes are savage and can never assimilate because the images they show of blacks in their native environment are so alien to whites, therefore easily believable. For Negroes, the education, language, laws, and even the country were so alien that even when given freedom, they didn't know where to go or how to start. This confusion about being in a foreign land without assistance added to the whites' belief that they didn't belong. They would never be considered eligible to accept the gifts of knowledge and rationale that whites believe they hold the keys to."

Fessa was a little unsure how to respond to Major Vetter's revelation. He knew what the major had just told him was something that could get him in a lot of trouble if any other whites heard his true feelings. The fact that he had opened up to Fessa to let him know his true feelings wasn't lost on Fessa. He couldn't help but be reminded of the verbal traps his former master had used to lay for him to get him to expose his intelligence, then beat him for it. This conversation was refreshing and very uncomfortable at the same time. He hadn't had a good conversation with a white man since the night his adopted father died. Showing his true intelligence had gotten his master killed. Here was another white man offering him equality and talking to him as an equal. Major Vetter had always been honest with Fessa, so he felt the right thing to do was to respond in kind for the honesty and trust the major had just handed to him.

Fessa responded, "I have also seen how my education has helped me better understand and maneuver through the slave system that has been set up. I admit my initial introduction was brutal and violent, something no rational man should ever have to experience, friend or foe. The fact that I was treated less than an animal, less than a slave, and gleefully exposed to indecencies designed to take away my manhood because of my education gave me true insight into the true beast of a man. If I were to put it into gospel terms, the white men would be the evil Egyptians and the Negroes would be the downtrodden Israelites."

Fessa's brutal, honest, and well-voiced response had Major Vetter drop his mouth open a little too long. Surprised would have been an understatement. Vetter knew Fessa was smart, but here he was having a collegiate-level conversation with a former slave. The explanation was so profound that he found himself fascinated by the response, fascinated like a dog owner was when he taught his dog how to catch. For some reason, the last thought bothered Vetter. If what Fessa said really surprised him, then maybe he was no better than the racist white men who believed Negroes were incapable of such thought. All this he thought a few seconds before he responded.

"Fessa, I apologize. I correct myself, Lieutenant Phoenix. You are very right in all your observations, and I appreciate your candor. I have served long enough with you to know the type of man you are. Hopefully, through my actions, you will learn to understand that I am not one of the Egyptians. I believe in you and your potential to lead men. Let me help you help me."

For some reason, a deep wave of comfort came over him. He felt that he had done something noble and useful to the continued existence of the United States by promoting Lieutenant Phoenix and giving him his trust. It also confirmed his decision that the man before him was the right choice to be the face and voice of the Negro soldiers. It confirmed Vetter's choice for Fessa to lead the platoon.

Fessa, with a tear coming down his eye, simply responded with a heartfelt, "Thank you!"

TEN

Second Lieutenant Plato Phoenix— Bye, Fessa

BEFORE ACCEPTING THE promotion, Fessa briefly thought about returning to the school where his adopted father had instructed him, if only to inform his family of the professor's demise. The betrayal of seeing his adopted fathered murdered by Senator Jackall, a man he had invited into his home, weighed heavily on his soul. He hoped the death of master Jackall was some solace to his dead adoptive father's soul. Senator Jackall had been a man of many passions and sadistic pleasures, which had been visited on Fessa too many times to count. Fessa's ability to read, his culture, and the fact that he could hold a conversation set him apart from other slaves. With horror, he remembered countless parties where he had been the entertainment for the evening. He had been made to read poetry and plays, dance, and asked thoughtful questions. Once the "entertainment" was completed, he had been handed over to the guests for whatever sadistic pleasures they could dream up. Most of the time it involved sodomy and some sort of sexual perversion to make sure he knew that, even with his knowledge and upbringing, he was less than a man. Fessa knew Senator Jackall didn't like women, because there were never any women involved in those despicable parties. He viewed women simply as breeders and ornaments. He found enjoyment in the domination of men, both white and black. In fact, Fessa had never been with a woman. The horror he had witnessed and endured as a slave still haunted him.

The violation of his body and soul made him a completely different man. He wasn't the wide-eyed young man full of questions and seeking to understand the world. The world had been violently thrust on him, and it was something he no longer wished to see. His life as a soldier had given him new hope and purpose. As a soldier, he could defend himself and never need to be violated again. As a soldier, he would never again be viewed as a slave; he would be in service to the country that had given him his freedom. What better way to show the white man that Negroes are capable and competent, not the subhumans they had been portrayed as. He could start again.

As his first command from Major Vetter, the soon-to-be Lieutenant Fessa was ordered to pick a name for himself. Major Vetter told him he couldn't go around calling him Lieutenant Fessa; that would be like mixing oil and water, a slave name mixed with his new job title. He also told Fessa to inform the men of the same.

Fessa knew the only last name he could keep was his adoptive father's name, Phoenix. The name's reference to the firebird rising from the ashes also fit his story of a slave rising to freedom. His adoptive father had also given him his first name, which was Plato; he didn't see any reason to change that either. So he would be Lieutenant Plato Phoenix.

ELEVEN

First Sergeant Amra

FOR AMRA, TRYING to make his way back to Africa was at the forefront of his mind. The thought of free Negroes roaming the countryside would be a new phenomenon in the United States. The mood everywhere they traveled was one of apprehension and anger. There were rumors of men in white sheets, called the Klan, roaming the South and looking for helpless Negroes. The thought of navigating a war-torn country where hangings, burnings at the stake, castrations, and mutilations were commonplace didn't make sense to Amra. As desperate as he was to find a ship to leave this country, he knew that for now, staying in the military until things calmed down was his best option. Besides, he had already started to get more responsibility; the major had acknowledged Amra's natural leadership abilities and the respect the other men gave him. For now this was the best place for him.

Major Vetter, along with the newly promoted Lieutenant

Phoenix, had called Private Amra in for a meeting. Private Amra had been key in teaching the men various hunting-type techniques he had learned as a child in Africa; the unit heavily relied on them to confuse and bewilder the enemy. Amra had taught the unit, including the major, about the value of sitting still and utilizing senses other than sight when navigating the forest. He had taught the unit how to distort the human body image with burlap bags, tree limbs, and foliage natural to the environment, something he had been taught as a child, so prey couldn't recognize the hunter's form. The hunter/predator mentality Amra taught, combined with the strict military regimen, was integral in creating the lethal, silent, and deadly unit they had become. Major Vetter had explained all this to Private Amra before offering him the rank of the first sergeant for the unit.

Lieutenant Phoenix, now standing beside Major Vetter, smiled and said, "It is well deserved, and the men respect and fear you just as much as we do. The two qualities a good first sergeant need to have."

Amra was completely taken aback by the offer. He was focused on going back to Africa to see what was left of his tribe. He had never thought about leading men, even though he knew was a born leader. His initial thought was that he wasn't qualified for such a responsibility, but that was immediately tossed aside.

Major Vetter added, "I don't know where our unit will be going, but I do know that I want to train and lead the men."

Private Amar simply smiled, overwhelmed by the rush of emotion he was feeling. "I accept, sir, and thank you for believing in me."

With that complete, everybody smiled. Lieutenant Phoenix asked Amra whether he wanted to change his name. Newly promoted first sergeant responded, "No, Amra is my birth name, so it will be my name for the rest of my life. I don't need a first name. Just call me First Sergeant Amra."

Major Vetter thought it was a strange request but understood there was more going on here than just a name change. Amra was African at heart and would always maintain his African heritage. Keeping his name ensured he always remembered where he had come from and what he'd had to go through.

TWELVE

Sergeant Hall: A Journey Back for Fieldhand

SHORTLY AFTER PRIVATE Amra's promotion to first sergeant, Private Fieldhand approached Major Vetter and First Sergeant Amra to discuss his return home to look for his family. When they had offered to let soldiers leave the military, Fieldhand decided he wanted find out whether his wife and child, Wanda and Tarrie, were still alive.

Captain Vetter listened to Fieldhand's request and responded, "The South is in turmoil, and such a journey will be extremely dangerous. Since the war has been over, lynchings and burnings of blacks have increased. Wandering groups of white men are roaming the woods, raping and murdering any 'free' blacks they find. A lot of blacks are even being forced into slavery at gunpoint. It is a very bad situation."

First Sergeant Amra, arms crossed, just stared at Fieldhand and nodded. He knew decisions of the heart had to be worked out. Everything Major Vetter had just told him was true and, in First Sergeant Amra's mind, all that needed to be said. He was a man informed with more knowledge than most men could claim. He would make his decision for himself and his family; the first sergeant believed he had a small advantage.

Private Fieldhand looked at both of them and smiled. This was something he thought he would never see, a white man and a black man standing side by side, sharing in a decision. It felt right. He responded, "Sir, I am very afraid to go back, but I need to know if my family survived. I am still married to my wife, and as her husband, I owe it to her. As a former slave, just living was dangerous. On numerous occasions, I witnessed a slave lose life, limb, or a family member on the whim of a master or one of his brood. Often the life-changing decision for the slave was based on the master's mood. However, due to all the training and experience I have received as a soldier, I now feel confident enough in my abilities to defend myself. By God, I am more than a man. I am a husband and a father. What is a husband without his family?"

Having never had the opportunity to have a family, Captain Vetter couldn't respond to that question. He admired the commitment to family Fieldhand showed. He was willing to put his life on the line for his family.

Captain Vetter informed Fieldhand that all the soldiers were changing their names now that they were all officially free. He asked Fieldhand whether he also wanted to change his name as a sign of a new beginning.

Fieldhand thought about what Captain Vetter had just asked him. He had never known any name other than Fieldhand. Who could he be now if he had the choice? The only names he knew were those of his former master and the people he had met since his escape and freedom. He didn't want to use a name he had just learned because it could cause some confusion. He remembered that when he had been a slave, the master gave slaves two days off on a holiday's special to the master and his family. It also became special to the slaves because the master was in a good mood and was free with his favorite beer. The holiday was called St. Patrick's Day. The master and his family wore their best clothing, and he noted everyone had some color of green. Patrick seemed like a lucky name to him, and it always reminded him of good times when things were bad.

Patrick would be his first name. As for a last name, Fieldhand remembered the first free black man he had ever met. His name was Jesse Hall, and he had come through to do some seasonal work for the master. He was the first man to tell Fieldhand about the world beyond the plantation. Jesse claimed he had over twenty children, but he had never seen any of them; they had all been sold off before he could see them. He was a good and honest man, the first man who had befriended Fieldhand. Fieldhand had to admit that in reviewing his emotions about Jesse, he just realized he was the father figure Fieldhand had never had, even if for a brief moment.

Jesse had started a relationship with one of the slaves at the plantation, something the master promoted. More babies, more slaves. Jesse knew that when the baby was born, he would have no fatherly rights to the child. Instead of losing another child, Jesse had used his freeman status and escaped north with the woman. Fieldhand had never seen him or the woman again and didn't know whether they had made it to the North. To discourage other slaves from running, the master made up false accusations against Jesse and told the slaves he had been hanged and the woman had been sent to another farm, notorious for its abuse. Fieldhand knew the truth of how Jesse had escaped and decided right then that he would honor old Jesse by taking his last name.

Where Fieldhand had once stood, Private Patrick Hall would now claim the space. It was a good name filled with both luck and honor. A new name for a new man. There was a huge chasm that separated the difference between Patrick Hall and Fieldhand. It was like comparing a baby to a grown man. If Fieldhand was threatened, he would stand there and take whatever abuse was dished out to him, like a good slave should. The new man, Patrick Hall, would kill any man who tried to hurt him or the people he loved. He would die fighting rather than be a slave. He knew in his heart that in whatever came his way, he would face it head-on. He no longer feared the lash; nor would he accept it.

He informed Captain Vetter of his name selection and his plans to continue to look for his family. Captain Vetter begrudgingly said he understood and wished him luck on his journey. Captain Vetter also told Private Hall that if he wanted to stay in the military, he would have a promotion waiting for him. He needed more sergeants, and both he and the first sergeant believed Private Hall was perfect noncommissioned officer (NCO) material and that he would always have a home in the unit.

Private Hall responded, "Sir, I have already made the decision—to bring my family out of the South and return with the unit. I want them far away from any memory of being a slave. If I can find them, I will also return. Being a soldier has helped me be the man I am, and I have to trust in what God has given me. Until he tells me different, Sergeant Hall will be returning."

Everyone smiled, and Sergeant Hall departed for his family.

THIRTEEN

The Encounter: Saving Lives

SERGEANT HALL, FORMERLY Fieldhand, had left the camp two days ago. So far his trip was uneventful; he traveled mostly by night and stayed off the roads. Captain Vetter had given him a map of the South to use, so he had a good idea of his location. Captain Vetter had required that all his men, regardless of color, learn how to read. This requirement included reading maps. It was because of all the training. Sergeant Hall felt the unit had experienced only twelve deaths since the time he joined the unit some time ago. He felt comfortable in his knowledge and experience at not being seen when he didn't want to. In either case, he had an answer strapped to his side.

It was near sunset on the fourth day of his journey when he heard a woman's scream in the distance. The dense forest and foliage prevented him from clearly seeing anything in the distance.

His initial placement of the sound was directly in front of him, on the current path he was traveling. He slowed his mount to listen and heard the scream again. This time it was at the two o'clock position up ahead, a little distance away. As he got closer, he noticed a small hint of smoke, and the screams became mostly muffled with a random shriek thrown in.

He drew as close as he dared before halting his horse and dismounting. He tied his horse to a nearby tree and put a scarf over the horse's mouth. When the scarf was applied, the horses were trained to be silent, walk stealthily, and not react to any noise. That also included not panicking when a gun or cannon was discharged. As a slave, he would never have dreamed of owning a horse like this, one trained to be more than just an animal but also a companion. His horse was his most valuable possession and best friend; he made sure to tie the knot so the horse would be able to work its way free in case he never returned.

Once he was off the horse, his mind briefly flashed back to the training fields they had used. The horses had also received extraordinary training from a Sioux warrior turned scout named Piyahma Atula or Pit. His abilities with horses were considered almost phenomenal, and Captain Vetter was quick to assign him as the unit's horse trainer. After being put in charge of the horsemanship training for the unit, Pit used training techniques based on the same horsemanship training young Sioux warriors were required to go through. Pit's horsemanship techniques required that each individual was comfortable with his or her horse prior to actually mounting the animals. This involved days of just walking and leading the horse around through a maze of obstacles Pit had designed, training on how to properly care for your mount, and using numerous other strange training techniques that bonded horse to rider. Once a rider was allowed to mount the horse, all his or her time riding was done bareback, utilizing only his or her knees to guide the horse. After a rider was able to navigate a complex riding course Pit had designed, using only his or her knees, only then was he or she allowed to move forward in training.

In Pit's tribe, the training stopped after the rider was able to navigate with his or her knees, since the tribe didn't believe in saddles. With guidance from the captain and quiet recommendations from Amra, Pit had created training for mounted men in the saddle that required soldiers in the unit to engage targets with rifles and pistols using only the knees to navigate the animal. The captain had said they would probably never use the skill, but it couldn't hurt to have it. Amra believed the confidence the men gained from the training in their own combat abilities was invaluable. Most of the men assigned to the unit, who ranged from very poor white men to slaves before being assigned to the unit, were afraid of the horses. Before being assigned to the unit, the only people associated with horses in their lives were plantation owners or masters. Hall was more inclined to agree with Amra; having his own mounted animal added to the feeling of being his own man.

Sergeant Hall couldn't see himself now without his horse, Vengeance. Vengeance was a jet-black Morgan stallion with a unique, cream-colored mane. He was strong, fast, smart—and he was Hall's best friend, the only friend Hall could tell his darkest secrets to.

Hall wondered what would happen to Pit now that the war was over. Hall had enjoyed the small conversations he had on occasion with Pit. Pit's use of the English language was atrocious, so the conversation they had was minimal. However, the feeling of comfort and comradery he felt when around Pit couldn't be ignored.

Once his horse was secure, he approached the sound on foot. He could see movement through the trees, so he dropped to the ground and slowly started to crawl toward the noise.

The sun had already begun to set by the time he inched his way close enough to where the trees started to open up a little more. He used a large tree to screen his approach. The flickering light cast an eerie shroud over the large trees. He peeked around the tree, and the scene that unfolded before him was something he hadn't seen since he was a slave.

There was a naked black man tied to an old, desiccated tree. Placed at his feet and going around the small tree were hand-size pieces of wood. The smoke Hall had previously seen was coming from the small fire, which a dirty, young white man was coaxing at the slave's feet. He could have been between the age of twelve and twenty. He was young and scrawny with a very hard look. His long, disheveled, dirty-blond hair was stuck to his face and looked matted in some parts. He was lean and gave the appearance of someone who hadn't eaten regularly. He had a short, gray, dirty coat that had holes in the left sleeve and was missing the right sleeve below the elbow. It was an old rebel officer's jacket. About ten feet to the left of the burning tree, a half-naked older white man was on top of a screaming, young black woman. The screams he had heard earlier were coming from her. Upon closer inspection, the young black girl was very light in color, and Hall could tell at a glance that she was a "half-breed" child. Her light-skinned face was already turning an ugly black with bruises, and her dress had been pulled almost over her head. The man also had on a rebel officer's coat.

Hall had learned the Confederate ranks as part of their training. They had been trained to take out the highest-ranking officers to sabotage the enemy's leadership. It was always a bonus during an attack if you killed one of the high-ranking enemy officers. It was a proven fact that, if those in leadership of the Confederates were eliminated, the soldiers would quickly lose heart without their officers and fall into disarray due to a lack of leadership and guidance. Most of the men didn't want to fight anyway; most were looking for an opportunity to better their miserable lives, which was a little bit better than those of the slaves.

The scene of the older white man's bare buttocks as he thrust into the screaming black girl reminded Hall of his daughter's rape and murder. In a flash without thinking, he pulled out his Remington Model 1858 and shot a single round into the back of the man's head. Brain mass and blood exploded across the screaming girl's face and mouth. The man's buttocks were still moving as the life ebbed out of his body.

A loud shout reverberated across the area, and the young man near the tree jumped up to see what was going on. He saw all the blood streaming down the naked man's back and screamed, "Pa!" The second shot exploded, and the boy's face turned to mush as teeth and brain matter exploded into the fire at the burnings man's feet. A brief "scaaahhh" sound could be heard as the blood hit the fire. He crumpled to the ground almost in slow motion, first to his knees and then finally on his shattered face. His life was gone before he hit the ground. The large hole in the back of his head glistened in the departing sunlight. The event was all over in a few seconds.

Sergeant Hall released the man from the tree before the fire got to him. His name was Zebadiah, and he was pretty broken up; there were a lot of bruises from the beating and two or three broken ribs. His nose was probably broken, and his feet were blistered from the burning wood. A few minutes more, and he probably wouldn't have been able to walk anymore. The woman, Nan, his wife, quickly recovered from her ordeal. Hall knew a woman as pretty as her probably had to get used to being abused whenever it suited the wrong white man. Hall could tell she was traumatized; she was trying to fix the already-tattered dress and cover her young breasts. Her right eye was closed, but no blood came out; she probably would be able to see.

The brief surprise at being alive was short lived; former slaves didn't have time to celebrate living. She frantically started shifting her head left and right in a wild fashion. Sergeant Hall knew she was afraid the gunshots would bring more people. He quickly untied Zebadiah as Nan gathered their meager belongings. Sergeant Hall had to assist Zebadiah, and he told Nan to grab any weapons, food, or anything of worth from the men. Nan refused to touch the weapons.

Hall simply looked at her and said, "I wasn't asking." He turned his back to try to get Zebadiah's feet ready for travel. Hall heard Nan rifling through the bodies as he gathered Zebadiah to his feet. Hall looked around and identified a few more things in the dead men's gear he thought they needed, including boots, pants, and shirts. When they left, the bodies were partially naked. Hall thought about stringing the two bodies up to the tree as a final revenge, but the evil of the act didn't sit well in his gut.

Zebadiah told Hall he was a runaway slave and that he and Nan were heading west. Nan had been a house slave for the master and one of his many daughters by a slave woman. Zebadiah and Nan had fallen in love, and the master had promised Nan to Zebadiah for his work as an armorer. After the master's second wife died and Nan's mother died, the master had started to show his attention to Nan, his own daughter. At that time, Zebadiah and Nan had decided to take a chance and leave before the master had his way with Nan. With all the attention on slaves heading north after the war, they felt they had a better chance of going out west to the frontier or Mexico.

Zebadiah's former master had been an arms dealer, and Zebadiah knew how to fix weapons and had some smithy skills. Hall told Zebadiah his soldier's story and described how he had just come from the West and hadn't witnessed many patrols. Hall recommended that going out West was probably the best option for Zebadiah and his beautiful wife, Nan. Hall would have given him some directions and distances, but like most slaves, Zebadiah was ignorant of distances and directions. Any slave who knew distances and directions was a real threat of running away. Hall told them to follow the road they were currently on but only to travel at night and to stay off the road in the woods as much as possible. He understood that it would be difficult to travel, but it was the safest way to get out of the South. He also informed them of the camp of his unit some nine to ten walking days away. Since Zebadiah didn't understand how to read maps and terrain details, Hall did his best to give a detailed description on how to get there and informed them not to let anyone know about their destination. If he was to spot the camp, Hall informed Zebadiah to pass along his name and let them know of his skills. He could possibly find a little work. Captain Vetter was always looking for people with skills on how to fix weapons.

Hall gave Zebadiah the murdered white man's pistol and knife, then provided brief instructions on how to use the pistol. He gave Nan a large hunting knife that had belonged to the young man and told her that the rape and abuse she had experienced today wouldn't compare to what would happen if she got caught again for the murder of these white men. He told her not to be afraid to use the knife if cornered, and he showed her where to stab. They departed ways that evening, and Hall's thoughts returned to finding his wife and child.

FOURTEEN

Going Home

A SMALL PART of Hall wanted to believe his wife and daughter were still alive, but the rest of him understood that his former master's desire for vengeance would be great after he found out Hall had murdered his son. He understood that the loss of his son, coupled with the scandal resulting from a slave murdering young, white noblemen, would send the whole community in a frenzy. The knowledge that his homicidal actions in his grief over his daughter's tragic death had probably resulted in the deaths of both his wife and daughter weighed heavily on his soul. The thought would haunt him every day, but the satisfaction in slaying his daughter's murderers would always provide him a little comfort on his cold and lonely nights.

The night he ran from the plantation was all a blur in his mind. When he ran away, his knowledge of the world was limited to the master's plantation and a few adjoining plantations he had traveled to for his master. Every time slaves left the plantation, they were transported in covered wagons so they couldn't see which direction to run if they tried to escape.

Since he had run away and joined the military, his journeys as a soldier had given him general knowledge of how the Southern states were situated. The unit, because of its secretive mission, had comprised slaves and whites. Hall had listened and learned a lot from individuals in the unit. A few of them had known the name Lewis, the name of his old master. From his findings, Master Lewis's plantation was in Tennessee near the border with Alabama. Before leaving the camp, he had asked Fessa to help him find his way using a map. Fessa worked with him for about week before he felt Hall had a good accounting for the direction he needed to go. Using the map had Fessa provided and looking for pre-plotted landmarks helped give Hall a general idea of where master Lewis's plantation was located.

The last couple of years had transformed him. When he was a slave, he thought he had a decent life with a wife, kids, and a small place. After killing the master's son and his friends in his rage, he thought he had destroyed the little happiness he found. His training and traveling had exposed him to the world and given him an education he would never have received on the master's plantation. He had unlearned so many wrongs he was taught as a child, the two most significant being that a man should be judged by his deeds, not his words. He had witnessed black men who were as equally vile and cruel as whites when dealing with other blacks. He also learned that, given the knowledge or education and opportunity, he could be on equal footing with any man, white or black. He had found friends in Amra and Fessa, two distinctly different men, but both with good hearts after all the abuse they had been through. However, with every enemy soldier he killed, he imagined he was getting revenge for his lost happiness and paying for the lives of other slaves who had probably been murdered because of his vengeance. Now he was harder, calmer, and decisive. He had become deadly. He would never lie down again and pray for some God to save him while he was abused. He would fight back to keep the small amount of manhood and freedom he had gained while serving as a soldier. He would fight for his freedom with every tool and trick he had learned.

After a week of hiding out in the woods, eating cold meals, and avoiding numerous patrols, Hall started to see signs that mentioned Master Lewis's plantation. Inwardly he smiled, thinking about all the signs with words he had seen during his escape. The night of his departure had been pure terror, but he vividly remembered seeing the signs when he was fleeing and pausing in his panic to wonder at the strange, flat trees with symbols and how truly amazing the world was. At the time he didn't know how to read, write, or barely hold a conversation due to his ignorance. After carefully poking around, he finally found the location where he had killed the master's son and his friends. He decided to leave his horse in the woods near the location and make his way by foot to the plantation during the night. In retrospect, he now viewed every step of his escape as a new door opening for him. Because of the traumatic experiences in his life, he had become the man he was today. Not the slave but the man. He just hated that his beautiful daughter had to die for him to evolve. He started for the plantation.

Entering the old plantation during the night seemed surreal to Hall; the last three years were a blur, and it seemed like he was right back to the night he had killed the master's son and friends. Not much had changed, except everything looked unkempt; the grass was longer, and some of the slave houses seemed to be burned out. His slave house was still intact, and he could see a small flicker of light through the only window in the small hovel. He remained in the bushes, waiting for everyone to settle down for the night.

It was a little after midnight when Hall approached the slave cabin. The candle had gone out a few hours earlier. Hall had seen movement in front of the candlelight, but no one came out of the cabin. Before the war, it was common for slaves to remain inside the house at night. Any slave seen after dark would be considered a runaway, unless he or she had specific guidance from the master. Hall didn't think they would break habits so soon after the war. Besides, it was a lot more dangerous now with all the Klan members roaming the night, burning and hanging blacks.

He approached the cabin from the back. This was one of the few cabins that had both a front and back door. He knew the door would be open because slaves weren't allowed to have locks on their doors. The room he entered was completely dark, with a little moonlight coming through the small hole serving as a window.

He had his firearm out just in case the cabin had new residents. He could see sleeping bodies on the dirt floor, lying on top of blankets. He counted five bodies in all. Approaching the nearest person lying down, he put his hand over the individual's mouth and pulled him or her close. It was a young man, who immediately began to thrash. The others started to wake upon hearing his thrashing. Hall put the barrel of his pistol to the man's head and told him to quit moving, or he would be dead. He told the others to shut up and not move, or he would kill them all. The individual lying next to the young man whispered, "Daddy." When he heard those words, Hall slowly removed his hand from the young man's mouth and almost dropped his pistol.

After the initial confusion, Hall informed everyone in the small cabin that he wasn't there to harm them, but he was looking for his family. Hall informed them not to light a candle because he didn't want anyone to know he was here. Tarrie was in the room, and so was Wanda. The man Hall had grabbed was Wanda's new man, named Lee. They had been put together after Lee's wife died after Union troops tried to attack the plantation. Lee had two kids from his previous wife and had taken the last name Wilson.

They had been together for just over a year and hadn't asked to marry because of the war. Hall was introduced to the two children, Noony and Charl. Noony was a young girl, around five years old, and Charl was a young boy of about twelve years old. Wanda was happy to see him but told him the old master was still looking for him, even after the war. There were no hugs or tears. Being alive was its own accomplishment.

Wanda informed him that Master Lewis had put out a $500 reward for his capture or killing. That was a considerable amount of money for a runaway slave. She also told Hall that after the master's son and friends had been found, they had initially believed another slave named Hurl was to blame and murdered him in front of his family. After Hurl's murder and burning, Master Lewis proceeded to round up various slaves, both men and women, for questioning to see how much any of them knew of the incident. She said it was horrible; the master was in such a fury that he used hot metal branding on all parts of the slaves he was questioning, large iron clamps on the genital areas of men, and other mind-breaking atrocities put on their children to get them to talk.

When Wanda realized the focus of Master Lewis' pain and anger at losing his son started moving toward her and Tarrie, her remaining daughter, she hesitantly approached Master Lewis, who was watching his men beat a slave named Earl almost to death. The flexible, hard leather batons the men used made wet *thunk, thunk* sounds as each baton made impact with Earl's back and side.

Master Lewis noticed Wanda approaching him and yelled for his men to stop. The yell scared her a little bit; she could hear anger and a sort of madness in his voice. As she drew closer, she started to move a little slower.

"What the hell do you want, Wanda?" Master Lewis asked in anger.

She explained to him that her daughter had come home all covered in blood and that she hadn't seen Fieldhand since that day. She claimed that since that day, Tarrie hadn't uttered one word. The initial shock of seeing so much blood on that fateful day had scared her silent. Wanda explained that Tarrie had just recently started talking, and Wanda pieced together what had happened.

She told Master Lewis she had run over to tell him as soon as she figured it out.

Master Lewis raised his hand as if to slap her but instead turned to his men and told them to stop beating Earl and to grab Wanda. In his rage at what Wanda had just told him, he had her tied to a whipping post. He had his men commence to beat her. It wasn't long before the loud *thwap, thwap* of the hard leather and wooden batons started her back to bleed. It wasn't until Master Lewis saw blood that he asked his first question. Wanda told her master what had happened on the fateful night, including that young Master Jeremiah and his friends had raped and murdered Cassia. She told him that Hall had been covered in blood and that young Tarrie had thought he was the devil come alive.

Master Lewis asked her why she had lied, and she told him that Hall had threatened to kill young Tarrie, whom she informed the master wasn't his child. She also told Master Lewis about the blood and gore all over Hall.

Master Lewis had seen how his son and friends had been butchered, so he knew the fear Wanda explained. He had felt it himself when he had first seen the atrocities committed. The fact that Wanda was more afraid of the deranged Hall than him was completely understandable.

Master Lewis had Wanda untied and helped her to her feet. He told his men to immediately start the hunt for Fieldhand. He told Wanda he wanted to check her home for clues and that he would walk her home. The gleam in his eyes and the bulge in his pants told Wanda otherwise. It would be a while before she could take care of the bloody gashes in her back. As she walked away, she looked down at Earl and thought she had just saved his life.

Wanda informed Hall that the Master Lewis had initially thought another slave did the murders. In fact, the other slave was the young boy, Charl's father. Charl had been given to Wanda after Master Lewis killed his mother and father.

The reunion was bittersweet. He was happy to find out that this family was still alive but sad that Wanda had already moved on. He didn't blame her; it was hard for a slave woman to live with no man around. He asked them whether they wanted to leave with him and that he was heading back west to rejoin his unit.

They were amazed by everything about him—his gun, his confidence, and the fact that he didn't act like a slave. Wanda and Tarrie both said they didn't want to go. After the war, things had gotten very dangerous for Negroes. The new Klan was running rampant throughout the South and finding any reason to hang or burn Negroes. The thought of leaving and going into the big world where the Klan was always on the prowl for stray Negroes was too much for them. The master liked Lee, and they were given better food than before the war. The master was real kind to slaves who wanted to stay.

The boy Charl wanted to leave with Hall and was busy rolling up a blanket and gathering his meager possessions. Hall asked Lee whether it was safe to take the boy so they wouldn't be punished for it. Lee informed Hall that slaves were running away every day after hearing about President Lincoln's decision to free them. Lee informed him that he wouldn't report the boy missing until late in the afternoon and that he would put on a good show of being extremely hurt by the boy leaving such a good life.

It was still dark when Hall and Charl left. He hugged Wanda

and Tarrie, shook Lee's hand, and melted back into the forest. It hurt him to leave Wanda and Tarrie; he wished they weren't so scared to leave the plantation. He understood how the big world away from the plantation could scare a former slave who had never been anyplace. Just a few years ago, he had been in the same situation. Leaving them was the hardest thing he ever had to do, but he knew there was nothing he could do, short of kidnapping them. Besides, Wanda appeared to be happy with the man Lee and seemed to be afraid of Hall. After seeing him so long ago with blood all over him, it's a wonder she could even look at him at all.

It was just starting to get light when he got back to his horse. He informed Charl that they would sink deeper into the forest and rest through the day and head out that night. The boy was extremely scared and jumped at every sound. Hall gave him a bayonet knife and instructed Charl that if anyone came, he would have to use it. Hall gave Charl his first real lesson on how to defend himself and kill a man with a knife. Charl was a quick study, and after about an hour, he knew the key areas to stab a man.

Once they had found a dark spot deep in the forest, Hall shared a few of his rations with Charl and lay down to rest in preparation for the night's journey. As he was falling asleep, he imagined his daughter Cassia smiling at him; it was the first time since the night she died that he had seen her without all the blood and gore on her.

FIFTEEN

Charl's Story

AS CHARL GAZED at Hall's broad back, he couldn't believe he was actually with the man he had heard about all his life. Up until this point, the man had been part hero and part monster. This was the "demon Fieldhand." According to stories told on the plantation, Hall had brutally murdered Master Lewis' son and friends. The bodies had been so torn up and abused that everybody thought he had turned into some kind of animal and tore them apart. However, when Master Lewis found out his child had been murdered, he had assumed the guilty man was a slave named Hurl, the man Charl thought was his father, who had committed the atrocities. Master Lewis had fathered a child by Hurl's wife, Becca. Only after his father was beaten to death, his mother brutalized and hanged, and numerous other slaves were beaten and hanged did the truth come out.

He remembered the night as one of death and truth. Master Lewis brutally murdered the only man he had ever known as his father in a fit of rage. He also learned on that night that his real father was the murderer, Master Lewis. He remembered that horrible night as if it just happened yesterday.

The loud *bang* of the small wooden door being smashed open had awakened young Charl out of his sleep. He could hear multiple booted feet come into the room, and men start screaming his father's name, Hurl. There was a brief sound of tumbling, and he started to hear the meaty sounds of men beating someone. One man kept screaming, "Why, nigga? Why, nigga?" He could hear his father responding, "No, sir! No, sir!" and understood that the men were beating his father.

Charl and his two younger brothers were situated in a small, partitioned area next to the fireplace. The little space, separated by an old broken door, was used as a small wall for the children. Charl could easily stand up and see what was going on, but he was so afraid of all the noise that he was frozen in place like a small deer, avoiding an approaching predator. He was terrified of the sounds of his father's beating. Almost as soon as the sounds started, they suddenly stopped. The sudden quiet caught Charl by surprise, and in that instant, one of his brothers whimpered. The small door screening the children was violently pulled away.

There were at least three white men in the room with Charl's mother and father. One of the men was Master Lewis, who repeatedly beat his father on the back with a wooden cane. Another white man Charl didn't recognize held his mother by the hair, and she knelt at his feet. She also showed signs of being beaten; there was blood running down her face from a large gash in her scalp that showed the white meat skin beneath it. The last white man was busy trying to tie Charl's father's hands while at the same time avoiding the master's cane, which continued to rise and fall. The loud *thunk* sound as the cane met backbone was unsettling. His father was barely moving. He could also hear other men outside the door and see glimpses of torches.

Once the man had finished tying his father, he grabbed him and pulled him up. Master Lewis looked at his father and raised his cane for a brutal swing across his jaw. Charl could hear the bone crack. "You will die for killing my son! We know how much you hated the fact that your wife was my bed warmer. You know that boy of yours is mine, and it just kills you knowing that."

Soon after the loss of his mother and father, Charl was placed with the slave woman Wanda, who treated him like he was her own son, and Tarrie became his true sister.

SIXTEEN

Integration

A MONTH PASSED after Captain Vetter informed the men that the war was over. All the men who wanted to stay with the unit had left, come back, or just stayed the entire time. Some men brought people back with them, mostly family members, but this included a few former slaves, who just wanted to try a different life. Initially Captain Vetter was a little weary about having the newcomers in his camp. Second Lieutenant Phoenix handled the situation with minimal issues. He had the new people corralled in a location close to the camp but not close enough to interrupt daily military activities.

Major Vetter had the pickets moved in a little closer but still maintained vigilance. The Klan was reportedly hanging and burning entire encampments of free blacks, and the men were on edge. Some wanted to go hunt Klan members. Once he got wind of what some of the men wanted to do, Major Vetter quickly informed them that they were now soldiers and subject to the orders of the United States; they couldn't abuse their power as vigilantes. He informed Second Lieutenant Phoenix that no one was to leave this camp unless expressly given permission by Major Vetter. The whispers became grumbles, but the men decided it wasn't in their best interest hunting Klan now that they were soldiers. It pained most of them that they were now capable of defending themselves and couldn't help the former slaves.

Except for the few who wanted to go hunt Klansmen, most of the men had been taking the month off since they were briefed that the war was over, so they could clean up and enjoy the time they had now that the war was over. This was something new to the former slaves; they'd never had the opportunity to just relax and basically do nothing. Major Vetter noticed that the men maintained their composure and didn't start acting like a bunch of "monkeys" now that they didn't have a war to fight. It was another thing that proved to him that Negroes were no different from whites.

Lieutenant Phoenix was everywhere at once. The men saw him as Major Vetter's second in command and gave him due respect. It also helped that he made the former giant Amra his first sergeant. He was now First Sergeant Amra.

Major Vetter was impressed by the names his subordinates had chosen for themselves now that they were free. Fessa or Second Lieutenant Phoenix had chosen the name Phoenix because of his former adoptive father and because, like the fabled bird that rises from the ashes, he felt like he was a new person and set to rise. Amra or First Sergeant Amra paid homage to his ancestry, which Major Vetter was informed by Lieutenant Phoenix was from the line of Nubian kings and queens of history. It was a good sign that the men wanted to be more than they were and now had the chance. He would make sure the men under his command could be the best they could be, black or white.

SEVENTEEN

The Move to Port Hudson, Louisiana— Captain Vetter's Concerns

CAPTAIN VETTER KNEW his men had changed and grown. They had fought hard for a country to recognize them. Unfortunately, Vetter just didn't think the country, particularly any place in the South, was ready to see their change.

These were his thoughts as he prepared his men to get ready to move out to Port Hudson, Louisiana. He had to admit to himself that he was extremely concerned about the move to Port Hudson. He honestly believed this move, if not managed appropriately, could be more dangerous than any battle his men had faced.

Almost every single man under his command had been a slave

before joining the service. When they first arrived, they had all possessed the slave mentality when talking to or being addressed by whites. With heads down, they appeared as humble as possible to avoid incurring the master's cruelty for some perceived threat. Now, to a man, they exuded the confidence of men who have been forged in the fires of the struggle of life and death and had come through as hard, sharp weapons. Looking at his men, he noted that they all exuded the confidence of men who were comfortable in their own skin, and they were capable of defending themselves against anyone who would try to take their freedom away. Heads that were too comfortable looking down were always up now, alert and sharp.

Each man had to come to terms with the horrors and heart-breaks of slavery and the Civil War. They had endured both and had learned since that, regardless of a man's color of skin, each man bled and died the same way. They rode horses like men who were seasoned in the saddle and held their weapons like men who are comfortable using them.

Vetter knew that the confidence his men exuded was defi-nitely something white men in the South had never seen from blacks before. The atrocities of the war were still too new to give men like his an honest chance. After years of treating Negroes like pets and cattle, white men weren't ready to witness blacks, known for killing other white men, still living. This was some-thing Southerners believed no good white citizen in the South should be comfortable with. Vetter also knew without a doubt that his men would rather die than be put back in any semblance of slavery.

Many of his men possessed a lot of hatred and anger the war couldn't heal. They had now broken the taboo of killing white men and had been working or fighting side by side with them. The truth of the matter, which was revealed in war, was that a man's value was determined by his heart and will, not by the color of his skin. Blacks knew this because they had seen whites run at the thought of dying and quit when they were too tired; as their executioners, they had seen the light dim in their eyes as their lives departed. The blacks may have been illiterate, but they weren't ignorant. Wasn't the master always supposed to be greater than the slave? Vetter knew the blacks had already figured out that wasn't the case; the battlefield had taught them that the only master they had to answer to was themselves. Given opportunity and knowledge, they could manage their own destiny.

EIGHTEEN

Lieutenant's Phoenix Concerns

THE ANNOUNCEMENT OF the move to Port Hudson, Louisiana, gave Lieutenant Phoenix pause. The unit would need to come out of the shadows and function as a normal unit. Major Vetter had warned everyone that his mission was never to be spoken of, and the fact that they were responsible for so many white men's deaths must never be found out. He warned that if it became public knowledge, white men would stop at nothing to kill them and their loved ones as revenge and a lesson to other blacks.

In his mind, moving a large group of colored men through Port Hudson, Louisiana, immediately after the war was a very dangerous idea. No training could prepare him or his men for what to expect in a post-Civil War city in the Deep South. However, the thought of a skirmish with white people who refused to acknowledge the black soldiers brought a smile to his face. The perceived violence from white people wasn't what scared Lieutenant Phoenix. Violence from white people was a way of life for Negroes, and besides, he was armed now; any violence could be quickly dispelled. Let them come; if there was anything he was confident in, it was his men's ability to defend themselves and their comfort with killing white men. This was a taboo for every other black man in the country.

Going back to Port Hudson, Louisiana, was a conflict filled with multiple emotions for Lieutenant Phoenix. Slavery, a way of life in the South, was now banned and considered illegal, and blacks were now supposed to be equal. Southerners were being forced to accept the "animals" who had worked their fields as equals. In their minds, it was like accepting a pig to dinner or inviting a cow to a wedding. He predicted that the threats, once they started to enter Port Hudson, Louisiana, would grow; the nearer they came to the city, the situation would only get worse the longer they stayed. Even though the war had resulted in the freedom of Negroes, the South was furious about the "Yanks" winning the war. The few news reports they had received indicated that Negroes were being hanged and burned all over the South for the smallest infractions. His understanding of strategy and tactics had taught him that his unit would be viewed as invaders and part of the new reality, which was too new to most Southerners. They would be viewed as uniformed slaves come to seek retribution for the perceived wrongs of slavery. Now anybody who tried to cross them would find out that being a slave was an aspect of who they used to be, and they would find out in fatal fashion who they were now.

His personal journey through slavery had taught him that men who truly embraced slavery would always be a threat to black people and that they would continue to spread that hate to everyone they come in contact with. The war had changed him, and he'd had to learn some hard lessons. They had told the men that it wasn't okay to go out and hunt Klan members, because they were soldiers of the US government. But if the Klan members put themselves in the way of him and his men, he would ensure that no threat remained. He would never leave an enemy alive who showed himself to be dedicated to the destruction of the black race.

NINETEEN

Major Vetter's Thoughts on Lieutenant Phoenix's Concerns

LIEUTENANT PHOENIX VOICED his concerns to Major Vetter. He felt that the safety and comfort the unit had shared in hiding would be shattered when whites outside the unit saw Negroes leading. Major Vetter didn't distinguish his leadership under a white or black division; platoon sergeants were placed in their positions based on capability and with the general consent of the platoon. When Major Vetter had initially told Lieutenant Phoenix about his desire to promote him as a platoon leader, he went to Lieutenant Phoenix first to discuss in detail the possible issues that would be associated with the elevation and his desire to have leadership be colorless. Meaning, could Lieutenant Phoenix get comfortable managing white men under the scrutiny of other white men?

Lieutenant Phoenix had initially had serious reservations about being put in charge, but Major Vetter explained to Lieutenant Phoenix that even though it was a hard position to be put in, he, Lieutenant Phoenix, was the best representative to show white people that Negroes were capable of leading. He also mentioned that with Lieutenant Phoenix's unique upbringing and education, they made him the perfect representation of the Negroes' capabilities for both white and blacks to witness.

The last part of what Major Vetter told Lieutenant Phoenix had the most impact on him. Lieutenant Phoenix's other concern was that he wasn't immune to the fact that he was considered a role model for every black man and woman in America. He had never considered himself a role model for anyone. Hell, he was too worried about living to think about what others thought of him. But the more he thought about it, the more he could see Major Vetter's view. He was the only Negro in the camp who could read, and if you hadn't seen him first, you would have thought he was a white man based on how well spoken he was. He also made a point of keeping his uniform clean and tried to take a bath every time he had the chance. He had never considered his education and upbringing to be a beacon of hope for other blacks. He was a little worried that the few gains or accomplishments he had made in his life were nothing outside his unit and that everyone would see only a slave when things became difficult for the unit. His new confidence as a leader of troops as a black man was a double-edged sword, which would be tested at every opportunity. On one side, every black man and woman would see him and be counting on him to show them what this new America looked like for free slaves; and the pro-Negro white people would be expecting him to set the example for other blacks to keep the peace.

On the other side, both the uneducated whites and rich whites of the South would be extremely intimidated by this new way of life for the Negro but for completely different reasons. The rich whites would lose free labor and money. They in turn would tell the poor whites that newly freed blacks would take their menial jobs at cheaper pay and that they now had to face possible hunger for their families.

The educated whites simply didn't want the cattle to be educated on their plight. This would be a threat to their investments and other slaves, and it would mean the death of the "Southern Belle" culture. Their wealth depended on slaves working and toiling in the fields as a way of life with no other options. Education would make Negroes wise to their plight, and that couldn't happen at any cost. Exceptions could be made for certain slaves, particularly those with the master's blood running through their systems. However, these exceptions were far and few, and they weren't enough to give any other Negroes hope.

His mind, when not on the duty of work, spent time sorting out and making sense of the things that had happened in his life. He had been witness to, and often was the subject of, horrors and abuses no man or woman should ever have to endure. More times than he would like to admit, he reverently wished for the sweet silence and peace of death. However, his understanding of history gave him a perspective that bad things happened all the time to good people and that life still moved on. He knew of ancient characters like Spartacus, the plight of the Hebrews and their struggles with the Egyptians, even the current decimation of the American Indian. Bad things happened to people all the time everywhere. He had also witnessed the overwhelming sense of hopelessness that made some people accept their fate or became stronger because of their suffering. In his mind, he had been forged in the fires of slavery and become hardened, stronger. He knew that once they left their current encampment, his education, pain, suffering, and war experience would make him even stronger. He wouldn't wish slavery on anyone, but just like God made Moses get a slave's perspective by living the life of a slave, he felt the slavery he had experienced had made him stronger to defeat it. To be strong for the future, they needed to ensure that they carried the burdens forward so they would never happen again. Would his men recognize the leadership in him when things got bad? He smiled, remembering an incident when he had taken his first baby steps in giving orders. He remembered the fiasco that involved First Sergeant Amra, who at the time had also just gotten promoted to his position, when he incorporated the cleanliness rule.

After about a week of officially wearing uniforms, Lieutenant Phoenix had approached First Sergeant Amra about incorporating a cleanliness rule in the unit. After a recent inspection, he had noted that some, if not most, of the men were rancid with stink after months and months of buildup and no baths. First Sergeant Amra jokingly said that the people of Port Hudson, Louisiana, would smell them before they could see them; the only welcome they would get before being strung up was a hot, boiling bath. First Sergeant Amra had the same reservations as Lieutenant Phoenix about cleanliness, so when Lieutenant Phoenix advised him of his new rule, he exuberantly went about his task of "cleaning up the pigs," as he called it. He took all the men to a nearby river and had them all plunge in and soap up with a lye-based soap, which one of the men claimed to know how to make. Common advice was to let the soap sit on their skin and eat up the dirt, when in actually it was eating up their skin. The results were minor burns on some of the men near their sensitive areas. One man was so dirty that he was reported missing for three days. A review of the platoon roster after the platoon had returned from perimeter duty identified a man with the same name as the missing person, but he had been listed as a new recruit. His transformation to clean had been so complete that everybody thought he was a new recruit.

The questions, as he fondly remembered that day, were still there. Was he strong enough to be the leader they needed? Would he have the leadership the men needed in these tumultuous times? First Sergeant Amra was the best soldier they had, and Lieutenant Phoenix felt he had proved himself to him that day; it was something he now understood—that he needed more than Major Vetter's approval. There were so many questions, and the answers were yet to be known. Well, good or bad, he would soon find out. They were leaving in two days.

TWENTY

Sergeant Hall

HIS TRIP BACK home to find his family and the return trip with young Charl in tow were the first time Sergeant Hall had ever been by himself. The little time had given him a rare moment to think about his life and all things that had happened. Looking back at his life since his escape from the plantation, he could hardly believe the man he had become. Hell, just the thought of being able to consider himself a man was like the first breath of air to a newborn. As a slave, he'd had as much knowledge of the world around him as the cats, dogs, and cows on the farm. Just like the farm animals, a slave's place was to live and die on the property he'd been born on. Even worse, he was to be upended from the only thing he knew and sold to another plantation, where he had no family, friends, or anyone with any sort of re-lation. Abandoned and alone in a world already ugly with the oppression of one person by another for personal gain, there was nothing to hope for in a slave's life.

In just a couple of years, he had been transformed into the man of confidence, skill, and death as a soldier. His attempt to find his family, though unsuccessful, had taught him much about himself and the man he had become. He now knew that he would never be a slave to anyone again. As long as he had a gun in his hand, a knife in his belt, and breath in his lungs, he would fight to the death to keep the freedom he had gained.

He could even see the change in the young boy, Charl, in the short time since freeing him from his former slave plantation. Just being out in the world had started to transform his demeanor and appearance. Sergeant Hall smiled as he remembered how scared the young boy had been during the first couple of nights out in the dark woods. Charl had snuggled under Sergeant Hall like a young dog pup, shaking and shivering and jumping at every sound. He held the boy tight all night, and it was the first time since his daughters had died that he had felt anything fatherly. The situation was warming and gut wrenching all at once—enjoying the comfort of providing security for the young boy but dying inwardly, wishing it was his daughter once again. He then realized that young Charl couldn't be any older than ten. A little big for his size but still just a little boy.

When he arrived back at the camp, he informed newly promoted First Sergeant Amra that young Charl would join them and asked whether he had anything for him to do. First Sergeant Amra had been talking to another soldier when Sergeant Hall approached. As he introduced himself and started to speak, First Sergeant Amra turned around and acknowledged Sergeant Hall. He looked down at the object of Sergeant Hall report and immediately reached down and grabbed the young man like a father holding a son. He picked up young Charl in his arms, smiling the whole time. He lifted the boy into the air and simply looked at him, still smiling.

It was the strangest thing Sergeant Hall had ever seen. After a couple of seconds, First Sergeant Amra gently put the boy back down, still smiling, and said, "Welcome." He told Sergeant Hall to get the boy settled and bring him back in the morning. Charl would be under Sergeant Hall's supervision; they would occupy the same tent, but during the day, when Sergeant Hall was doing maneuvers or drills, First Sergeant Amra would put young Charl to work.

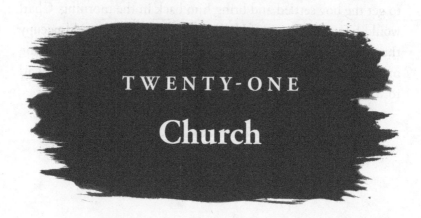

TWENTY-ONE

Church

SERGEANT HALL HADN'T given much thought to the move to Port Hudson, Louisiana, because he was so preoccupied with getting Charl situated. In his mind the move was just like any other order or task he had ever been given in his life; he would follow without question. As a slave, he had never questioned his master or the rules he laid down. As a soldier, he would go wherever the army sent him, but now he would be armed as a man and defend himself as such. Being his own man was a dream he had never had and never thought possible. He had been born a slave, and until he had run away and become a soldier, he had believed he would die a slave. Since his freedom, he had taken to learning how to read in classes Lieutenant Phoenix offered.

One day, when speaking to the men, Lieutenant Phoenix told them all, "Now that you are free, you will need to learn how to read to navigate from one place to another and to make sure nobody ever tries to take advantage of you. As all of you know, white people start learning how to read as kids, and we Negroes needed to start making education and learning a part of our lives. The slaves before us never thought to be free or what that would mean. They died, not knowing that one day their children would be free. We need to respect and honor the sacrifices of all the former slaves. They endured so we could endure. They gave us strength. The first thing we need to learn is knowledge. Our African ancestors were enticed due to their ignorance of world affairs. They played tribe against tribe, because the tribes couldn't see past their front doors. We need to make sure our ignorance of the world never makes us slaves again."

This made a lot of sense to Sergeant Hall; a slave didn't need to know how to read, but a freed man should know how to read. One of the main reasons he wanted to learn to read was so he could learn the good word of the Lord for himself and learn to read the Bible.

Sergeant Hall, considered a Christian, had learned to love church because it was the only place and time where he felt like a man. When he had been on the plantation, church had been the only place where the master wouldn't harass the slaves and leave them completely alone. During this time, slaves congregated, talked about the things going on throughout the plantation, and shared any news. This was the only time the slaves had some semblance of normal lives. The women and men wore their best, and the children get cleaned up for church services. It was because of this experience that he felt the need and desire to learn the good word of the Lord himself.

Sergeant Hall remembered his slave pastor, Pastor Bill, who had been very respected by the slave community and had been the main source of information to other slaves about what was happening in the world. He was the only black man who had any semblance of freedom on the plantation. He could even go to other plantations.

Pastor Bill was the slave of a white reverend and had learned the word of the Lord from the reverend. The rumors were that the reverend liked little boys, and when the boys had gotten too big, they had made him a slave pastor, because he could read. Pastor Bill could preach only what the reverend told him to preach and nothing else.

Sergeant Hall remembered that Pastor Bill was the only black man any of the slaves knew who could read. He had privileges most slaves couldn't even imagine. He traveled from plantation to plantation, so he was also the most current form of news the slaves had on what was happening around them. Pastor Bill was always better dressed than everyone else. He usually had handed-down suits. He was well spoken and the definition of a man to other slave men. Because of his ability to speak and dress, most white people treated the pastor with a little deference, which was better than any treatment given to any black Sergeant Hall had ever seen. He could approach white people and talk to them about the Lord and his ways. Some white people even deferred to him for religious guidance. Slave pastors also didn't work in the fields, and they walked about during the day, doing a manner of services near the big house. A lot of times, the pastor doubled down as a driver since he was required to go from plantation to plantation to "tend the flock."

Sergeant Hall remembered that Pastor Bill had been treated like an aristocrat. Pastors often drew dirt maps on the ground and tried to show slaves where they were in relation to other plantations, because most slaves had never traveled past their own plantation grounds. Pastor Bill traveled back and forth between three other plantations. Hall remembered that the pastor had a wife at each plantation he visited. Each of his slave families was given deference over other slaves. Each of the pastor's families worked in or around the big house, not in the fields. Now, in retrospect, Sergeant Hall realized there was even a hierarchy among the slaves.

Now during Sunday services, Sergeant Hall delighted in the word of the Lord the pastor preached. He remembered the pastor starting every sermon off with "Servants, be obedient to them that are your masters according to the flesh, with fear and trembling, in singleness of your heart, as unto Christ" (Ephesians 6:5 KJV). Saying this phrase had always made the weight of seeing the abuses and tortures of slavery seem to melt away. He had been doing the Lord's will by humbly serving his master, taking the abuses, and never raising a fist. He had felt that by keeping Christ in the forefront of his mind and heart, he would eventually find his peace and happiness. He believed the Lord was recording the abuses his masters had visited on him and other slaves around him and that God would judge accordingly. This was what had kept the peace in his mind as he witnessed one atrocity after another done against slaves. But now, after attending the reading classes and talking to Lieutenant Phoenix about his belief in the Bible and why he wanted to read, all that had changed.

Sergeant Hall and Lieutenant Phoenix's relationship came about only because of Sergeant Hall's urge to learn how to read. Sergeant Hall was considered a field slave, who toiled in the fields his whole life. A black man like Lieutenant Phoenix was likened to a house slave, because he could read and write, talk well, and usually had a better selection of clothing. In his old life, there was a clear distinction between house slave and field slave, and Sergeant Hall, being the good field slave, always kept the distance. His initial conversation was interesting because when Sergeant Hall asked Lieutenant Phoenix whether he could attend the class, Lieutenant Phoenix asked why he wanted to learn how to read. Sergeant Hall told him he wanted to hear the Lord's word for himself. Lieutenant Phoenix's response was interesting; he told Sergeant Hall, "Only if you first promise to learn to better yourself and only preach to others how the word has impacted you personally." Sergeant Hall understood the first part about making himself better but didn't understand the second part about preaching to others. His look of consternation probably said so. Lieutenant Phoenix just laughed and said, "Welcome."

Over time Sergeant Hall began to look forward to the teachings and ask questions of Lieutenant Phoenix. They were simple questions at first and mostly about the future of the company, but as he learned more and more and thought about things, his questions began to become more complex. Lieutenant Phoenix gave him all the time he needed, since they were in sort of a standstill. The first things Sergeant Hall learned how to read were the old newspaper articles Lieutenant Phoenix kept for Major Vetter. Sergeant Hall asked him whether he had a Bible, because that was what he wanted to learn how to read, and Lieutenant Phoenix told him that words were words in any book. If you can read one book or magazine, he said, you can read them all. But Sergeant Hall was adamant about learning how to read the Bible. Lieutenant Phoenix looked at him and said, "Just like the Lord told Moses when he was at the mountain, they have bowed down to it, offered sacrifices, and said that it is the God who brought them out of Egypt. The Bible is a tool to learn about the faith you need in the Lord; don't make it the crutch you need for faith."

Sergeant Hall asked Lieutenant Phoenix, "Who was Moses?"

The question took Lieutenant Phoenix completely off guard. "What do you mean, who is Moses?"

Sergeant Hall replied, "I have never heard that name before."

That statement started a long conversation about what Sergeant Hall knew about the Bible. Lieutenant Phoenix realized there were major portions of his religious education missing. What Lieutenant Phoenix learned was that the limited knowledge Sergeant Hall had of the Bible he could almost recite word for word. They talked for days on how much Sergeant Hall knew about the Bible and the large gaps in his knowledge of details.

Two phrases, in particular, Sergeant Hall knew by memorization. They included the issue of Negroes being descended from the line of Ham, those identified in the Bible as blacks and as the reason slaves were cursed to being indentured from birth.

> Noah planted a vineyard, overindulged in the fruit of his labor, got drunk, and "lay uncovered in his tent." His son Ham, the father of Canaan, "saw the nakedness of his father," and told his brothers, who respectfully covered their father. When Noah woke up from his stupor, he condemned Ham's bad behavior, saying, "Cursed be Canaan; a servant of servants shall he be to his brothers." (Genesis 9:25 ESV)

The other verse stated that slaves should be obedient to their masters unto death, that slaves, would have their happiness in the afterlife, and that hardships in this life were just a test for the next. "Servants, be obedient to them that are your masters according to the flesh, with fear and trembling, in singleness of your heart, as unto Christ" (Ephesians 6:5).

He expressed to Lieutenant Phoenix that these two scriptures were core to his belief and justification for his servitude and compliance. He then confessed to Lieutenant Phoenix his murder of his master's son and friends; after killing them, he'd known he would be condemned to hell for raising his hand against his master. Now that he was a free man, he wanted to learn what the Bible had to say about him being a free man and whether there was a way to get redemption for the killing of his master's progeny? He had killed many men since that day, but killing the master's son was the only killing for which he felt he had to face Jesus on the day of redemption.

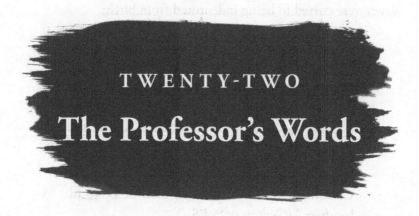

TWENTY-TWO

The Professor's Words

LIEUTENANT PHOENIX LISTENED to Sergeant Hall's story with a sense of detachment. This same conversation had gotten him one of the most brutal abuses of his life with his former master. He had been well versed in Bible verses, and his adoptive father had always warned him about knowledge. He fondly remembered him saying, "The first lesson God taught man was that he wasn't ready for knowledge, and that since then we have been blindly destroying ourselves with more and more knowledge because the cumulative *we* are not ready. Remember, the Bible was written at a time when 99 percent of the population was illiterate, with a large portion of the literacy rate being in the church. The only way to get information across to the people was in the form of a story. Like most stories before the Bible, the reader was supposed to glean a lesson or moral from the story. Because the church basically held a monopoly on the distribution of the Bible, the lesson or moral of the story was dictated to people versus being internalized. Now, over time the world has learned their faith based on another man's perception or internalization. The most basic tenet of the Bible, the Ten Commandments, which the church couldn't deny, man has chosen to ignore, in favor of taking the stories and arguing over the intent or trying to get everyone to see things their way."

Lieutenant Phoenix's former slave master had hated him for his intelligence and known Lieutenant Phoenix to be extremely intelligent. Playing ignorant in front of his master would never work because he had witnessed Lieutenant Phoenix's true intelligence when he was still free and so proud of it.

He painfully remembered the event like it was yesterday. Lieutenant Phoenix had been polishing the master's study, while his master was looking over some paper. His former master had jokingly said to Lieutenant Phoenix, "I wonder if you will still be my slave when we are both in heaven."

Lieutenant Phoenix didn't want to answer the question because he knew that either way, the answer would define the degrees of pain he would receive. Initially, he acted as if he hadn't heard the question and kept working. The master said it again, this time with a little anger in his voice. The calm before the eruption, Lieutenant Phoenix responded, "The Lord willing."

The master smiled and asked Lieutenant Phoenix to come close to his desk. Lieutenant Phoenix walked over and stood in front of the desk. The master asked Lieutenant Phoenix to come around the desk and stand closer to his side. Lieutenant Phoenix obliged.

When he got next to his master, the master asked Lieutenant Phoenix to pull his britches down. Lieutenant Phoenix began to sweat and knew immediately this wasn't going to turn out well. Lieutenant Phoenix untied the string holding his britches, and his pants dropped. His manhood was exposed. The master grabbed the letter opener on this desk and pressed the pointed end against

Lieutenant Phoenix's manhood. Then he asked, "Now tell the truth. Do you want to be my slave in heaven?"

Lieutenant Phoenix knew anything he said would be wrong; he knew he couldn't play dumb, so he said the only thing that meant something to him. "Evil men do not go to heaven, so you being my master there is not my concern!" Lieutenant Phoenix vaguely remembered getting the words out before a large explosion in his groin caused him to pass out.

When he came to, he was leaning over the front of the master's desk, with both hands tied in front of him. He was totally naked. The master was sitting at his desk, writing, apparently waiting for Lieutenant Phoenix to awaken. When he saw Lieutenant Phoenix was awake, he smiled and said, "Glad to see you awake. I thought a lot about what you said, and even though I didn't like what you said, it did have a large ring of truth to it. For some of the things I have done, there will be a reckoning, and I will have to answer for it, but I'll be damned if a slave tells me where I belong. Since you are so well versed in the Bible and its punishments, you should also be familiar with Leviticus 18:22. 'Thou shalt not lie with mankind, as with womankind: it is abomination.'" (KJV). The master looked past Lieutenant Phoenix and motioned for him to come forward.

Lieutenant Phoenix heard a scuffle behind him, and from his left, a huge slave by the name of Bamba came into view. Bamba was the master's enforcer slave, who did all his dirty work, anything the master tasked him to do. The problem with Bamba was that he enjoyed hurting slaves, because he had been so brutally abused and beaten over the years. He saw beating other slaves as a way to relieve some of his pain.

The master said, "Ole Bamba here is going to give you some good ole man loving. That way when judgment day comes and if I find myself in hell, I know that after Bamba finishes with you,

you will be guaranteed a place in hell also. Like Leviticus says, laying with a man is an abomination."

Master pointed to Bamba, who in turn looked at Lieutenant Phoenix and smiled as he turned and walked to the rear of Lieutenant Phoenix. The ropes holding Lieutenant Phoenix didn't allow him to move. To his embarrassment, he remembered every painful and horrific moment the master put an abomination on Lieutenant Phoenix's soul.

The embarrassment and pain of that tragic day brought a constant fight to his mind. Even though that hadn't been the first time his master subjugated him to this type of punishment, it was the first time religion was linked. It was a whole new type of pain for Lieutenant Phoenix. Afterward, Lieutenant Phoenix's mind and soul were in turmoil. Was he destined to be an abomination, and was he hell bound? Only after becoming free and being provided the chance to read and discuss his belief with Major Vetter in depth was Lieutenant Phoenix able to internalize the Bible's passages. He learned and felt that no man could put an abomination or sin on a man whose heart was with God and didn't voluntarily do so. Also, people in power were using the Bible as a weapon to control and abuse a race of people. This was never more evident than now, as Sergeant Hall repeated line for line the only verses he had ever been taught. Sergeant Hall had never been witness to the full gospel because of the church's manipulation to control the slaves and keep them in servitude. In his channeled ignorance, Sergeant Hall, because of the church's need to control the slaves, had dedicated his life to the abbreviated gospel and found peace in slavery. In Lieutenant Phoenix's mind, this was a calculated and monstrous deed, a deed in which the Satan the Bible warned of would be gleefully appreciative of.

Lieutenant Phoenix came out of his thoughts and informed Sergeant Hall that he understood his concerns and that he had also often had the same questions. However, he told Sergeant Hall, "No man can tell you if your soul is in peril or is not worthy. Your relationship with God is yours alone, and to make that relationship stronger, you need to learn to read everything. You don't need to learn how to read just the Bible but to learn to read everything. The challenges to your faith will be learned from the Bible but experienced in the real world."

Lieutenant Phoenix also explained to Sergeant Hall that he had been given only a portion of the Bible in the form of a "Slave Bible" and that the full gospel had been denied to slaves. Sergeant Hall stated that he didn't understand what Lieutenant Phoenix meant by a "Slave Bible." Lieutenant Phoenix told him to hold on and disappeared for a few minutes. When he came back in, he had two books; both had the same cover, but one seemed smaller than the other. Lieutenant Phoenix explained to Sergeant Hall that the original Bible had been edited for slaves to make them feel like their lives of servitude were the only lives they were entitled to. He explained that the edits had been designed to prevent slaves from revolting; by teaching enslaved people biblical lessons about obedience and accepting one's fate, masters helped them "be better slaves." Lieutenant Phoenix explained that certain books, such as the Exodus story, could inspire hope for liberation, so they were deliberately removed. Instead, the creators of the "Slave Bible" stressed only the parts of the Bible that justified and fortified the system of slavery and kept the slave docile and malleable. The last two words had to be explained to Sergeant Hall, and his face took on one of wonder and anger.

The conversation had taken place a couple of days ago, and Sergeant Hall now took to learning with a new passion. He still didn't understand why people from the church had tried to keep the word from slaves. Wasn't God a God of all people? Why had he let them violate his word and use it as a weapon to keep a race in ignorance? When he had asked Lieutenant Phoenix how God could let this happen, Lieutenant Phoenix answered, "God didn't edit the book. Man did. Remember, Satan is the master of lies, and if he can get man to corrupt the word, then that would be his greatest success. You have been informed that your education on religion was lacking and abbreviated. Do you blame God or take on the responsibility of learning for yourself what God intended?" Lieutenant Phoenix added, "Remember, the first lesson God taught us with Adam and Eve was to be weary of knowledge and basically that we weren't ready for it. Remember that and make it your goal to be worthy of the knowledge the Lord has provided."

Sergeant Hall felt better after talking to Lieutenant Phoenix; he was more confused but happy that he knew there was more to the Lord's word. After a week of learning how to read and talking to Lieutenant Phoenix, he had already increased his knowledge of the Bible and felt stronger in his testimony. The talks with Lieutenant Phoenix helped him to better internalize what he was reading. He had also started doing one-on-one sessions with other soldiers, who were part of Lieutenant Phoenix's reading group. They had all heard the story of the "Slave Bible" and felt the best way to get their truth about God and the church was to create their own Bible among themselves—not a church but a group of men dedicated to learning about God and sharing their concerns and revelations.

TWENTY-THREE

First Sergeant Amra

NEWLY PROMOTED FIRST Sergeant Amra was at the top of his game. He was doing something he was most prepared for: being a soldier. Major Vetter told him the men both respected and feared Amra, and that fact could be put to good use in getting them ready. Lieutenant Phoenix revealed to Major Vetter his background as a warrior in Africa before being captured and sold. Major Vetter had often leaned on Amra's knowledge of guerrilla warfare to develop their attack plans, and now the hunting-like techniques could be explained.

After First Sergeant Amra informed Lieutenant Phoenix of his original plans to head back to Africa to see whether any of his tribe was still alive, Lieutenant Phoenix's historical curiosity was stirred. He asked his first sergeant about it, and that was when First Sergeant Amra informed Lieutenant Phoenix of his unique lineage, that he had been the firstborn prince of his tribe and that if any of the tribe was left, it was his responsibility to go back and try to put the tribe back together. He informed Lieutenant Phoenix that his tribe could accurately trace their lineage back to the first men, whom ancient rulers believed to be giants among men. First Sergeant Amra's mastery of the English language was limited, but he was an inherently intelligent man and learned quickly. Over time Lieutenant Phoenix was able to decipher Amra's story, and it was amazing.

Amra had been from a rarely mentioned noble Nubian tribe, which traced its lineage back to the ancient king of Sumeria, Gilgamesh. Gilgamesh was purportedly a giant and demigod. Amra's tribe was also mentioned in the Bible; the book of Genesis claimed that Abraham descended from Egypt's Upper Nile region and was of Nubian descent. Amra's tribe's average height, even among the women, was six feet. Amra was six foot, seven inches tall, and he had 250-plus pounds of solid muscle. His tribe in combat was awesome to behold. The tribe's weapon of choice was the giant khopesh, a huge Egyptian curved blade. Throughout Africa's history, his tribe had become feared and respected. Their unnatural size and almost mythical reputation as indestructible fighters in battle were respected throughout the African continent. Feared in battle because of their size and ferocity in dealing death with the large blades, they were highly respected because they chose to fight only when threatened, instead of using their size to dominate other tribes.

It had been his tribe's voice that regulated how other Africans treated prisoners of war. They had initiated a rule that set guidelines on the general treatment of prisoners; those guidelines received universal approval of all tribes, small and large. The rules allowed a prisoner to be an indentured servant for a year in a tribe. After a year, the prisoner was free to go back to his tribe, or he could choose to stay in the tribe he had been a prisoner in as a new tribe member. There were strict rules on the way they could treat a prisoner, and over time these had become a huge tool in integrating tribes and lessening their warlike natures. It was hard to go to war with someone with familial links. There was always the small tribe, which wanted to get more respect or better land, but centuries of relevant peace was maintained.

Amra informed Lieutenant Phoenix that all this had changed with the introduction of the gun. The little tribes demanded respect now that they had the gun, the means to get respect. The established rules were thrown aside as they ascended through slaughter and terror. In fact, it was while on his way to a meeting to address the terror the small tribes had spawned that Amra was captured and brought into slavery.

TWENTY-FOUR

Amra's Capture

AN INFORMAL TRIBE gathering had been called to discuss recent accounts of the white men trafficking with smaller tribes and trading slaves for weapons. With the new guns, the smaller tribes were slaughtering other tribes for slaves and territory. This practice was completely against the rules all other tribes had agreed on. The other tribes were looking to the Kushites to bring some wisdom on how to handle the situation. Only the tribes that dealt with the whites had guns, so individually each tribe was at a disadvantage.

Young Amra had already shown much promise as a young chieftain with his physical prowess and believed that only by uniting the tribes could they hope to have an advantage over the rouge tribes. As the senior son of his tribe and future chieftain, Amra's father had sent him to represent his tribe at the huge gathering. This was his chance to prove to his father that he was also a capable and wise leader. He would bring the tribes together and defeat this challenge to their way of life.

Already the stories of slavery to the whites had reached his tribes, including the degradation of the women and the treatment like animals. The idea of being taken away from their land to a strange place, never to return, was incomprehensible to the Kushites. Their land was their life, and they lived to nurture and take care of it. The plateau the Kushites lived on had been given to them through their ancestors. The land was fertile from volcanic erosion; it rose from the ground almost two miles in the air. From the edge of the plateau, it seemed like they could see all of Africa. It was their sacred duty to protect and watch the lands and the people. Their size wasn't by coincidence, and their lineage wasn't an accident. They believed their link to the first man gave them a responsibility to watch over the rest of the other tribes—not to rule but to watch over them and advise. His father always said, "Man must learn to increase his sense of responsibility and the fact that everything he does will have its consequences." His tribe had once ruled the earth with great cities; a small portion of the tribe had decided to break away to the current plateau area and had chosen to give up the life of ruling and domination. They were peaceful people, but they prided themselves on their warrior skills. Children, both boys and girls, were taught to be warriors and fight as soon as they could walk. They were taught multiple weapons, and yearly games were held to see who the best warriors were. They not only learned to be proficient in various weapons but also discussed ancient battles to learn strategy. An old African proverb states, "Don't beat the drums of war unless you're ready to fight." The Kushite tribe was always ready to fight, and with their signature khopesh, they were fearsome to behold in battle.

The route to the gathering would take about eight days of travel. Amra's father had given him a ceremonial guard of twelve warriors, all armed with large khopesh strapped on their backs, bows and arrows, and javelins or short throwing spears. Amra had trained with each warrior while growing up, and he knew them like brothers. They were the best warriors of the tribe. They had planned to meet up with the leadership of the tribe bordering the Kushite land, the Tigrayans.

The Tigrayans were mostly nomadic farmers, who primarily relied on the bow and arrow as their primary weapons. By being a boundary neighbor with the Kushites, they benefitted from the fierce reputation and protection. Amra's father had unified his neighbors in a treaty that stated that if someone attacked any tribe that signed the treaty, other tribes would come to that tribe's aide. His father knew that years of slaving in the South would find its way North; the tribes needed to unite to defeat this effort. Amra would enforce his father's plan.

The meeting Amra attended was enforcement of that treaty; there were reports of two tribes already being attacked. Nothing had been verified; one child had escaped, and there were reports of white men and guns. Scouts had gone to verify. The scouts hadn't returned in two weeks, so the meeting was being called as a precaution.

The boundary between Kush and Tigray was a natural river, which was two days' run from the base of the plateau. Kushites traveled at a light jog; they never walked when traveling. The men took pride in being able to run from sunup to sundown, it helped add to the fear and mysticism of their tribe.

Amra and his men were a few hours out from the river boundary when he heard the first pop. The man on his left went down, blood exploding out of the back of his chest, almost immediately after the noise. Amra knew immediately that someone had fired a gun; he had never heard one fired before but had heard about the destruction they caused. Amra had his men stop and drop to their knees. He told them to put their shields up. The fallen man had a huge hole in his chest. Behind Amra and his men, a huge fire erupted; someone had thrown large straw heaps in the middle of the trail they were on, and he could see men rise to the left and right of the fire with long sticks held up. Guns!

Amra had two of his men get their bows and point them toward the men he had seen rise; they were within killing range. While his focus was on the fire and men in the back, a voice called out in Tigrayans. "Kushites, put down your weapons. We do not want to kill you. You are surrounded by guns. We want to talk." Amra knew that if he was surrounded by guns, these men were either rouge tribesmen or slavers; either option was bad for Amra and his men. He also believed that if they already knew he was a prince of his tribe, they could use him as a ransom or, even worse, a tool to enslave his tribe.

Amra smiled inwardly; his father had told him that he would have two men following a day's travel behind him after they departed. They followed so they could verify that Amra and his men made it to the link-up point with the Tigrayans. If he could head their way, they could provide cover with their bows while he and his men tried to escape. Going forward was no longer a consideration; he had to ensure his tribe's safety. All this passed through his mind in a brief second. Taking decisive action, he told four of his men to identify two targets, fire two arrows, and take off toward the fire. They would use the thing they thought would trap them to escape.

With a tribal signal for attack, the first volley of the four bowmen went off. Corresponding with the shots, three of the four targets with weapons silhouetted against the fire immediately fell. True to their disciplined training, all men jumped and took off toward the fire at the same time, shields up and facing back, heads below shields. Forming a tight, oval-shaped shield wall, they took off at a full sprint. Immediately the pops heard earlier could be heard again; one of the men grunted but kept running. As if on cue, the four men dropped flat to the ground, secured their bows and arrows, and fired. Two more arrows toward targets silhouetted by the fire went down; the pops had stopped.

Amra knew the guns would have to be reloaded; his men's six-foot-plus frames jumped up and covered the remaining distance in seconds. The smoke was thicker the closer they got to the firewall. They all braced to breach the firewall they were all almost through. After a momentary blast of heat, they were through. Amra told his men to keep running. Suddenly, the ground beneath them came up, and a large, heavy net of rope, which was the thickness of a man's arm, encircled the entire team and lifted them briefly in the air. They were all gathered together—shields, equipment, everything—and then slammed to the ground, bound in the net.

Before Amra and his men could even start to cut the rope bonds they were trapped in, strange white men appeared with short sticks called induku (short sticks with a large knob at one end thrown at animals during hunting or used for clubbing an enemy's head) and started indiscriminately beating his men with them, aiming for their heads. The last thing Amra remembered about his homeland was hoping that his father's men, who were trailing him, had witnessed everything and had time to get away.

The first thing Amra felt upon waking was pain. It was mostly in his head, but he could feel pain in his back, shoulders, and arms. He had been beaten pretty badly. He tried to move but could move only his arms about two or three inches before the chains around his body encircled him, prevented him from moving farther. He tried to move his legs and found the same restrictions. Then the smell hit him; the stench almost made him gag. It was heavy in the air, strong with the stench of human excrement, piss, blood, and rotting flesh. Though he was free to breathe, every breath was labored, heavy with the taste of despair, loss, and pain.

The rocking back and forth made him realize he was on a boat of some sort. He could barely discern the salt air in the stench. He could also hear the lament of women and children, so he knew both men and women were on board. He called out in the Kushite language for any of his warriors. One answered, barely. Amra waited for what seemed like an eternity before he heard the man's voice again. It was Kasm, one of his schoolmates; he told Amra his arm was broken and that they had been captured about three days ago. The white men had separated Amra and his men into separate groups of slaves. They almost left Amra behind because of the head injury; they thought he was going to die. They had brought him only because of his size.

Amra sat in darkness and gathered himself for what was to come. He and his men had been captured into slavery. Everything his father had feared had come to pass, just faster than he had anticipated. He hoped his tribe had been warned and were safe. He had to worry about himself now and about surviving what was to come. At the time, Amra didn't know there was nothing in his life that would prepare him for the white man.

Thoughts of the past helped put things in perspective for First Sergeant Amra. He had come through slavery a stronger and smarter man. Yes, he had been abused, beaten, and degraded to less than an animal, but for a man born free, his mind had always stayed free. He had seen the mass slavery of Africans on his way to America and held little hope that his tribe had remained untouched by the brutal practice of slavery. But the hope to find people of his tribe again was strong in him, and he felt he had an obligation.

Lieutenant Phoenix gained his composure and informed Amra that recent intelligence reports had reported that the naval blockade the North had made around the South was recently being lifted and that traffic out of the United States was very limited to the extremely rich and very hard to secure. Lieutenant Phoenix told Amra to hold off for a month or two to see whether things would change. Lieutenant Phoenix understood the historical impact and import of what First Sergeant Amra had just told him.

A big part of the first sergeant's duty was to take over the responsibilities to train the unit. Amra would be responsible for integrating all the new men into the organization and teaching them the unique rules they would follow, both in combat and in camp.

Since taking over training, Amra had incorporated a rigorous training regime that started early in the morning, right before the sun came up, and went till late at night. The men were conducting constant patrol, doing guard duty, or learning how to ride horses. Not all the men were proficient at horsemanship, Amra included. He reveled in the power and strength he felt when he was riding horses. He knew a good horseman was worth three to five infantry, if trained right.

Taking over as the training sergeant was like food to Amra's soul. He had the opportunity to do what he had been trained for his whole life, but now he was also leading men. It hurt his soul that he couldn't go back to his home in Africa and find out whether his tribe still lived. He had done a lot of soul searching and had finally come to the conclusion that his tribe wasn't a place or land; it was in his blood. Wherever he went, his tribe went with him.

His new assignment as a first sergeant gave him relative freedom. He wasn't a fool; the white men, Southern or Northern, weren't prepared to acknowledge black men as equals. But by letting them serve beside them, they had inadvertently opened up Pandora's box to the black man's future possibilities. Already, his upbringing as a warrior and leader was starting to show as he became more and more comfortable with army life.

Lieutenant Phoenix had seen Amra's excitement about horses and told Amra a story about a tribe of men called Huns, one of the most destructive armies to ever walk the earth. He explained that their claim to fame was their unique ability to shoot arrows from horses in hit-and-run-type tactics. This information fascinated Amra, and he felt that, if given enough horses, he could make his men into that same type of force. He had already started to notice the difference in training and competencies between the men who had been with the major's team the whole time and the men who had just come into camp. Amra had started taking the men into the woods on training exercises, where he would have the men do mounted and dismounted operations. For the men who didn't have a horse, he came with a type of technique where one man controlled the horse and the man behind him fired his rifle. He had gotten the idea from what Lieutenant Phoenix had told him about the Huns; he thought it would be better to have one man control the horse in a fight and the other take aim and shoot. So far, the technique worked okay for short distances and on flat terrain. The older musket rifles Amra had started with wouldn't work on the backs of horses; the newer cartridge and revolving rifles would work better. Amra liked the fact that one man controlling the horse allowed for constant movement and a harder target to shoot while allowing for a moving "platform" for the shooter. This was how Lieutenant Phoenix explained the Hun method or warfare, except they had rifles. Even Major Vetter had come to watch the drills. He asked Amra questions on how he thought this type of battle tactic could be used and whether other types of weapons could be incorporated.

Amra wasn't numb to the fact that weapons or superior weapons could make a weak man strong. As big, strong, and wise as his tribe was, guns destroyed all the advantages that had been the Kushite strengths through the ages. He had witnessed firsthand the carnage and destruction modern weapons wrought when unleashed to their full, destructive potential. The Africa he had grown up in would never be ready for this type of warfare unless they learned to embrace the brutal nature of this weapon as their own. He hoped his countrymen and family had still survived. He had his own gun now and was probably the most proficient man in the unit on how to use it, next to Sergeant Hall and the snipers. He would master this new way of warfare, and if he ever got to go home again, he would teach it to his people; the future depended on it. Amra would never let himself be captured or enslaved again.

Another bright light in Amra's life had been the introduction of the young boy, Charl. The boy reminded Amra of his people; Charl was already large for his young age, and the hard work they had put him under had already started to give him a warrior's physique at just ten years old. Amra's tribe prized children above all else, and Amra had immediately taken to the child. Amra was surprised that Sergeant Hall had also grown close to the boy. Amra respected Sergeant Hall and had witnessed him on the battlefield. The men feared Sergeant Hall because of his cold and unnatural way in battle. They whispered that he was possessed when fighting; bloodshed and danger meant nothing to him. The other men mentioned a word Amra had never heard before: *berserker*. When Amra asked Lieutenant Phoenix what this word meant, Amra knew what they were referencing. Amra's father had talked about men like Sergeant Hall; the African word was *ukuthukuthela*. These were men who walked the battlefield, doing something with great zeal or energy, attention entirely focused on killing. Their previous mission to disrupt and try to cause fear among the enemy lines fit Sergeant Hall's mindset perfectly. What made him so scary was that he killed in silence; and could use anything as a weapon. The one saving grace was that the men felt that he received no enjoyment in killing. Amra was glad Charl could also be such a ray of light to Sergeant Hall.

TWENTY-FIVE

The Encounter

THE MOVE TO Port Hudson would take just under two weeks of travel by marching. Fortunately, they had been issued enough horses that all the soldiers could ride if they doubled up on the horses. First Sergeant Amra had recommended that they double up for travel to shorten the pace. Lieutenant Colonel Vetter liked the idea of getting there faster and realized the trip would help all the men understand the value of horses. This would also help them get away quickly in case they needed to avoid any unforeseen drama. Lieutenant Colonel Vetter didn't know what to expect on the journey and believed that having all the men mounted increased their chances of getting to their destination quickly.

The country was in turmoil. There were reports of displaced Negroes living in the woods throughout the South. Small villages of poor Negroes trying to eke out a life with their newly granted freedom were sprouting up all over the South. Reports also indicated that former slaves were living in terror because large groups of white men were roaming the countryside and randomly killing Negroes. They were mostly rogue Southern soldiers and displaced Southern former slave owners. They were terrorizing Negroes wherever they encountered them. Hangings, castrations of men, and the burning of women and children were becoming common throughout the South.

Major Vetter knew this would be the first time for the unit to actually be out in the open since its inception as an army unit, and he didn't know how the men would react or how people would react to them. He would lead from the front of the formation as they traveled. He had also forewarned his men to be ready for anything and to be on the alert during the entire trip. Before they departed, he held up his hand to get everyone's attention. "You men are the last thing in the world the defeated Southerners needed or wanted to see. You are triumphant blacks marching through their streets. I need each of you to understand that even though the war is over, there is still a war in the South."

They had identified rally points along the route in case anything happened and men became separated. Vetter even went so far as to identify shooters in case of a confrontation. He pulled his leadership together and asked who would be the best individuals for shooters. Outside of the two sharpshooters who had joined the team, Sergeant Hall and First Sergeant Amra were the unanimous choices by his men. Vetter knew Sergeant Hall to be a good, quiet soldier, who kept mostly to himself. After the meeting was over, he asked Lieutenant Phoenix his thoughts on Sergeant Hall, and he also agreed that they were a solid choice.

Vetter knew his men had killed before. To be honest, most of the white men they had killed had been either asleep or unaware of their presence. This would be the first time his men had to engage white men face-to-face. How would they react? A few of his soldiers had briefly fought in the shoulder-to-shoulder type of warfare and knew what it meant to see a white man in their sights and pull the trigger.

Their war mission was to run clandestine, guerilla, warfare-type tactics behind enemy lines to break the spirit of the Confederate army. He knew white men in the area wouldn't be happy to see a bunch of Negro soldiers with weapons traipsing through their land. Vetter knew this would be an affront to their attempt to terrorize blacks from trying to exert their freedom in the South. Southerners held in their hearts that blacks were no more than slaves, that they were less than men and didn't deserve the same God-given considerations as white men. The slaughter of slaves was likened to culling a herd or removing (and usually killing) inferior animals out of a herd to reduce numbers or remove undesirable traits from the group as a whole. A lot of Southerners believed the undesirable trait in Negroes was simply existing. The North had given Negroes freedom, but even that was a new concept to a lot of whites: Negroes being human beings. The difference between the North and South was that the North understood that Negroes were different from, and not like, whites but human. The South also understood this fact but chose to ignore it because of the economic need to preserve the cotton dominance the South maintained throughout the world. Slaves enabled the South to maintain dominance and reap maximum profits by not paying their workers.

Besides, Southern plantation owners felt they were capitalizing on a trade that had already been established in the Caribbean and in Africa. It was commonly understood among the whites that Africans were always at war with each other and that slavery was a way of life among them. Vetter had often heard the statement "What is the difference between being a slave in Africa or a slave in America?" Hell, Vetter had felt the same way until he was ostracized in the military because of his Southern upbringing and because he was forced to lead Negroes. It wasn't until he started to dialogue with Lieutenant Phoenix about the slave experience that Vetter understood the difference between being a slave in Africa, where most slaves were considered indentured servants, and it was often possible for them to earn their freedom. He learned about things like the "Slave Bible," "buck breaking" of black males, and the mass breeding of black females for a slave workforce. Lieutenant Phoenix had informed Vetter that now that Negroes no longer held any monetary value to the white man and had assisted in the South's downfall, the vengeance on free Negro families trying to find their way would be merciless. In return, Vetter informed Lieutenant Phoenix of the current drive to ouster foundational Southern government control by getting the Negroes to vote and how that effort had been received with violence and death. They both concluded that the South wasn't about to concede the power they'd held since the inception of the United States.

Before his discussion with all the men, Vetter wanted to update his officers and NCOs, both black and white, on current activity in the area and gain their thoughts and concerns on the upcoming move. He started his meeting by briefing them on the scout's recent report of the route ahead and possible areas of contention. Also, a recent intelligence report had warned them to be on the lookout for bands of white men roaming the countryside, murdering former slaves. He had read a detailed report of an incident in Opelousas, Louisiana, in which groups of white men indiscriminately murdered over 250 men, women, and children. The local paper had called the slaughter epic. Captain Vetter read,

September 28, 1868, Opelousas, LA, The St. Landry's Massacre—A small group of armed African-Americans assembled to search for a missing white school teacher, Emerson Bentley, who taught free black children. The black men were met by an armed group of white men, mounted on horses, outside Opelousas. Of those men, 29 were taken to the local prison, and 27 of them were summarily executed. The bloodshed contin-ued for two weeks, with black families killed in their homes, shot in public, and chased down by vigilante groups. An editor of a local newspaper was also murdered in the early days of the massa-cre, with his body displayed outside the Opelousas drug store. By the end of the two weeks, estimates of the number killed were around 250 people, the vast majority of them blacks. Local reports claim a new secret Democratic organizations called The Knights of the White Camellia & the Ku Klux Klan were responsible for the carnage.

The men were silent, each lost in his thoughts. Captain Vetter finished by saying, staring directly at the black men, "Listen, men, the South is still at war with blacks, even though the war is over. I only tell you this so you know not to ever let your guard down. As black men, always consider yourself at war in the South. Stay alert to stay alive." Staring at his white officers, he said, "I don't believe in keeping any information from the men. What's going on around here is bigger than the military. The black man will have to fight for any respect he is going to receive in the South. Just like in the war, you will still be targeted for your association with the blacks. If you would like to be assigned someplace else, I will respect your wishes."

He then asked their thoughts on how he should address the men. The consensus was that whatever he said had to be somewhat motivational. Vetter looked around at his men and could see the firelight glint off their eyes. He noticed Sergeant Hall in the corner; as usual he quietly and intently listened to everything Vetter was putting out. Unexpectedly, even to Vetter, he asked Sergeant Hall what he thought he should say to the men. Sergeant Hall looked surprised by the question, but so intent was he on the conversation that he simply replied, "The truth." Everyone in the room seemed surprised to hear his voice and even more surprised about what he had said. Vetter asked him what he meant. Sergeant Hall replied, "Even though we are free, we are not free. Negro freedom is new to both whites and blacks. There are those who like it and those who don't. If Negroes want to keep freedom, we have to fight for it and act like men to keep it. To keep it, we will have to mean it."

Listening to Sergeant Hall speak, it was then that Vetter began to truly understand how precarious the newfound freedom for the black man was. For black men, this was a fight for their lives, souls, and existence. Every step for them would be to prove that they deserved something that should have been theirs from their first breath of air. The old stamp of slavery and dehumanization was still too fresh to just wipe away. How long would it take before the repercussions from the systematic destruction started to diminish? How do you recover when every aspect of being a man or woman is beat and whipped away into fear? How do you recreate a race of people who, for hundreds of years, have been bred only for slavery? Vetter knew a lot of his men had been subjugated to physical, sexual, and mental tortures most men couldn't even fathom. He knew the wrong spark could ignite a flame of retribution that would put a nail in the coffin for any chance of America to have a peaceful future. If vengeance for the atrocities of slavery were to be realized, America would drown in blood. A lot of innocent people who had received little to no value out of the slave trade would die.

Captain Vetter thought, *What does a free American Negro look like?* American Negroes were a hodgepodge of black men and women from all over the world, and like cattle, they had been bred and mixed to produce the strongest and most exotic. Their original African link had been washed away in the breeding cycle. Traditions had been beaten out of them. What should be their new distinction? Most blacks had no history in America other than slavery. How did a race of people build from that?

Vetter began to understand his role in this new America, where the Negro was free. He had to show them that not all white men viewed them as animals and would judge them as men, not by their color, something he felt totally comfortable with. He had some things to learn to provide the leadership and guidance they felt and knew was in their best interest, to protect his men like any other leader would. He had to make sure he moved cautiously ahead to avoid the dangerous fires of hate and anger his men would exact on white men if given the chance. They knew how to kill white men now, justifiably so, and they wouldn't hesitate to do so again.

He informed the men about his concerns and explained to them that if they were accosted on the way to Port Hudson, they would need to make a statement. They needed to let men in the area know there was a legitimate American force to handle situations, if need be. If that were to happen, he wanted Sergeant Hall to initiate the response they would make. The table was stunned by that comment.

Sergeant Hall asked, "Sir, what kind of statement should I make?"

Lieutenant Colonel Vetter looked at Sergeant Hall and simply said, "We represent the United States and are on official business. Any men who show a dangerous intent or criminal activity represent a danger to the US. The crimes they are committing now must cease, or countless other black people will pay. Mind you, our mission isn't to go looking for these bands of men, but if we do encounter them, as the only authorized representatives in the area, it is our duty to address them, and we will address them!" In reality, Vetter wanted the men to understand that the only way they could kill white men was with orders.

Lieutenant Colonel Vetter gathered all the men on the night before their departure. He had thought a lot about his conversation with his leadership a few nights before and hoped he could frame the situation to his men correctly. He started his brief to the men in a conversational tone. "We have come a long way since our inception as a unit. I don't think anyone expected much from us, but I do believe that each of you has proven over and over again that minorities—black, brown, and red men—bleed and fight just like the white man. However, even though freedom has been bestowed on you, the war to be integrated into American society as men is just beginning. We have secretly performed our duties in the shadows, and this will be our first move as a unit in the open. Before we move out, the leaders and I felt there were things you needed to know. First, since black men and men of color no longer hold any monetary value to the white man as slaves and since you also assisted in the downfall of the South, the vengeance on the free Negro will be merciless in the South. Second, even though the Thirteenth Amendment has directed that all black men are free, each of you needs to consider yourself at war, at least until you leave the South. You need to constantly be alert to stay alive and to keep your comrades alive. I tell you this because we have recent reports of large bands of white men roaming the countryside and murdering former slaves. Black families all over the South, who were trying to make their way from slave owners and looking for a new way of life, were being murdered throughout the South, and the slaughter was epic."

He had Lieutenant Phoenix read a detailed report of an incident in Opelousas, Louisiana, in which groups of white men had indiscriminately murdered over 250 men, women, and children. Lieutenant Colonel Vetter could physically feel the tension and anger generated in the room as Lieutenant Phoenix read the report. He finished by telling the men, "In no uncertain terms, if you encounter any of these men and if the signal to fire is given, I expect you to perform your duties without question. Even if that means having to kill white men, do not hesitate. But remember, you are now soldiers representing an entire country, and all the black people in this country maintain your order and discipline. This may be the first fight of many."

The silence following his statement was deafening; the whinny of horses and the readjustment of equipment were the only sounds heard after a brief pause. Lieutenant Colonel Vetter went on to say, "I know a lot of you thought that once the war was over you wouldn't have to kill again. I understand that killing in war is one thing, but killing in peacetime is completely different. Under normal circumstances, you would be right. However, we now occupy today what was called enemy territory yesterday. The unification effort to bring this country back together will take some time, and until then men who represent the unified government will be called on to enforce laws in the absence of new government representation. As I said before, free black men in the South are the living representation of the Southerners' loss. For the masters, you represent the loss of financial earnings and the end of their plan to subjugate and keep a race in total ignorance. They have been judged wrong in the eyes of God and this new country. They now have no one to look down on in their own misery. For both of them, you also represent how wrong and shallow they are in their minds and lives. You show their hypocrisy in their faith in God and as human beings. Be ready, be fast, and be deadly!"

All the men responded with a loud "Hoorah!" Major Vetter mounter his horse and started to move.

For three days, Major Vetter led his group of just over eighty men, mostly colored, through most of their trip without incident. It was close to evening, and the unit was about ten miles from their destination, Port Hudson. They had identified a place to rest for the night; they didn't want to finish the final leg of their journey in the dark. They could be mistaken at night and attacked. Their scouts were just leading them into their destination when one of the men sounded and pointed. Everyone also pointed in the direction the man had pointed so everybody else knew where the threat came from.

Since the men had been traveling double, each second man on the back of his horse jumped down and assumed a shooting position on one knee. The men remaining on the horses simply faced the threat, hands near their sidearms.

Captain Vetter could describe the men in front of him only as a mob. All the men were white, ranging in ages from teenager to grandfather. Only six of the men who greeted them were mounted; all others were dismounted. It was close to nightfall, and the men had a few torches ablaze. Vetter could feel the air get thick with tension, and everything seemed to go silent in his mind. He immediately recognized that many of the men had vestiges of Confederate uniforms as the diminishing sunlight glistened on uniform buttons. A few had the standard-issue rifle and kit handed out to Confederate Soldiers, and only two seemed to have sidearms.

His scouts had identified the group about two days ago and reported back to Vetter. His scouts had informed him that there were about fifty men in total and that they had recently burned twelve Negro men, women, and children who were traveling along the road. The scouts had also informed him that the men had tortured and raped the travelers before they burned them. In fact, his men had just informed him that the camp area they had selected was near the same spot. It seemed that travelers picked the spot because of its easy access to a nearby stream. It seemed the men had been preying on everybody who stopped in the area.

Earlier in the day, First Sergeant Amra had broken off with about thirty men to flank the bandits and make them think they had superior numbers. He had received word before they arrived that the first sergeant was set and had eyes on the bandits. Captain Vetter had briefed his men on the scout reports, particularly about the savagery these men had visited on a black family just recently. He had finished his briefing by stating, "Remember, dead is dead and no longer a threat." The men had nodded in silence, each with his own thoughts to contend with.

The remaining men with Captain Vetter approached the bandits in a wedge formation, the horse out front in a triangle formation. Vetter was at the point, with Sergeant Hall and Lieutenant Phoenix to his right and two of his white officers, Captain Sturgis and Lieutenant Reeves, to his left. The rest of the company followed in a two-man column, with the remaining leadership mixed among the column. Everyone had his orders and knew exactly what to do in the event of any issues.

Vetter raised his right hand, and the entire formation stopped moving. Vetter could hear the slight adjustments behind him, which he knew were the readjustments of rifles by the mounted men behind him.

Inwardly he cringed a little because he knew at this exact moment that if there were any enemy on the flanks, trying to entrap his men in an ambush, they were either already dead or quietly being eliminated by the two scout teams led by First Sergeant Amra. Lieutenant Colonel Vetter told First Sergeant Amra that no mercy or quarter was to be given to these men, but no harm was to be given to any women or children. There were two teams of fifteen men in the burlap uniforms they had perfected during the war flanking his formation. The burlap bags also allowed for maximum concealment in the woods.

All this flashed in Captain Vetter's mind before he dropped his hand to his side. He didn't say anything; he simply waited. One man in the front of the formation raised his voice and shouted to Lieutenant Colonel Vetter, "We represent the Knights of the White Camellia, a new organization designated to monitor and maintain law and order during these turbulent times. We ensure that former slaves understand what it means to be free in the

South and that they understand the new laws they fall under. We believe some of the more undisciplined free slaves are responsible for recent attacks in the area and may have fled to Union army lines. We are looking for two in particular and believe they may be in your formation."

Vetter had to give them credit for their creativity. They put Vetter in a difficult position; he could satisfy the local white populace and hand over two men, which in turn would show his soldiers that even though they were in uniform, they were still slaves to the white man's whims. If he refused, the men in the woods they had strategically placed would open fire on Vetter's group and kill them all.

Still facing the men in front of him and speaking softly in a voice only his men could hear, Vetter simply said the name Sergeant Hall. Without hesitation, Sergeant Hall freed his side-arm, strapped in front of him, and discharged a single round. As if in slow motion, the smoke from the discharge seemed to slowly come out of the weapon. Across the distance, about fifty yards, the impact against the head of the man talking was almost instantaneous and witnessed by a large red explosion. A cloud of blood sprayed the men behind him as his head exploded. Immediately after the shot, the woods to the right and left lit up with the smoke of multiple weapons being fired at the same time. Captain Vetter and the men around him had their sidearms free and added to the carnage in front of them.

The sound of multiple Pattern 1861 Enfield (.577) caliber muzzleloader carbine rifles and the revolvers in front and flank firing was deafening. The first and second ranks of the Knights of the White Camellia were totally decimated. The four horses neighed and backed up; one horse received multiple shots for wildly turning and running in front of the dismounted men. The remaining men, some ten to fifteen after the initial carnage, didn't know what to do since their immediate leadership had been destroyed. What had started off as a sure-fire ambush had been turned around into a full-out slaughter. A few tried to fire back and were immediately taken out in the next volley. Others tried to get out of the kill zone and galloped or ran away. Vetter informed his snipers and scouts to hunt them all down and kill them. He knew the retribution for this attack would be on innocent people.

Lieutenant Phoenix could see the men come out of the woods and instantly knew most of the men were former Confederate soldiers. The scouts had been very graphic about the evil and carnage these men had brought on the black families just a few days before. For Lieutenant Phoenix, the battle itself was uneventful, because it was over so fast. Once Sergeant Hall fired the first round, it was like a scythe of bullets swept across the enemy front. The men in the immediate front and a few behind died without even a chance to lift their weapons. The fire from the wood line totally caught the dismounted troops by surprise, and they fell like wheat; small explosions of blood in the dimming light could be seen by the few torches being held. The men in front of them had underestimated the uniformed Negroes and died very quickly as a result.

For Lieutenant Phoenix, the more interesting aspects of the whole drama were the development and growth of Lieutenant Colonel Vetter. Lieutenant Phoenix knew Lieutenant Colonel Vetter was a friend to Negroes. He was the first white man in the military who had looked at a man based on his capabilities, not his color. This was the first time Lieutenant Colonel Vetter had faced an enemy after the war. He thought he might have some reservation or turmoil with the decision to kill these men, but he finally realized that for every one of these men remaining, innocent black people would die. Surprisingly, Captain Vetter wasn't concerned about the prospect of killing other white men; he had seen them for what they were, traitors to the Union and losers in a cause they were willing to die for. The war was over, and they still chose to fight for the cause that sought to separate a country. In Vetter's mind, these men were already dead when they chose the path to continue to separate from this country. Lieutenant Colonel Vetter viewed it as his legal duty, as the only authorized representative in the area for the United States, to exterminate them. No, Lieutenant Phoenix realized after much conversation that Vetter was more concerned about how the recently freed Negro would be perceived if it was common knowledge that armed Negroes were roaming the countryside, seeking justice in the name of the United States. Even though the former enemy's actions warranted arrest and death, the simple fact that Negroes were involved wouldn't be accepted by anyone white, North or South. Lieutenant Phoenix informed Vetter that no court in the South would hold these men accountable for the horrific crimes they had committed, and if left unchecked, they would ruin any possibility of a "more perfect Union." Black men would never feel unified in this country as long as white men allowed this type of abomination to exist. It was then that Vetter made the complex decision that no man would escape and that no mention of this incident or any other like it was to ever take place. It was then that he told Lieutenant Phoenix something he would never forget for the rest of his life. "Tell the men we will erase any possibility these men may have on the Negroes' future."

Sergeant Hall could see the men in front of him and knew they were responsible for the horrible deaths of travelers a few days before. The scouts had mentioned that these men had tortured the men and raped the women before finally killing them. For Sergeant Hall, in this mind this was like reliving everything that had happened to his daughter all over again. Again, in his mind he could see the horrid and brutal gang rape of his lovely and innocent daughter like it had been only yesterday. The calm that always came over him before killing was the first indicator that he was going to a place in his mind where violence reigned. When they had killed his daughter, he had blacked out; when he came to, the massacre at his hands was horrendous to behold. In his anger and hate, a demon had been unleashed that dismembered and abused dead bodies. He promised himself that he could never let the demon be released again; it had hurt his soul upon his realization of what he had done. Becoming a soldier had given him ample opportunity to let the demon out but had also given him time to understand and control it. Their war mission of wreaking havoc behind enemy lines had allowed him to release the demon indiscriminately on the enemy soldiers. Each of the rebel soldiers he killed had been abusing his daughter all over again, and he destroyed him. Over time, by giving his demon freedom, he had learned to manage and control it. He learned to manage his rage, and his trance-like transition was part of it. It enabled him to focus on the task at hand and nothing else. By doing this, his rage could be focused and somewhat contained. Everything in front of him became crystal clear, as if viewed from a telescope. The leader of the group was talking, and Sergeant Hall could clearly see the hate in his bright-blue eyes. The leader had a short, black beard that seemed more kept than the others around him. He leaned forward in his horse at the ready. He held his bridle in one hand, and the other hand was to his right, near his sidearm.

Sergeant Hall knew this man was in a position to attack and kill. His entire body language spoke of aggression and violence. He distinctly heard Lieutenant Colonel Vetter call his name. The image of his daughter passed in front of his mind. Without thought, in one fluid motion, he pulled the loaded, large-caliber pistol strapped across his chest out and aimed it at the leader.

As if in a dream, Sergeant Hall could see the leader's left eyebrow lift in surprise before his face was obliterated by the lead ball that penetrated his skull. The explosion of smoke from the initial shot and the explosion of bright-red brain matter and chunks of skull erased his memory of this man. Time to be mean.

First Sergeant Amra had left with his two teams earlier in the day before sunrise. Before their departure, Lieutenant Colonel Vetter had come to see the men off. He reminded the men that this mission was like any other mission they'd had during the war and that it was probably more dangerous now because the enemy wasn't required to reveal who he was. First Sergeant Amra had a white NCO, Sergeant Michaels, who would lead the second fifteen-man team. He told the men to be careful and for all of them to come back. Before he walked away, Lieutenant Colonel Vetter pulled First Sergeant Amra and Sergeant Michaels aside and told them that if the mission went awry for any reason, he wanted the men to hurriedly make their way to Port Hudson for safety. He reminded the men of his no quarter, no mercy rule; if any of the enemies escaped, they put the whole unit in jeopardy from reprisal. Both men nodded, and Lieutenant Colonel Vetter departed.

First Sergeant Amra's team was outfitted for concealment and secrecy. During stealth attacks, the goal was to perform their task in complete silence, to get in and out without being seen or heard. Each man had burlap bags tied intermittently around their person to break up his human silhouette in the dark. They were all armed with a sidearm and some sort of edged or blunted weapon of choice. Most of the time, the guns would be used only as a last resort and only if commanded. For this mission, guns would lead. First Sergeant Amra had his khopesh strapped to his back.

Because of the guerrilla-type warfare they had performed during the war, each soldier was encouraged to choose an edged or blunted weapon that would allow him to kill in silence. The soldiers started calling them "silent" weapons and were instructed to become proficient in their use of them. Most chose knives, short and long, a few picked hammers, and there were a few who became extremely proficient at the bow and arrow. A few small checks of the men, and they were on their way.

They had to cover only about twelve miles. They didn't take the most direct route because they wanted to come upon the group of men from the flank. Two of the six Native American scouts in the unit were assigned to Amra's team and had mapped out all the sentry areas the night before. They would drop the horses off about two miles away from the closest sentry and finish the rest of the mission on foot. Amra was proud of his men as they swiftly and quietly moved through the woods. Amra had trained his men hard, and each was competent in the abilities of the men around him.

First Sergeant Amra was intently focused on stepping silently in the murky, dark path ahead when he heard the raccoon call in the dark. He put his hand up, and immediately every man in the group went to a knee. The raccoon call was a preset warning or alert that let the team know they were extremely close to the objective. Nobody moved as they waited for the next command from the scouts. The raccoon sound came again, this time as if it were angry; that was the sound to move forward but to stay down and be silent. Amra moved forward on all fours and slowly approached the location of the raccoon noise. He heard the sound of a pig grunt, stopped, and waited. That was the sign for the scouts to let Amra know they had seen him, and one was moving to his location.

The small Native American scout materialized to the right of First Sergeant Amra and tapped First Sergeant Amra's arm four times. Four of the enemy were near. The other scout materialized out of the dark, and they waited for the remaining men to catch up. The rest of the men gathered around on all fours, and the scouts quietly informed First Sergeant Amra that there were two teams ahead, one team of four men and another team of five on the other side of the road. The scouts informed them that the men had arrived right before darkness to set up for the ambush they expected the next day.

The enemy soldiers were so confident in their ambush that they didn't even build any defensible positions and were using the trees as cover. The men had set up in an ambush position and weren't very quiet. The scouts pointed to two points of light in the woods, small campfires from the two teams. Amra informed his men that two teams would break up and station themselves as close to the enemy as they could without being seen. He informed one of the scouts to go back the way they had come and inform them when the rest of the unit was in range. They wouldn't attack the ambushers until they had sight of the unit. The ambushers would also be focused on the unit coming and wouldn't think to look behind them. On the raccoon signal, they would eliminate the ambushers and reorient their weapons in their team. No one was to escape alive, and all bodies needed to be accounted for when the attack was over. Each man knew his task and grimly moved out to get ready to execute it.

About midday, the scout sent to watch out for the ambushers arrived back to inform First Sergeant Amra the enemy was close. First Sergeant Amra gave the raccoon sound and moved toward the five-man enemy ambush team. He crawled on all fours toward the known location and could barely discern the heads of two men in the woods ahead. The enemy men were totally focused on the road ahead and were busy trying to move logs and tree limbs around to conceal their fighting position. The enemy soldiers were set in position but still making quite a bit of noise. This clamor allowed First Sergeant Amra and his team to get close enough to smell their cigar smoke. First Sergeant Amra could distinctly see all five of them now and gestured to his men. The enemy tried to space themselves out to confuse anyone trying to get a bead on them for returning fire, which also worked to First Sergeant Amra's advantage.

On cue, the two men on the flanks were brutally taken out with their throats cut. Simultaneously an arrow materialized in the back of the head of one of the men in the back, and First Sergeant Amra and two other men rushed the ten to fifteen meters to finish the other two. First Sergeant Amra's khopesh appeared in his hand as if by magic; he covered the distance to the last two men in seconds, and the first man's head came off with a mighty heave. Surprised, the other man started to turn his head to see what happened; with a grunt, stopping the mighty swing, Amra reversed the swing back, and the sharp, curved portion of the khopesh split his head at the cheek. The top of the head flew away.

It seemed like the attack was over before it began. Two bird calls informed him that his other team had taken out the smaller team across the road. They had been told to try to capture one man alive to get whatever signals the enemy had worked out for the ambush. Two bird calls also meant they had a captured a prisoner alive.

Amra had to smile at the sheer fear he saw on the captured prisoner's face as he walked toward him. Like his men, he was covered from head to toe in black soot, put on to diminish any sheen their dark skin might put out in the darkness. The bags protruding from various points on his body, coupled with his giant size and the large khopesh in hand, must have made Amra look like some vengeful forest god. The prisoner was so scared to see the approaching Amra that he passed out. As Amra got closer, he could see the dark stain grow in front of the man's pants, and then the stench of sewage hit him. The prisoner had both defecated and urinated on himself in terror.

First Sergeant Amra had staged his men around the prisoner before he woke him up. He wanted to capitalize on the man's fear; he didn't have a lot of time before the unit and the rest of the enemy approached. Amra had to admit they did look terrifying. One of his men started to lightly slap the prisoner's face.

The prisoner came to and looked around. He immediately

tried to get up and run off. Amra said, "Tell the truth or else." He had all the men cover their faces with burlap bags so the man didn't know who had made the statement.

Amra went on. "Where are the rest of your people?"

The man lied and said they were the only ones, just robbers in the forest. Amra nodded, and one of his men grabbed the prisoner's hand and told him to hold his fingers up.

"I am going to ask one more time. Lie again, and then I will start cutting a finger at a time."

The questioning went smoother after that, and they got all the information they needed. After the questioning, First Sergeant Amra told the men to release him and get him a horse. The soldier's hands were released, and he immediately pulled his two cauterized fingers close to his chest. He rolled over to get up on all fours, and that's when First Sergeant Amra's khopesh took the soldier's head clean off.

The surprise at the unexpected move was still on the dead soldier's face as his head rolled away. Nobody said a word; everybody understood what no quarter meant. First Sergeant Amra also knew these "soldiers" fought for a way of life that didn't include men of color as equals. Just like Sergeant Hall had claimed, for black men to be free, they would have to be mean. The men took positions aimed in the opposite direction and waited.

After the battle, the men gathered any usable weapons and equipment from the dead bodies. The equipment would be used for the family members left behind, waiting for the unit to get them on their return west. Lieutenant Colonel Vetter had the men burn all the bodies; in his mind, a small part of him hoped his own men would sleep better tonight and tomorrow, knowing that no memory of these evil men remained. It was the least he could do.

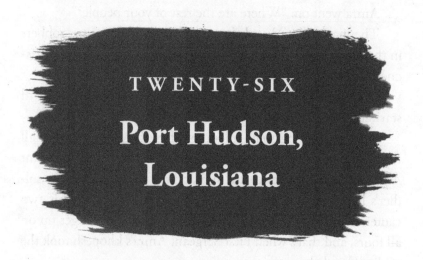

TWENTY-SIX

Port Hudson, Louisiana

VETTER CONSIDERED THE arrival to Port Hudson uneventful after the brief conflict. He settled in the officers' barracks away from his men after he saw to them being settled. While among normal Union troops, Vetter had to play the game and separate himself from his men. Any perceived familiarity with his men would be perceived as another negative against Vetter. His assignment to lead Negroes was a direct consequence of him being born and raised in the South but choosing to fight for the North. Even Lieutenant Phoenix agreed that this was the only course of action. Vetter was surprised by the thought of the duplicity of being a black man. You have to be one way with the master and another with your own—always guarded, never understood.

The short battle had definitely changed things with the unit; he could feel it. As they had gotten closer to Port, they started to see more people, mostly black families, on the road, headed in the opposite direction. Vetter noted that the men stood taller, chest out, and straightened up their uniforms. The future of the black man was represented in his unit for both blacks and whites. They were the first representation of the free black man in the United States. The true weight of their positions started to settle on their shoulders. Good or bad, white men would have to look the Negro in the eye and have discourse with him, just like two white men talking to each other. Seeing Negroes in uniform was the first time a white man had to acknowledge the Negro as an equal. Vetter was proud of his men and knew they would be more than ready to face whatever challenges lay ahead for them.

Port Hudson still showed signs of the ravages of the forty-eight-day siege that resulted in the enormous loss of life for Union troops. Port Hudson was the nail in the coffin for the confederacy. Once Union troops gained control of Port Hudson, they owned the entire length of the Mississippi River. It was also the spot where Negro soldiers in the regular Union army first participated in a major assault and demonstrated that they would and could fight with discipline and valor for their freedom from slavery.

TWENTY-SEVEN

Fleur

VETTER'S BRIEF MOMENT of respite at Port Hudson was briefly interrupted by the surprise of his life, which brought the old world of family to the forefront. The surprise presented itself in the form of his childhood friend and sweetheart, Fleur de Bourgmount, cousin to famed French explorer Étienne de Veniard, Sieur de Bourgmont. Vetter hadn't seen Fleur since the night he departed for West Point. They had stayed in contact as much as they could via the postal service, but during the war, communication had been minimal. Messages of his recent promotion and assignment to the West had been sent home to his family as standard procedure. He knew his family had made it through the war mostly unscathed but didn't know whether they had ever gotten the messages. Seeing Fleur was a breath of fresh air and confirmed that his family knew he was alive and thriving. His father had disowned him when he refused to come home and serve the Confederacy. Vetter hadn't spoken to any of his family since then and had mostly picked up whatever information he could from people he met from the few messages from Fleur or people he had met from the general area.

Fleur had changed little since the last time he saw her, she was still the most beautiful and exotic woman he had ever known. A mix of French and Indian or Métis, she was a descendant of the Missouria Indian tribe and was always at the forefront of any conversation whenever she was around. She had a rare beauty that made snobby French purists look past the mixture and see only the result. Like a diamond, you forget it was formed from coal.

Her raven-dark hair shined with a dark-blue tint. Her eyes were the brightest amber and seemed to almost glow. She was always a tomboy, competent with shooting pistols and archery, activities forbidden to most noblewomen. Her family honored their Indian heritage; it was now unique in French history and set them apart from all other Frenchmen. She had acquired the best of both bloods, aristocratic and strong. She was one of the few women who would brave such a trip with only two bodyguards during such turbulent times. They had never been intimate, but Vetter had always had feelings for her. Their small group of friends had all gone their separate ways, and only a few survived the war.

His temporary office/room door opened, and she stepped in, wearing a dark-blue satin dress with silver accents and a small fascinator hat tilted over her left eye. He stood. She yelled, "Robert!" and covered the two to three steps before being swept into his arms. She smelled of her namesake—flowers and lilacs this time. The hug was long and probably the best thing Vetter had experienced in the past two to three years. It took all his power to let her go.

Fleur hadn't seen Robert since the night he had his going-away party for West Point. She remembered him as a very sweet young man, quiet and composed, not someone to raise a young woman's temperature. Unlike a lot of her friends, she enjoyed Robert's companionship; he wasn't ugly and absolutely praised the ground she walked on. He was also very honest; when he didn't show support for the Confederacy, he was ostracized by everyone, including his family. Maybe that was her attraction to him, the fact that he chose to be different from everyone else. She was definitely not like the normal aristocrats and was accepted only because of her famous name. Inside the French community, she was an aristocrat, and the new Confederacy aristocracy had to recognize her family and their connections if they planned on keeping positive relations with the French. Most women of her exotic beauty were highly sought after as a master's bed warmer. She had taken a chance by coming here to see Robert, but when she heard he had gotten promoted and would be so close, she had to take a chance. Besides, her father was trying to marry her off to some Frenchman from the home country. She had traveled back to France shortly after the war had started and had only just returned to see the downfall of the Confederacy. Since she had been back, she had volunteered much of her time assisting French families impacted by the war. Hearing about Robert's promotion was a good opportunity to get out and see an old friend.

She had to admit that the combination of events leading to the opportunity to see Robert again wasn't to be missed. Her father was near Port Hudson on business, and when Fleur had heard that Robert was nearby, she forced her father to give her an escort to go the fifteen miles to see Robert again. She had to admit that seeing Robert after all this time had definitely been worth the effort.

The man who stood to greet her when she came in wasn't the same Robert she remembered. He had grown in every way since the last time she saw him. He was tall but always thin; he was still tall but filled out with muscle and age. His quiet and composed nature as a young man was now being carried like an aura of confidence any woman could instantly see. His hug spoke of strength yet tenderness. He was still the same but much more now. This intrigued Fleur.

They babbled back and forth for the first hour or so, catching up on what had happened to old friends, with Fleur spending the majority of her time talking about France and Europe.

Robert listened to her speak like his life depended on her every word. Up until now, he didn't realize how lonely he was for his friends and acquaintances. The life before the war seemed like a dream now that he had been blooded on the battlefields. Hearing Fleur talk brought all his life before the war back, and he wondered about his own family and wished he had tried to keep in better contact with them over the years. With that thought in mind, that's when he heard Fleur mention that his father hoped he would come home and lead the family.

She looked at Robert, waiting for a response.

The only thing Vetter could think to say was, "I don't understand."

Fleur relayed the story of how she had gone to visit his family to congratulate them on his promotion, when her dad pulled her aside and told her that Robert's standing with the US government as the victors could be put to good use for the family. That is, if she ever saw him, she should tell him he had betted on the wrong horse. He needed Robert to come back home and help him fix his error. His father also told her that Robert's actions, although abhorred at the time, gave the family an opportunity to have good business relations with the US government and that none of their assets had been messed with because of it. She explained that Robert had basically given the family a pass for their dealings with the Confederacy because of his service. She explained that since President Lincoln's assassination, the new president, Johnson, was "Southern friendly" and didn't demand the same amount of fealty from the Southern aristocracy that Lincoln would have proposed.

"Your father wants you to come home," she said, "and use your influence with the new government to gain an advantage."

Initially, Vetter was surprised by his father's sudden forgetfulness at disowning his son because he had chosen to join the side of the "enemy." It made sense; like then, it was a business decision. Vetter's support of the North had hurt his father's business back then, but now since the unlikely hero was on the right side, his father wanted to exploit his decision to follow his heart and do the right thing. Inwardly he smiled. His father hadn't changed and was still protecting family interests with no apology.

He simply replied that the issue was something he would have to do some thinking about. Right now he felt he had an obligation to his men and getting them out of the South. He then went on to tell her about his stint at West Point and about how much he'd had to go through as a Southerner who chose to support the North. His assignment to lead Negro troops had been a direct reflection of the Northern leadership's mistrust of him because of his Southern heritage. Over time he had come to learn that maybe this was a blessing in disguise.

He went on to explain how he had met his men and that he felt they had grown over time. He explained to her what he had personally witnessed with the black man and some of the horrors he had learned about how they were subjugated. He explained that just about every bad thing they had heard was true. He went on to explain that black men had been brutally raped and often been forced to rape other black men to take away any semblance of manhood so they wouldn't resist. He explained that women had been told that if they had fourteen babies for the master, they would be freed. Those fourteen babies would be sold into slavery and probably never be seen again. For a long time, he talked about the things he had learned; he was able to share with her his successes and failures as their commander. Over time they had evolved into a cohesive unit that looked out for each other at every turn. Without getting into details about his wartime mission, he explained that because they were colored soldiers, they had been required to perform differently from other soldiers. He felt that their unique mission had made them forge a bond that was stronger than that of most units. He told her about his happiness upon seeing the men become more than they had ever thought they could be. He had to admit that he had grown fond of the journey he had started and didn't see much of a possibility of going back to a life with his father, but he would still think about it.

Fleur was mesmerized by the story that unfolded before her. Robert had seen so much in the few years since they departed. His passion when talking about the Negro was something to behold; he really believed what he said. Nobody in her circle would dare speak like this; it could get him or her killed. Even with Indian blood running through her veins, she would never voice any support for Indians or acknowledge the fact that she was Indian to a nobleman's face. It was a silent understanding, a unique exception to the nobility rules because of her name. She could also feel strength and purpose in his voice, and they started a tingle in her body.

She was so entangled in his story and her own internal thoughts that when he stopped speaking, it was like a physical shock not to hear his voice anymore. That was a new feeling to Fleur, to be so caught up in a man that she lost sight of herself and her surroundings.

They talked long into the night and early into the morning. Fleur could only spend a day with Robert before being missed in such violent times. Sounds of early morning started to make them aware of the time. It felt pleasant being here with Robert; Fleur felt safe and comfortable. One of her guards knocked to inform her that they would have to leave soon. Fleur felt a dead weight in her heart at the thought of leaving. She didn't want to go and didn't understand why.

Vetter wanted to tell Fleur that everything in his life mattered and didn't matter if it just meant her being here a little longer with him. He didn't realize how much he had missed her company. At first, he likened it to the fact that she was a woman and he hadn't been around a lot of women in the last few years. But, upon closer inspection of his feelings, he realized it was simply Fleur. She had always made him feel like he could do anything when she was around; she always made him feel like he had to be more for her. It surprised him that, after all the savagery and brutality he had witnessed since joining the military, he could still have a sweet feeling for someone. He hated that their meeting had to end but knew that the less that was known about her presence, the safer she would be. She was a target for all the poor and desolate people in the area. It was not only dangerous for former slaves to travel; it was dangerous for anyone with money to travel during such perilous times.

He stood up and beckoned Fleur to him. She came as if magnetized. They held each other as if it was the last time, each understanding that something had just happened that neither was prepared for. Robert applied a long, lingering kiss to the top of Fleur's head, hoping with all his might that this moment would be remembered for the rest of his life.

First Sergeant Amra walked the grounds of Port Hudson in awe. He stood in one of the first places where Negroes had been given the opportunity to fight for their freedom. They were among the first all-black units mustered into the Union army. Even though the leadership at the time didn't believe in the abilities of the Negro soldiers, they valiantly died fighting and dying for a country that barely recognized them as men. They died trying to create a diversion. Two regiments of black troops, the First and

Third Louisiana Native Guards, were ordered to charge across six hundred yards of open ground against a strongly defended portion of the Confederate line. The men of the First Native Guards were mostly free men of color, while those of the Third Native Guards were runaway slaves. In less than fifteen minutes, about half of the one thousand blacks were killed or wounded. Their chance at success over six hundred yards of open ground in a kill zone had been doomed from the beginning.

First Sergeant Amra didn't understand why any commander would jeopardize their troops on such a hopeless mission. The siege eventually worked, not because of direct military action but because of starvation. They waited the rebels out until they eventually surrendered. First Sergeant Amra was fascinated by the ways of war. To imagine that thousands of lives could have been saved simply by waiting an enemy out and letting nature take its course. No weapons or violence involved. Ever since Lieutenant Phoenix had communicated the strategy tactics of the Huns, he had found himself absorbed in the different ways to fight a war. He was growing wiser in the ways of war.

———

As one of the few black officers in Port Hudson, Lieutenant Phoenix was welcomed back to the harsh realities of racism and being perceived as less, even though he maintained the rank. White enlisted men were required to salute an officer when approached. No such consideration was given to Lieutenant Phoenix, and any white soldiers who would think about it would probably be out of favor. Both he and Lieutenant Colonel Vetter had agreed that it would be in the men's best interest if they were contained to a certain area while at Port Hudson. They had chosen a campsite between the Bayou Sarah Creek and Thompson's Bayou, a bombed-out area from the previous siege outside the main Port Hudson area but close enough that Lieutenant Colonel Vetter felt they were safe. Because Lieutenant Phoenix was one of the officers, he was required to go about and work on resupplying the unit before its departure in the next couple of days. His interaction with both white and black soldiers brought to the forefront how different his unit was, compared to others. With the white soldiers, his lieutenant rank meant little, and they showed disrespect at every chance. The only thing that mattered to him was that his commander, Lieutenant Colonel Vetter, was one of the few senior officers at Port Hudson at this time. There was even brief talk of assigning him as the commander of Port Hudson until his Southern background became known. They gave Lieutenant Phoenix barely recognizable acknowledgment for the simple reason that they didn't want to incur disfavor from a possible future commander. Lieutenant Phoenix received all the supplies they needed.

Lieutenant Phoenix was lost in thought about the significance of Port Hudson to the black soldiers. They were some of the very first to get the opportunity to prove they were men and not animals to be bred and beat. They had died ignorant, poor, abused, broken, and beaten but men. They showed that they deserved to have a place at the table in the new Union and shed blood to prove it. It was a sacrifice plain and simple to go forward, knowing you wouldn't return—not for yourself but for your people. It was a very noble sacrifice and couldn't be forgotten. Lieutenant Phoenix didn't see the value of walking to his death, but he understood the sacrifice those men had given. He mused that if his unit had learned to fight the same way, they would probably be in the cemetery with the other Negro troops who had died so valiantly, walking to their deaths. Lieutenant Phoenix also understood that the sacrifice these men had made magnified his position as one of the few black Union officers.

The black soldiers saw Lieutenant Phoenix as the future. They saluted him when he walked up and gave him the deference his rank deserved. Some didn't know what to think of him. Before the war, most black men in positions of power were simply extensions of the master's rule. Anything they had seen or heard would be told to the master. In some of their minds, Lieutenant Phoenix was the evolution of that. They acknowledged the rank more out of fear and distrust rather than respect. The men were all enlisted; all their officers were white and located at different locations. Lieutenant Phoenix understood all this when he approached the men, his previous reflections on responsibility still fresh in his head.

Lieutenant Phoenix returned the salutes and responded with "Good afternoon, men!" This seemed to have a physical impact on the men; they didn't expect to hear that. Lieutenant Phoenix didn't give them a chance to answer and continued to explain who he was, told them a little bit about the unit, and described how they were departing to go West. Without giving the exact details of what the unit did, he explained that the men had to develop unique skills outside the normal shoulder-to-shoulder, walk-to-your-death form of battle other Union troops were used to. Lieutenant Phoenix told them he had been given the authority to recruit other blacks, who were interested in the unit. He explained that they would depart in about two days and that for those interested in talking to their superiors and showing up tomorrow morning, all questions would be answered then.

Lieutenant Phoenix saluted the men, acknowledged salutes, and departed. He knew that to gain these men's trust, he had to be what they expected him to be, a leader. He came to give them information; he was short, concise, and to the point. He gave them information that allowed them to have options. He didn't come to "heck and jaw" about everything that was going on in an effort to gain their trust. He was a soldier and had been given a great trust; he would ensure that he would do his part.

———

The ride into Port Hudson was the first time Sergeant Hall had ever been in any type of parade. That's what the colonel called it. The black people around the Port had come to see the all-Negro unit.

Sergeant Hall was still struggling with what had happened in the encounter with the former Confederate soldiers. It troubled him that they had looked to him to initiate the action. He knew why they had chosen him, and that was what really bothered him. He wanted to be a godly man, not a killer. But how was he to be a godly man if he could kill so easily and without remorse? His one saving grace was that he didn't feel any joy or satisfaction in killing; he just felt like it needed to be done.

Seeing the Negroes lined along the street to see them made him realize that every man he killed was one less person to torture and maim the people who were looking to him for hope. The little kids along the street looked up in amazement and wonder at the black men in uniform. For a majority of them, they had never seen their own people in anything other than slave garb. Now they were on the backs of horses in uniform and with weapons. For the more religious in the group, the heavens had parted, and God was finally shining a light on his persecuted children. The import of the position they held and the realization of the responsibility thrown on his shoulders slowly seeped into Sergeant Hall's mind. Maybe a killer was what his people needed to be safe. For them, the world would hold new wonders, a world where a slave was nonexistent and a man would be allowed to live his life unjudged by the daily optics of life but by how well he navigated the obstacles of life.

Looking around at all the black faces made Sergeant Hall sit taller in his seat. If the Negro was to be anything in the United States, men like Sergeant Hall would define what that would look like.

Sergeant Hall had to admit that he was ready for this battle. He would never be a slave again; he would fight every day, every minute, and every second of his life to stay free. Yes, he was an impassionate killer, but it was only for those who felt the success of their lives came from the whip marks on slaves' backs.

TWENTY-EIGHT

Departing Port Hudson

LIEUTENANT COLONEL VETTER was surprised when Lieutenant Phoenix reported that over sixty-six black soldiers had volunteered for the mission out West. Another twelve white soldiers also volunteered, to the dismay of their fellow white soldiers. For a lot of the white soldiers in the Union army, the distressed South was an opportunity to gain land and earn a new life. Especially for the officers in the group, there were a lot of rebel lands in the South that were being confiscated as a result of supporting the rebel cause. Whatever the reason, Lieutenant Colonel Vetter thought this was a small step in the unification of black and white. Everyone understood this was an all-black unit, and for white men to volunteer to be in it meant a lot, at least to the black men in the unit. In total, he had about 120 men, not including the families they had left behind.

TWENTY-NINE

Jian Chiy

VETTER WAS ALSO surprised by a meeting with a middle-aged Chinese nobleman named Jian Chiy. He was residing at Port Hudson and had learned of Lieutenant Colonel Vetter's mission to go out West with his colored troops. He was a Chinese dignitary brought to the South at the onset of the war to help the rebels improve their metal-making techniques as they sought to develop their navy. He claimed to be a direct descendant of an ancient Chinese leader, named Chiyou, who was from a clan of blacksmiths who had discovered the process of casting and were responsible for introducing stronger and advanced weaponry throughout Chinese history. He had been brought to the South under a lot of pomp and ceremony. His presence had also been used as an indicator that China was favorable to the rebel cause. Initially, the Chinese delegation were treated like nobles. He was given a small farm in New Orleans near the industrial location planned for shipbuilding facilities. He was also given three slaves, a small family. The man was Jian's manservant, the wife was to manage the home, and the young boy would do whatever else was needed around the house. Jian could work on his metal research, primarily building stronger cannons with a longer range.

Jian understood metal in all its intricacies. He knew how to make metal stronger or weaker depending on what it was used for. He wasn't a weapons maker, but because of his family's extensive background with the military, he understood how it functioned. Since being in the South, he quickly learned that the Americans had gained a creative edge on weapons of destruction. Their ability to create new and more efficient weapons of war outstripped their knowledge of the metals needed to contain the growing energy dispensed from the weapons. China had always been a leader in the advancement of weapons, and it only made sense that when the South first thought about seceding from the Union, they started to look at ways to increase their military powers. They had realized early that naval control of the sea and the Mississippi would be paramount to the continuation of the way of life in the South and the continuation of the war. The South's logistical links to the world would be critical once they seceded. Control of imports and exports, chiefly cotton, via the sea would be paramount to their future. Unfortunately for the South, the Union initiated and maintained a blockade that put a stranglehold on the South.

He had planned on staying at least a year and had brought his family and a small entourage of Chinese citizens, totaling twenty-five people. A few were noblemen and noblewomen in their own right.

He explained that even though the Chinese were embracing and changing to western ways and getting rid of the sword to embrace the rifle, the need for strong metal was even more critical. They led the world in developing long-range cannons and enhancing the metals to contain the growing need for larger and stronger cannons. Jian had helped the South develop the first ironclads of the war and the destructive power they brought to the new battlefield. The South had the initial surprise in ingenuity with its initial ironclads and better cannons, which could have been a factor had the North not constricted the influx of additional metal with the blockade. The South didn't have the steel-mining capabilities needed to keep up with the demand the ironclad required. With the blockade also came the need for more money as the South became cash strapped, and the rebel dollar lost value.

Jian and his entourage, who were so formally welcomed, now found themselves being held for ransom. Only with an extreme amount of money were any of the Chinese in Jian's group allowed to go back to China. Only six were able to go, and Jian had a suspicion that they didn't make it. Jian felt the only thing that kept him and his family alive was the fact that they could still ransom him, his knowledge of steelmaking, and the fact that his skin tone didn't have a definition in the Southern code; they closely resembled whites. Fortunately, they had moved him and his family to Port Hudson for "protection." Due to the port's location, it was the perfect place to create a weapons factory both for maritime and land use. The plans to break ground on the weapons facility never came to fruition due to the redistribution of both money and supplies. Since being here, he had helped recast the few cannons at the port and increase their range. During the siege, they had been told to stay inside their facility; anyone seen outside would be shot and killed. They had run out of food within five days of the siege and resorted to eating the family pets. The only thing keeping them alive was the slave family that had been given to them. The slaves had more access to materials during the siege than the soldiers and the white families in the area. It had gotten so bad that one white family had threatened to cut the necks of little black children if their parents didn't bring food to feed them. That threat was quickly given up after one night of intense bombing; the family was found with their throats cut, and nobody had witnessed anything.

Initially, Jian had no interest in the new American country and its issues with slavery. China had always had some form of slavery or caste system, and this was nothing new. However, the enslavement of Africans in America was something different to Jian. When Jian first met the slaves who would be working for him, the first thing that stood out was the smell. The smell was like a physical weapon; it was so strong. They smelled worse than farm animals and literally had rags on for clothes. The mother's hair was the only thing about her that seemed orderly. She had it braided in long cornrows, and they fell to the middle of her shapely back. The mother's breasts were barely hidden under the rags she had put together to cover them. Pieces of what might have been a dress were pinned together and covered the bottom half of her body. She had an extra string wrapped around her waist and breast as an extra precaution. The father was the only one who wore shoes, and they were from two different types of shoes, and his toes were exposed on the left side. He had on a burlap bag for a shirt, with holes cut in the sides for his arms to stick out. His pants were also made of some burlap-like material and sewed together with the string normally used to hold the bags together. The little boy was eight years old and still wore clothes that were better suited for a baby.

Even in China they recognized slaves as human beings; they just basically held that if you were born a slave, you would die a slave. However, you could live a somewhat decent life. The Americans wanted their slaves to think they were equivalent to animals and didn't want them to feel any semblance to humans. Jiang had his wife and her maids immediately wash and clothe them. Jian thought it would be best to clothe them in Chinese clothes so his slaves were recognizable among others. They didn't even look the same once they were cleaned and shaved. The woman cried and kept saying she was in heaven. She had never seen such nice clothes and said the material had to be from heaven. Jian hated to admit it, but if it weren't for his slaves, his whole family would have been dead by now or taken as slaves. He owed his life and the lives of his family to them and wanted to make sure they had a chance at life. The strife and struggle of the siege had made them all one family now. When the Union army found them, they didn't know what to do with them, since they were obviously prisoners of the rebels. Jian was given a special status and left to his own means until some word from the official government could be gained. Everything was still in shambles.

Jian offered his services to the Union army, helping with the armorers and smithies. When he had heard of Lieutenant Colonel Vetter's upcoming move to the West, he wanted to offer his services for passage and security for himself, his family, and the former slave family. They were no longer his slaves but close friends and family. They had all agreed that going someplace else and rebuilding were the best options for them. They would work hard and provide wherever. The former slave was interested in becoming a soldier and would love to join Lieutenant Colonel Vetter's unit if he would have them.

Vetter immediately liked Jian and could feel that he meant every word he said. Having additional help with weapons maintenance and general repair of stuff around the camp would be useful. Vetter had to admit, though, that he was fascinated with Jian and where he was from. He knew very little about China and the Far East. This was a very unique opportunity, especially during a time when everything was in such disarray. He agreed and told him to be ready in about two days. They would leave here and link up with the small contingent of family members they had left at their camp, which was on the way West. Jian stood, bowed, and thanked Vetter. Vetter stood and reached to shake Jian's hand. Jian grabbed Vetter's one hand with both of his, and with a tear in his eye, he thanked Vetter.

Jian for his part felt he had finally found a man in this country who was honorable at heart. He felt relieved and good that he had found such a person for his family. He knew this man would always be honest with him.

Lieutenant Phoenix woke Lieutenant Colonel Vetter at 0300; everyone was ready to leave Port Hudson. The unit had been up most of the night, preparing for the early-morning departure. They had agreed to let Lieutenant Colonel Vetter sleep in since he had been up for the last two days, organizing the leave and doing final coordination with the remaining leadership at Port Hudson. Vetter dressed, ate, and closed the door on Port Hudson. Outside, he walked down a long line of mounted soldiers, two abreast. All his men had horses now. Each man silently acknowledged Vetter with a nod. The unit was under orders to move and work under as much silence as possible overnight and this morning.

Toward the middle of the formation, there was a huge shadow, which turned out to be a large, ornate two-wheeled carriage, pulled by four horses. This was unlike anything Vetter had ever seen. There was a small window toward the back, which briefly shined a light as if a curtain had been pulled back. Jian was seated in the most comfortable-looking carriage seat Vetter had ever seen. Vetter couldn't wait to learn more about this contrivance.

At the front of the formation, his leadership was already mounted, and young Charl held the reigns of Vetter's horse. The young man had grown so much. He grabbed his reigns and thanked Charl. Young Charl hurried away to get on his own horse. Vetter mounted his horse, turned it around, and looked at each of his men. Each nodded. He turned his horse back around and started forward.

The dim glow of the early-morning sun was at the back of First Sergeant Amra when he noted the place where they had attacked and killed the men days before. There was no sign of the brief and bloody battle. The men had named the place Cockcrow Point. When Lieutenant Phoenix had asked what the Cockcrow meant, First Sergeant Amra had told him the men had thought of the battle as a wake-up call for black Americans. They felt it was the first time as Americans that they had to defend their country.

THIRTY

The West

THE DESTINATION OUT West was an abandoned Confederate outpost on the Mexican/American border called Fort Quitman. The trip was just under one thousand miles. Lieutenant Colonel Vetter and the team planned on at least twenty miles a day of travel and figured it would take at least three months to get to their destination. The plan included picking up the additional families and wagons they had left behind before coming to Port Hudson. First Lieutenant Phoenix had informed Lieutenant Colonel Vetter that they had 156 soldiers or little over two troops and an additional eighty-five family members in tow for a total of 241.

The actual trip took just over eight months to make. Navigating through the West was still new and hard due to a lack of landmarks. The extreme heat, being the most critical factor, made Vetter change travel to late nights and early mornings to avoid the worst of the day's heat. Also, the travel had to coincide with the mapped-out watering holes. This was something Vetter felt should have been the driving factor in deciding how much travel they would do from day to day.

The trip would have taken well over a year if not for the addition of about six Seminole-Negro scouts. Lieutenant Colonel Vetter had heard of black/Indian scouts who were serving the military. He knew they had initially served with the rebel forces and in Texas before the Civil War and had been treated harshly by rebel forces and the Texan civilians in the area. Despite being treated so harshly, they had become critical to navigating the vast and markerless western frontier. Their loyalty to the army had been proved over and over again against the harshest treatments. Even under the harsh desert heat, Vetter could tell these men served with their heads held high; they were proud of themselves. The men were immediately accepted among the ranks. Vetter's men knew the value of scouts and how mastering the terrain in any area was always crucial to a soldier. First Sergeant Amra immediately put them to work by teaching his men the ways of the desert.

Added to the constant battle with the heat was the need to maintain security at all times. In the early days of the trip, as they were leaving Louisiana and heading into Texas, there were a lot of rebel bands roving around. Most of the time the scouts reported seeing groups of men in the distance but nothing else. However, one group of about thirty men thought a large group of free Negroes was just too much a target and had attacked the rear of the caravan, where they thought the caravan would be the weakest. Unfortunately for them, the last three wagons held soldiers who were sleeping or resting for their shift as roving guards. Scouts had warned them about the pending attack, and the decision was made to pretend negligence in the rear of the caravan and lure them into a trap.

The attacking band had only enough time to yell their attack charge before fifteen rifles opened fire on them. Over half of the rebel band was cut down on the initial volley. The attack was so unexpected to them that they didn't even try to fire back; they immediately stopped their horses and tried to turn around and run. The second volley finished the remaining band off. All this happened without the caravan even stopping. Vetter ordered a group of men to see whether any of the horses were still alive and to take all firearms off the dead. He ordered the men to leave the bodies where they lay; he hoped the sight of the bodies would deter any future bands from attacking.

As they got deeper into Texas territory, they started seeing more Mexicans and a few Indian stragglers. They weren't the first black unit in the area, but they could tell some of the people had never seen blacks before. Scouts reported being monitored by various bands of Indians in the distance. Fortunately, after the first event, the only things the caravan had to deal with were dealing with the heat, finding their way in a markerless terrain, and discovering the next waterhole.

PART TWO

PART
TWO

THIRTY-ONE

Jian's Impact

THE IMPACT OF Jian's presence could already be felt in the new shirts the men wore. Immediately upon entering the Texas territory, it became evident that the wool clothing wouldn't be sensible in the desert heat. First Sergeant Amra had forecast the heat issue in early planning. He had stated that if the western heat was anything like the African heat, they would all die in their wool uniforms. Having been one of the senior officers at Port Hudson, Lieutenant Colonel Vetter was able to acquire large rolls of tan-colored, eleven-ounce canvas made of cotton duck fabric; it was waterproof and coated with linseed oil. The canvas covers were intended to be stretched across arched wooden bows of the wagons to protect the contents of the wagon from rain and dust.

Vetter had originally intended the canvas to be used as tent material. The material was lighter and cooler than the wool issue, and the color didn't absorb the daily heat. After the first couple of soldiers passed out from the extreme heat, Lieutenant Colonel

Vetter stopped to assess the health of the rest of his men and make
sure they didn't get any mortal injuries. This was when they identified the need to travel more at night and less during the day to
avoid the worst of the sun's heat. The additional tent material was
brought up as the solution to daylight tents to avoid the heat. Jian
brought up the fact that in the deserts of China, people dressed in
light colors to reflect more of the sun's heat; they were cooler as a
result. First Sergeant Amra, the only black male in the group actually born in Africa, confirmed that even in Africa, they followed
such rules to avoid the desert sun. Maybe with lighter clothes,
they could travel more during the day. Jian also noted that his wife
was from an ancient clan of exclusive Chinese seamstresses, who
had created the coveted "qipao" for former emperors and their
relatives. With the help of Jian's wife and the other women in the
camp, a good portion of the material was repurposed and used to
make shirts for the soldiers. The shirts were fashioned after the
Union cavalry shirts with the "bib" in front.

Lieutenant Colonel Vetter had been given the shirt as a gift
because his family knew of his passion for the mounted cavalry.
The replica shirt had a thin wool strip, fashioned from some of the
less desirable blue shirts among his men, and had been sewn along
the sleeve of each shirt. The look gave the shirts a very unique but
durable look. After the first couple of shirts were seen throughout
the camp, the demand from the men was such that they required
an additional day to get shirts for all the soldiers.

Vetter could feel the morale and the sense of the men change
almost instantaneously. The new shirts, though crude in their
make, gave the men a real, fierce look. The tan color seemed
made for this environment, and the blue stripe added a sense of
legitimacy like the blue coat. Lieutenant Colonel Vetter made
sure they added the ranks on the sleeve like the real shirts. The
men loved the shirts, and each couldn't wait until his shirt was
completed. Women were also given large headscarves or shawls

out of the material to protect their faces and heads from the extreme desert heat. Soldiers mounted, heads held high, and families readied wagons with smiles. Who would have thought something as simple as a clothing change could have such an impact on the overall morale of the whole team? The move into Texas felt lighter.

Even before giving the order to move out, Jian immediately knew the men around him weren't average soldiers. The composition of the unit was the normal mix he would have expected to see in a black unit, with the leadership positions held primarily by the all-white staff and the majority of the soldiers being former slaves. White soldiers were also equally numbered among the enlisted ranks and primarily all the leadership positions. The addition of Native Americans made sense given the mission they were getting ready to embark on. No, the sense of purpose was prevalent throughout the camp. Jian noted that every man had some sort of sharp instrument as a side weapon. He hadn't seen so many large knives, throwing knives, or throwing axes since he left China.

The men trained every morning, worked throughout the day, and played skill games with their various weapons to include firearms. Jian could tell the men were lethal. The whites worked side by side with the blacks, and he noted a lot of light banter and laughter in the performance of their daily tasks. Everywhere he went, there was some sort of skills match going. When Jian had initially brought up his large wagon, two men explained to him what was expected as far as distancing and that one man would be near him at all times to assist his needs, by Lieutenant Colonel Vetter's orders. Jian was impressed; everything had been thought out in advance, and everyone knew his place. Along the route, there were constant movements of men coming in and out at regular paces, a very cautious group that didn't take much for granted. It was like they were always at war.

It was the roving bands of security that had given early

warning on the attacking band of men. Jian didn't realize they were being attacked until the men in the front of the formation started firing their rifles. The noise was tremendous; smoke was everywhere from the black powdered weapons. His wagon never stopped moving, and the formation never slowed. As soon as the smoke cleared, so did the enemy. It was like a brief thunderstorm, and the sun decided to pop back up like nothing had happened. Just like that, it was over. Immediately after the first volley, a group of about twenty men broke off and rode off into the distance. Jian could hear sporadic reports of gunfire for a few minutes, and then everything went silent again. The only noises were the intermittent neighing of horses and the loud turning of the huge wagon wheels.

The attack was sort of surreal; it happened so fast. It was now a few hours later, and he was just started to get a sense of reality when he noted men riding back and falling in line with the caravan. He noted that as they passed, they dropped off additional equipment and supplies they had scavenged on a wagon in front of Jian. The men were practical and didn't leave anything to waste; considering the harsh environment they were headed to, that was a good trait to have.

THIRTY-TWO

Hell

SERGEANT FIRST CLASS Hall (Fieldhand) had never felt heat like he experienced now. In his early life as a slave, he had worked the fields in Alabama and had no fond memories of the blistering, hot, and steamy summer days. He had spent days in and day out in the cotton fields. He had believed then that the Southern heat was the other torture from slavery no one ever talked about. The threat of the lash was always prevalent while working the field; the added heat was excruciating. However, he always had the green to provide a little shade in the brief moments of respite. The beautiful and deep green of the South, nourished and toiled on by the rich sweat and blood of slaves, was green everywhere to behold.

The desert heat was nothing Sergeant First Class Hall was ready to understand. Since they had crossed into Texas over three days ago, he felt as if he were witness to what the pastors often talked about. Hell! The heat was unbearable. In fact, he expected to see Satan come out of one of the rocky outcrops or strange-looking plants, called "cactus." There were no trees any-where. There was no green anywhere—not the rich, dark green but a dirty, light green. He smiled inwardly; did this mean no black blood had been spilled in the desert heat? The "hell," as he was apt to call the desert, made him more cognizant of his surroundings. With the dominant green of the South gone, he was never more aware of the different colors around him. The desert was a mixture of mostly browns to red. He missed the greens, but being in the desert made him realize how unaware of his surroundings he had become. Even as a soldier in the South, he could find his way by well-worn roads or trails. Here, no such indicators existed.

He was leading a security patrol with five other men. They had just come from a mountainous area about two days ago. It was a little cooler in the mountainous terrain, and the open plains caught everyone off guard. The heat was like nothing they had experienced until this point. They were about fifty miles from a place called Fort Phantom Hill, according to one of the Seminole scouts attached to his unit. He had been having stomach cramps and sweating profusely since they entered the plains area. They were heading back to the caravan when Sergeant First Class Hall slumped over in his saddle; he was falling off his horse when one of his men caught him.

Sergeant First Class Hall came to in a tent; there was a candle burning, and he could instantly tell that it was dark outside. He didn't remember what had happened. He had a damp cloth on his forehead. The little candle illuminated the small tent. Sergeant First Class Hall could see four to five other men on cots in the tent. He tried to sit up and felt a little queasy. He lay back down, thinking to himself, *Hell has won.*

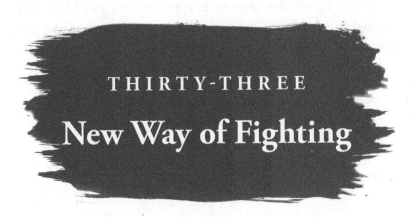

THIRTY-THREE
New Way of Fighting

IT WAS EARLY in the camp. Hints of the sunrise were just barely starting to light up the night sky. First Sergeant Amra liked this time in the morning. It was the only time he had for himself. He remembered when he had been a child, and his father would get up in the morning and go through his sword maneuvers. His father's khopesh had been huge, a giant's weapon compared to that of normal men. It had been handed down for nine generations and was supposed to be a normal sword for the original owner. Another myth to add to their mystical heritage.

His father's technique for using the giant sword involved constant movement. When he was young, he thought his dad was the strongest man in the world because he could lift the huge sword so effortlessly. After years of studying weapons, he finally realized how strong his father actually was and the strength and discipline it took to effortlessly handle and control such a huge weapon.

He was looking for a clearing a little ways from camp so he

could swing his sword without any concern for others' safety. He was walking around a small rock outcropping when he noticed the Chinese man, Jian, and his family going through strange exercises with their hands. Jian seen Amra approach and asked him if he wanted to join. It was then that Amra and the rest of the unit learned about martial arts.

THIRTY-FOUR

Fort Quitman

IT TOOK THE caravan a day to finally recognize they were at the Fort Quitman location. The scouts had informed Lieutenant Colonel Vetter and the leadership of what to expect once they arrived and were right in their assessment. The fort, if that is what you want to call it, consisted of a small brick wall surrounding the fort, a few broken down buildings, and some old graves. Lieutenant Colonel Vetter could immediately tell by the reaction of the men around him that the end of their journey was a big letdown.

Vetter thought using the word *fort* to describe this place had probably started out as joke and gotten taken out of context. Vetter didn't think this place was worthy of the name of fort, post, or station for US troops. The buildings were made of what appeared to be mud and had been stripped of all wood, including roofs, doors, and window frames. Jian informed him that the mud material was called "adobe," usually a mixture of mud and straw. The buildings that were supposed to be barracks for the men didn't have doors or windows. There seemed to have been attempts at some sort of garden; the west end facing the river showed plow marks, but the sandy soil and dry, hot climate had frustrated attempts to cultivate a post garden.

Based on the scouts' earlier update, the plan had been for the caravan to immediately go into a tight circle around the dilapidated fort upon arrival. The circle would allow for 360-degree security while providing a modicum of safety in the interior for families.

Once the wagons were settled, a small heavily armed team escorted the water wagon to the river to gather water. The "fort" was less than a mile away from the Rio Grande River and the border with Mexico. Fondly remembering his terrain analysis training while a cadet at West Point, Vetter surveyed the area and observed that the land slightly sloped down toward the west, going toward the river; as expected, the land was definitely greener as he came closer to the river. There was gradual elevation while heading northeast toward the Quitman Mountain Range some fifteen miles to the northeast, which seemed to be the focal point of the area. Going north brought mostly washed-out sloping plains for miles and miles. This wasn't a very defensible position in Vetter's mind; this place was out in the open and had no walls.

Vetter's main mission was to maintain order in areas disrupted by Native Americans, many of whom were frustrated with life on Indian reservations and broken promises by the federal government. They would then go seek land off the reservations, which now belonged to white men. Under the Texas law of 1845, all "unoccupied" land was the property of the state. Since the Indians weren't citizens of Texas, they were considered trespassers and should be militarily expelled. In conjunction with expelling Indians and putting them back on the reservation, they were also tasked with expelling Mexicans who had also taken up residence in Texas territory and preventing Mexican bandit excursions into the United States for the purpose of harassing and murdering white settlers in the area. First Lieutenant Phoenix had informed Vetter that it was ironic that the blacks were facing their own forms of discrimination throughout the United States, predominantly the South, and were now tasked with removing another minority group in that government's name.

THIRTY-FIVE

News

VETTER SHARED ALL his intelligence missives with his leadership in their meetings. He had promoted the idea that all his leadership team should learn to read. The intelligence he had been receiving clearly showed that the newly freed Negro in America wasn't doing so well. There were reports of constant hangings and burnings in the South. The freed Negroes were being used as pawns for the voting but were given the protection needed to vote safely. For blacks in the South, things had gotten worse; Northerners had conceded authority in the South to a lot of former slave owners, who weren't required to take any oaths of loyalty and basically continued slavery through the use of penal codes.

The penal codes resembled laws from colonial times, which placed severe restrictions on blacks. Blacks couldn't vote, serve on juries, travel freely, or work in occupations of their choice. Even their marriages were outside the law, white legislators in the South saw little reason not to continue the tradition of unequal treatment of black persons. Vetter knew the white South strongly believed there was such a radical difference in the mental and moral (nature) of the white and black race that it would be impossible to secure order in a mixed community. He could personally discredit that belief but knew his perspective had been gained only after being forced to work with blacks as a sign of distrust and through shared hardship. How many other whites were being provided the opportunity to work alongside blacks, let alone acknowledge that they were humans? How long would it take for the white race to get the same perspective he had? A man or a woman should be judged on merit and character.

THIRTY-SIX
New Place

ONCE EVERYTHING WAS somewhat settled, Vetter immediately gathered his leadership team to assess the next steps. As his team gathered near one of the tents set up in the middle of the encampment, Vetter noted that even with the harsh conditions, he could sense that the men felt relieved to finally be at the end of their journey. He also noted that the men kept looking around as if expecting something to happen. He was in a similar straight; getting used to the openness was going to take some time. He felt exposed.

Once everyone was settled, Vetter started the meeting by saying, "We are currently the outermost military unit in the whole United States. There is no other unit deployed as far as we are. If we are going to survive out here, we will have to rely on all of our skills to make it. I am not a desert expert, and I know a lot of you have prior backgrounds in desert environments. The camp followers and family members will have to be included in any plan we make. We need to make sure that we query them for any desert knowledge that could be useful to our survival. I remind you that our primary mission is to expel non-American citizens from American territory and to protect American citizens. Our scouts report roving bands of at least three Indian tribes in the immediate area. There are no signs of permanent settlements yet. As you know, this place was formerly run by the rebels, so I do expect to see some white families in the area who are former rebel sympathizers. Be on guard. I don't have to remind you of the backlash across the country at freed blacks. Right now my biggest concern is our defense and the safety of everyone who is with us. What are your thoughts?"

Immediately First Sergeant Amra stated, "We need to maintain our current security patrols but increase the teams from three men to five." Everyone agreed with this recommendation.

It was Jian who noted that the current site wasn't acceptable as a defense; the mountains to the northeast would provide a better vantage and give more cover and concealment from the elements and any prying eyes. All agreed about the current area not being defensible, but they weren't sold that the mountains were the best spot. Many wanted to move closer to a water source. Jian chimed in. "If you look at the lay of the land, you see that there are rainy seasons and that all the rain from the mountains drains to this area. Earlier settlers tried to plant crops but weren't successful, as evidenced by the dried-out fields."

Once again it was First Sergeant Amra who replied and seemed to take on the mantle of security for the unit. "If we are the only unit in the area and have no current support, then we need to ensure that we can survive on our own and provide for our own. This area only has water that can benefit us. The mountains have water and cover, and they can provide us with an early warning if anyone is coming to try to attack us. Moving there may be extra work, but it will be better for everyone."

Vetter was impressed. First Sergeant Amra had laid out every reason to move, which Vetter had already decided on. He wanted the idea to be his men's; he didn't need to tell them how to protect themselves. He had already talked to Jian, and the plan required a significant amount of work to see them safe in the mountains.

The next couple of months were busy for the unit. Everyone who wasn't on patrol was working on building fortifications. The mountain, identified as Quitman Mountain, was steep and rocky, with a few narrow canyons with flat bottoms and vertical walls. There was a combination of shallow, stony soils with some clay and sandy loams. The sandy loam was the best soil for growing root crops where the roots needed unobstructed, even soil. The lower elevation supported live oak, pion, juniper, and grasses. At their higher elevations, there were Douglas fir, ponderosa pine, maple, Arizona cypress, and madrone.

First Sergeant Amra took the lead in executing the plan for developing the defense for the organization. Controlled blasts with TNT were used to clear a road to the top of the mountain. Additional blasts were used to level off the top of the mountain, where the main base would be housed. The newly blasted road was cleared of debris. First Sergeant Amra advised everyone to save all destroyed wood and not to cut down any wood on the mountain. First Sergeant Amra knew that if this desert was anything like the African desert, wood would be highly prized.

At the top of the mountain, men used a mix of mud and straw, called "adobe," to develop large mud bricks, which were laid out over pits for drying. Wood debris was used in the pits to burn under the bricks to increase their strength. As the bricks dried, the barracks building and the HQ building started to take form. Near the center of the mountain off the road, dwellings were being developed unlike anything Vetter had ever seen. Instead of just letting family members live in the fort, it was decided that families should live closer to the bottom of the mountain. The design was similar to the medieval fort layouts, with towns falling under the shadow of the fort. Under Jian's direction, a small road was cleared out around the side of the mountain. Off the road, areas were cleared out, with particular attention put on how the layout was viewed from the bottom. Careful detail was given to make sure the dwellings were hidden when viewed from the bottom. The adobe clay was mixed with the normal rock layout, and some wood was added to increase the stability of houses. The results were cozy, little, cave-like structures built into the side of the mountain. A dwelling wasn't considered complete until Jian couldn't view the newly created dwelling from the bottom of the mountain at night with a fire lit inside.

THIRTY-SEVEN

Visitors

ALL THE DEMOLITION to clear the mountain and the smoke from the bricks being made could be seen for miles in such an open environment. One early morning just after sunrise, a small group of people was reported coming in from the Southwest. It, wasn't long before the men found out they were heading directly toward the fort's location.

A squad of eight was sent out to engage and investigate; there were no reports of any weapons other than sidearms. By noon the group was identified as a small delegation of Mexican farmers visiting from across the river. Lieutenant Colonel Vetter decided to meet the delegation at the bottom of the hill near the entrance of the newly developed fort. He didn't know the intentions of the farmers and didn't want them to understand their defenses until their intentions were known.

There were six men in total. Two were immediately identifiable as priests due to the brownish robes they wore. The older and taller of the two monks introduced himself as Padre Anthony Morales, and his shorter and stouter friend was Padre Cristobel Garcia; both were Catholic priests at a small monastery a few miles on the other side of the river. The other men were introduced as farmers and miners in the area near the monastery. Vetter had little intelligence from the other side of the river, so knowing a mine was in the area was new to him. The older priest was designated as the speaker because he knew English, but Vetter could clearly see that all the direction was coming from a middle-aged-looking Mexican man introduced as Señor Guadalupe Perez.

If the men were surprised to see the black soldiers, they didn't show it. The men were simply dressed but clean; they seemed to have some wealth, and their clothes were well made, not the simple homespun of the locals. Vetter's men were setting up a tent to get the men out of the heat. It was cooler near the mountain, not as hot as the heat from the trip that had brought them here.

Padre Morales opened up the conversation, saying he would speak for the group since he spoke the best English. He mentioned that he knew of the previous owners, the rebel masters who were in the previous location, called Fort Quitman, and conveyed that they had tried to enslave all the natives in the area to work for them. The only thing that had saved them was the onslaught of the Civil War and the fact that they couldn't sustain themselves while they were here. The natives in the area had quickly moved to the Mexican side of the border to get out of enslavement.

Until recently the area had been a prohibited area to the local populace because of its bad history. They hadn't known anyone else moved into the area until they heard the blast and saw the smoke. They had watched the unit for about a week before deciding to approach. They had seen the black soldiers from afar and noted that they worked and were treated like equals. That fact was what finally made them approach, hope that they had amicable neighbors.

Vetter knew of the previous rebel owners but had never heard of rebels trying to enslave the populace. It made sense; if the owners believed in slavery, then everyone they met who didn't look like them was a possible slave. That was the whole reason for the Civil War: to prevent the spread of slavery. Vetter informed the Father of his mission to expel non-American citizens from American territory and to protect American citizens. He assured him that he wasn't here to enslave the local populace.

Father Morales also talked about the conflicts on the Mexican side of the border. Recent wars with France and follow-on wars within Mexico with different factions had left the country with a lot of uncertainty. The people of Cajoncito had been relatively forgotten in the remote Mexican wilderness because they were hidden behind a long mountain range and lived so close to the US border. The rebels had also raided Cajoncito multiple times, looking for the Indians who had escaped to the Mexico side. It had gotten a bad reputation, and ever since, Mexicans stayed away. They had lived a relatively quiet and unobstructed life.

The Father informed him that they had originally been sent to Mexico from Spain to spread the word of God, like Fathers before him since the late 1500s. Because of the recent independence of Mexico, contact with Spain had become more and more tenuous until there wasn't communication at all. The two padres had become so enamored with the people they served that they had decided to stay and make the place their home. Most of the people were farmers with a small population starting to look into mining. The miners, because of the amount of wealth they had generated, were the designated leaders of the community. The town had started out with mostly indigenous Mexicans in the area, but it had recently seen a large influx of Indians to the area, who were escaping the American Indian reservations or the rebel forces seeking to enslave them. Until recently they had been untouched by all the conflict in Mexico.

First Lieutenant Phoenix listened to the monks as they talked to Lieutenant Colonel Vetter. They didn't notice anyone else in the room but Lieutenant Colonel Vetter; everyone else might as well have been furniture. Their initial look of humbleness and righteousness was instantly dispelled upon Phoenix's closer inspection. The first thing Lieutenant Phoenix noticed was the clothing. Most of the people in the area had some sort of rough homespun in various shades of tan to dark brown. As a former man slave to a very narcissistic master, Phoenix had become very familiar with the types of exotic and expensive clothing. The padres' robes were a dark brown, but they had a dark sheen seen in clothes made of the finest materials and quality. Only noblemen had this type of material. The other things that were completely out of nature were their hands; they were immaculate. Phoenix also knew a manicured hand when he saw one; his manservant training had included taking care of his master's hands and feet. He saved his thoughts for himself and listened more to learn what was in the wind.

Father Morales explained that since the war had ended, three former rebels had come back and started up a bandit band. These men had gone to Cajoncito, burned two buildings, and taken over thirty women and children with them as hostages. The padres had been told they would be given back two women a week if they provided their weight in silver every week. The bandits knew of the silver mine and had decided that instead of robbing the people, they would extort them. They were safe on the American side of the border, and the people of Cajoncito couldn't hope to try to save the hostages, even if they had the means, which they didn't. The only weapons in Cajoncito were pistols and a few rifles, but they weren't enough to stop a heavily armored outlaw band.

Vetter already knew what the men wanted, but something about the padre just didn't feel right. However, if such a bandit band did exist, it was in his mandate to address it. If what the padre said was true, they were basically an autonomous city operating outside the Mexican government. That was what bothered Vetter. Why didn't they go to the Mexican government first and have them try to work out this problem in their behest? He told the padre that his unit was new to the area and had just started using long patrols. Their focus had been on establishing dwellings and mapping out the immediate area. He mentioned that if such a band did exist, then he was duty bound to look into it and address it accordingly. He told the padre that he would like to take a moment to discuss the issue among his men. Vetter excused himself to discuss with his men.

Lieutenant Colonel Vetter nodded to his men, and they all stood and walked back toward the mountain, out of earshot of the visiting padre team. Vetter found a waist-high rock and sat down. His men immediately formed a semicircle, blocking the visitors. He started the conversation simply by saying, "Thoughts?"

Captain Matthews, one of his white officers, was the first to speak up. "If they are extorting the people, there must be a lot of silver in the town. The bandits must know something more." Everyone nodded.

First Lieutenant Phoenix chimed in. "The robes the padres are wearing are of the finest European quality and not any homespun from around here. They also have manicured hands, which could indicate they have servants. Not something a humble priest would have."

Finally, First Sergeant Amra chimed in and stated that if the women and children were saved, "it would be a good gesture with our new neighbors. There could be an opportunity for some sort of trade, considering the harsh environment we are in."

First Lieutenant Phoenix watched as everyone's interest perked up at the idea of the trade option. The unit had just received its first resupply, which had taken four months to receive. Everyone, both black and white, felt the disappointment in the resupply. Half of the requests had been filled with bacon and ham of such poor quality that it was barely edible. The live animals were primarily inferior, and nearly all the fresh vegetables quickly spoiled. As former slaves, they were used to eating the scraps from the master but didn't expect to be treated like this as new citizens of the country. Even the white soldiers were amazed by what had been sent. One white soldier went so far as to claim that the quartermaster sent their trash because the quality of the food was so bad.

During the war, the unit had had to rely on its own survival because of the clandestine mission they had behind enemy lines. But they had always been near water, and the woods had more abundant life than the desert, so the resupply was critical to the unit. Therefore, the idea of a trade to help their situation was tempting and needed. First Lieutenant Phoenix mused that quite honestly, every black man there didn't give a damn about the quality of food; the fact that they had control of their lives and destiny was more than what they ever thought they would have. Let the white man keep the good food; the black soldiers would survive of their own volition. Nothing was worse than slavery. If they didn't even need a chance, they would make their own as long as they were free.

Vetter contemplated the input from his men and was honestly surprised by their observations. He realized their lives as slaves had given them some unique perspectives and survival skills that made them keen and wary in the ways of men. Even though they couldn't read, they had to learn to watch the mannerisms, attire, and everything outward about a person to develop a comprehensive profile of an individual. Snapped out of his musings, Vetter liked the idea of possible trade as a goodwill gesture. If he could help benefit the unit and people under him by simply doing their jobs, then those were ideal conditions. If there were rebel soldiers in the area working clandestine operations, he wanted to make sure he put them out of operation.

Vetter told the men, "Thank you for the honest assessment. I don't feel they are trustworthy either. However, the need to establish other means of supplies is tempting, and we are still new to the area. Any possible 'friendlies' could be a good thing. Inform the scouts to be prepared to follow them when they leave; I want a full report on the town of Cajoncito. He had to admit the town intrigued him. He had told Jian to stay behind, and now he hated that he hadn't gotten a chance to get his perspective. Lieutenant Colonel Vetter asked, "Any other issues?"

Captain Matthews reiterated his earlier concern about the town being extorted for silver. Which brought up another question from Lieutenant Colonel Vetter. How would they get the extortion money to the bandits and return the family members? Vetter amended his earlier order and added an additional two-man scout team to follow the visitors back to Cajoncito. The additional scout team was tasked to follow any personnel leaving the town of Cajoncito and heading toward the US border. Lieutenant Colonel Vetter believed this should be the ransom payment leaving the town. Lieutenant Colonel Vetter directed them to follow the payment back to the bandits' base and verify the location if they got there before the rescue team did. He warned his men to be extremely careful, because the bandits knew the area and would probably have local Indians or Mexicans working with them and would be on watch.

I don't want our knowledge of them to be known," he said. The remaining team needed to stay at Cajoncito to get more information about the mines and the people of the city.

Discussion was complete; as a group, they turned and walked back to the padres. Lieutenant Colonel Vetter informed the padres of his decision to assist them and wanted to thank him for providing him with the information on the bandits, even if there was an underlying motive. He informed them that he looked forward to trading with the men and needed as many details about the bandits that they knew so they could get started. He apologized for having to do business out in open but informed them that the area was still littered with rocks after the controlled explosions, and they hadn't established any resident building yet. Makeshift tents, tables, and chairs that could be spared were brought out; and Lieutenant Colonel Vetter and the team discussed a plan with the padres. The padres explained that they could help the unit by providing some goats and pigs for supplies. They also had tools and other supplies that would be useful in helping to establish the fort. They explained that there was a total of thirty-two women over eighteen years of age; there were twenty-two kids, mostly young girls under eighteen years of age. There were also fifteen elderly. He mentioned that the bandits had taken some native Indians women living in the area but didn't know the count; they had killed all the Native American men.

Lieutenant Colonel Vetter thought that to be a significant number of people and that this was more than just a happenstance ransom. The bandits had taken on the responsibility of the care of all those people, or their intent wasn't for any of them to survive, which posed an even worse situation. There was a lot more going on in this situation, which needed to be learned.

The padres wanted to leave one of the miners behind to assist and stand in as a liaison. Vetter noted that the identified individual seemed startled by the statement and a little upset. Vetter pushed back and stated that his men traveled faster alone and that the liaison would be a hindrance, and there were no livable quarters to support his staying at the fort. Vetter informed them that this could be an option once they had dealt with the current situation. However, Vetter did recommend to the padres that one of his officers should return with the padres and start the preparation for the supply transfer and get a good account. The padres agreed, but Vetter could detect a moment of hesitation at the initial request.

Captain Matthews was introduced to the padres as the representative and one other individual, to be identified shortly. Vetter had thought to ask Jian to be that other person and to go undercover to get both his perspective on the town and to keep an eye on Captain Matthews, who seemed very intent on the silver.

The planning continued into the evening with a final call for quitting right after sunset. The Midwestern sunset lit up the sky with a fiery red, orange glow, nothing like First Lieutenant Phoenix had ever seen his life. It was like a huge door had opened, and a hot furnace was revealed behind. Heaven was on fire, and it was beautiful. He smiled at his internal musings. He was still poeticizing about life and looking at the beauty of things after all he had been through. The new desert environment was a new journey each day. He was fascinated by everything he saw and couldn't see. Where he would have thought death ruled, there was life. This wasn't life like the in South, where everything was green and lush, but it was life in a desert environment, where water or the lack of it ruled everything. He also mused that the native Indians were as exceptional as the land, in that they also were defined by the amount of water or the lack of it. They lived within their means within the land. They didn't seek to change it but to live within it in harmony. They had been in the area for hundreds, if not thousands, of years, and there wasn't destruction of the land or tracks of civilization they could see in the South and East in a fraction of the time.

First Lieutenant Phoenix was brought out of his thoughts by one of the visiting miners, a Señor Guadalupe Perez, a Spanish Indian who had been born and raised in the town of Cajoncito. First Lieutenant Phoenix immediately liked the man; he had an easy smile, which came from his eyes. The other men, including the padres, were very furtive and watchful. Señor Perez was the first to try to talk to anyone while the meeting area was being developed. He personally introduced himself to all the men in the area and thanked them for being here. He even shook the hands of the black soldiers on guard in the area. First Lieutenant Phoenix thought that if this was a tactic to gain trust, it was an effective one.

When Señor Perez approached First Lieutenant Phoenix, he leaned in and whispered in his ear, "Can we talk someplace private?" First Lieutenant Phoenix was surprised by the request but remained calm and seemed unfazed by the request. He simply nodded and started walking toward an area a few feet away, where some of his soldiers were providing security for the meeting.

As soon as they started to walk away, Padre Garcia told Señor Perez not to go far because they were getting ready to depart. As they walked, Señor Perez whispered under his breath so only First Lieutenant Phoenix could hear. "Please, my daughter is among the people captured. She is fourteen years old and a hand servant to one of the ladies who was captured. Her name is Genet, and she is deaf. Please bring her back."

First Lieutenant Phoenix was surprised, but his demeanor or face didn't betray his emotion. He responded under his breath, information only for Señor Perez, by asking why he felt Phoenix wouldn't save the girl if she was one of the people missing. Señor Perez smiled and put his arm around First Lieutenant Phoenix to make it seem like they were having a jovial, friendly conversation. He mystically stated, "There is much more going on here than meets the eye, and I don't want my daughter sacrificed for others' safety. Ask to leave a liaison back from the group, and I can explain all. Otherwise, please be careful, and when I can, I will explain further. Please find Genet."

First Lieutenant Phoenix introduced Señor Perez to one of the soldiers guarding the meeting, and Señor Perez spoke a few kind words, laughed aloud, and turned around to walk back to his group. First Lieutenant Phoenix thanked him and walked toward the larger gathering, where Lieutenant Colonel Vetter was speaking.

Padre Morales wanted to leave immediately after they had made all their coordination efforts. It was early in the evening with the sun setting. The moon would be bright and good for walking in the dark. However, Lieutenant Colonel Vetter informed the padre that his people wouldn't be ready to travel until the next morning and requested that they spend the night. The padre reluctantly agreed, and soldiers prepared a makeshift camping spot in the area. Captain Matthews and a small security force would spend the night with the padre and his men.

The sleeping preparations were completed in a few hours, and Lieutenant Colonel Vetter and the rest of his team retreated up the hill to their pre-constructed fort site. A lot had happened today, and the men were tired. However, he needed to make sure any information the men may have gained was discussed while it was still fresh on their minds. He sent a runner ahead to get Jian to meet at the meeting. He led the group to a large campfire, where the meals were made for the soldiers. Light at night was limited to a few small kerosene lamps, which were lit randomly throughout the camp. The whole camp had taken on trying to ration everything they had, using them only out of necessity. He waited for Jian to show up. He called Jian over and gave him a quick brief on the events of the day. After giving Jian a quick rundown, he turned to the team.

They all stood around the kerosene lamp, which gave off a dim, yellow light in the pitch darkness. Lieutenant Colonel Vetter noted that in the dim light, the men seemed larger than life. Their shadows projected in the darkness behind them. Lieutenant Colonel Vetter stated, "That was a lot to take in, and the information they provided asked more questions than they answered. What are your thoughts?"

First Lieutenant Phoenix was the first to open up and relayed the incident with Señor Perez earlier and his mystic comment. "There is much more going here than meets the eye, and he didn't want his daughter sacrificed for others' safety." He also mentioned that Señor Perez had asked to stay back as a liaison, and he could explain further.

Lieutenant Colonel Vetter contemplated his previous decision not to allow any of the padre's men to stay behind. If he suddenly changed his mind, it could seem suspicious. This request could also be some sort of a preplanned scheme by the padres and a ruse to provide misinformation to his team.

Lieutenant Colonel Vetter informed his team of his thoughts. They all nodded in response to his concerns. First Lieutenant Phoenix mentioned that this was their first positive contact with people living in the area. The opportunity for any information could increase their chances of survival, and keeping peace in the area they controlled couldn't be ignored. Already, what was happening on the Mexican side of the border was affecting them. However, First Lieutenant Phoenix warned, "As a primarily all-black unit, we need to be concerned about the view by some of a black military unit dealing with Mexican nationals with a silver mine." Everyone's head snapped up at that; it was something nobody had considered.

Even Lieutenant Colonel Vetter was surprised by the statement and immediately understood the truth in it. He had already had reservations that Captain Matthews had seemed too concerned about the silver. First Lieutenant Phoenix must also have picked up on that. Would he start to feel the same way about all his men who had questions about the silver? This presented a new dynamic his men had never faced: greed. He would have to make sure he paid close attention to his thoughts on each of his men.

He looked around at the men around him. There were a couple of new faces among his officer ranks, all white. However, his senior NCO core, primarily black, was the same one he'd had during the war and indoctrinated in the guerilla-type warfare they had used in the war. A few white senior NCOs were also veterans; however, the majority had come over with the new officers and understood only the more formal army tactics. Until he knew more information about what was going on, he wanted their efforts to be as clandestine as possible.

Coming out of his thoughts, Lieutenant Colonel Vetter looked at his men and addressed the group. "First Lieutenant Phoenix and First Sergeant Amra will set off tomorrow and lead a team of up to thirty heavily armed men to go rescue the hostages. They have already delivered ransoms, and we have a general idea of where they are."

First Sergeant Amra broke in. "I will send a scout team out tonight to guide us in. If there is any bandit reconnaissance in the area, the scouts will deal with it."

Lieutenant Colonel Vetter nodded and continued. "I will inform the padre that I have reconsidered having a liaison from Cajoncito travel with the rescue team. I will try to get Señor Perez to travel with them since he is comfortable with First Lieutenant Phoenix. I honestly think it will be good for the hostages to see someone from their own town when they are rescued." All the men nodded at that.

He continued, "Captain Mathews and six other soldiers will travel to Cajoncito to set up the supply and logistics exchange. Jian has agreed to follow along; his logistic skills can help set up the trade with the town. Sergeant First Class Hall will lead two scout teams, doubled with horses, and trail Captain Matthew's team traveling with the padres. Along with following the ransom money and surveying the area, Captain Matthews will use the scout team for any relevant intelligence he feels needs to be immediately relayed back. The rest of us will remain here and prepare to continue building defense and be prepared to support either effort. I need the new lines of communication we set up strictly adhered to." They had established a form of communication that used bow and arrows and mirrors, which gave quick updates on the danger level. He reiterated the point of keeping to the reporting timelines and always trying to use discretion.

Lieutenant Colonel Vetter ended the meeting because there was a lot of planning they needed to do if they planned to leave tomorrow. Not many people would sleep tonight. He was walking back to his tent, head down, when he had a moment of panic, heart beating faster. He just realized this would be the first time his men would perform a mission on their own and without his direct guidance. Once they started their mission and identified the enemy, the decisions from that point on would be entirely theirs. Would they make the right decisions? He smiled; they were free, and they were trained. Whatever decision they made, they would make as free men.

THIRTY-EIGHT

Captain Matthews

CAPTAIN MATTHEWS COULDN'T sleep the night before the departure. He was prepared to go in less than an hour. He had to admit that he had been prepared to go for a long time. His current assignment wasn't what he had envisioned for his military career; he definitely wouldn't have predicted his current predicament or curse as he thought about being assigned to lead Negro troops. He had envisioned a career of leading white soldiers and having his name associated with the greats in military history. Now his career would forever be tarnished with his record of leading Negroes. He had spent two years as an enlisted soldier during the Civil War and had been battlefield promoted during the end of the war because he simply picked up the fallen American flag and refused to let it drop during a short and intense battle. A lot of men said he had inspired them during the battle by refusing to drop the flag amid all the carnage. His officers had thought it was a good idea to promote him since the men thought he was some sort of good-luck charm. His fame and stardom among the men had been both a blessing and a bane. If fact, it was the jealousy of the other lieutenants that had gotten him sent to lead Negro soldiers. The other lieutenants had felt that his fame was ill gotten because he hadn't displayed any true leadership skills. Senior commanders thought it was a disrespect to them to accept him among their leadership and that he didn't have the school training in problem solving and tactics to properly lead soldiers.

His fame quickly receded after the war, and he was assigned to Port Hudson. He had been given charge of the kitchen and cleaning staff, who maintained the military buildings. Initially, he was excited at the prospect of leading in any capacity, but he soon learned that the assignment wasn't a sign of confidence in his abilities but the complete opposite. Other officers ridiculed him, and the few peers he had on Port Hudson labeled him the "mess bitch." When he found out Lieutenant Colonel Vetter was looking for men to go out into the western wilderness, he viewed that as an opportunity to get out of his current situation and hopefully get some real soldiering. He had to admit that he had taken a liking to the little bit of immediate respect he received from subordinates. Even if the other officers didn't now see his value, the subordinates had to respect his rank, and that in itself was a win for him.

Coming to a unit of colored soldiers, he figured he would stand out with his combat experience and his battlefield promotion status. He understood he was part of a small, unique population of men throughout history who had been promoted during wartime. The distinction was something a lot of enlisted men admired and respected about him. It gave them something to strive for and made them believe that being an officer was more about qualities than about upbringing. Even at Port Hudson the enlisted men often stopped him and made sure they believed he was one of them, who had made it. They would try to get him to stop for a drink and give them insight on being an officer.

All that had changed upon coming to Lieutenant Colonel Vetter's unit. Any expectation of instant respect in this unit was hard won. Yes, the soldiers acknowledged that he was an officer, but that was where it ended. These were hard men used to doing what needed to be done without supervision and with minimal guidance. Everyone in the organization, including the families who followed them, had trained on some sort of weapon and had responsibilities in the camp; nobody was ever idle. Captain Matthews had to remind himself that these Negroes were probably the only government-employed Negroes in the entire country and that damn near all of them had been touched by slavery. Even First Lieutenant Phoenix, which Captain Matthews had a little respect for, had been born out of slavery but was captured and put into slavery.

Lieutenant Colonel Vetter made no secret that the Negroes' comments and suggestions held a lot of weight with him and most of the time over the suggestions of his white leaders. Initially and even now, this fact upset Captain Matthews every time he thought about it. How the hell could he ever put a colored person's opinion before a white man's? He had to grudgingly admit that his white counterparts often gave suggestions aimed more at incurring favor with Lieutenant Colonel Vetter. Hell, that had been the way it was at his last unit because competition among officers was so high. Here it was no nonsense, and he proved himself by his ability to perform. The Negro NCOs had free reign in the organization and were highly respected by the men, not by the tyrannical leadership he had so often seen. He had to admit it was a good place to be a soldier but not a good place to move up in the ranks in hopes of making a name for himself in the military.

Once Captain Matthews had found out that Lieutenant Colonel Vetter's family was from the South, he realized there was nothing he could do to help advance his young career. Lieutenant Colonel Vetter was basically in the same predicament; they were both in a system that didn't trust them because of their history. The fact that Lieutenant Colonel Vetter was probably one of the best officers Captain Matthews had ever worked with didn't mean anything because he was from the South. His career, if he called it that, would always be overshadowed by his interaction and command of the Negro. Commanding or leading Negroes in any capacity was something every commander in the army looked on with complete disdain. He had seen them fight and knew that tenacity in which they fought. Their fight had been for the survival of the black race and the opportunity to exact legal revenge on the tyrannical rulers who had tried to erase them from any account of history.

When he had heard the padre explain their plight, it became very clear that there could be an opportunity, and it could involve a lot of silver. Maybe there was a way to get some notice out in the desert. He viewed this as another opportunity to get out of his current situation and hopefully better his situation this time. He had found out at the meeting that the Chinese man Jiang was going to accompany him. This was great, even with his little bit of management of the servants at Port Hudson. Captain Matthews knew he didn't know anything about real business. Lieutenant Colonel Vetter trusted Jian's business skills, which worked out well for Captain Matthews; any failures would be Jiang's, and any successes would be his. He smiled inside; he had wished for more soldiering earlier and had gotten more than he expected—and in a totally different direction. He would be very careful about what he wished for this time. He had to get some sleep. Tomorrow started a brand-new day for him.

THIRTY-NINE

Departures

IT WAS STILL dark when Lieutenant Colonel Vetter was awakened. He was informed that it was about two hours before sunrise. However, the early morning in Texas was bright enough to move around. He was still fascinated by the beauty and danger of the desert. Nothing was wasted, and everything had a purpose. He either learned the rhythm of nature or died trying to bend it to his will. Water was life, and having it just wasn't enough; you had to manage it. Use it in excess, and any gains you thought you had would blow away in the dust.

The previous owners of Fort Quitman had tried to make the new home like the old home, using growing and building concepts of the East and South. Any attempt at growing crops and building a settlement was now under the dirt, evidence of their short-term fix to a long-term problem. He had realized that any success at survival would need to be centered on how the natives currently lived and the control of the water. He quickly pushed these thoughts to the back of his mind as he grabbed his hat and stepped out of his tent into the semidarkness to see his men away, some for the last time.

There were three groups in total leaving, but Lieutenant Colonel Vetter held Sergeant First Class Hall and his detail of scouts back and out of view of the padres' team. Their mission to follow the padres and do reconnaissance on Cajoncito was known only by his leadership. He didn't want the padres' party to know they were being watched. He needed to find out whether they were honest and trustworthy men. He had too often seen the greed and corruption of church officials and the abuse of their so-called God-given powers.

He went directly to the team led by Captain Matthews, who was already having a conversation with some of the mining men with the visiting padres. He noted that Jian had already introduced himself to the padres and was currently talking to Padre Garcia. He found Padre Garcia speaking to one of the farmers; Vetter remembered the farmer being introduced as Señor Harold Montoya. Señor Montoya noticed Lieutenant Colonel Vetter first and pointed him out to the padre. The padre seemed relieved and a little nervous to see Lieutenant Colonel Vetter.

Lieutenant Colonel Vetter gave his "good morning' and immediately told the padre about his change in mind about having an individual from Cajoncito go along with the rescue party to provide a familiar face to the hostages upon release. The padre didn't seem prepared for this news and immediately looked at the closest man to him, who was Señor Montoya. Señor Montoya informed the padre of the upcoming harvest, which he was responsible for. The padre seemed to think about this for a second and nodded in agreement, thanking Señor Montoya for reminding him of such an important upcoming event.

The padre then called all his men over to explain Lieutenant Colonel Tobias's request, which he told his men made a lot of sense. There was a silent pause, in which the slight early- morning breeze could be heard; then it seemed like the other sounds of the camp breaking down and other parts getting ready to move out broke into that brief pause. Señor Perez spoke up and told the padre that his young daughter was with those captured, and even though he was scared to go, he wanted to volunteer. The padre seemed pleased and put the whole thing behind him. Lieutenant Colonel Vetter thanked the padre for supporting his request and told him he hoped the rescue mission would turn out okay and that his men would do their best. The padre said he felt extremely better about the whole situation and didn't feel so hopeless anymore. Any support the town could provide to support the effort would be provided and would be considered the beginning of a prosperous relationship.

The padre and his men mounted their horses along with Captain Matthews and the few men going with him. Captain Matthews turned toward Lieutenant Colonel Vetter, saluted, and quickly turned his horse around. All conversation had been done the night before. Jian also mounted and smiled toward Lieutenant Colonel Vetter as he started to depart. He gave an imitation of a salute and nodded. Lieutenant Colonel Vetter smiled at the salute and felt a little better about the nod. It was a nod, and he would do his best to make sure Captain Matthews and the situation in Cajoncito went well. Lieutenant Colonel Vetter watched as the small group rode away, west toward the Mexican border.

Sergeant First Class Hall also watched the group depart. He would be following them about one to two hours behind. His small team consisted of just four men. Pit and his small team of trackers were probably the best in the army at tracking. The two other men with Pit had been recently trained as snipers. First Sergeant Amra believed the value of snipers in the wide-open terrain was critical, so he had introduced sniper training.

Now every soldier in the unit had gone through sniper training, which focused mostly on how to use cover and concealment as well as the techniques of shooting to his advantage. Even some of the women were required to learn how to shoot the weapons. They initially started out with two Sharp sniper rifles and modified a few of the other rifles for sniping capability. Not everyone who tried long-range shooting was good at it. Most of the people in the unit couldn't see past fifty yards. It was a common joke in the unit that if the enemy stayed more than one hundred yards away, he or she could throw rocks, and half of the unit wouldn't see them.

He drew his thoughts to the present and mounted his horse. Now there were ten men and three women who knew how to shoot the sniper rifles, and more were learning. He smiled. Now the enemy would have to stand a little farther back. He looked at the three other men with him and nodded. Pit led the way.

First Lieutenant Phoenix and First Sergeant Amra would leave within the hour after the padres' party left. Phoenix briefly talked to Sergeant First Class Hall to make sure he was ready to go. First Sergeant Amra was busy checking the men who were going. During the planning session, the padres pointed out the general location of the hostages. By map reconnaissance, the trip shouldn't take more than four to seven days of careful travel. It would be a much quicker trip, but secrecy was important. Phoenix noted that First Sergeant Amra had his khopesh strapped to his horse's side. Jian had shown him some martial arts sword techniques, and the already-dangerous weapon was now lethal in his hands.

First Lieutenant Phoenix had a little apprehension about the upcoming mission; this was the first time he had led an excursion on his own. It wasn't lost on him that this was an all-black-led mission. Yes, there were a few white soldiers among the ranks, but he and First Sergeant Amra, the Negroes, would make all the decisions. He was happy to hear that Señor Perez was coming along on the trip. He felt there was a story that needed to be told, and he was the one who needed to hear it. He had been up since dark and walked with First Sergeant Amra with the men to check on them.

This was the first time they would perform a task in support of their mission to protect the people of the area. If these men were taking hostages out of Mexico, there was no telling what else they could be doing. The padre made sure to mention that the men were rebels. There wasn't a black man in the unit who wouldn't love the opportunity to get some revenge for the wrongs of slavery. First Sergeant Amra was the one to note that the men seemed a little bit too high spirited, and this had him concerned. He told First Lieutenant Phoenix that he needed to remind the men that they were soldiers first and that everything they did would be a judgment against all Negroes.

First Lieutenant Phoenix felt relieved when First Sergeant Amra told him his concerns. The last thing he needed was a revenge mission to paint Negroes as men and women who lived only for revenge, and if given positions of leadership, they would kill whites. But then the rebellious and revengeful side of him had another thought. Why should he give a damn about the way white people felt about Negroes? Any retribution they got was well deserved and more than justified. As quickly as he thought, the thought came; it was immediately drowned out by the knowledge and fact that innocents would die for his brashness—some as reciprocal repercussions and others through inspiration to fight back against the former oppressors. Either way, the educated man in him knew that until they could all stand together in a cause, none would be safe. He mounted his horse and moved toward the front of the line of men, where First Sergeant Amra and Señor Perez waited.

First Sergeant Amra was anxious to be off but knew he had to ensure that his men were ready. This was the part of leadership he didn't relish; he would rather be out front, leading the men instead of checking their equipment. He didn't understand why grown men needed someone to tell them something that could keep them safe. He had finally attributed it to fear of the unknown. But time and time again, he had seen men fall apart, even when there was no imminent threat. After much thought, he thought he had finally figured it out.

FORTY

Amra's Insight

WHEN AMRA WAS a boy in Africa, his father taught him the importance of hunting the animals that wouldn't hurt the overall health of the herd. He taught him to watch the herd, seek out the older bulls or animals, any animals that seemed injured or hurt, and try to avoid hunting the bull leader of the herd or the healthy females. He told Amra, "We need to mimic nature and how the animals hunt. In nature the strong survive, and the weak and frail, unprepared, and older die. It's not good or bad; it just is to maintain balance. As hunters we need to keep the same mentality, because in times of drought, fire, or extreme hardship, only the strong and healthy will survive in the herd. As long as we keep in harmony with nature, we better our chances of ensuring we also have food in times of hardship."

This was the rule all tribes were supposed to follow. However, because of man's ability to rationalize and think, his greed, laziness, and overall concern for himself allowed him only to hunt anything at any time and lay traps that were indiscriminate of how healthy an animal was. In times of hardships, the same tribes would have to resort to thievery and raids to stay alive, because they had lost their ability to effectively hunt, and all local animals had departed. This caused an imbalance in the harmony of the tribes.

Amra always kept this philosophy that everything was interconnected and that maintaining balance was the key to survival. However, since being a slave, he had seen so many things about man and the bigger world that made him understand that man was the biggest threat to the balance. He didn't say that because of the evil acts of slavery or anything remotely associated with the deeds that men do. No, what he had learned was that man's ability to rationalize was the biggest threat to nature and balance. In nature the old and infirm would eventually either be eaten or die trying to survive; in the world of man, old people lived longer and held positions of power longer. In nature the positions of power are given to the physically powerful. Man attains power through mental discipline. Call it cruel or unjust, but in nature the mentally unstable and physically deformed don't live past the first year of inception. In the world of man, the mentally unstable and physically deformed live to longer ages, but they often procreate, something nature doesn't allow under normal circumstances. Hence the phrase that only the strong survive.

However in the world of man, the strong were defined by money and power, and the weak were simply those who didn't have access to money and power. Amra believed that over time this continued allowance in the human world to allow the weaker, as defined by nature, had tainted and weakened the spirit of man in such a way that his God-given ability to think was now clouded by all the bad and cruel things weak men could think of, with no concern for the pack or tribe, simply for self-absorption. The abuses he had witnessed while in slavery were a direct result of the unnatural allowances gone unchecked and the taint on man's soul.

As a child Amra grew up in a society that understood the value of the elderly and was somewhat compassionate to the disabled and infirm. He witnessed how man's immense rationality and ability were used to live in harmony with nature, take care of the sick and elderly, and be completely and totally brutal and violent when the need called for it. He also knew it had taken centuries for his people to arrive at such a place, but they had arrived nevertheless. They had done it by finally understanding to embrace and seek the good values in a man—honor, integrity, family, discipline—and to stay forever vigilant against the bad in all men, even themselves. They even took it one step further by establishing their courts and laws based on these same tenets. Yes, their justice was sometimes violent and without compassion, but to save the society, some bloody sacrifices had to be made, especially by those willing to break the law.

His leadership role with his men portrayed his beliefs in the values he believed the newly freed slaves needed to see. If they were going to be a contribution and part of this country, the best thing he could bring to the table were men and women who judged based on character, not on money. To right the current wrongs in this country, he would have to lead the way in developing the standard of expectation in all men. Since he had started learning how to read in First Lieutenant Phoenix's reading classes, he had taken it upon himself to read a copy of the Constitution First Lieutenant Phoenix had acquired. The men who had founded America said all men were created equal, which was true. However, Amra also understood another truth—that all men weren't born equal. There was no way to provide immediate equality among the poor and rich. The only way to establish equality in the poor or in the rich was to establish a standard of expectation that had naught to do with being rich or poor. A good man was neither rich nor poor; he was just a good man. He knew he would need to develop good men if they wanted to survive, and First Sergeant Amra would do his part to develop good men.

He rode to catch up with First Lieutenant Phoenix and Señor Perez.

First Lieutenant Phoenix was ready to get along with the mission. First Sergeant Amra was almost done checking on the soldiers. Phoenix walked around and nodded to a few soldiers; he wanted to see how the men's spirits were this morning. He had learned the best way to find out how men were feeling was to listen to what they were talking about. This was hard, because most soldiers cleaned up whatever conversation they were having when an officer walked around, so the key was to be seen only when you wanted to be seen. Yes, it sounded sneaky, but Phoenix thought it was necessary. The few conversations he heard were about freeing the hostages, and one soldier even mentioned they now had the opportunity to free some captured souls. Phoenix thought this sounded good for the most part, but he could see how "freeing captured souls" could escalate into some sort of revenge mission. He had to admit the idea of getting retribution on people who still devalued life, even after slavery was banned, was high on his list of things he wanted to do. But he also knew that even though they were in a remote part of the country, any word of Negroes doing anything bad against whites would be publicized all over the United States. The eyes of every white in the United States were looking at every Negro to see whether they deserved the hard-fought freedom that had pitted brother against brother and had nearly destroyed the country. He made a mental note to talk to First Sergeant Amra about his concerns.

Señor Perez was standing by his horse, looking all alone, when Phoenix walked up to him. Phoenix had assigned a soldier to him to ensure he knew what to do, but the soldier didn't see the need to befriend Señor Perez. That was okay; Phoenix hoped Señor Perez was in need of some conversation. Phoenix could use the four- to seven-day ride to get him to talk and tell him more about the hostages and the city of Cajoncito.

Phoenix greeted Señor Perez with a "good morning" and a smile. He told Señor Perez he would be honored if he would ride with him. Señor Perez was more affable toward First Lieutenant Phoenix after their brief conversation yesterday and seemed relieved to see First Lieutenant Phoenix. Phoenix found that he genuinely liked the man, so that meant he had to be even more careful when talking to him. They walked their horses to where First Sergeant Amra had the soldiers in a tight semicircle. Lieutenant Colonel Vetter wanted to address the soldiers before they departed. They had a man hold their horses and went and stood behind Lieutenant Colonel Vetter as he began his speech.

"I cannot tell you enough that even though you are servants for the US government, the people you are serving do not see you as such. They will hate seeing you and still see you as nothing more than dressed-up slaves. You are still defining what a free you looks like, and for a lot of you, falling back into slave status will seem normal."

The men mumbled a little at that; none of them wanted to be known as possible traitors.

"I tell you this because that is the reality that you will have to face, and I want to be honest with you at every opportunity." A few men nodded.

"For most of you, I have been your commander since both during and after the war. I have seen you grow and struggle. I hope you don't get offended, but I feel like a parent watching his children grow. I have seen you fight for a cause in which you didn't know whether the outcome would see you a free man or a slave again. But you fought with the hope of freedom in your hearts and the determination, savagery, and nobility seldom seen in armies of the world. My pride in you is unimaginable.

"Now I see you fighting to define your future, with the challenges of a country still divided dogging your every breath. I know that every single one of you is now the ambassador for the whole Negro race. Good or bad, you will be judged insufficient. If you want to survive, you will have to make your own way. This is a hard and ugly truth but the truth just the same. I ask you to be careful and use all the tools at your disposal to come back safe.

"I have total faith in First Lieutenant Phoenix. He has been with me since the inception of the unit and has earned my respect multiples times. All of you know First Sergeant Amra and his abilities; his skills as a soldier are unparalleled. Listen and learn.

"For the new men in the unit, as you know, we are not a typical army unit. Our mission during the war required the unit to fight a different way. The tactics and training we have put you through since you have been here have been designed to fight the way we have found to be the most successful. If you want to live, listen and learn. Also, understand that any disobedience against my leadership is disobedience against me. Does everyone understand?"

A solid but quiet "Yes, sir" echoed through the group.

Speech done, Lieutenant Colonel Vetter saluted the men, who in turn saluted back. He then turned to First Lieutenant Phoenix, saluted him, and said, "Remember, when in charge, be in charge."

First Lieutenant Phoenix saluted back and simply replied, "Thank you." Lieutenant Colonel Vetter turned and walked away.

First Lieutenant Phoenix mounted his horse, and everyone else followed. The sun was just starting to peak its orange and red glow in the distance. He looked around briefly at the mountain home they had started to develop and briefly wondered whether he would see the place again. He smiled; these were probably the same thoughts of soldiers in all the stories he had read. Now he was one of them; he would have never imagined that. He never would have imagined slavery either. As he raised his fist in the air to start the movement, a cold chill briefly took him. Fist in the air, he pointed forward, and his horse and the entire formation started to move. Silently, two by two, the rescue party was on its way.

FORTY-ONE

Pit

PIYAHMA ATULA, OR Pit as everyone in the unit called him, was following a small party for three days after they had left the town of Cajoncito. Sergeant First Class Hall wanted all activity out of the monastery to be monitored; the four of them would be separated for any groups larger than eight. He said eight seemed like a good number. The party he was following consisted of fifteen men with two on a hooded wagon. They didn't seem to be in a rush and didn't think anyone was following, as evident by the lack of urgency and security. He followed at a comfortable distance, out of sight and out of the smell of the animals.

While he followed, he had time for some reflection. He couldn't believe he was on the Mexican side of the border. His travels as a soldier had taken him many places, but Mexico was never a place where he thought he would be. He had been in the unit during the war and had stayed with it because it was a good place for him until he could find something better. He had briefly left the unit after the war to find his mother, but when he arrived at his childhood home, the whole place had been burned down. He had searched for a week for possible clues to where they might be, but the war had changed the whole landscape of the area to included new inhabitants. He went back to the unit to bide his time until he could find something better, but deep down he knew he came back because the unit had started to feel like family. He had missed it as soon as he left it.

He was half Sioux and half Comanche. On his mother's wedding night, Comanches had grabbed her during a raid, but her new husband and his small band of Sioux warriors had rescued her after a two-week hunt. During that two-week time of capture, the Comanche leader raped his mother. Eventually, the newlywed husband's war band caught up to the Comanches and rescued his wife by killing all the Comanche in a sneak attack. She found out afterward that she was pregnant, but by then she had already consummated her relationship with her new husband. He was the only one who knew about his interesting parentage, besides his mother. She had kept the secret of the rape and told her son only when he turned ten years old due to his affinity for horses and the fact that he looked just like the Comanche leader.

Piyahma had become one of the best horsemen of the tribe at a very young age. By the time he was thirteen, he could accurately shoot his bow and rifle while mounted. At the onset of the Civil War, the Union army was actively recruiting Native Americans as sharpshooters. Their exceptional skills at hunting and moving silently through the underbrush made them perfect for this type of warfare, and it kept them away from some of the more prejudiced soldiers. Before joining the unit, Pit had over seventy confirmed kills as a sharpshooter.

After joining the unit, Pit was primarily used for his hunting and tracking skills. Back then, the unit's mission was causing disruptions among the enemy ranks in hopes of hastening the rebel need to quit the war. The unit primarily operated behind enemy lines, and Lieutenant Colonel Vetter felt their success depended on remaining hidden, not in seeking out some sort of confrontation. Firing weapons during this time wasn't considered the best way to do this unless forced to do so. Lieutenant Colonel Vetter had always wanted the attacks to seem like they were retribution from the slaves, some otherworldly force attacking the rebels indiscriminately. Pit had respected the commander's discipline in keeping to his plan, which ultimately made unit casualties almost nonexistent. How could the enemy fight back at what they couldn't see or hear? He had only three confirmed kills since he had been at the unit. Pit had never worked with Negro soldiers before when he first joined the army; they were all white units, and they made sure to keep the Indian scouts away from the regular army soldiers. They didn't even want to give Indian soldiers uniforms, which the Indians didn't mind at all. The Indians thought it was very funny how the white man fought the war; they lined up on a field and walked toward each other, shooting. The Indians refused to fight this way; the white men called it honorable to stand and get killed; the Indians thought it was stupid. There was no skill in the shot, no hunting of the prey, and no game of wills.

Since joining this unit, he felt that they fought more like Indians. The focus was on being hidden, silent, and deadly. They planned the attack, focused on each man doing his part and returning safely—and most importantly, being silent. Each man had a sidearm, and most had a rifle, but each man was also required to be proficient in a silent weapon. There were long knives, axes, spears, swords, crossbows, bows, and some big swords First Sergeant Amra carried. A sense of personal pride in weapons ability permeated the unit and resulted in constant mock combat training and practice in weapons abilities. Pit often heard the former slaves say that training with different weapons increased their chances of never being slaves again. Even after the war was over and freedom was declared for the Negroes, they still felt the need to be able to fight. Pit understood; he had seen both Indians and Negroes in slavery, and it was something he would never want to be in or put somebody in. Pit smiled inwardly; he didn't know where his journey was going, but he felt he was in the right place. He put his thoughts aside and focused on the huge mountain monastery in front of him.

They had been in the area for two days and had started quietly looking around the area without being seen. The initial entrance to the town was breathtaking. The town itself was mostly composed of buildings partially built in the mountain on the road leading up the mountain to an old Spanish monastery built into the side of a mountain. The entrance to the monastery started at a jagged edge in the mountain, where two huge ornate wooden gates stood. They were about twelve feet tall and looked to have ramparts on the top. They had scouted out men appearing in some sort of uniform at the top of the gates. After the gates, there was a slender walkway, funneled by the mountain walls, which led to another smaller but still ornate door.

The monastery had been etched into a natural cavern. There were two levels above the main door as indicated by the large windows and ornate walkways above the door. The windows and walkways were ornate, but they also controlled all traffic into the monastery, a kill zone. Guards were also posted on the walkways and were changed daily. Captain Matthews and his team were viewed while giving a tour of the place after a couple of hours upon entry.

It wasn't until two days later that Captain Matthews and the team, Padre Garcia, the miners and farmers, and six additional armed men left the monastery and headed south. The armed men wore the same livery as the gate guards. Pit and one other scout followed Captain Matthews's team entourage. The reasoning was that they were returning the miners and farmers to their mines and farms. There was minimal space in the current area to support such functions. Sergeant First Class Hall and the remaining scout stayed behind to see whether any ransom payments were collected, which was another part of their mission. As the party headed south, Pit paralleled the party to the east along a mountain range. The party was following the easier traveled terrain at the mountain's base.

On the second day of travel, Pit and his scout were surprised to find the tracks of men and women in the mountain range. They were on the Mexico side of the border and didn't have any reconnaissance on this side, so they didn't know what to expect. Pit and his man immediately and carefully maneuvered around the area; there were no other Indians. They came upon two older Indians, crouched behind some small boulders and watching the party move below. They would be invisible to the men passing below. There were no other Indians in the immediate area, so Pit figured this wasn't an ambush, simply Indians watching or hiding. He passed the capture hand signals to his counterpart but needed to wait until the caravan moved farther down the road.

Once Pit felt the caravan was far enough down the road, he gave the attack signal, and they both pounced on a man separately. The old men didn't have a clue what was happening and immediately went still upon capture. If Pit and his man were going to do violence, the men would have quietly given their lives. Pit immediately understood that they had entered close to the men's home and family. To be captured this close to the home was a disgrace to any Indian, regardless of the tribe. Pit and his man simply tied the men up and sat them down against some rocks. Pit needed information and didn't relish the fact of killing any Indian. He tried to talk to them in his native language, then Sioux, then a little Comanche. One of the men understood the Comanche and replied to Pit. The man seemed happy to be talking to Pit.

Pit found out that the men were from the Rarámuri tribe, the original inhabitants of the area. The man, whose name was

Tepor, said his tribe had retreated to the high sierras and canyons after constant war with the Spanish colonizers. Tepor told Pit that he had thought Pit and his man were slave traffickers, who had depleted his tribe to just old men and women too frail to work. All the younger men or women of the tribe had been captured and enslaved to work in either the mines or the farms. Pit asked Tepor whether he knew anything about the recent kidnappings in Cajoncito. Tepor explained that heavily armed men had herded all the women and children off about two weeks ago. Tepor and his partner, Arnulfo, had followed as far as the American border but didn't cross. Arnulfo said something to Tepor in their own dialect, and Tepor told Pit that the men were soldiers from the gray side. Pit knew he meant rebel or Confederate soldiers. Pit had his companion release the old man and his friend. They seemed relieved and invited Pit and his friend back to their village; they hadn't seen any other Indians in a while and wanted to know more about Pit and his companion.

There were only ten to fifteen Rarámuri in the camp, all senior in age or infirm. Tepor told Pit that the tribe had had over three hundred people before the slavers came. His tribe had thought they were safe in the mountains, and it had been a long time since they had any contact with the outside world. They had established homes in the natural caves and cliff overhangs. They had even established a small farming community up in the mountains, hidden from view from anyone not knowing what to look for.

Pit asked Tepor how his tribe had been found in such a remote spot. Tepor explained that a hunting party had been captured and tortured to provide the location of the camp. Ever since, they had been coming back in regular raids to take people from the camp until the only ones who remained were the few elders. Pit explained that they were sending men to go release the captives back to the padres from the church. Tepor or the remaining clan members didn't know who the padres were but felt they would be releasing the tribe members back to the men who had originally captured them.

Tepor and the remaining tribesmen offered Pit and his man, Chatan, a former Sioux Indian, their ceremonial drink, tesgüino. After two sips of the drink, Pit had to decline for himself and Chatan. The men didn't seem to take any offense to the refusal. Tepor told Pit, "God taught the Rarámuri how to make corn beer, so the Rarámuri make offerings of tesgüino to God himself, and he drinks it also." The drink was a homemade corn beer; the corn kernels were soaked, ground up, boiled, and spiked with a local grass to help the mixture ferment. Tepor said they had mixed theirs with the local agave plant, and it was a sacred mixture. Tepor took a deep drink of the liquor out of the earthenware jar and spit into the campfire. *Whoof!* The large blue blaze was immense and made both Pit and Chatan, who were closer to the campfire, jump back. The heat was intense. The other tribesmen seemed unfazed by the miniature explosion. Now Pit understood why they drank well away from the blaze of the campfire. As Pit's eyes refocused, the normal orange blaze of the campfire came back into view. What were they drinking? The old men seemed very comfortable sitting around and drinking it.

He didn't like the alcoholic drinks; he had witnessed firsthand how they had been used to destroy Indians. He knew the decline of the Indian nation and way of life, coupled with the flooded accessibility of alcohol, was a major contributor to the complete destruction of the Indian way of life. He pulled his mind back to the present; given the chance, he would do better for his people. In some small way, if he could help the other tribesmen to return, it would be a good start. He looked around the campfire; Tepor and his small group were smiling and laughing, oblivious to the dramas of the world.

They drank well into the night and told Pit and Chatan of

the Rarámuri history. They had once been proud people who expelled the Jesuit priest from their land. They had eluded the Mexican government all these years in the mountains. They were glad to once again have a reason to celebrate. Pit smiled inside; he didn't think anything would keep these men from drinking their ceremonial drink, and any reason would be considered a reason to celebrate.

Their drinking left Pit to his thoughts for the future. These were good people, but like most Indians tribes, they were dying out little by little. If there was a future for the tribe, then the hope was that there were still tribesmen alive among the hostages. They had lived an isolated life in the mountains and didn't have the defenses to keep their people safe. From this vantage point in the mountains, the tribe could control the entire valley below and beyond. The mountains had provided everything for them, including freshwater wells within the caves. Like most Indian tribes, they didn't care about the world outside them as long as their stomachs were full. He couldn't blame them; finding food was hard enough in the wild. But the mentality had left them vulnerable to the world and its evils. They needed help, and Pit would recommend they come back to meet Lieutenant Colonel Vetter in the morning. Even though they were on the Mexican side of the border, they still needed help. He also wanted them to show the liquor that explodes.

In the morning Pit asked Tepor to go back to the fort, speak to Lieutenant Colonel Vetter, and explain the situation, particularly about the enslavement of his people. Pit also told Tepor that the hostages would go back to the fort before being released, and it would be good for Indian hostages to see familiar faces. The remaining Rarámuri were so excited about possibly seeing other tribesmen that they all agreed to go back. Pit didn't say it, but he believed the padres ran the mines and farms; they were the ones enslaving the Rarámuri.

FORTY-TWO

Cajoncito

THE TRIP TO rescue the hostages was uneventful during the first three days. During that time, First Lieutenant Phoenix had the opportunity to develop a friendship with Señor Perez. Señor Perez was always smiling, even when though he was under obvious stress. His family had been in the town of Cajoncito since control of the town had been transferred from the government of Spain to the Franciscan missionaries before the Mexican independence. He explained that they had converted a majority of the local Indians but had faced fierce resistance from a small minority. Over time the area was settled, and the Indians were pacified. Cajoncito was established as a remote getaway for Spanish aristocrats. The mountains in the area were filled with caverns and hot springs, an ideal getaway for the rich. The original Spaniards had also brought artisans and stone builders to reshape the area into a secretive system of swimming pools, elaborate rooms etched into the mountain with hot spring baths inside. The Spanish also found freshwater springs and silver mines south of Cajoncito. They fought a long battle with the local Indians in the area, the Rarámuri, and eventually enslaved the Indians to work the farms and the mines.

The actual town of Cajoncito was behind the current Franciscan church and used to house over one thousand people, descendants of Spaniards and native Indians, who had been made to maintain and serve the rich Spaniards. Shortly before the war between Mexico and Spain for Mexico's Independence, the Spanish government turned the area over to the Franciscan church and had the elaborate church built in Cajoncito. The church was a reminder to the locals in the area that Spain was still quietly in control of the area. When the Mexican government took over, the priests were very reassuring to the Mexican government and were considered a minimal threat. Coupled with the remoteness and being considered pretty much worthless, the area over time became an invisible point to the Mexican government. The Franciscan church still maintained its contacts with Spain, and Cajoncito became a hiding spot from time to time for rich Spanish families still residing in Mexico and wishing to hide or passing through on their way back to Spain.

Señor Perez claimed that before the hostages had been taken from town, townspeople had started to disappear on a trip to and from the farming pastures. Most of the townspeople blamed the disappearance on the raiding bands of Comanches in the area. Señor Perez claimed that he had repeatedly gone to the padres to ask the Mexican government to intercede and deal with the Comanches. Each time, the padres said the Indians were only passing through and wouldn't be coming back. Only after they took the women as hostages did the padres get interested in the whole situation. When the padres found out that the women had been taken to the US side of the border, which was when they had decided to go to the old fort and ask for help.

He went on to explain that his daughter and other children had been brought to the monastery to serve two Spanish families passing through. Señor Perez claimed he didn't know who the families were, only that they had to be of some import. Soon after their arrival, a request was posted throughout the city for all young men and women in the town under the age of thirteen to come, serve, and provide entertainment for the visitors. He claimed it was normal for young ladies and men from the town to be hand servants to visiting Spanish nobility. It was considered a great honor to the people of Cajoncito. They had been doing it for so long that it had become almost ritual in the town. His daughter, Abiana, was only nine years old and the only child between Señor Perez and his wife of fifteen years. With tears in his eyes, he related the last day he had seen his child; she was so happy to go to the monastery. She wore a bright orange and white dress her grandmother had made for her. It was beautiful, and she was so happy to wear it. She twirled and twirled all morning, and she was smiling when they left her at the monastery. That was the last he had seen of his daughter.

They didn't hear about the kidnappings until hours after they had gone. The monastery bells were ringing, and that meant there was something important or dangerous in the area the people needed to hear. They had been rung only one other time during a flash flood. The villagers had hurried to the monastery, only to find that most of the children had been taken, along with the people responsible for the daily monastery maintenance for the day. Almost one hundred in total were gone.

Two days later, one of the fifteen men who had gone after the kidnappers hurriedly returned, stating that the others had been captured and that the kidnappers were coming back. When his wife heard this, she started packing, planning on giving herself up to the kidnappers. She wanted to be captured so she could be with her daughter. In his panic for his wife's safety, Señor Perez clubbed her senseless and hid her so she wouldn't be taken. When his wife came to, the kidnappers had left with the remaining women and children. His wife hadn't spoken to him since the incident some two weeks ago and was now contemplating suicide. He believed that if he could bring his daughter back, his wife would get better. He told his wife to be strong and that he would bring their baby back. He gave his wife a reason to live and now had to make it a reality.

First Lieutenant Phoenix listened to Señor Perez's story in stony silence; he was giving Señor Perez the respect to share his raw emotions on the loss of his family and the sense of betrayal by the padres. First Lieutenant Phoenix could see the mix of emotions playing on Señor Perez's face as he talked about the hope of being reunited with his daughter. He was under a lot of duress and was extremely agitated as he spoke. Phoenix realized Perez was depending on him to remedy the situation.

He quickly assessed that the town of Cajoncito had been created as a resource pool for the elite in Spanish aristocracy, and the people of the town were held in subservience to render services. When Spain gave control to the padres, the subservience had also been transferred to them. It was a form of slavery that left alone became a way of life for the townspeople. Only after their livelihood and way of life were threatened did they take the time to take a hard look at their lives.

First Lieutenant Phoenix could hear the slow realization from Señor Perez that his life, his family's lives, and the lives of the townspeople were solely dependent on the whims of the monastery. The townspeople didn't even have weapons to defend themselves, since they were so dependent on the church. Now all the roads of their current misfortune seemed to lead to the padres.

First Lieutenant Phoenix also noted that Señor Perez didn't mention the silver mines. First Lieutenant Phoenix asked Señor Perez about this, and he stated that he had never met the miners

before their departure to ask for assistance. He had been introduced to the miners on the day they set out. Prior to that, he had
never known there were mines in the area. Apparently, the mines
were farther south from the town of Cajoncito.

This was interesting news to First Lieutenant Phoenix; the
padres knew about the mines, but the townspeople didn't. Was
there a link between the missing townspeople and the mines?
Could there be some other sinister reason? It seems Cajoncito was
a lot more than it seemed. He made a mental note to put all his
thoughts together along with everything he had heard and send
a message back to Lieutenant Colonel Vetter. He needed to be
appraised of the situation.

This was a unique experience in First Lieutenant Phoenix's
life. Señor Perez was talking to him as an equal and seeking his
assistance. He viewed First Lieutenant Phoenix as a representative
of the United States and a person of authority. He had to stop and
take a moment to reflect on the strange yet comfortable feeling
he suddenly had. He couldn't explain it. He should be terrified by
the thought of accepting any responsibility. What training did he
have to direct people and give judgment over anyone? Did putting
on a uniform make him the judge and jury over men and women
who didn't wear the uniform? He had seen white men and women
who couldn't even read or make life-ending decisions about black
men, women, and children simply because they were white. Yes,
he could read, but did that give him the authority to say to the
ignorant what was right and wrong in their lives? Phoenix couldn't
help but be fascinated by his own journey from freeman to slave
and now to freeman again. He noted that each time he was
purportedly a freeman, he had never felt the freedom of his own
worth and power until now. This was the first time as a freeman
that his decision and choices would guide or decide someone else's
life. The molten, white-hot anger over the abuses he had received
during slavery was suddenly less painful due to the realization of

a future realized by his own choices and actions, a future where he would be whatever man he wanted to be. The forge would always burn hot, the brutality of his slavery never forgotten and etched into his soul, but he had an opportunity now to remake himself. He could take the energy of anger and revenge and turn them into weapons of life and hope, or burn in the intense flame they created and disappear.

He should be bitter and angry about his misfortune in life, but just simply breathing was proof that he was stronger than any evil thrown against him. His will to survive and be better than the monsters around him burned bright; he now had the opportunity to fix a wrong. He was his own man now, and his future was his to shape, good or ill. He didn't believe in religion; he had personally seen how men could bend words to subjugate others into submission. But he did believe he was a spiritual man, a man humble enough to give thanks for the simple opportunity to breathe each day.

FORTY-THREE

The Padre

PADRE MORALES COULDN'T believe his good luck in meeting the new army unit. He knew it was composed of mostly Negro soldiers and had been in the area for only a couple of months. He had never seen Negroes in positions of authority; he had always seen them as slaves. From what he had witnessed during the brief meeting, they seemed to be proficient soldiers. He noted that all the soldiers were armed to the teeth, with sidearms and other weapons. It took the padre a minute to recognize them, but each soldier had a variety of additional weapons at his side. The padre noted axes, swords, and crossbows along with sidearms. The men looked very comfortable with the weapons and looked like they knew how to use them. What were they so afraid of?

The padre was glad the white officer, Captain Matthews, had been sent back with him. The padre had taken a chance by mentioning the silver mine to Lieutenant Colonel Vetter to see what his reaction would be. Lieutenant Colonel Vetter had taken the knowledge with a stony face; however, Captain Matthews showed interest at the mention of silver. He had shown immediate interest. The padre hoped he could use this to his benefit. He was taking a very calculated risk by coming to the Americans for assistance. They were new to the area and were committed to the safety of people in the area. The less they knew about what was really going on at the monastery, the better.

The padre was one of the last men who knew all the secrets of the monastery. He was scheduled to head back to Spain in less than three months. Careful coordination for the past two years had enabled him to maneuver the movement of all the riches they had accumulated from the mines and from ransoms collected over the years. The Mexican government had agreed to escort him and the sarcophagi of five former priests. Their remains wouldn't be incurred on Mexican ground but be back in Spain with their families. The sarcophagi, normally constructed of stone, had been made from melted silver and painted in multiple layers to appear as stone. The craftsmanship was so real that the padre originally couldn't believe it was silver when he first viewed it. Padre Garcia was an artisan of exquisite skills, learned as a young monk. They had known each other since seminary, their feeling toward each other forbidden by the church and the world. Their friendship was scorned, and they had to learn to keep their secrets. It was no wonder when they both found out they would be assigned to a "wilderness" assignment. Mexico had lost a lot of its allure, and Spain was almost completely withdrawn. The only reason the place was kept and maintained was because its history and remoteness made it a safe place for the remaining Spaniards still in Mexico. Over time they had basically forgotten the place existed, and it became the old monastery.

They had found about the silver mines about five years ago. The mines were in a ruinous condition, choked with debris; the place flooded almost to the surface, and the remaining miners and their tools were dispersed. The padres formed an agreement with the miners there to provide more manpower and assistance to unload whatever riches were still there. Padre Garcia knew new mining techniques that would assist the miners. They had thought the mine was almost dry; however, with Padre Garcia's new mining techniques and the miners' renewed commitment to mining, they started to see an increased output from the mines. The miners informed the padres that with more manpower, they believed they could increase output levels never previously achieved. Initially, the padres along with the miners captured the local Indians in the area and subdued them into compliance by starving them off. After the Indian population started to dwindle, some well-placed kidnappings of healthy citizens from the town of Cajoncito helped augment the Indians, who were dying off from the harsh work in the mine. One of the miners had heard of slaves being sold in Texas. They had taken a small portion of money and headed a small expedition to America to purchase additional manpower for the mines.

In retrospect, he should never have agreed to deal with the rebel filth, who were selling the slaves. Their commitment to slavery after it had been made illegal in the States made them very dangerous men. The rebels must have seen the padres as an easy target. The fact that they were from the other side of the border made any crimes committed against them the Mexican government's problem, so they sent men to follow the padres. On their return trip to the mine with the slaves, the padres briefly stopped at the monastery, keeping the newly purchased slaves away from the town of Cajoncito. The trailing rebels, seeing the monastery for the first time, believed the monastery was the final destination for the padres, returned to their leadership, and informed them of the grand monastery in the mountains. The brief stop kept the rebels from finding out about their final destination, the silver mines. That in itself was a win for the padre, but now he needed to close the loop on their deceit and keep the knowledge of their complacency in giving up the townsmen as slaves a secret. He needed the destruction of the rebels. Only then could he and Padre Garcia safely complete their plan and escape the hell they had been in for the last eight years. They would leave Mexico and the church, and head back to Spain with enough money to make them rich and powerful men.

FORTY-FOUR

Underground Railroad

SERGEANT FIRST CLASS Hall received Pit and his small entourage at the hidden location they had established outside the town of Cajoncito. Pit introduced the Rarámuri tribesmen and gave Sergeant First Class Hall an update on why he had brought the tribesmen back. Sergeant First Class Hall agreed with Pit's entire assessment; Captain Vetter needed to be assessed of the findings. Even though they were on the Mexican side of the border, the town and Indians needed assistance. He also believed they were interconnected.

The trip back to the fort from their hidden position was less than a day of travel. But it would take some extra time; traffic around the monastery had increased. Captain Matthews and the small group that had gone south had just returned with a loaded wagon of unknown supplies. Whatever they had gone to the mines to get, they had succeeded. The next morning after their arrival, two men on horseback arrived at the monastery. They were too far away to get good descriptions of the travelers, but they stayed for only a few hours and were on their way, headed west. Each had two heavily loaded saddlebags.

Sergeant First Class Hall sent Chatan to follow the two men, whom he assumed were the ransom party based on the direction they were going. This close to the border, they could be only part of the group that had kidnapped the people of Cajoncito. He sent Pit and the Rarámuri tribesman back to the fort to update Lieutenant Colonel Vetter on everything he had learned. That left only him and one scout at the town of Cajoncito.

Sergeant First Class Hall thought they needed a better picture of the area near the mines. The Indians had explained that they had never seen where the silver from the Indian labor went. There was no traffic, other than the padres coming and going in small groups, similar to the group Pit had followed. They always came with a wagon and loaded only saddlebags. If it was silver in the bags, it was very little for the effort being accomplished and the number of people dying to work the mines. The tribesmen claimed they had observed there was another location further south of the mine, but he had never seen it. Pit said he had also observed men still at the mine; this made sense since the hostages had been taken from the town. Sergeant First Class Hall decided to leave the remaining scout to monitor the town of Cajoncito, and he would find out more about the silver mines and the numbers there. He had overheard Lieutenant Colonel Vetter tell First Lieutenant Phoenix that a solid reconnaissance of the territory could save lives by preventing surprises. It was one the smartest things he had ever heard, and he had taken it to heart.

The terrain west of the mountain range where Pit had found the Rarámuri tribesman was situated between the mountain range the Rarámuri tribesman called home and the Rio Grande River, the natural border between the United States and Mexico.

In the distance, just over the border, he could see more mountain ranges extend off into Texas. The terrain was very rocky, with the water-runoff trails from the mountains etched into their sides. They looked as if they hadn't seen water in a long time. At the lower levels of the mountains, there was sparse vegetation, but it was considered ample for this type of terrain, which was so different from the wooded south, which he had grown up in. If it wasn't for the mountains, they could see for miles and miles.

It was then that he noticed the buzzards in the distance. That could mean only one thing; something or somebody was dead or about to be dead. It was in the direction the Indians had given him about the other side of the mine. It was a few miles off; he would find a good spot for his horse and go investigate.

The smell of rotted, infected meat was the first sign that he was near something dying; the smell was very familiar to Sergeant First Class Edwards. It wasn't quite the same smell a dead body gave off, and the birds above knew it, which was why they still circled. It was the smell of infected, dying skin or gangrene.

Sergeant First Class Hall had seen it many times when he was a slave. The first time he had witnessed it was when a young slave girl was beaten for hiding from the master when he wanted to have sex. She had hidden for two days before they found her and beat her so bad that a broken bone in her left arm had punctured through the skin. The master had refused to get help for her, and the slaves were afraid to help, for fear of retribution from the master. The only thing she could do was try to fix it herself or hope to heal naturally. Days passed, and she continued to work. She became more and more fevered as the days went by, but she didn't want to stop working for fear of getting another beating. The young Fieldhand (Sergeant First Class Hall) remembered seeing her a week or so after she had been injured. She had wrapped the arm in a dirty rag, and she was obviously still in pain; she had a sheen of sweat on her face on a cool morning. She carried a bucket of water in one hand, something she would normally use two hands for. Every few steps, the weight of the bucket caused her to stop and recalibrate; the broken arm was useless. She tried to level it with her injured hand, and the immediate pain caused her to whimper, too afraid to scream her agony for fear of retribution.

That was the last time Sergeant First Class Hall had seen her alive before she decided to take her chances and run away to seek medical help from another town. She understood that her arm would never heal with the bone sticking out and that it needed to be reset. The master still refused anyone to get close to her, even though he was regularly calling her to him, broken arm or not. She didn't make it very far during her escape; she had been in the woods for about a week before she was found. He has been tasked to retrieve her body and bring it back to the plantation for a proper burial. At the burial, the master showed up, and Sergeant First Class Edwards heard him speak of his dismay and wonder that he had the slave who would rather run away than accept the gifts and love he tried to give her. Sergeant First Class Edwards never forgot the true sense of sadness he had witnessed on the master's face at the loss of his slave. He had caused her death but felt it was her fault because she didn't want to accept the slavery and abuse he had put her under. It didn't make sense then, and it still didn't make sense now.

Sergeant First Class Hall came upon the man from behind. The surprise at seeing another black man on the Mexican side of the border caught him completely off guard. What was a black man doing, apparently dying here in Mexico? The man's condition was dire. He had a huge gash along his left leg, which started about mid-thigh and ran down to the mangled bottom portion of his leg. The bottom portion of the leg looked as if it had been shredded; he could barely discern a foot. The smell of the gangrene coming from the wound made him want to gag. He was over the man now, and he could see a dirty-looking, foul-smelling discharge coming out of the sores or blisters that were bleeding out and around his leg. The man was in a fevered state and didn't even notice Hall had walked up to him. This man was going to die real soon; if there was any hope for him to live, the leg would have to be cut off.

He had only the long knife most men carried to do the job with; luckily the man was out and wouldn't feel much of the pain. Hall pulled the man deeper into the mountainside; whoever he was hiding from could come back. Also, he needed to start a fire; the only way for him to help this man was to burn the wound closed after he had taken the leg. He wasn't sure why he was doing this, but here was a black man in need, and he would do his best to help. He was also very interested in why the man was here in the first place.

The man was still alive after three days. Cleaning the wound was one of the worst things Hall had ever done, and he was still in wonder that the man was alive. He had found a small stream about a mile away; once he collected his horse, he loaded the unconscious man on the horse and took him to the stream. When he picked the man up, maggots fell out of the wound. Hall just put the man in the water and let the cool water wash as much of the dirt and debris out as it could. The man didn't even wake up when his body hit the cool water. Hall cut the tattered clothing from around the leg; it had been stuck with dried blood. He wasn't too worried about being careful; if he didn't take this man's leg off and get the gangrene under control, it wouldn't matter. Upon closer inspection, after the water had time to clean the wound, Hall found that the man's legs seemed to be crushed; there were no cuts or signs of any type of gunshot wounds. Cutting the leg off was much easier than he had thought because of the crushed bones, but it was still a messy affair. He had tied a tourniquet above the leg to stop the bleeding.

He started a fire close to the water and used one of the two knives he had carried in to cauterize the leg wound. He cut the leg in the water and hurriedly pulled the man out to cauterize the wound. When the hot metal hit the bloody skin, the man let out a groan, but that was all. It took Hall about an hour to cauterize the wound with the two knives. The smell of roasting meat permeating the air. Once complete, Hall took a quick bath to get all the blood and gore off him. He located a small cave well away from where he had amputated the man's leg; he wanted to get away from wild animals who would be attracted to all the blood.

Hall didn't have any medical supplies to treat the wound, but he used some local plants the Indians in the unit had advised were good for healing. He found a few of the aloe plants in the mountain area and smothered the wound in the aloe's clear gel. He then used the aloe leaves to wrap the top of the wound. He cleaned part of the tattered leg clothing he had cut from the wound in the stream, and he added more aloe gel to the rag bandage before tying it over the aloe leaves. Since he had been a soldier, the use of plants to heal wounds had become a necessity because some of the smallest scratches could kill a man, if left unattended. The strange plants in the desert were different from those in the South, and without the Indian's advice, they could be deadly. He smiled inside; hell, he never had the time as a slave to think about plants, other than cotton. He broke out of his thoughts; he hoped this makeshift medical remedy would work. Only time would tell.

While the man was fighting for his life, Hall decided to use the time to finish his reconnaissance of the area. What he found was very disturbing. He followed the trail he had seen earlier, which he realized led straight back to the camp. A little ways from where he had found the man, he found the rest of the bodies. There was a pile of ten to twenty bodies in a mountain crevasse, which had apparently being used as a mass burial grave. No one had taken much effort to bury the bodies; they had been thrown into a hole, with lime thrown on top. They were all coated with a heavy layer of white dust. That would explain why he didn't smell the bodies. The bodies were all Indians, with one or two Negroes. None of them had gunshot wounds, but all had some sort of bone break or crushed limbs.

He left the bodies and continued to follow the trail. The miners probably didn't think there was anything in the area that could affect them, but it didn't hurt to be cautious as he moved forward. Eventually, he came upon what he assumed was the other side of the mine, which apparently was where the ore was smelted. There was a large cave entrance, which seemed like a huge, dark hole in the earth. In front of the hole, placed randomly in front of the cave entrance, were four large devices, each with two large flat stones, which a donkey dragged around a circular pit made from flat stones. The drag stones were attached to a central point, which allowed them to be dragged repeatedly over the ore, which the slaves randomly brought out of the cave and disposed of among the four ore breakers.

Hall had never seen anything like this before, and he watched as slaves, both men and women in chains, brought out heavy bags of rock or ore in backpacks. The weight of the heavy rocks loaded in the packs was back breaking, as evident by their constant dropping to knees and staggering. Once they dropped off their loads, the relief was evident; each looked around in amazement at being outside in the open sky. It was at this time that the whips were tactfully used to remind them of where they needed to go, back in the mine. The women were chained only at the ankles, but the men were chained at the ankles and wrists to limit their movement.

Hall watched for over two hours, and he didn't see the same people come back and drop loads off in that time. The distances and the number of people in the mine had to be large. He was just starting to leave when he felt the ground beneath him shake.

It had to be the aftershock of some sort of explosion. Soon a large plume of smoke could be seen coming from the mine entrance. They were also using explosives in the mine. That didn't sound good for the slaves. Hall packed up and went back to the recovering man.

He had been gone for almost a whole day. There were still a few hours before the sun went down when Hall made his way back to the little gap in the mountain, where he had left the one-legged man to heal. The man's eyes opened as Hall entered the little gap. There was just enough remaining sunlight to clearly show the man's sweat-sheened face. The rag of a shirt he wore was drenched in sweat. He was clearly surprised to see another black man enter the makeshift shelter. In a crackling voice, the man said, "I must not be in heaven because there is still too much pain in my body, and you don't look like blue-eyed Jesus."

Hall smiled and hurriedly got the extra skin of water he had left behind to quench the man's thirst. The man drank long and deep before lifting his hand in a cease manner. He took a couple of deep, tense breaths and said, "Whoever you are, thank you. The last thing I remember was hoping I would die before animals ate me alive.'" The man drank greedily from the water skin Hall had provided. Hall had him slow down and drink it little by little, but eventually the man drank it all.

He continued, "They left me to die in that hole with all those other poor souls. I was crushed during a mine explosion. They thought that by using small amounts of dynamite, they could limit the damage to the mines. The backblast from the explosion loosened the support where we were hiding, and the tunnel collapsed. They only found me because they had to get access to the area the explosion had opened up. I was immediately pulled out, and a tourniquet was put on my leg. I was put aside until they finished clearing the rubble and the bodies that didn't make it. I was in the hole for at least a day before they came back to see if I could get up and work again. When I could not, they decided to take me to the doctor."

Hall didn't immediately respond; the man seemed like he needed to speak. Hall also just realized he had never had to face the dire aspect of dying before. Yes, he had been in slavery, but he was always mindful of the rules and had never been in any life-or-death danger. It wasn't until they had raped and murdered his daughter that his life was put in peril. Even then, he hadn't faced death directly in the face like this man had. Hall respected what the man had been through; if the man needed to speak, he would let him.

The man continued. "My name is Wyatt, originally a manservant for a slave trader named Master Isaac Franklin from Natchez, Mississippi. The war saw me and my Master Franklin on many a perilous journey. Many nights I never thought I would see the sunlight again. I served Master Franklin but never served the South! After the war, I was kept at a plantation in Natchitoches Parish, Louisiana. Even though slavery was abolished, we were told not to leave the plantations or risk being killed."

The slaves started trickling out one by one until all routes that led north were manned continuously, looking for runaway slaves. He had heard of slaves escaping to Mexico on the "great Nacogdoches road," where they didn't have to worry about the white man at all. This had appealed to Wyatt and a few other slaves. He had never married, and there was a slave woman with him, Addie, with whom he felt he could have a life if they got away. She was the master's favorite, and he had fallen in love with her.

They planned their escape well; there were families along the route, and they heard they could link up with the Los Mascogos, a group of freed blacks and Seminole Indians. "After we crossed the borders of Louisiana and Texas," he said, "we crossed over from heavily wooded areas to large open areas and low hills. We hid in the thick growth of the bushes. The closer we got to Mexico, the more desolate, dry, and barren the land became. There was a lot of thorny vegetation and a lot more rugged, rocky hills. We even had to swim a river to get over to the Mexico side. We thought we had made it safely into Mexico, only to be caught by ex-Mexican rebel soldiers, who had been slave catchers during the war. They had retreated to Mexico and now worked for the priest who needed slaves to work the mine. Most of the slaves in the mine were Indians, but there were also blacks and Chinese being worked to death in the mine. Nobody left the mine alive that I know of."

Hall was fascinated by what he was hearing. There were black men and women in Mexico who were still being treated as slaves. There had been an underground railroad for slaves who wanted to go to Mexico. And who were Los Mascogos? He had never thought about other men being slaves. He didn't know how to feel. He knew slavery was wrong; he had seen it and lived it. But what about the Indians and the Chinese Wyatt had just mentioned? Could they also do something for them?

Stop, he thought. What was he thinking? Slavery, regardless of what skin color was involved, was wrong. He had lived in subjugation his whole life and knew the hopelessness of knowing he would never be more than a slave and that the life given to him on this earth would be as a slave. It had been a murder of his soul every minute of the day and enough to kill himself over. Living as a slave had been like breathing water; he couldn't and shouldn't, and his mind and body told him in every conceivable way that it wasn't right. In the water you drown; in slavery, you shrivel and diminish every day. Hall shook himself out of his thoughts and remembered he wasn't a slave anymore.

He asked Wyatt, "How many guards do you think were in the mine?" He waited, and Wyatt didn't reply. He asked again, this time looking at Wyatt for a response. Wyatt didn't even move when he asked him. Hall went over to check on him and realized he had stopped breathing. He was dead; the injury had probably been too much, and the gangrene had done its job.

Hall closed Wyatt's eyes. Wyatt had lived long enough to tell someone about his trials and his journey to be free. Hall had heard him and would make sure Lieutenant Colonel Vetter knew what was going on in the mine. He would block up the place with rocks so the animals didn't get to him; he would pay his respects again when he came back to help free the slaves.

FORTY-FIVE
The Camp

FIRST SERGEANT AMRA looked down on the site where the hostages were being held. They had arrived about a day and a half ago and had placed their camp about nine miles away from the actual site. He was on reconnaissance with two other scouts, who were positioning themselves at other points around the camp. They would all watch for about five hours, just observing the location.

They needed information on the camp, particularly how much traffic was around the area, if any. The place was pretty desolate and well hidden. They had to travel up and down a bunch of small hills to reach the location to stay hidden. Amra had positioned himself north of the camp, ever watching the entrance. The location was deceptively well hidden and would have been extremely hard to find without the directions the padre had provided. The place had only one entrance; left and right of the entrance were large rocky outcrops of huge boulders, which provided a natural funnel to an old, ruined wall.

There was a partially built structure, which didn't resemble anything Amra had ever seen before. There was a small trail from the partial building, which led to another. It was a long, slender building, which looked more recently built. It was a type of log cabin of rough timber and rocks. The bottom portion was built of small boulders held together with some sort of mortar. Logs had been roughly stacked on top of each other with slots for randomly cut-out windows. The roof was also built of logs but seemed to be under some sort of repair, being replaced with clay tiles. Behind the building was a huge pit that may have been some sort of open mining area. The dirt in the pit area was of some pale substance, lighter than the topsoil around it. Amra could see a trail lead from the house directly through the middle of the pit. To the side of the trail were random lean-tos, which provided shade from the hot sun. He could see people on the ground; from this distance, it looked like they were chained. He would wait until his other scouts came back to finish the picture.

The other two scouts arrived back and gave their descriptions of the camp. The total picture was very disturbing to First Sergeant Amra. The trail he had witnessed went deeper into the pit and eventually leveled off at the bottom like a *T*. There was a fifteen-foot wall at the end of the trail, and then it went left and right. At the top of the fifteen-foot wall was another wooden or rock building, similar to the one at the entrance. There were guards in the building, watching the slaves below; and large dogs could be seen with some of the guards. The dogs looked like they were a mix of wolf and some other large breed; whatever breed they were mixed with, they weren't normal-sized animals. They were huge. The women were all to the left of the main trail in a large cavern, and the children were to the right in a similar cave-type structure. Neither the women nor the children were chained.

Both scouts believed the structures were the result of explosions; they weren't natural. The debris from the structure had created walls, and the ends of the trail went left and right, sealing the slaves perfectly. The men were in the lean-to structures, chained sporadically along a line on the main trail, and they were all chained to the floor in irons at all times. There was a variety of races in the pit, mostly nonwhite. There were Indians, Negroes, and Mexicans all herded together. The women and children weren't chained but separated into two separate areas. Women were to the left of the trail, and children were to the right. The caverns they were in went back into the cave, and neither of the scouts could discern how deep the caverns went and how many people were being held. On the surface, there were about one hundred people; the majority were women. He noted in the women's area that they had put themselves in their own small groups, according to race.

As night started to fall, activity in the camp started to increase. Bonfires were lit around the camp. Moonlight made the night bright, and coupled with the bonfires randomly lit around the camp, portions of the camp Amra couldn't see during the day started to appear. At the building's front entrance, there were two underground cave structures at each end. They were well hidden in the day and could be seen only now because of the light beaming out of them. This indicated that there was possibly more than one entrance into the camp.

To the right of the structure, horses and other farm animals were located in caves almost directly under the end of the house. To the left, there were a dry storage area and an off-loading ramp for supplies. There was a lot of activity; male slaves were being dragged to the ramp and being chained in a line along it. There was other movement throughout the camp; women and children were being selected and dragged out, chained in a long line together, and marched out of the pit toward the building in the front. They were led to the entrance, where the farm animals and stables were located. Each was stripped naked, had his or her body rubbed with rags dipped in some thick substance, and rinsed in the animal watering troughs. The women were then herded to the middle of the stables and made to sit. Amra had his men posted to watch the activity.

Throughout the night, guards came, pulled women into empty animal stalls, and raped them. After they were done, the women were put back in line. Some unfortunate women were raped more than once, since the guards didn't know which women had been visited. One of his men reported the same thing was going on near where the children slept; guards with a different taste were taking the children off into the night.

THE SCREAMS AND moans of both the women and children could be heard into the night. It reminded Amra of when he had been first brought to America; his new master had sent him to a slave-breaking house in Virginia. He didn't immediately understand the language of the whites, and it took him some time to learn. But he didn't need to understand what they were talking about because his eyes told the whole story. The place he was in had bars on the windows and doors made of steel. He came to learn this was an old jail where criminals had been held. It had been transformed into a place of slaves. Amra had never seen so many black men and women chained up like animals and treated even worse. The first night, he had seen a group of men walk among the slaves and pick black women out. They would probe them with their fingers, smell them, and look at their teeth, just like Amra would do when looking at the health of cattle. Some women, new to this treatment, fought back in response to the touches, only to be beaten with sticks.

It hurt his heart to see women treated this way. This was just the beginning of a long and heartbreaking trail of systematic misery and degradation of women he would see and be made part of. He learned the place was run by a man named Master Lumpkin, who had purchased the jail to be turned into a slaving house, a place to buy, train, breed, and punish slaves. Slaves were bought, sold, trained, and broken at this location. It was at this place that Amra learned about the true hate and disdain the white man had toward the African race. He had seen atrocities in combat as a young man that were truly horrific—seeing men separated in half by the giant khopesh, observing headless bodies, slipping on the entrails and guts of the enemy on the battlefield. He had seen savage things done to another man in the name of war.

But the things he witnessed in the slaving pens had nothing to do with war. They were the savage and brutal things most men would dream about but wake up and call a nightmare. It was horrid to be a witness and part of the brutal and vile aspect of a man, who debased another man to less than an animal simply to enact the horrid and monstrous depraved things his dark nature could conjure. After all, they were slaves and considered less than animals. Beatings and whippings were brutal and freely given to maintain complete dominance over the slaves. He quickly learned that there was no limit to the decadence and vileness that could be heaped on a human soul. There was constant traffic of both white men and women in fancy clothes, anxious to witness or be part of some new decadence or degradation. Certain parts of the prison were partitioned off, and there was the constant sound of music and laughter always emanating from the area day and night.

Amra had been part of the "parties" in these areas and dreaded them. He also learned that for the right price, any decadence of choice was available. He had been witness to the raping of little girls and boys, barely in their walking stages, and hearing the laughter in response to their squeals of pain. He had seen the glee and pleasure in the sweat-soaked face of a slave owner as he took the manhood of a teen boy. Due to his unnatural size, Amra was considered a novelty, which was a blessing because he was beyond being beaten, but his size was a curse because of the things he was forced to do. He was forced to breed with girls as young as twelve years old. The first time he refused, his left foot was soaked in burning grease. He almost died from the infection he received from the burns; the only thing that saved him was his value to Mr. Lumpkin as a breeder. They made sure he understood that his only value was in impregnating women. That's why they had chosen to burn his feet; they didn't want to hurt the parts they needed to breed.

They became very creative about how to punish him if he refused to give the brutal and heinous things they wanted from him. They also used him to break other slave men, an experience that still haunted him today. They didn't want black men to feel the basic need to be a man. Once, he learned the basics of the language from one of the women he was forced to breed with; if she had fifteen children, she would be given her freedom. For some reason, that fact hurt Amra more than all the other things he had witnessed or been part of. The young girl couldn't have been more than fourteen years old, and for her to feel her only value in life was to have fifteen children for her master sent a jolt through his soul. She saw children as a means to an end and not as the blessings they were. To devalue a child's life to a transaction seemed horrific on a whole different scale. The currency for his survival during this dark time made his soul forever darkened by the association with white men and their "civilized" ways.

He was abruptly brought back to his current reality when one of his men reported that a small caravan was en route to the camp. The sunrise was a few hours off, and the caravan would arrive right around sunrise. Activity around the camp also started to increase. The slave men located at the loading dock started pulling out a makeshift platform and setting it up just inside the courtyard between the main gate and the longhouse in the front. The few remaining guards were hurriedly trying to get their remaining time with the female slaves. The other female slaves huddled together in a large bundle to keep warm. The previous separation of individuals by race was forgotten.

The caravan arrived right before sunrise and consisted of four wagons and two stagecoaches. There were about fifteen guards, not including the two drivers for each wagon and stagecoach. Two of the wagons were empty, and the other two were loaded with supplies. The wagon with the supplies went to the left of the longhouse to be unloaded. The empty wagons were placed inside the gate near the platform the slaves had erected. Amra had seen this situation before and knew a slave auction was about to happen. He decided to pull his men in and head back to brief First Lieutenant Phoenix on the dire situation they had observed.

FORTY-SEVEN
The Deal

JIAN COULD DESCRIBE the monastery at Cajoncito as only breathtaking. He could tell by the artistry and design that the place had been created for the rich and not designed to be a church. Upon close inspection, a lot of the frescos depicted nude people and warlike scenes. These were things he understood the Christian churches would never condone. The padres provided Captain Matthews, Jian, and the others who accompanied them rooms normally reserved for Spanish nobility. They were lavish, and the hot spring tubs in each room were something he had never seen before, even in some of the richest Chinese nobility. The massive amount of water eluded to underground springs in the area. The place was lavish but not gaudy, and Jian felt it was designed to give those visiting a sense of relief from all the trappings of nobility without losing the feeling of luxury.

Two days after their arrival, Jian, Captain Matthews, Padre Garcia, and a small group of men headed to the mine in the

South to get the silver needed to pay the ransom. They had to pass through the actual town of Cajoncito en route to the silver mines. Seeing the town for the first time, he realized it had also been designed with thought and care like the monastery. The town was built into the side of a plateau of volcanic rock in neat and structured lines. A road, at least three carts wide, zigzagged back and forth up the mountain, with the monastery at the bottom and the town a little higher but deeper into the plateau. It was a beautiful place, and Jian was instantly drawn to it. Each house was uniform in structure; some were larger than others, and the shops bore signs in front, but the overall structures were the same.

He felt that it was best to let Captain Matthews do all the talking for their team, since he was here at the request of Lieutenant Colonel Vetter and had no authority to make any decisions. He purposely stayed in the background during the ride to Cajoncito and subsequent stay in the monastery. He pretended his use of the English language was limited and often asked for things to be re-stated. He was actually very proficient in the English language but found it useful to be otherwise. Padre Morales instantly disvalued Jian when he tried to ask Jian a question and Jian pretended that he didn't hear him. It wasn't until Captain Matthews tapped Jian and relayed the same question that Jian responded. Jian's response was choppy and confused, and he could see the disdain in the padre's face. Since then, all conversation was with Captain Matthews; Jian listened and learned.

The people of Cajoncito came out to meet the small band before they even arrived. There weren't many people left in the town, and only a few of the men came out. Jian could see relief on the men's faces to see Padre Garcia, but the look was quickly replaced by one of concern for their families. A portly, graying Mexican man asked the padre a question in Spanish. The padre responded and pointed at Captain Matthews; the soldiers and said a few more things. The men looked at Captain Matthews,

252 | CHRISTOPHER "CHRIS" NUELS

and all started bowing and nodding, saying, "Gracias." The padre informed Captain Matthews that he had told them that Matthews and his men were here to help get their families.

Trays and tables were brought out, and food was laid out for the padre and his visitors. Jian could tell the town was totally subservient to the padre's needs. Captain Matthews seemed to think the same thing and asked the padre about this subservient attitude. The padre informed Captain Matthews that the people in the town were descendants of the original caretakers of the monastery, which at the time had been a retreat for rich Spanish nobility. They have always been in service to whoever ran the monastery. "It is similar to medieval feudalism," Captain Matthews replied.

Jian thought that even though the padres, the current masters of the monastery, didn't keep their responsibility to protect the citizens of Cajoncito for their loyalty, they still treated the padre and his friends like royalty. Jian realized these were good people and wanted to help them.

They stayed only half a day in the town of Cajoncito before moving farther south toward the mines. The people of Cajoncito wished them well and provided supplies for their trip. The padre gave a speech, in which the people gave a loud cheer upon completion. After a few moments of happiness, he bowed his head and said a prayer. They departed onward to the mines that evening; there was a resting place the padres wanted to make before nightfall. The resting place ended up being a small opening in a hillside, where an underground spring briefly burst through the ground. They spent an uneventful night there and headed for the mine at first light.

The mine wasn't very hard to find; the reverberations from the underground explosions could be felt right before the sun began to rise. The rugged terrain required a bunch of loopbacks to avoid going up and down the mountain. The opening was a large, rectangular slot in the mountain, about one hundred feet wide and roughly ten to twelve feet high. Two railroad tracks ran parallel into the darkness of the mine. Crushed rock and boulders of varying sizes were scattered in front of the mine. A large piece of tarp or tent was strung between two large boulders and appeared to be a dwelling of some sort.

As they drew closer to the mine, they noted a wagon coming up a well-kept road to the right. The padre mention that this was the welcoming party from the miners. The mining village was about a mile to the southwest of the mine at a higher altitude; the people there had a view of the men as they rode up.

Captain Matthews's trip to Cajoncito had been everything he expected and more. The monastery was the most elegant place he had ever witnessed in his entire life. The rooms they stayed in were those he expected a dignitary or nobleman to stay in; he was neither. The actual town of Cajoncito was the prettiest city he had ever been in. The place was clean; there were no smells, and he didn't see any poor people. He was treated like royalty, and his little bit of Spanish was just enough to gain the respect of the padre.

Added to his happiness was that Jian hadn't been any problems since they departed. He barely spoke, and that suited Captain Matthews fine. He suspected Lieutenant Colonel Vetter had sent the man to either keep him honest or spy on him. Matthews couldn't say for sure which he thought the real reason was. Right now it didn't matter; they were at the mine, and Padre Garcia said he wanted to talk to Matthews alone tonight after they had settled. He said he had something very important to ask him, and it would be very lucrative for him if he agreed.

That was all Matthews need to hear; this had to be his destiny if not his fate. He knew his duty as a soldier and didn't believe · anything he had said or done was against his country or his oath.

He was brought out of his thoughts when Padre Garcia led the way into the darkness of the mine.

Padre Garcia had decided to show the soldiers the full extent of the mines. It didn't matter at this point; they would be leaving this hellhole in a month. He had hated this place ever since he found out he was being assigned to this desolate and God-forsaken place. The only thing that made the trip to hell so heavenly was his love for Padre Morales. He had come to terms with his love for his fellow padre a long time ago. His faith had to believe that love in any form was good. He knew the physical act was a sin, but the act of loving another with his heart and soul, and only that person, had to be held to some account. He knew the good book was written by men and therefore guided by the values and judgments of men of that time.

This was the last ransom payment, and hopefully after this introduction, he would have the security to make the first and most arduous portion of their journey to happiness. Either way, he was ready to meet God and explain his reasoning for having his one and only love and no other in his life.

Jian was disturbed by the senseless death of the slaves in the mine. His surprise at finding out that the padres had been using enslaved Indians and runaways to run the mine was quickly put aside by the bodies laid out in the dark mine, bodies that had been alive until the first blast this morning. Those in charge had tried to tie them up in tarps to prevent the blood from soaking up the narrow area, but it hadn't worked. The coppery, metallic scent of blood and feces permeated the small area. Crushed body parts, entrails, and pieces of skull were all over the place.

Padre Garcia called it a tragic accident and the first of its kind. Jian didn't believe him; since they had come to the mine this morning, two other explosions had sounded. Even as he was thinking about the damage done, another body, still bleeding, was pulled out of the darkness. The padre immediately started back toward the front, claiming that they had hit an extremely unstable area; it would be better to be outside the mine. Everyone hurried out.

Once outside, Captain Matthew asked about the mine's production. The padre claimed the mine had given most of its riches long ago, and that was why the miners had gone to using dynamite. The silver coming out of the mine now kept the miners' families well kept, and the miners paid a small tribute to the monastery, nothing significant. The padre claimed they had saved a significant amount of silver to pay for escorts back to their homeland. Captain Matthews's ear pricked up at this. The padre stated that his superiors informed him that his time in Mexico was up and too bring back the buried bodies of the former priest to Spain. The church also informed him to leave the monastery to the people of Cajoncito. The padre informed Captain Matthews that they would pay a king's ransom for a safe escort to Port Valesco in Texas. Captain Matthews believed this was a viable option for him, but he didn't want to discuss this matter further in front of Jian. He told the padre that such plans were for Lieutenant Colonel Vetter to decide, that he would sit down with the padre and formally put the plan to paper and present it to Lieutenant Colonel Vetter for approval. This way, Matthews thought, he could let the padre know his true intent without Jian listening.

Jian, for his part, had heard everything and knew Captain Matthews was definitely interested in the endeavor. He acted as if he were interested in something else and walked away to give Captain Matthews the privacy he needed. Jian had already heard the offer from the padre; now all he needed to do was wait and watch for the reaction.

FORTY-EIGHT
Pieces of the Puzzle

AFTER THE DEPARTURE of the rescue party and the small detachment sent with Padre Morales back to Cajoncito, Lieutenant Colonel Vetter had the rest of the camp amplify their efforts to obtain solid security around the camp and to work more at getting the dwellings completed. The limited amounts of wood in the area had forced them to look at building residences inside the mountain. Lieutenant Colonel Vetter made sure that, before any dwelling was started, it met the guidelines he had set for the defense. Vetter viewed the current setup as too open and very hard to defend. The mountain gave them the advantage of looking down, but if they didn't have the defenses set, then it wouldn't matter.

There was still a large migration of Indians and Mexicans in the area, displaced after the Treaty of Guadalupe Hidalgo. The recent civil war had put a trickle on migration to the West; now that the war was over, more Americans were moving west to the newly acquired area, primarily for gold but also for land. Also, there was the threat of large bands of rebel soldiers, who had also migrated to the Texas/Mexico area to avoid surrendering their way of life and start it anew in the frontier. At West Point, he was taught to always improve his defense. Jian had assisted a lot in helping create mortar composed of the dried-up cactus and local plants and added to mud and sand. The few families with the unit were busy day and night, doing the work their men couldn't do while they were on the various missions.

Vetter was proud of the community-type environment that had developed within the unit. He knew that for a lot of the men in the unit, this was all they had and nothing else to fall back on. This was their first attempt at being Americans or being part of anything for the last two hundred years. Just yesterday they were equal with the animals; now they were expected overnight to have all the civility and resourcefulness of white people. They had no knowledge or education, no family business or trade to start with. Nothing. Yet he had to admit it was amazing that overnight they had eagerly stepped into the void of nothingness to escape the reality that was slavery. He smiled inwardly as he realized he was probably among only a handful of white men who had the opportunity to work with blacks as men and not as slaves or lessors. His men had learned early that he judged them based on their contribution to the unit and abilities. On numerous occasions, he had chewed out asses of white men and black men alike and stopped abuses in his unit.

When he was first given his unit, they had sent him all the white soldiers they felt were sympathetic to black soldiers or were pains in the asses to the units they were in. This had been fine with him because their guerrilla-type warfare made conventional soldiers problematic, and any who had problems with blacks usually ended up in a bad state. It wasn't a coincidence that two of his white officers, who were loose with the word *nigger*, were part of the few mortalities he had in his unit. Everything was justified

258 | CHRISTOPHER "CHRIS" NUELS

in how they had died, but his gut told him they had overstepped their welcome and had been dealt with. He couldn't say either way, and because it was justified, he decided not to address the issue. Wouldn't he be just another white man questioning the integrity of what was justified in front of his face? Would he address the issue if white soldiers had done the same thing and everything was justified? Each time the answer came back no; he wouldn't even second-guess it. He put those thoughts behind him and started to focus on the problem at hand and in getting the area he was assigned to under control.

Four days after the different units had departed, one of Sergeant Hall's scouts, Chatan, arrived with some Indians Lieutenant Colonel Vetter had never seen before. Chatan introduced them as the Rarámuri tribe, and their speaker was an older man named Tepor. Tepor told Lieutenant Colonel Vetter the story of his people and why they had decided to make the trip here. Outwardly, Lieutenant Colonel Vetter nodded as he listened to Tepor tell his story. He agreed with the reasoning of why they had come and assured him that he would do everything he could to assist them.

Inwardly, he shivered at the possible treachery he had gotten his unit in. If the padres were making slaves of the Indians he had helped in their return, then he and his men would be accomplices to a horrible act by assisting in the enslavement of other men. He didn't know whether his leadership and the relationship he had with his men could survive if he ordered them to assist, knowing they were slavers.

He was just putting his thoughts together and getting ready to order a good portion of the men in the camp to prepare to move so he could push forward and assist First Lieutenant Phoenix and his men in making sure the rescued hostages didn't get let back to the padres' care.

A runner from First Lieutenant Phoenix asked to see

Lieutenant Colonel Vetter and said he had an important message from Lieutenant Phoenix. The man introduced himself as Corporal Charl and started to relay the story Señor Perez had communicated to Lieutenant Phoenix, referencing the town of Cajoncito and Lieutenant Phoenix's concerns that the padres were using the town as a resource pool for either slaves or mining. Lieutenant Phoenix also relayed that First Sergeant Amra had eyes on the objective and would soon be reporting his findings; he would send another messenger soon after. Lieutenant Colonel Vetter thanked Corporal Charl and told him to get some rest and something to eat; he would have a return message first thing in the morning. The young soldier saluted and departed.

The news was good to Vetter; it confirmed his suspicions about the padres and put his mind at ease, knowing Lieutenant Phoenix was also aware of the padres' possible treachery. Vetter now understood why the padres had been reluctant to go to the Mexican government after the hostages were taken. Their possible complicity in the kidnapping and slavery of the Indians and the people of Cajoncito was at risk of being found out. He had a better understanding of the situation and could react accordingly.

Lieutenant Colonel Vetter was just starting to depart and do a walk-through of the camp when he heard another fast horse ride up to the front of the new headquarters location. There wasn't a door to the new building, but two guards were always posted when Lieutenant Colonel Vetter was inside. He briefly heard voices but couldn't discern what they were saying. He heard the sound of boots walking toward the opening to his current location. One of the guards from outside walked in, and another, a blue-shirted Union soldier, entered behind him. The guard introduced the soldier as Sergeant Nance from Fort Concho. The sergeant saluted and stated that he had come to deliver a message to Lieutenant Colonel Vetter; the Fort Concho Commander requested Lieutenant Colonel Vetter come to Fort Concho to discuss local issues in the areas. He finished by saying his message had further details attached. Lieutenant Colonel Vetter acknowledged the message and told him to get some rest and something to eat, that he was welcome to stay the night and return in the morning if he liked. The sergeant thanked him and departed.

Lieutenant Colonel Vetter read the missive and couldn't help but believe the incident with the hostages and slaves—and now the first request from his command to come and discuss issues in the area—was more than a coincidence. The missive also contained a map of the Texas state and identified places the civilian governor said were off limits to the military and private property. To avoid a possible confrontation with private property owners, the commander believed the meeting was pertinent. He didn't know the exact location of the hostages but believed it was in one of the restricted areas identified on the map. A brief moment of concern enwrapped his entire body, but as quickly as it came, it was gone. He would trust the lieutenant and his men to save the hostages, an act he could see no wrong in. If there were civilians in his assigned area doing criminal acts, then in the absence of law and order, he and his men would provide it.

FORTY-NINE

Rise of the Phoenix

FIRST LIEUTENANT PHOENIX had just finished receiving the reconnaissance brief from First Sergeant Amra. They were in his tent alone; the first sergeant had requested that he brief him alone before the rest of the team heard the news. He had to agree; the news was grim, and he could already start to see the problem when the rest of the team found out there was a slave-holding area in the middle of the desert with primarily blacks and Indians being enslaved. When they found out about the abuse of the women and heard about children being raped and abused daily, they would see this as a direct threat to themselves and their families, and he had to agree. Of all the news Phoenix expected, this was the furthest from his mind. The fury was hearing over again that even with the ratification of the Thirteenth Amendment to end slavery, there was still an attempt to keep it alive. This had to be dealt with, and it needed to be dealt with now!

First Sergeant Amra watched the expression on the lieutenant's face. He could see him dealing with the same emotions he had struggled with when he first learned of the slave camp. He knew the need for vengeance was great, but they were no longer slaves; they were US soldiers, so they had to handle this situation like soldiers. Amra told the lieutenant they needed more information on whom they were dealing with and thought the first thing they should do was capture someone to question. Amra believed the sale of the slave presented the perfect opportunity. "We could wait till the caravan departed with their new merchandise, capture the leaders and question them, and release the slaves. Once we learn more, we can plan the attack."

Lieutenant Phoenix's anger dissipated as he listened to the first sergeant's plan. Until this moment, he hadn't realized how much pent-up hatred and anger he had and how easy it was to let it take over his feelings. He had to be more careful. The plan had merits and was the right thing to do. They would use the guerrilla warfare tactics they were comfortable with and attack at night. They would wait on the night after the caravan departed and attack it then.

Both the lieutenant and first sergeant decided they should attack with the burlap sack camouflage they had used during the war to break up their silhouettes. For some reason, they both felt it was important for the unit to remain anonymous for now. There wasn't a lot known in this area about black soldiers, and they wanted to keep it that way in case something went wrong. They both spent the next couple of hours planning the attack. At some point in the planning, a silent agreement was made that, just like during the war, there would be no one left alive to support slavery.

The lieutenant decided to brief the men on the findings from the reconnaissance of the slave camp. He didn't leave anything out and let the full horror of what was going on settle among the men. They were deadly silent, each imagining his own history of slavery. The fact that there were other nationalities in the slave camp other than black didn't matter; the only fact that mattered was that the propagation of slavery was continuing. The display across their faces showed that they were going through the same internal struggle both the first sergeant and lieutenant had gone through in reliving their old horrors of slavery, the indignation, terror, uncertainty, and hopelessness. Then there was the realization that "You are no longer a slave. You are a survivor, forever marked." Finally, there was the white-hot anger at realizing that this time they had a weapon in their hands and the ability to change the outcome. This time there would be no second chance for them if given the opportunity. They had the silence of death and the commitment to deal with it.

In the silence, the lieutenant added, "In the war we silently killed the enemy in hopes that they would lose their heart for the war. We don't know if our techniques were the reason the war stopped, but that is how we learned to fight and how we learned to survive. The men we will capture tonight and the men we will fight at the camp have all decided to continue the cause for the rebels here in our new home, in our backyard. I know a lot of you have thought about it, and I want to make sure I answer your questions and ease your mind. There will be no quarter for the men who have chosen the continued path to enslave other men. We still need to acknowledge that we are soldiers, and for that reason, we will act in our old covert manner. In keeping with our old covert manner, I expect us to be silent and the kills to be silent. No torture or unnecessary maiming of the slavers. Unlike our old techniques where we left the bodies to be found, we need to ensure that we erase all evidence of their existence. I don't even want the vultures to smell out the bodies."

Phoenix could see the relief in the men's eyes at his comments. He felt that if Lieutenant Colonel Vetter were here, he would have done the same thing. The evil of slavery had to be stamped out wherever it was found. This was frontier territory, and no formal legal system had been set up to support criminals. There were no prisons or jails to contain the men once they captured them. Also, helping the hostages while keeping security on an unknown number of dangerous men didn't make any sense. He had made his decision based on the best information he had, and he would stick by it.

The capture of the slave caravan after it departed went off without any unit casualties. They didn't expect anyone to be out in the desert and didn't expect to be attacked. The empty wagon they had come with had fifteen slaves in the back—men, women, and children. They had stopped about ten miles from the caravan camp to rest and enjoy the purchases. The men had to watch as the women and children were abused, and the guards went to sleep. The tension in the air was thick enough to cut.

Once the leader's tent had been identified, he was safely secured and dragged away from the area. Once the okay was given that he was secured, the men quietly went through the camp, dispatching the guards. Amra noted that the anger at having to watch the abuse of the prisoners before the attack was evident in the knife, ax, and mace swings of his men. Throats were gashed open, or heads were entirely decapitated from their bodies; skulls were crushed to mush and pieces in one swing. The silent thud of metal hitting meat could be heard throughout the camp. Not one voice rang out in fear or warning. The massacre was over in a matter of seconds.

A selected group of men already started to pull the wagons out of the area along with the slaves and all the extra horses. The men swept the area one more time before sheathing weapons and starting to drag bodies away. There was a cave in the area where they would put the bodies and seal it up. The dead men were searched for equipment and any items of use. In less than an hour, all evidence of a camp disappeared into the night.

FIFTY

The Missive

FIRST LIEUTENANT PHOENIX couldn't explain the emotions that were going through him. It was like he was walking in a dream of reality. As he peered through the eyeholes of his burlap bag, he couldn't believe he was seeing the white man in front of him, again. He had gotten older and fatter, with a little more balding on the top, but this was still the same disgusting man Phoenix remembered. The last time Phoenix had seen this man was when he was going by the slave name, Lieutenant Phoenix. Martin Gutsgell was Master Clement Jackall's first cousin. His mother's sister had married one of her third cousins, and Martin was the creature born of the unblessed union. Martin or cousin "Gutter" had been the master's primary enthusiast in all his sexual decadence and spent more time at the plantation than any other relative. Young Lieutenant Phoenix had been abused at the "Gutter's" hand on multiple occasions. To see him here in the frontier of hell was a morbid sort of comedy. He expected a man like him to be in a hell like this but not in the hands of one of his abused.

Phoenix told First Sergeant Amra about his dilemma. Amra listened to the whole story without saying a word, and when Phoenix was done, Amra simply looked at Phoenix and said, "You have already told the men and basically ordered that everyone was to die. They have carried out your orders, and this is the last man alive. What is the difference now that you know who he is? Take care of it personally to get rid of your demons and be done with it!"

Phoenix agreed that this was something he had to deal with himself.

The "Gutter" had been knocked senseless, and Phoenix had time to go through the things they found on him. He was still seething inside as he went through some of the travel bags; he noted a decorative envelope that simply said "Brother" on the front in ornate calligraphy. His fiery anger at being sexually abused by the animal in front of him, masquerading as a man, dwindled briefly as he began to read something he believed gave insight into his future and the future of every other black man.

In the envelope was a letter from an anonymous source, and attached to the letter was a pamphlet labeled "Walker's Appeal, in Four Articles; Together with a Preamble, to the Coloured Citizens of the World, but in Particular, and Very Expressly, to Those of the United States of America, Written in Boston, State of Massachusetts, September 28, 1829." The letter attached said,

Brother,

I hope this note of hope and resurgence finds you well. The recent setbacks with the surrender of the war may have been repaired with the death of Lincoln, and we may have reaped more than we have ever known. The "Great Deceiver" Lincoln has found his place in hell, and his successor is known to us. The war is not over. It has only just begun, and our way of life will be advanced. Texas is a new, unrealized frontier capable of bringing new gains and power to our continued fight. I write this letter to revivify the importance and value your continued endeavors are to the cause.

One thing that has definitely set us back is the freedom of the nigger. Fortunately the "Great Deceiver" did not get to enact any of his save-the-nigger programs before he was destroyed by the righteous. Plans are on in effect that will make the black man in the South either a criminal or a slave again, but they will never be free. Just like the cockroaches that they are colored after, they persist and survive to try to come out of the darkness we have put them in. The pamphlet I have enclosed is old writing we thought was suppressed, but it has come back to light. They have become smart to our ways of subjugation and manipulation, even among their own kind. Read it and understand how your enemy views you so that you have no misunderstandings about their intent. The blacks, our enemy, our workforce, our slaves, are evolving, and we must also. Don't let me remind you that the worst thing for the white man is an educated and united black man. If they ever become united, we will lose our free workforce and be forced to pay wages to the animals. That must never happen. Read and learn.

With that said, we must continue to make a concerted effort to breed blacks and Indians.

You have the opportunity to make a new slave. Your mission to create a new slave training and breeding location in the frontier is critical. The demand for slaves has risen since they have been given their freedom, and your supply of slaves to our clandestine slave owners throughout Texas and other bastions of slavery still in the South is critical.

As I mentioned earlier, plans are in effect that will make the free black man in the South a criminal, and the effort to survive in the South as a free nigger interminable. The south will never accept the free nigger!

The south will rise!

kkk

Lieutenant Phoenix folded the letter back up and put it back in the envelope. He continued to read the pamphlet and was amazed by what he read. This was the first writing he had read by a black man. Phoenix found the pamphlet to be enlightening on its own, but when it was added to the missive he had just read, also from the mysterious "kkk," he believed he had insight into how the white man was going to diminish the black man's ability to integrate into American society and fully become American.

Even though Walker had been born a free man, he found the oppression of fellow blacks unbearable. He stated, "America is as much our country as it is yours. Treat us like men, and there is no danger, but we will all live in peace and happiness." He truly believed America belonged to all who had helped build it. He rejected the white assumption in the United States that dark skin was a sign of inferiority and lesser humanity and a former slave. Since he had been born a free man and had access to education similar or better, Walker's Appeal showed what an educated black man was capable of and was meant to instill pride in its black readers and give hope that change would someday come. He even went so far as to urge slaves to rebel en masse and asked, "Had you not rather be killed than to be a slave to a tyrant?"

Having just read the missive from the mysterious "kkk," Phoenix realized that Walker's incendiary rhetoric terrified already-paranoid white masters. The fact that blacks were now free men, coupled with the belief that the country was also theirs, would lead to equal wages, loss of land, retribution, and all sort of privileges every white man was born with. But now they had a race of people willing to work hard and break their backs to earn their living. The missive clearly validated that their indispensable rule was that they would never pay wages to the animals, the blacks. It also showed that their circumcised view of any human beings living in America, other than white, was that they would always be lesser and never have the same rights as whites.

Now their strategy to offset Walker's Appeal and the freedom of slaves was to make every black man who chose to live free in the South a criminal or fear of being a criminal. As criminals, they would be put to the same slave labor they had been subjected to during slavery at no cost, and the government would pay for their incarceration. Any freeman that they arrest inside the South, whenever possible, assign a crime and send them to one of the new slave farms in frontier country of Texas. The new slaves would be quietly distributed to an exclusive list of slave owners in the frontier, where slavers had control of the township.

Phoenix couldn't believe what he had just stumbled across. There was more documentation that identified another slave farm in the Colorado area, which was entrapping local Indians. They were being sold off to mines in the new California area to work for the gold miners. There was a lot of information that would take Phoenix some time to go over. He started packing the information and getting it ready to be sent back to his tent. As he was packing, the question that kept unsettling him was, how were black men going to be citizens in the United States if the whites were going to make criminals out of them?

FIFTY-ONE

Awakening

MARTIN GUTSGELL COULDN'T understand what was happening. One minute he was having the most delightful time with two of his newest slave women, but then everything went black. His head was throbbing on the left side, and his eyes were still foggy. He could smell wood smoke, and as he opened his eyes, the flickering light of a campfire came into view.

He was lying spread eagle on his stomach, with his face turned over his right shoulder. His left and right arms were tied at the wrist and then to pegs in the ground beyond arm's reach. The ropes had been pulled tight at a forty-five-degree angle, so his arms were outstretched. His legs were in the same manner, tied at the ankles and attached to pegs anchored in the ground. He wasn't on dirt but on small rocks, which cut into his soft underside and his groan area. He didn't feel any wounds other than the bruise on his head, so he felt good that he hadn't been hurt further. Maybe there was hope.

Martin could barely opened his eyes, so whoever had captured him wouldn't know he was awake. He was in some sort of cave. The flickering campfire blinked along the walls and made the place warm. In his range of view, Martin could see a hooded individual sitting down in front of the travel bags that had been stored away in his carriage. The man, Martin assumed, was reading something out of Martin's saddlebags and would take it out and put it in another bag. Even in the dim light from the campfire, Martin could see that the man was engrossed in whatever he was reading. He couldn't discern what papers were being moved around, but he was very concerned about the information they contained. There was enough information in the bag for someone to have a nice payday for ransom. Martin hoped this could be of use to him. Maybe if there was something of interest to this man, Martin's chance of surviving this capture increased.

The prisoner, formerly known as "Gutter," was awakening as the last of his travel bags were being packed up. Phoenix could hear him groan a little and get a sense of his surroundings. Phoenix was still in his burlap bag and didn't want Gutter to know who he was. Phoenix had rearranged the documents into four separate packs. He finished his last one and turned his attention to the man who used to abuse him.

Martin could see that the man now focused on him. The man didn't say anything; he just stared. Martin knew that if he waited, the man would eventually talk. The man didn't say anything, didn't even move.

Martin had been sitting and waiting on the main to tell him his demands for the past two hours. The man didn't say anything. Martin started to feel a little uncomfortable; if he wanted to increase his chances of living, he had to hear the demands. So far the man hadn't made any attempt at making demands. Martin decided to speak first and asked the man in the most commanding voice he could make, "What are your demands?"

The words seemed to energize the man, who stood up and walked out of Martin's view. From the noise he was making, it was apparent that he was at the fire; the flames in the cave briefly grew brighter, like the fire source had been moved.

Martin asked again, this time in a louder voice, "What are your demands?"

The man walked back into Martin's field of vision. The first thing he saw working its way up from his feet was the cherry-hot end of an almost sword-like knife. The man still had the same clothes on, but while going up, he now had his hood off. The prominent features of a young to middle-aged nigger were looking back at him. He had a barely grown beard, and his hair was close cut. He looked vaguely familiar, but Martin couldn't remember where he had seen him before.

Martin immediately went into an angry tirade at the nigger. Told him that, whoever the hell he thought he was, if he didn't let him go now, a hanging would be the nicest thing in the world to him. Martin was just winding down when the nigger walked toward him and stood over him. The man stopped a few inches from Martin's body, his right boot in Martin's face.

The man didn't say anything; he just stood there. The man walked away and headed back over to the fire. The light in the room brightened for a brief moment, then went back to normal. The man walked back over to Martin; this time he walked past his head and stopped near his legs. Martin didn't know what to expect; the only sounds in the room were Martin's loud breathing and the fire flickering.

The pain of the hot iron hitting the crack of Martins ass was the most intense pain he had ever felt in his life. The scream he let out almost tore his voice out; the pain was unbearable, and he wanted to faint. The removal of the hot iron may have been worse than the initial burn; the burned and melted skin came off with the hot iron. The room immediately smelled of hot, burning meat. He became dizzy. The man walked away and returned a second time with a newly heated iron. This time there was pain in his groin area and he blacked out.

Martin woke to the pain and horror of what had happened to him. He was now on his back and pinned to the ground. Even as he woke, his body tried to release the urine and feces he had stored, only to have the entryways blocked by the seared and burned skin. He screamed in a hoarse voice and almost passed out again in pain.

On cure the nigger came back into view. Martin didn't know who this man was but realized this man had no intention of taking him hostage. Martin spat at the nigger and told him, "No matter what you do to me, you will always be a nigger." The hot iron inserted into Martin's mouth and was the last thing he remembered this time.

Phoenix initially wanted to kill the "Gutter" by decapitating him. However, he didn't plan on hearing the man's voice again, and his arrogant demand to be let go brought all the horrors back to him.

He was a slave again at one of his master's decadent parties. The slave, Lieutenant Phoenix, was tied to the back of a chair, naked, bent over, and available for any person to try. The "Gutter" had made it a point of coming back more than once because he said the sight of the nigger with his ass up in the air kept arousing him.

He went back to get the iron bar out of the fire in hopes of burning the memory from his mind. The first burn that had sealed the "Gutter's" anal canal almost made Phoenix vomit from the smell. The "Gutter's" scream of agony and distress quickly dissipated all thoughts of Phoenix wanting to vomit; the scream was like a soothing lotion to his mind and soul. Each scream of

"Gutter's" agony erased a memory of Lieutenant Phoenix's agony. In his mind, it was a fair trade; he had to have another.

Later, Lieutenant Phoenix couldn't remember when he stopped burning the "Gutter." He became lost in his own depravity. The "Gutter" had stopped screaming a long time ago; the burns had stopped, and the chopping and cutting with the knife had begun. There were pieces of the "Gutter" everywhere in the cave. Even his guts and been chopped into.

Phoenix looked around and smiled; this was ugly, but he would no longer have to dream about his man again, and if he did, he would dream about his expiration. Phoenix got his stuff together and crawled out of the narrow entrance leading to the cave where the "Gutter" would remain forever. He placed rocks over the entrance and walked away.

FIFTY-TWO

Destroy

LIEUTENANT PHOENIX ARRIVED back at camp, and First Sergeant Amra had everyone ready to attack the slave camp. Amra and Phoenix locked eyes, and Phoenix simply nodded. Phoenix was glad Amra understood what needed to be done. He didn't know whether it was right, but he felt more at balance with himself. He went to his tent to get ready for tonight's attack.

First Sergeant Amra could tell by the look on the lieutenant's face that he had come to terms with whatever monsters were troubling him. Amra smiled wickedly on the inside; it always helped to have the monster, the actual tormentor, as your captive.

The main attack on the slave camp had already commenced before his return. Two of the white soldiers had changed into the clothes of the caravan guard and had taken one of the recently captured caravan wagons back to the slave camp under the guise of needing more water.

Amra briefly remembered his talk with the four white soldiers before their leaving. He had asked them whether they had any reservations with the upcoming battle and the fact that there wasn't going to be any quarter given to the slavers. Amra understood that if they had any trepidation or just felt it was wrong, they should please let him know. He promised his men that he wouldn't hold it against them but would understand. To a man, they were offended that he felt the need to talk to them. They had all been with the unit since the war, had worked side by side with blacks and others, and had killed other white men before. One even joked and said the only difference he could tell between blacks and whites was that blacks could dance better. Amra thanked the men and told them he felt he should discuss this issue with them and wanted them to understand there was nothing he or they couldn't talk about.

The initial assault team had left early in the morning and had already signaled by mirror that they were okay and set. Their primary task was to drug the dog food and get the dogs out of the fight. The guard at the camp fed all the dogs every day around lunchtime; they would add the poison to the dog food to disable them. Amra didn't want to kill the huge animals; he wanted to try to save as many as possible. He even went so far as to tell the men to muzzle the larger animals, but if they became too unruly, they should kill them. He also added that all the puppies had to be saved. If he had to plan around the animals, he figured they were a formidable enough threat, something the unit could possibly embrace. He had a strange concern for the animals and couldn't understand it.

Instead of filling up the wagons and departing, the men would claim they wanted to stay until morning because they had such a long way to go. At night they would take out the front gate guards, signal the unit, and let the rest of the unit in. Three teams would go through the camp and quietly dispatch all the guards. Once completed, the men would load gunpowder and dynamite into the two primary structures. All the guards' bodies would be piled on top of the gunpowder and dynamite. Once everybody was out, the building would be set on fire. By the time the fire reached the ammunition, most of the bodies would be burned to be unrecognizable, and the explosion would incinerate the already-burned bodies. The explosion should also fill the gap in the ground and erase all history of the slave camp.

The attack went off almost as if it were predicted to happen. Phoenix watched the attack from an overwatch position along with Señor Perez. The moon was bright enough in the desert that he could clearly see the shadowed shapes of his men as they made their way to the slave camp. The burlap bags they wore distorted the vision, and they looked like a stream of ghouls just come from the dead.

The most intense moment of the whole attack was getting the gate open and ensuring that the dogs were asleep. There seemed to be a little turmoil earlier when it was time to put the dogs on duty. The men in the wagons had poisoned the dogs, and when it was time to change the guards out, there was some concern about the dogs. The turmoil lasted only a few minutes, and it seemed like the decision was made to have guards without the dogs. The justification seemed to work for the night; the threat of the enormous dogs was resolved. Watching the men move through the camp reminded Phoenix of when they had been in the war, and he and Lieutenant Colonel Vetter would overwatch as the men attacked. He now understood the stress of leadership; these were his men, and their safety was on him.

The shadows moved from the main building and were now making their way down the long narrow path where the men were chained. A few men broke off with the intent of calming the men down. They didn't want them to panic and make noise; they still had one more building to make it to. In front of the main building, a cloth was waved back and forth in front of a lantern to let him know the first building was secure. The attack had been going on for only a few minutes.

Suddenly, a shot rang out at the bottom of the hill, near the intersection. Only a few men had guns; the rest carried edged weapons. There were three more shots, and all else was quiet. Thirty minutes later, another cloth was passed back and forth in front of a lantern in a window in the second building to let him know it had been secured. Hostages and slaves were all released and moved out of the camp to a location about two miles away. The first fire would be set on the second building to let him know all the slaves were out and released. The first building would be lit by First Sergeant Amra, the last man in the unit to leave the camp, to let him know everyone was gone.

Once all the slaves and hostages were evacuated, the men would go through the camp, take weapons and knives, and make sure the farm animals were herded out. Nothing was left to waste, and anything they kept was considered a present from the slavers.

The whole attack, including stripping the place of anything of use, took just over four hours. The sun would rise in another two hours. The first explosion when it came was huge and lit up the predawn night. Additional ordnance found in the camp was added to the two buildings. The explosion ripped apart the side of the mountain and covered up the areas where the children and women had been enclosed. The second explosion was even more impressive; the front gate of the camp blew out about fifty feet. The destruction was total; there was no indication other than a large burned-out piece of the wooden gate and a plume of smoke.

Phoenix smiled; only he knew how the loss of this slave facility set the rebels back on their long-range plans. There were other locations he knew about. What should they do about those? Would Lieutenant Colonel Vetter support going after these people, or would he consider it someone else's business? The more he thought about it, the more he asked himself, *Who will deal with these people?* The government was in a state of rebuilding; according to the missive, they were already incorporating laws and measures to keep the black man a slave. The more he thought about it, the more he realized he was probably the only black man to ever be witness to the information he contained.

He wrote a brief letter to Lieutenant Colonel Vetter, explaining the night's activities. He decided not to mention the missive he had found in the letter; it would be better if information like this was shared face-to-face. His gut told him to keep this matter as secret as possible. He would get Corporal Charl to deliver the letter in the morning. He sat back; it had been a long night, and he had a lot to think about.

FIFTY-THREE

Hostages?

IT HAD BEEN two days since the attack; the first day was primarily about safely moving the former hostages or slaves away from the area. They moved them back to the original staging area. Since the battle, Phoenix had been informed of a small group of Indians being escorted into the camp from Fort Quitman. A small detachment had escorted the Rarámuri tribesmen from Fort Quitman after delivering the initial message. The speaker for the Rarámuri, Tepor, informed Phoenix that he believed some of the former hostages could be Rarámuri tribesmen. It was late, and Phoenix knew it would be hard to discern some of the faces in the dark. He explained this to Tepor and told his people to get something to eat and rest after their long journey. He told Tepor he knew he was excited to see his tribesmen and was glad he had come to be here for his people, but they were safe for the night and resting. He also informed them that they were free to go through all the rescued hostages in the morning to find their people. Tepor explained that he understood and thanked Lieutenant Phoenix for everything they had done. Lieutenant Phoenix told him it was their duty and that he was glad he could help free people who were being enslaved.

First Sergeant Amra watched from a distance as Señor Perez was reunited with his daughter. It was a bittersweet reunion; her tender age of nine years old hadn't saved her from regular sexual abuse by the men in the slave camp. Amra had seen the blank look on her face when she first saw her father as he picked her up and hugged her; the girl had been severely traumatized. Amra had seen this before and knew the only cures were time and activity to fill up her young mind with better images and memories. It took her a while before she recognized who he was; even then, she still acted numb to everything around her. It would take her a while to get over the shock she had been through. Amra noted that she still held the knife he had given her upon her rescue. That brought a small smile to his face; maybe she would get through this and be stronger for the experience. The night he had rescued her still played over and over in his mind.

He had been the first person in the area to rescue the children. One of the guards had just returned from one of his checks and was leaning against a side wall with his back to Amra. Amra silently entered the cavern and could hear a little girl crying a few feet away. The "sssssh" was the only alert the unsuspecting man had as the khopesh swept his head completely off. The body dropped, and the sound of whatever metal he had on made the young girl immediately go quiet. The killing was swift and violent; it had all the anger and frustration of not being able to help sooner by releasing them all at once.

The sound of the falling torso also alerted the other guard, who had been sitting by the fire. Before he could even rise, Amra closed the distance and had the khopesh at his throat. Through the burlap bag over his head, he told the guard not to move and to put his hands where he could see them. His men were gathering the other children. The girl who had been crying started screaming when she saw the men with the burlap bags over their heads. Amra gave custody of the guard to one of his men and walked over to the little girl. He could imagine how the burlap bags over their heads would scare a young child. He took off the bag over his head and gently wiped the blood off her face. The girl looked at his exposed face and screamed again. He smiled, his white teeth against his dark skin glowing in the darkness. He didn't know whether taking the bag off scared her or the sight of his black face, but she started screaming more.

The sight of his teeth seemed to settle her down just a bit. In the darkness, he couldn't tell her nationality. Amra began to rock the little girl in his arms. He also took out a small dagger and handed it to the girl, hilt first. The scared girl stopped crying at the sight of the dagger and just stared at it. Amra put it in his palm and handed it to her. She put her small hand around the hilt and quickly pulled it away. Amra continued to rock and simply watched as she looked at him to decide what to do. After a few minutes of her not doing anything and seeming to get more comfortable in his arms, Amra looked at his men and started to move. As he walked out of the room with the girl in his arms, he could hear a *thunk* sound, like a meat cleaver chopping meat, in the background and what seemed like thrashing. Then all was silent. The guards who were part of this camp had decided their fate.

Seeing her father and hearing his voice brought some light to her abused eyes but not much. Amra didn't get a chance to talk to Señor Lopez, but due to the brief conversations he had with the man, he felt he was a good man. The hurt, pain, and anger Amra saw in his face now would change him. He was facing the plight of thousands of slave fathers who could live only in hurt, pain, and anger as they realized there wasn't a damn thing they could do to relieve their family member's hurt and pain as a result of constant abuse.

He knew he had children, but he didn't know any of them. He had been used as a breeder and hadn't gotten the opportunity to even see his children. It hurt him all the time that, even as big and strong as he was, there was nothing he could do to save his kids, let alone find them. As a man, this made him feel helpless, something no father should have to feel. Amra had seen young slave women with the same look and knew that only time and care could heal the wounds she had gained. Amra couldn't help but wonder what the lack of fatherhood for black men would do to the black family over time. It couldn't be a good thing when men could no longer look forward to being fathers and women viewed birth as a tool to get out of slavery. What would be the long-term impact? Amra watched a little while longer, glad that he at least could help this family see a better day.

Lieutenant Phoenix was awakened by the bright light that entered through the opening of his canvas tent. His men must have let him sleep. It seemed like it was late morning, not the usual predawn darkness he was usually greeted with. Corporal Charl informed him that he had some men and women from the hostage group who wanted to talk to him and that the Rarámuri had been out since first light, looking for their people.

Corporal Charl had become Lieutenant Phoenix's most trusted confidant after First Sergeant Amra and Sergeant First Class Hall. His growth as a soldier was phenomenal, and Lieutenant Phoenix considered him prime officer material. He was a quick study in everything he had been exposed to, from horse riding, shooting, and scouting. He was on his way to doing it all and always wanted more. Charl had had no education or training before being brought to the unit. He had escaped being a slave with the help of Sergeant First Class Hall, whose slave name was

Fieldhand. Corporal Charl knew only the life of being a slave and now the life of being a soldier. Charl had been incorporated in the unit as a messenger; he had attended all Lieutenant Phoenix's reading classes. He was an excellent rider and had quickly picked up on scouting skills.

Phoenix had hated to send him back with the initial message because Corporal Charl had missed the entire battle. Phoenix understood that playing a soldier and being a soldier were two different things; some men didn't handle the stress of combat well, and Corporal Charl hadn't killed a man yet. Phoenix hoped he would never have to, but killing was a soldier's only reality, and in combat, killing was the one thing that would save a soldier's life. Phoenix didn't think it would be a problem for Charl, but it was always good to get more perspective on his abilities. Combat and stress are the quickest ways to get a good bearing on his abilities to lead.

Phoenix came out of his thoughts and told Corporal Charl to get some rest but to be prepared to leave shortly; he had a return message to deliver. Corporal Charl saluted and departed. Now Lieutenant Phoenix had to meet with some of the rescued hostages and check on the tribesmen.

Near the main campfire, he met up with Señor Perez. He had a very solemn look on his face; he looked at Lieutenant Phoenix and mouthed, "Thank you." Phoenix couldn't begin to understand what the man was going through. His only child, though alive, was in an almost comatose state, and there was no guarantee she would come out of it. Phoenix simply nodded at him, and Señor Perez told him two women in the group were from Spanish nobility. They had been at the monastery as a waypoint for their trip back to Spain. The older woman, Señorita Gomez, was the grandmother, and the younger girl, Wendy, was her granddaughter. The mother had been raped and beat to death for her violent refusal at being raped all the time. He stated that the mother had killed two of the prison guards before her death. Señor Perez informed Phoenix that the two women wanted to thank the Americans for their rescue and desired to know what was going to happen to them.

Phoenix couldn't say for sure; he knew only the next step, which was to get the people out of the area and back to Fort Quitman as soon as possible. After they returned to Fort Quitman, they were originally going to be given over to the padre and the mining team who had first asked for their rescue. However, since that request, new information had been acquired that questioned the motives of the padres. Señor Perez relayed all this information to the two women, who nodded at everything he said.

Lieutenant Phoenix also added that they were free to do whatever they liked. They were free women, and he didn't want them to think they had traded one bad situation for another. He told them it was probably in their best interest to stay with them until Fort Quitman, and they could seek assistance from either government or however they saw fit.

Señor Perez relayed the additional information, and Phoenix watched the reaction on the women's faces. They nodded and smiled at the information Señor Perez was giving them. They responded to Señor Perez in Spanish. Señor Perez translated and stated that the women were grateful and thanked the lieutenant for his kindness. He also said, smiling, that they had heard that all black men were savages, but the actions of the unit had made them understand that to be a lie. She said the Lieutenant and the men were the most civilized soldiers they had ever seen in their lives and that they were a true credit to the black men. Phoenix didn't know how to respond to that; he just nodded and thanked them. Señor Perez's solemn look broke for a second, and he informed Phoenix that the last part was only for his ears. He told Lieutenant Phoenix only out of respect and because he thought it was something he should know. Phoenix thanked him.

Phoenix then asked Señor Perez about the missing people of Cajoncito and how they were doing. Señor Perez told Phoenix, "Five of the thirty or so people from the village died as hostages. The five dead bodies were supposedly going to be taken back to Cajoncito as the first ransom payment. The men would tell the people of Cajoncito that they had been attacked on the way back and that people had died as a result, which was a lie. The remaining people were happy to be going home, but they would be forever changed for the experience." Phoenix knew that to be a fact.

After meeting with two Spanish Noblewomen and getting their arrangements modified, Phoenix and Señor Perez went to where all the rescued hostages were being kept. They met the Rarámuri tribesmen, who had come to find out whether any of their tribesmen were part of the rescued hostages. Their new chieftain, Tepor, updated Phoenix and said that the Rarámuri had found over forty-five of their tribesmen among the rescued. He also stated that he had opened up his home to other tribesmen in the group as long as they agreed to follow the Rarámuri laws; a majority of the tribesmen had accepted. Tepor even opened up the invitation to other individuals in the group including the rescued black slaves. This was good news to Lieutenant Phoenix. When he asked Tepor why he did it, Tepor told him, "My tribe has been dying for the past ten years. After they started taking our people away, a lot of our old prejudices among our own tribe were cast away when we realized that few remaining tribesmen were all we had. Now I see people who need a tribe. Once again I cast off old prejudices, because I realize again that we are all we have."

Lieutenant Phoenix found his statement both profound and a relief. One of his concerns was how they were going to take care of all these people after they got back. There were over two hundred rescued people of all colors; now some had a place to stay, and they would try to put their lives back together.

Señor Perez, who had been listening to the whole exchange,

was also touched by what Tepor had told Lieutenant Phoenix. He had heard rumors of a tribe of Indians south of Cajoncito, but he had never seen them. He told Tepor and Lieutenant Phoenix that maybe the people of Cajoncito would welcome in some of the former hostages and slaves. He also stated that he could see strength in a unity between the Cajoncito and the Rarámuri tribes. Lieutenant Phoenix let Señor Perez and Tepor finish the conversation. He was sure Lieutenant Colonel Vetter would like to hear the news of a plan to assist the hostages already bearing fruit with minimal military involvement. Phoenix also understood that Lieutenant Colonel Vetter was extremely limited in his ability to assist the former hostages once they crossed the Mexican border. If the leadership among the hostages could figure out their problem, that was a win for the unit.

The day had been long, and Lieutenant Phoenix felt good about everything that had happened. He put together a quick note to Lieutenant Colonel Vetter, leaving out a lot of what had unfolded today but making sure he understood the battle was over and all evidence had been destroyed.

He called in Corporal Charl and told him to get the message only to Lieutenant Colonel Vetter.

The missive he had read earlier as well as the pamphlet still gnawed away at his mind. How could blacks ever feel free to be citizens if they were going to be constantly criminalized for anything they did? It was interesting that in this battle, it was the slavers' own white supremacy attitude that allowed First Lieutenant Phoenix and his men to so easily destroy such a valuable asset to their movement. They didn't think any other man, especially a black man, was a threat to their plans. Even worse, they knew that route they were taking would prevent any dispute as to the legal or moral correctness of what they were doing. If they wrote contradictory and frivolous laws that were enforced only on black people, how could any black man with no education or standing dispute them?

Lieutenant Phoenix knew history and understood that the open confrontation that had recently ended was just the beginning of a war for control of a country and its resources. In their minds, the industry of the South would be reimagined in the West, starting with Texas. With the country in reform after the war and the lawlessness of the frontier, it was the perfect opportunity to establish slave-holding roots. They had also decided to change their mindset on eradicating the Indians; now they would also use them as slaves; they were better suited for the environment. *Well*, Phoenix thought, *the burning slave camp would go a long way to sending a message that their plan wouldn't be as easy as they had thought it would be. The men in the camp and the camp itself wouldn't be a threat to any more people of color ever again.*

FIFTY-FOUR

Seizing the Moment

CAPTAIN MATTHEWS AND his team made it back to the camp almost a half day after Lieutenant Colonel Vetter left to answer the summons from Fort Concho. Lieutenant Colonel Vetter had left a junior captain, Captain Dewalt, in charge of the camp in his absence. Captain Dewalt had joined the army toward the end of the war and was still considered green. He also didn't relish this kind of authority, as evident by how quickly he relinquished control of the camp to Captain Matthews, his senior, as soon as he returned.

Captain Matthews was briefed on what had happened and why Lieutenant Colonel Vetter had left for Fort Concho. Captain Dewalt explained that Lieutenant Colonel Vetter had left the request and attached information in his tent. Matthews eagerly read the request and the attached map. He instantly saw the conflict of interest, with Lieutenant Phoenix and his men possibly entering lands identified on the map. That also explained why Lieutenant

Colonel Vetter had taken off in such haste. This could prove to be a critical error on Lieutenant Colonel Vetter's part if Lieutenant Phoenix and the team caused any loss of life to the civilians in the area. Blacks killing whites, for whatever reason, wouldn't be received well, especially in Texas.

Matthews decided there was nothing he could do to assist Lieutenant Colonel Vetter in this issue; it was his problem to fix. However, he was more than happy to take control of the camp in his absence. It felt good to be in charge. His first order of business was to get a bath and clean up.

Once Matthews was cleaned up, he decided to do a walk around the camp to show the men that even though Lieutenant Colonel Vetter was out, leadership was still in the area. He had chosen to wear not the normal tan-colored shirts the unit normally wore but the original blue army officer's shirt. He didn't know why he did it, but it made him feel superior for it. He felt different from the others; besides, he believed the officers should be able to be distinguished in a crowd of soldiers, especially among black troops. The men seemed to take kindly to his presence. This was the first time Matthews had been in charge of the camp, and the sense of power was exhilarating. He had to admit the black troops were very good at being soldiers, but Matthews questioned whether they should have weapons on them all the time. He had seen the men in action and knew them to be extremely efficient.

He spent the whole day in the camp, making his presence known to everyone, providing his opinion on all aspects of camp life. He thought Lieutenant Colonel Vetter spent too much time working among the men, always willing to get down and do some sort of physical labor with them. He believed an officer's place was to provide inspiration through presence and appearance. Getting dirty with the men, in his mind, simply showed the men he was no better than they were. Over time, he believed that familiarity equated to a lack of respect and a failure to exuberantly follow orders. Hell, he had been a soldier and had lost all respect for the officers who tried to befriend the men in the unit they were supposed to order around. If given the chance, he would make sure to provide the example the men needed, particularly the black men, who had only Lieutenant Colonel Vetter as a template for leadership.

Captain Matthews had finished his walk hours earlier and had just eaten dinner, which was brought to him for the first time. It was amazing how something as simple as a servant bringing food to him could be so empowering. He usually didn't eat until all his men had eaten; that was an army rule, regardless of color. It used to be a rule for officers only in white units; when blacks first came to the army, they ate last after all the white soldiers, including officers, had eaten. Lieutenant Colonel Vetter had kept the tradition and added the regardless-of-color stipulation for the officers.

It was getting dark, and the first of the night sentries were getting ready to post. He had set up in Lieutenant Colonel Vetter's sleeping area, making sure not to disturb any of his personal items. He was just settling down in probably the only chair in the camp, a folding field officer's chair from the war. It was simply crafted, the type with wooden legs, a wrought-iron back, and a carpeted tapestry for the seat and back. The carpet portion of the seat had lost some of its color, but other than that, it was in a very good condition. Sitting down reminded him of how little the comforts of a normal life had been deprived for him. The room and bath at the monastery had provided the first time in his life that he had slept in a place of such quality. Most of his life, he had slept on the floor or on beds made of straw or whatever soft material he could find. He seldom, if ever, sat on a chair; he was usually on the floor or some bench.

It was very dark when he was awakened from sleep. He was still in the chair, and a small candle provided dim illumination. There was a loud "Sir, Corporal Charl reports!"

Captain Matthews asked him to come in. A young, black corporal entered and saluted Captain Matthews. He looked as if he had come a long way; he was dirty and breathing hard. When he saw Matthews, he seemed to be taken aback, probably expecting to see Lieutenant Colonel Vetter. Matthews told him to report. The courier informed him that he had a message for only Lieutenant Colonel Vetter from Lieutenant Phoenix.

Matthews seethed inside at the disrespect. Didn't this soldier see him in the seat? He calmed his inner fires; he needed information. He went on to explain the situation to the courier and said that Lieutenant Colonel Vetter had gone to Fort Concho to meet with his commander. He added at the end that Lieutenant Colonel Vetter had put the entire camp into his trust and to inform all people who came back to speak to him like they would Lieutenant Colonel Vetter. He then added, "So if you have a message, please let me know for the sake of the camp and because this is what Lieutenant Colonel Vetter wanted."

The messenger seemed to accept what Matthews had stated and finally handed him a letter. Matthews thanked the messenger and dismissed him, excited to open the letter alone. As soon as the messenger departed, Matthews read the letter from Lieutenant Phoenix.

Captain Matthews finished reading the letter and smiled. If what he had just read was true, Lieutenant Colonel Vetter had given the order for Lieutenant Phoenix to enter an area the state of Texas claimed was forbidden to soldiers. Lieutenant Phoenix had fought and killed whites on the forbidden land. The Texans needed to know that the land was being used as a slave camp. Once Fort Concho found out that Lieutenant Colonel Vetter had given the order, coupled with his Southern background, he would be lucky to get out of this without a jail sentence. The Texans would also want blood because black men had killed white men so indiscriminately.

Captain Matthews thought hard about what his next steps would be. This could be an opportunity to get out of the hot desert, away from the blacks, and get some respect from senior whiter officers. He would take Lieutenant Phoenix's letter as evidence and turn it into the command at Fort Concho, expressing his concern for black soldiers killing innocent white men on forbidden land. With his intimate knowledge of the organization, together with his status as a senior officer at Fort Quitman, he could possibly end up in command of the fort with a promotion. According to Lieutenant Phoenix, there were no witnesses remaining from the slave camp. If he left now, he could get the information to Fort Concho in two days and start the road to a new life and career. He would do it!

FIFTY-FIVE

Fort Concho

FORT CONCHO HAD been built along the banks of the Concho River to protect frontier settlements, patrol and map the vast West Texas region, and quell hostile threats in the area. Lieutenant Colonel Vetter had never been to the fort before and was surprised by the number of buildings that had been constructed. The fort was relatively new, being constructed in 1867, and it most recently housed the Tenth Cavalry, a primarily all-black regiment of infantry and cavalry. There was still a large black presence in the area; Vetter witnessed family homes for blacks en route to the fort.

The current commander at Fort Concho, General "Bill" Spoderly, a former Confederate officer from Texas, had joined the US military after the war. He had commanded Confederate cavalry at the brigade, division, and corps levels. He had even served briefly as a state representative for South Carolina. Many Confederate soldiers had joined the US military under the condition that they could be posted only to the frontiers, and if they fought, it would be only against the natives. Giving him command of black troops to fight Indians had been a very controversial decision; he was sort of in the same position as Lieutenant Colonel Vetter, except General Spoderly had fought for the South and at one time believed in the cause. Unfortunately for the blacks, they were also regulated to the frontier because white men weren't comfortable living among blacks who owned guns. Hell, he would be afraid too after all the things he had heard from his men about their former abuses. He was now glad that he had received the report from Lieutenant Phoenix before he left. He was pulled out of his thoughts when his name was called; he was ushered in to see General Spoderly.

Lieutenant Colonel Vetter's first impression of General Spoderly was that he wasn't a very old man, or he was an old man who was in good shape. He had a slender yet muscular frame; he may have been in some physical sport when younger. He was about five eight, but he had the presence of someone much larger. He was a man who was comfortable in a soldier's role and he exuded the confidence of a military man. He wore his Union uniform like he had been born to it; he looked like a soldier, and Lieutenant Colonel Vetter instantly respected him.

There were two other men in the room with him, civilians by their garb. Both were seated together on a small couch in the office. One was of middle age, very portly, and balding on top. He seemed very uncomfortable on the sofa. He kept wiping his forehead with a napkin. The other was older, gray haired, tall, and lean. He could have been a former soldier. He wore spectacles and had the look of a predatory bird. Vetter instantly disliked the man; he felt a threat in him.

Lieutenant Colonel Vetter saluted and reported. General Spoderly asked Vetter to sit in a chair opposite the two men. Both groups were situated in front of General Spoderly's desk, he sat in a large, light-wood, ornate chair with a rich, dark-blue cover. Vetter thought it was the chair for a king with all the carvings.

General Spoderly's first thought of Lieutenant Colonel Vetter as he walked into the room was of no consequence. Lieutenant Colonel Vetter was average size, about five nine. He was a little stout but not fat. He carried his weight well. His eyes were between green and blue, and when he looked back at General Spoderly, there was a keen intelligence there. His light-red hair was short, and his face was clean shaven. He couldn't have been older than thirty-five, if that old. General Spoderly had read his file and knew he had been born and raised in the South but had chosen the North when the war came. He understood why such a bright officer had gotten placed with the blacks and eventually the frontier. His file claimed that his unit had been overly effective in guerilla warfare and had almost become a legend among other black troops. Lieutenant Colonel Vetter's unit history and mission had never been publicized, but soldiers had their own lines of communication. As a leader of black troops himself, he had to be watchful of this man's popularity among his troops.

He personally didn't care whether the blacks liked him as long as they got the job done and stayed away from him. Even though they had proved in the war that they were more than animals, they still weren't white and should never have the freedoms of white people. No matter how smart or great they thought they were, America would give its bounty only to whites, the ones who had fought and died for it. His recent collaboration with the new slave holder's society had been very lucrative so far. All the natives—Mexicans and blacks—who had been captured or found were tried for crimes and sent to prison, the slave camp. They were then sold to underground slave plantations throughout the South. Slaves were also still being smuggled in through Houston; his white soldiers had the distinct charge of escorting them to the slave camps. As long as he focused his blacks on the north and the

Indians, they could develop a new South in the Texas area and maybe farther. If not, they could keep the secret and have their own piece of heaven.

Spoderly drew his thoughts to the present and said to Lieutenant Colonel Vetter, "Glad to see you made hit here so quickly. Did you have enough time to take in the information in the letter?" His voice sounded like a mix of English and Southern drawl, very distinct.

Vetter nodded. "I came as soon as possible, and I wanted to ensure there are not conflicts between my men and any civilians. I also believe good coordination between civilian and military leadership is critical, considering the makeup of our men."

General Spoderly was impressed; Vetter was very confident in his words and spoke matter-of-factly.

Like lions scenting another lion in their territory, the tall, lean gentleman introduced himself as Mr. Jasso and also thanked Lieutenant Colonel Vetter for his quick response to the summons. He also followed that it was great to meet a soldier who was so keen on following orders without haste and understood the need for cooperation in the complex dealings with civilians.

Vetter could already tell Mr. Jasso was trying to establish his authority in the room, which he had already figured out by the "summons." This amused Vetter inwardly at the choice of words. The military gave orders, and civilians got a summons, so who was in charge was established early. He thanked Mr. Jasso for the kind words and continued to watch his supervisor, Brigadier General Spoderly.

Everything was interrupted by a knock on the door and the sound of the door opening. Immediately, Brigadier General Sprodel and Mr. Jasso stood up. Lieutenant Colonel Vetter's back was to the door, and he couldn't see who entered the room, but he also stood out of deference for the unknown person, who demanded the respect of both of these men. He turned around to see who had entered and almost had all the air knocked out of him; he was so surprised by the sight of the individuals who walked into the room. In all his journeys, he had seldom experienced things that surprised him more than the surprise in front of him.

Standing in front of him were the two people who were at both ends of the spectrum in his life. One was his father, the man he hadn't seen since his departure to West Point and who had disowned him when he found out his only son had decided to support the North rather than come home and serve the South. The second was Fleur, the only woman he had ever thought about enough to consider being his wife. The sight of both of them here in the frontier, thousands of miles away from home, caused all kinds of questions to come to mind, but they were lost in his emotion and happiness.

He ran toward Fleur first and picked her up in a big hug. She laughed and said, "Oh, Rob, it is so good to see you again. I couldn't believe it when your father mentioned he was coming to surprise you." Fleur winked at Vetter so only he could see and smiled at him. He nodded and put her down so he could face his father.

Holding Fleur's hand, he faced his father and simply said, "Father."

Mr. Robert Lee Vetter Sr. looked at his son as only a father could. Vetter Jr. was touched by the genuine concern and love he saw in his father's eyes; the look melted away some of the hardness in his soul toward his father. Vetter Jr. understood that for his father to continue to survive and do business in the South, he had to do something significant to keep the trust in the South. Publicly disowning his son was the exact type of statement he needed to make to ensure the Southerners that he wasn't a threat to them because of his son's transgressions. Even after disowning his son, Vetter Sr. was still distrusted but tolerated in the business community. Over time the issue with his son had been put behind him like he didn't even have a son. Seeing him now with Fleur was something he could never have dreamed of, but even in his happiness, a small part of him warned, "Beware."

His glance and thoughts about his father must have lasted only a few seconds. In that time, Fleur cleared the distance between them and was in his arms. The sensation of holding her and smelling her overwhelmed all his senses; there wasn't much he could remember after that.

The rest of the evening flew by in Lieutenant Colonel Vetter's mind. Seeing Fleur and his father had taken him out of his military mindset and unhinged him. Every warning sign in his body asked, *Why?*

Reuniting with his father had been a wonderful thing. There was no need to go back to old issues and open old wounds. Vetter Sr. had healed years of misunderstanding and hurt by simply saying, "Even the best dads make mistakes, but there is no mistaking the love a father has for his children." Just like that, the storm in a son's heart was calmed in the waves of a father's love.

Vetter Jr, his father, and Fleur talked long into the night. At some point during the family reunion, General Sprodel and Mr. Jasso departed with promises to talk first thing in the morning. Drinks and food were brought in, and Vetter Sr. explained the journey and how they had come to be on the frontier. The first thing that seemed to stand out was that the meeting with Vetter Jr. wasn't happenstance. Right after his assignment to the frontier, his father had relocated all family business ventures to Galveston, Texas, which seemed like a new opportunity to establish business after the war. His father had no problem taking the so-called Ironclad Test Oath, which required him to pledge his loyalty to the United States, abolish slavery, and declare that secession from the Union had been illegal because he didn't deal in slaves. He said he had owned them only because, at the time, doing so was legal. Mr. Jasso had recently invited him to Fort Concho to look at establishing trade routes from Galveston to the fort. He had also been informed that they had invited his son to the meeting to discuss operations in the Fort Concho area. His father was excited to get a chance to be with his son again and work with him.

Fleur had agreed to assist his mother in setting up the new household in Galveston and had jumped at the opportunity to see Vetter Jr. again. Fleur explained that his mother would also have come, but her health wasn't good enough to travel the hard desert roads of Texas. She sent her love and said he should come to see her as soon as possible.

He hadn't seen his mother since his send-off to West Point. After his decision to support the Union, he hadn't been allowed to return home. She had sent him letters throughout his time at West Point, but they had stopped almost immediately after the war started. Any attempted contact with their "Union soldier son" would have been viewed as treason from a rebel's point of view and could have resulted in a loss of business and their way of life. As the only child, he had understood that his actions had a huge impact on his mother, who faced the possibility of never seeing her son again. Just to hear she was alive and doing well settled his heart immensely. This was definitely a reunion he hadn't expected, but he loved every second of it.

They talked long into the night. A little after midnight, a servant came and showed them to their rooms. The rooms were small soldier barracks converted with small furniture to make the place look more like a civilian hotel. The rooms were very sparse but considered luxurious in the frontier. There was a small porcelain basin and washstand for personal grooming. He washed up and lay down, drained both physically from the long ride and mentally from the family reunion. He fell asleep with Fleur on his mind.

It was still dark when one of his men came to wake him. He

had a standing order with the small contingent of men he had come with to be awoken if he wasn't located with them. That ensured that they were okay and that he had a chance to check on them. Even though he was considered among his own, something unsettled him; until he could make the feeling go away, he felt it prudent to be cautious. After all, never in a million years would he had expected his father and Fleur to be here.

The visit didn't appear normal or by chance; it had been planned. Why? He had the feeling that he would find out today; all the players had been set. As a precaution, he told Corporal Charl to change the contact time to every six hours instead of once a day. That meant that if he didn't get in touch with his men or if they weren't allowed to get in touch with him, a man was to return to Fort Quitman and let them know something was wrong.

He had just finished talking to Corporal Charl when a runner came and notified him that Brigadier General Sprodel had requested his presence in the raising of the flag. Lieutenant Colonel Vetter hurriedly made his way to the main building of the fort, where the garrison flag would be located. When he arrived, just about every soldier in the fort was neatly lined up in the parade field in front of the fort headquarters. Every man was in uniform and facing forward. The infantry were in front of the formation, and the cavalry were in the back.

Brigadier General Sprodel and Mr. Jasso were located on a small platform in front of the building. The color guard hadn't arrived yet, so Vetter had a few more minutes before the morning ceremony started. He made it to the platform and saluted Brigadier General Sprodel, who saluted back. Vetter nodded to Mr. Jasso, who seemed not even to acknowledge him. He didn't have time to think about his lack of response because the bugle started playing "To the Colors" as the US flag was slowly raised.

Lieutenant Colonel Vetter wasn't looking at the slowly-rising flag but at the two-hundred-plus men facing the platform. All the men except the officers were black, every single one. As the flag was raised, each hand was held up in salute, honoring the flag of the country that had made them slaves but had also given them freedom. He couldn't even begin to understand what these men had been through and that they could be here, honoring the same flag that had tortured them for so long. Where were the anger and hate normally associated with such abuse? Had the white man succeeded in breaking the souls of a whole race of people? Yes, they had gotten a chance to fight to gain their freedom and get the ultimate revenge. The Southern way of living was gone. The more Vetter thought about it, the genius of the whole situation revealed itself.

By offering the black man his freedom, something the white man knew to be inalienable, he had offered up nothing. However, he had gained the undying loyalty of a whole race of people. Like offering a starving dog food, you get his loyalty for life. Also, with no programs in place to assist the black man in his newly gained freedom, the only people who could help them move forward were their slavers. Genius!

The faces that looked toward the flag were full of hope. They had gone from being slaves to being men of purpose and honor by serving the country that had freed them. What would be the impact of arming the former slaves, something Vetter couldn't remember ever occurring in history? These men were now fighting and training, while the rest of the country was recovering from the massive damage of the war. They were learning to fight a type of war the conventional army had just started to grasp toward the end of the war, guerrilla warfare. What would be the long-term effect of that? These thoughts passed through his mind as the bugle played. The silence brought him out of his introspection.

Brigadier General Sprodel saluted the troops, turned around, and walked off the stage, followed by Mr. Jasso. Lieutenant Colonel Vetter followed.

Corporal Charl had followed Lieutenant Colonel Vetter when he found out Captain Matthews had hastily departed the same night. He had given him the letter from Lieutenant Phoenix. Corporal Charl's messenger title had ensured that he be placed with the messengers and not with the small team that had departed with Lieutenant Colonel Vetter. They were so used to seeing messengers coming in and out at all hours that they didn't even ask what fort he was from. He was put in the messenger quarters because they were always supposed to be ready to ride at a moment's notice. There were other messengers from a few other forts and smaller camps here with him. They were from places he had never heard of before, like Fort McKavette, Fort Griffen, and Fort Mason. Two of them were black, and one was white. The white messenger didn't like the fact that he was in a room with three black soldiers, and has asked one of the sergeants if he could be moved to the other white soldiers.

Once that bit of drama was over, the other two black messengers started to talk. The other two messengers were named Privates Poole and Evans. Both had arrived a day before Charl's arrival. They asked a lot of questions about duty at Fort Quitman and answered a lot of questions for Charl. It was quickly evident that life in the military units for black men was completely different from post to post.

Private Evans was on duty at Fort Griffen, and he claimed that all they did was hunt Indians. He claimed the white officers kept the black men in the field, hunting Indians, so they didn't have to directly deal with them. Private Evans claimed that was a good thing, because the men had learned to love their freedom in the wild and had even come to a respectful agreement with the Indians to stay away from the white settlers. They wouldn't hunt and kill them like their leaders wanted them to. Private Poole was at Fort McKavette, and he claimed that his units also had to hunt Indians but also deal with the local white people, who didn't want anything to do with the blacks and often went after the black soldiers. They wanted the blacks to protect them from the Indians but didn't like the idea of armed black men. When in town, the blacks had to lock up their weapons in the arms room; the white men targeted the unarmed black men to "keep them in their place." Private Poole said eight black soldiers had been missing, and three had been found hanged.

Corporal Charl couldn't believe what he was hearing. He told them about his duty at Fort Quitman, that they had a black officer, Lieutenant Phoenix, and that they got along with the whites. He told them that they were building places for the families and that everybody in the fort was required to learn weapons and take part in the fort's protection. Private Poole asked who had given Lieutenant Phoenix his name; he had never heard a name like that before. Charl told them Lieutenant Phoenix had chosen that name when he was freed. That news seemed to rock both men back on their toes. When Charl told them the rest of the story of how Lieutenant Colonel Vetter had the men pick their free names, they claimed he was lying. They said no white man had any time to take on letting black men choose names. They claimed they had been told to take the names of their former masters. Now Charl was surprised. Nobody had questioned the situation; when they were told to do so, they just did.

They had been talking when a loud commotion could be heard in the camp. There were a lot of men yelling outside. Everybody in the room froze to hear what was going on. Charl heard some man yell, "Put your weapons down." Charl and the other messengers approached the window to see what was going on. Charl heard voices and thought he recognized one of them. The same man yelled again, and Charl realized it was Captain Matthews, who was talking to the men who had come with Lieutenant Colonel Vetter. Charl thought to go and see what was going on but thought better of it; yet he wanted to see what was happening.

The men who had come with Lieutenant Colonel Vetter were all black soldiers; they came out of the small barracks area with their hands up, and all-white soldiers from the fort immediately arrested them. Captain Matthews ordered the men handcuffed and hurried away. Charl couldn't believe what he was seeing.

Lieutenant Colonel Vetter had been sitting and talking pleasantries with Mr. Jasso, while they waited for Brigadier General Sprodel. Mr. Jasso's strong Southern accent was something Vetter wasn't used to. The drawl almost sounded lazy and in some circles could be perceived as dumb or stupid. Vetter knew not to get lulled into complacency by the easy-sounding drawl.

Mr. Jasso had decided to talk to Lieutenant Colonel Vetter by himself, without Brigadier General Sprodel in the room. Jasso could tell Lieutenant Colonel Vetter was still in a state of dismay at seeing his father and his young female friend. He hadn't expected that, which was what Mr. Jasso had wanted. Jasso wanted him to feel off guard before bringing him into their plans.

They had started something great in Texas, something that could be bigger than the rebellion ever had been. They didn't need their plans jeopardized by a young, traitorous turncoat Southerner who had turned his back on his family and tradition for the nigger-loving North. Mr. Jasso was the one who had thought of using Mr. Vetter Sr. as leverage against the boy in case he didn't want to join the cause. The girl had been totally unexpected but an extra bonus. She would provide a different type of stress the young man had to consider. Mr. Jasso's plan of investing Vetter Sr. in the financial future of the new cause would put his son in a very precarious position if he decided not to go along with it. His son risked destroying his father's business if he went against it.

Mr. Jasso had thought about offering Vetter Jr a drink, but his research into the young man's background showed he was a dutiful soldier, if nothing else. There wasn't much information he had gleaned on his military career other than he had led black troops. Jasso had figured out that his background from the South had been a serious issue for the Northern army; the young man exuded confidence and control. He needed to be in front of troops. Even with everything that had just transpired, Jasso could still see some trepidation in Vetter Jr's eyes. Good; he was as good as he had assessed. Jasso was personally tired of men falling at his every word. Having someone in front of him who wasn't bowed by his position was a little refreshing—but only for a quick second; his mission to get this man under his foot was his primary task right now, and what he didn't need was resistance.

Mr. Jasso was just about to start in on Lieutenant Colonel Vetter when the door opened and Brigadier General Sprodel entered, followed by a blond-haired captain Jasso had never seen. Behind them were four armed soldiers, all white. Brigadier General Sprodel pointed at Lieutenant Colonel Vetter and told the men to arrest him. Jasso was stunned. What had happened to force this?

Lieutenant Colonel Vetter was still sitting and turned around to see who had entered. He was also surprised to see Brigadier General Sprodel; he had been told they would talk after he had his discussion with Mr. Jasso. When Brigadier General Sprodel pointed at him and told his men to arrest him, he was dumbfounded and didn't know what to do. Before he knew what was happening, the soldiers had him in cuffs. Now that he was secure, he was put back in the chair to face Brigadier General Sprodel.

Brigadier General Sprodel was furious with the information he had just been fed. The young captain, Captain Matthews, had just ridden overnight to inform him of a great crime committed by the black soldiers under Lieutenant Colonel Vetter's command. The blacks had destroyed and killed all the white men at what was described as a slave camp. The location was in one of the areas listed as off limits to the military sent to Lieutenant Colonel Vetter. Apparently, the men had been sent before Lieutenant

Colonel Vetter receiving the letter, and the slaughter of the white men wasn't supposed to be known to anyone but Vetter and his lieutenant.

All the slaves had been released and headed back to Fort Quitman. Brigadier General Sprodel knew Mr. Jasso would want blood upon hearing the news. He had to act fast, arresting Lieutenant Colonel Vetter and trying him and his men for the murder of the white "families." This move would get rid of the Lieutenant Colonel Vetter problem and put that part of Texas under his control. In fact, he would promote the young captain who had shown such promise and put him in charge of Fort Quitman. He would then have someone loyal to him there.

As he had expected, Mr. Jasso was livid upon hearing of the loss of the second biggest camp. He wanted to hang Lieutenant Colonel Vetter on the spot in front of the men for treason. Brigadier General Sprodel replied that this wouldn't be a good idea with his family on location. Mr. Jasso said to hang them; as far as he was concerned, the whole lot of them needed to die. Cooler minds prevailed, and Lieutenant Colonel Vetter was secreted away to a jail cell and would be under lock and key until they had time to get rid of him. His family would be told he had to handle an emergency with his men and had to depart before sunrise. Keeping his family in the dark would keep leverage over Lieutenant Colonel Vetter. Mr. Jasso's main concern was getting back all the slaves they had lost. This issue would cause a backlog in orders they had to fill for slaves if they didn't get them back. Mr. Jasso also added that the soldiers who had killed these white men needed to be brought in as treasonous. They had to pay for killing white men, right or wrong.

With all Lieutenant Colonel Vetter's men captured and secured, Brigadier General Sprodel called all his men to an emergency meeting and informed them of the unprovoked and inexcusable slaughter of a prison compound (and the guards involved) by the soldiers at Fort Quitman. Brigadier General Sprodel gave the order that all the black soldiers involved in the attack on innocent civilians be arrested and brought back to Fort Concho for trial. An expedition would leave in two days to arrest these men and secure the criminals they had released. Newly promoted Colonel Matthews would lead the expedition.

Corporal Charl heard the orders being given and couldn't believe it. The other messenger had said that some soldiers and the commander at Fort Quitman had been arrested for treason, but he knew that was ridiculous. Also, orders had been given to ride to Fort Quitman and capture the platoon responsible for killing innocent people. Preparations were being made to leave in two days to secure all the men responsible for the murders and to install Colonel Matthews as the commander. Corporal Charl knew Lieutenant Phoenix had been given orders to save the hostages. Nobody had mentioned anything about hostages in his or her explanation of the crimes; he or she just called them prisoners. Charl had to get back and warn Lieutenant Phoenix.

Charl waited until things settled down a little. Nobody knew he was from Fort Quitman. He had thought about how he was going to escape and decided he would simply leave like a normal messenger but give the name of a different fort as his destination. It was a really big risk for Charl; if he got caught, he would also be jailed, and all the men who had given him shelter as a young man and knew to be his only family would be facing imprisonment or death. Corporal Charl summoned up as much courage and confidence as he could and walked his horse to the front gate. He was terrified of being caught. There were four guards at the front gate; all of them turned and stared and Charl as he approached. Charl was so scared that he almost urinated on himself. He kept moving forward.

One of the sergeants asked him where he was going, and he

told him he had a message for Fort Griffen. All the men smiled at that and said they felt sorry for him. They had heard it was almost like slave conditions there. Charl simply smiled and said he agreed and would try to bring a message back as soon as he could get away. They laughed at that and wished him well. Charl, dizzy with relief at not being caught, mounted his horse, Sundown, a little ways from the front gate, waved at the soldiers, and took off like a lightning bolt. Lieutenant Phoenix had to be warned of his impending doom.

FIFTY-SIX

Revelation

LIEUTENANT COLONEL VETTER was kept in a cell built into a natural cave on the fort. They had simply dug or blasted out small niches and put bars on them. He was in a cell by himself, which was just big enough for him to lie down. He couldn't stand to full height and had just enough arm room to put his arms out in front of him. The small detachment of men who came with him was located a few feet down a small corridor. He couldn't see them, but he could hear them.

He replayed the confrontation and arrest by General Sprodel over and over again in his head. The only thing Brigadier General Sprodel had accused him of, which he could corroborate, was sending his men into a recently identified forbidden zone. As for the other comments about a prison camp in the area, he wasn't privy to that information and didn't understand the conflict. If the hostages were in the forbidden zone, he was sure Lieutenant Phoenix had gone in to save the hostages.

He heard some commotion at the outer area of the jail. He heard a few "Yes, sirs," and then Captain Matthews entered the hallway where he was locked up. He was the last person Lieutenant Colonel Vetter had expected to see. What did he have to do with everything that was going on?

Captain Matthews answered so many other questions he had never thought to ask. To realize he had an officer in his ranks who would stoop so low as to put the life of his fellow soldiers at risk was a profound disappointment. Lieutenant Colonel Vetter had always treated all soldiers, black or whiter, fair and equal, and he had always given the utmost deference to his subordinates. Up until hearing Captain Matthews's views, he had thought he gave his young officers the respect and courtesy deserving of their rank.

According to Captain Matthews, Vetter had played favoritism with the blacks and hadn't even considered the thoughts of the white officers. The fact that he had made his officers go on patrol with the blacks and not allow each a young soldier to assist in his daily needs was considered disrespectful. In other units, younger black soldiers were given the duty of maintaining officer uniforms and boots, and getting their meals.

Lieutenant Colonel Vetter didn't allow any of that favoritism in his unit; his officers took care of their own gear and ate after the soldiers.

The final straw, according to Captain Matthews, was making the white officers accept the young black Lieutenant Phoenix as a fellow officer. Matthews considered that an insult not only to him but also to the officer corps. Yes, blacks were free, but that didn't mean they were officer material. Matthew believed whites should always hold leadership over the blacks. He believed the choices for America were for white men to make, and those choices were theirs alone.

Lieutenant Colonel Vetter couldn't believe what he was hearing. Had he been around blacks so long that the unbridled hatred in Captain Matthews's voice was alien to him? He had witnessed Captain Matthews work among the blacks with no issue; the only signs of discomfort he had ever seen from Matthews was when he got his uniform dirty. The hate with which he spoke now was totally contradictory to his daily temperament. With one action he had turned his fellow soldiers over to the very people who wished them to be slaves again. According to Matthews, Lieutenant Phoenix had attacked and destroyed a new slave camp the South was building in Texas. He had unwittingly opened a hornets' nest. Mr. Jasso was an apparent leader of the organization, along with General Sprodel, in reestablishing new slavery in the frontier.

Now with Lieutenant Colonel Vetter out of the way, Matthews would be promoted to colonel and be given command over Fort Quitman. They would control Texas, and the new Confederacy would expand westward along the frontier. Without thought or consideration for his subordinate soldiers, he personally hand-carried a letter sent for Vetter, and he gave it to Brigadier General Sprodel. Vetter realized this wasn't about black or white; this was about unbridled recognition and greed. According to Matthews, Mr. Jasso was a major player and managed the movement of all merchandise or slaves.

Now Vetter knew what greed was. The unnatural light in Matthews's eyes as he spoke seemed unreal and out of place. It was as if something had settled over Matthews and was speaking for him. It unnerved Vetter a bit but didn't distract him from what he had just heard. Now aspects of this whole trip started to make sense. The appearance of his father and Fleur hadn't been a coincidence; it was part of a strategic move to get Vetter's cooperation in their scheme. Lieutenant Phoenix and his team had accomplished the mission he had given them; now they were wanted for the murder of innocent civilians, which was a lie.

The smug look on Matthews's face angered Vetter more than

he had ever been in his life. He realized that in his entire life he had never experienced hate before. Even when he had been abused at the academy for his strong Southern drawl, he had never harbored hate for any of his antagonists. Even when he had to take the lives of rebel soldiers, he had never hated them; they were just the enemy. Now, the man before him, Captain Matthews, his own man, had put the lives of the men he had trained and loved in a hangman's noose—all for his own personal gain and glory.

Holding back the seething, molten heat to smash the smug look off Matthews's face, Vetter told Matthews that Matthews had just signed the death warrant for Lieutenant Phoenix and all the men with him. Captain Matthews enlightened Lieutenant Colonel Vetter that Mr. Jasso claimed that eventually all the black soldiers would end up back in chains for the dedicated agents to the new South. Either way, they would serve the whites again.

Vetter didn't say anything more; the more Captain Matthews talked, the more he learned about the insidious plan. It seemed that in the short time Captain Matthews had been with Mr. Jasso and Brigadier General Sprodel, he had been fully vested of their plan. This had been validated when Captain Matthews informed him that he would be promoted to colonel in the morning and depart the next day to take command at Fort Quitman.

For a brief moment, Lieutenant Colonel Vetter felt a slight pang of remorse. Then he thought about his men, particularly Lieutenant Phoenix and First Sergeant Amra; they wouldn't be taken easily. Lieutenant Colonel Vetter hoped they had time to learn of the deceit and betrayal and have a chance to fight for their freedom. He wouldn't want any of his men to ever be slaves again; he had to help find a way to let them know.

Captain Matthews could see the defeat in Lieutenant Colonel Vetter's face when he found out about Matthews's promotion and assumption of command at Fort Quitman. He didn't relish the command at such a frontier fort, but he still held the information about the silver mines in Cajoncito to himself. He wouldn't share that with the Brigadier General Sprodel or Mr. Jasso, and he would use his troops to get control of the whole area. Given time, he would amass enough money to live wherever he wanted, maybe even take over the monastery at Cajoncito and make that into a town where rich Southern families could vacation.

CORPORAL CHARL RODE as fast he could and stopped only to give his horse time to drink water and eat a little. He wished he had two horses but knew that request would have caused more questions upon his departure. Fortunately, Lieutenant Colonel Vetter had posted watches miles from the fort; these had signal flares mounted on poles to be lit when something was afoot. The flares could be seen for miles during the day or night because they were so hot. They usually burned for about thirty minutes. Once a flare burned out, another was automatically lit, allowing for the blazing alert to be seen for up to an hour and a half. They also maintained two additional horses at each location and were current on most information; they would know whether Lieutenant Phoenix had arrived back.

Corporal Charl arrived at the watch spot in the middle of the night. He thought he had been quiet enough to sneak up on the sentry. Only someone familiar with this area would know how to find the lower level of the watch-out spot. He had just turned a corner when he heard the unforgettable sound of a pistol click. He stopped immediately and announced himself. "Messenger Charl, silent night, deadly night."

The tension noticeably dropped, and the sentry stepped out from the left of where Corporal Charl was standing. The password was tribute to the type of guerrilla warfare the unit used. Corporal Charl kept it strictly business with the sentry; the sentry didn't need to know what was coming just yet. Besides, he didn't believe it was his place to start warning soldiers about what was about to happen. He told the soldier he just needed a change of horse and wouldn't be staying till the morning. He had a very important message he needed to deliver back at the camp. As usual, the soldier wanted to know what was going on and whether there was anything he needed to be concerned about. Typical soldiers and gossip.

Corporal Charl assured him that everything was okay; it was just a message about some possible information about another camp. He told the sentry he hadn't read the messages; the gleam in the sentry's eyes dimmed a little at that.

Corporal Charl put together a small bag of food from the stored foods at the sentry point. As he walked down the winding path to where the horses were located, he started small talk with the sentry. Corporal Charl asked whether there was any news of a unit that had gone with Lieutenant Phoenix. The sentry told him that, as of yesterday, they were situated about three days from Fort Quitman. Lieutenant Phoenix had runners go back and forth to get Fort Quitman ready for the large influx of personnel. This was good news to Corporal Charl; his gut told him it was better to inform Lieutenant Phoenix while he was still out. It could get ugly in Fort Quitman if he told him the news there.

Corporal Charl gathered a little food and water, saddled the new horse, and thanked the sentry. He rode off into the dark night, hoping to intercept Lieutenant Phoenix with the dire news.

First Sergeant Amra was glad to almost be back to Fort Quitman. The journey for the last few days had become more difficult with each day. As the former slaves became more used to their newfound freedom, the request and complaints started up. The released men, both the Indians and the blacks, wanted weapons from some of the confiscated weapons for their personal use. First Sergeant Amra strongly forbade this request and told them that after they got to Fort Quitman, they would discuss options then but not before. His size and demeanor cowed most of the men from bringing the issue back up, but it didn't release them from trying to take out their anger on the weakest of the group.

One of the released Indian men tried to abuse one of the Indian women in the camp. Amra had been on his horse, watching from a distance, and the noise from the woman's rebuttal of the man who was trying to grab her made him look in that direction. Amra didn't know the complete story and didn't understand what was being said, but the woman clearly didn't want the man bothering her. After his few attempts to grab the young woman, she eventually tried to walk away from the man, which angered him. He forcibly grabbed the woman by the hair and yanked her back. The Indian was a big man and nearly lifted the smaller woman off the ground. As Amra forced his horse in that direction, the man had apparently decided to beat the woman into submission. Once he pulled her around, he leveled her with a punch, and she fell to the ground. The man stood over her and was about to grab her again when First Sergeant Amra closed the distance and launched himself from his horse at the man. The man never saw Amra coming, being so intent on the small woman in front of him. Amra hit him full on with all his weight.

Amra beat the man to within inches of his life, and the only reason he didn't kill him was because his men pulled him off his horse. Amra was visibly shaken for hours after the incident. He had to get himself together and realize what had just happened.

In his mind, the young woman had represented all the women and men in slavery who had seen abused, including himself. The man had become all the slavers he had wanted to destroy. The molten anger he had subconsciously kept on ice had exploded in a moment when he witnessed the abuse again. He had to admit that he even scared himself.

Fortunately, after that incident, they had no other incidences of abuse, complaints, or infractions. Amra felt bad that he had almost beat the man to death, but to see another former slave take advantage of a slave had been too much. At what point after being at the bottom and abused do you realize that becoming an abuser is not an option? You just perpetuate the hurt and pain, he realized.

Amra went to apologize to the man while he lay on a stretcher in one of the wagons. One of the Indian scouts translated for First Sergeant Amra. The man turned his head and didn't want to hear Amra's apology, but Amra made sure everyone within hearing distance heard him say, "Never again will I tolerate anyone becoming an abuser or anyone being abused while I am alive. If I have to beat the need to abuse another person out of each and every one of you or even kill you, then so be it!" He didn't know whether what he had said was the right thing, but he hoped he would possibly save lives by letting them know where he stood as a leader. The man he had beaten up was lucky that they had stopped him; one or maybe two more punches or kicks, and they would have been attending his funeral. The Indian scout who translated for Amra told him the man wasn't disrespectful, but he was ashamed of what he had done and had turned his head in shame. Amra didn't know why the man felt ashamed but thought that was a good start.

Amra was drawn out of his thoughts by a runner coming to let him know Lieutenant Phoenix had called a halt to the movement and wanted to see First Sergeant Amra immediately.

It was starting to get dark, so he figured he was stopping early on account of that. Whatever the reason, he could use the break.

Lieutenant Phoenix was talking to Corporal Charl when First Sergeant Amra arrived. They both turned to First Sergeant Amra with grim looks. Lieutenant Phoenix looked at First Sergeant Amra and simply said, "Lieutenant Colonel Vetter has been arrested for giving us the order to murder innocent white people, and we are now being hunted down for the murder of those people!"

Of all the things he had expected Lieutenant Phoenix to say, those words weren't it. Lieutenant Phoenix went on to tell him everything Corporal Charl had just reported, and the more he talked, the more dread seemed to set on First Sergeant Amra. If what they said was true, then they could face either being killed or being made slaves again, all based on a lie. Lieutenant Phoenix went on to reveal the missive he had found on the captured caravan master and explained how it was connected. Apparently, the leadership at Fort Concho knew about the slave camp and was upset that the black soldiers had destroyed it. This was knowledge they had gleaned from the turncoat Captain Matthews, who had intercepted Lieutenant Phoenix's update to Lieutenant Colonel Vetter.

First Sergeant Amra couldn't believe what he was hearing. He was actually scared. Their lives were over if they turned themselves in. Based on what Lieutenant Phoenix had just shared, there wasn't right or wrong in this situation. There was no mistake or misunderstanding; this was the elimination of a threat. Lieutenant Phoenix and his team had inadvertently stumbled on a hornet's nest of insidiousness. The plot involved the continued fight for slavery, and now, as black men, they were pawns in the middle.

The three of them sat silent for a moment. The only sound was the sound of the people in the camp setting up for what would have been their last night before heading to Fort Quitman.

Lieutenant Phoenix broke the silence. "We cannot let these people go back into slavery, let alone ourselves!"

First Sergeant Amra responded, "That would mean that we will need to raise arms against our fellow soldier and the United States. We have no one to speak truth to the lies for us."

Lieutenant Phoenix said, "We have the missive. We know their location and know who some of the key players are. If we get this to the right people, they will listen."

Amra admired the lieutenant's optimism and told him so. In the end, they both knew the powers they were fighting against required them to have equally influential and powerful people on their side, those whom black men in the United States just didn't have.

Overnight they had gone from soldiers to outlaws, all based on a lie. They had concluded that the country had just finished fighting the war for blacks, the apparent evil had been destroyed, and they wouldn't have the stomach to investigate this matter any further and risk tension flaring up again. This was the exact reason the new rebellion had decided to head toward Texas and consolidate their power and way of life in the frontier. While the country was recovering, they would secretly continue to maintain the establishment of slavery, keeping slaves both in the more common aspect as chattel and developing new laws to acquire them in a new way, which was as criminals. They would do this in the frontier before the United States recovered and expanded out West. There would be a huge need for human capital in the development of the expansion West. They planned on showing the continued value of slavery by showing it was still needed. They could also bolster their claim on the equality of blacks in a white society by showing how many had become criminals after given their freedom, ignorant and oblivious of the reasons they had been found criminal.

They talked long into the night, Corporal Charl listening

in wonder. He wasn't very smart, but he knew the weight and consequences of what these two men were talking about were very serious. The hairs on the back of his neck stood up, and he didn't know why.

Toward morning, the men decided to go before the men and the former slaves to let them know what was going on and in which direction they felt they needed to take. They all had a vested interest in this matter now, and it was only right that they have the same opportunity to decide their own future.

The noise normally associated with an awakening camp of this size was absent. Everyone—soldier, former slave, Indian, Mexican, black, man, woman, and child—was assembled in a tight circle around one of the captured wagons. Lieutenant Phoenix and First Sergeant Amra had gathered everyone in an emergency meeting. There was definitely tension in the air, a foreboding. There was a slight breeze, more heard than felt. A numbness settled on the crowd.

Lieutenant Phoenix cleared his voice and started to speak; he spoke slowly so the various interpreters in the group could translate what he was saying.

"I call you here to tell you about the news I just heard—news I feel affects each and every one of you and your future." The sound of the interpreters could be heard, followed by a slow rumbling and gradual increase in noise. People were yelling in different languages.

First Sergeant Amra held up his hand, and the noise immediately ceased. The lieutenant continued, "Please do not say anything until I finish telling you everything."

The lieutenant told them about the impending arrest attempt and that the former slaves had been identified as prisoners who needed to be recaptured. He read the missive and told them about the other slave camps that were being started. Speaking primarily to the blacks, both the rescued slaves and the soldiers, he said that being labeled as criminals, even when following an order, fell into the future they had planned for all blacks. He told them he and First Sergeant Amra had agreed that they wouldn't surrender and give up the new freedom they had just gained. Also, even if they did surrender, there was no one to fight for them, with Lieutenant Colonel Vetter also being arrested. This news caused a stir among the soldiers, and they started to talk among themselves; this was the first they had heard about it.

Finally, the lieutenant told them he understood that if people wanted to leave, both soldiers and former slaves, they had about three hours to get their stuff together and go. They needed to start to plan for their survival. He also said they would try to give them as much time as they could to support their getaway by keeping the focus on them as long as they could. But he wanted to warn them that fleeing people would be considered easier prey, and they didn't know who else had been informed of their sudden outlaw status.

Everybody was surprised when Señor Perez stood and said everyone, including the soldiers, would be welcome in Cajoncito, which was in Mexico.

Both Lieutenant Phoenix and First Sergeant Amra looked at each other and smiled. This was an option they hadn't thought of. It would solve the former slave issue, and that relieved a lot of stress for both of them.

First Sergeant Amra called for the scout Chatan, who stepped forward. He had been with the scout Pit on the reconnaissance of Cajoncito. Since neither Lieutenant Phoenix nor First Sergeant Amra had been to Cajoncito, they asked Chatan to share his thoughts and opinions on the idea of moving to Cajoncito.

Chatan told them, primarily the soldiers, about Cajoncito's size and location. Chatan explained that the place was huge enough to house all the people rescued, including soldiers and the few families still at Fort Quitman. This news caused a lot of heads to perk up. Those families were now in danger. He also explained that Cajoncito would be easy to defend given its small unit and its unique location. There was plenty of water in the underground reservoirs, but food was sparse. He went on to explain that its location also made it highly susceptible to artillery fire. The only other escape would be deeper south in Mexico or across the border back into the United States.

The leader of the Rarámuri, Tepor, spoke up and said he could teach them how to survive in the mountains and that there were underground fishing wells all over the mountains.

The Indian man First Sergeant Amra had almost beaten to death stood up and walked forward. Apparently, he was a leader among the Indian tribes; First Sergeant Amra hadn't known that. The man looked at the Indian translator and stated something in the Indian language. The interpreter said, "Chief Two-Axes says that if they are released on their own, the soldiers would find them anyway. They have no guns or weapons to fight back."

First Sergeant Amra was about to respond, but the lieutenant spoke before him. "Thank Señor Perez for your offer, and we hope you will let our families hide in safety in Cajoncito." He looked at the interpreter and said, "We understand your concern, but we cannot leave armed men at our backs and innocent people traveling who would be easily preyed on. We won't leave this country. We are Americans, and our blood has helped build this country. If they don't want to acknowledge us as men, then we must fight to live as men. We choose to stay here and fight for what we have." Looking at the soldiers, talking only to them, he said, "Any who wish to join us must agree to follow us and our direction. We will hold the lives of our brothers in our hands. Decisions have to be planned and made by those willing to make them. You soldiers who wish to leave, please separate yourselves from the others so we know how many we have with us."

First Sergeant Amra pointed to a location to his left of the wagon they were standing on. Eight soldiers out of the eighty-five separated themselves. All of them were white except the three black soldiers. A small silence ensued to see whether anyone else was going to separate themselves. First Sergeant Amra raised his hand, and soldiers with pistols encircled those who had decided not to follow them. First Sergeant Amra said, "Please disarm yourselves, and nothing will happen to you. You will be held until such a time that your information about us is not a threat. Right now, if you were to leave, you have too much information that would be damaging to us. I hope you understand."

Some of the men had already been given insight on what was about to happen, and the first sergeant had planned for this exact moment. The men looked stunned at the sight of the weapons drawn on them, but they knew enough about the first sergeant to know he meant what he said. If they were going to be harmed, the first sergeant wouldn't have gone through this formality. They handed their weapons, butt first, to a soldier who stood at the back of the wagon, ready to receive them.

One white sergeant stopped in front of the wagon and spoke to the first sergeant. "First sergeant, I changed my mind. I figured if you were stupid enough to let us go, knowing what your plans were, then you didn't deserve to be my leader. Now that I know you are smarter than the average, I choose to stay."

Quicker than thought and in one fluid motion, First Sergeant Amra grabbed the khopesh, which had been propped against the wagon seat next to the first sergeant. As if in slow motion, the blade was yanked out with such speed and violence that the scabbard didn't need to be held to release it. For a brief second, a silver blur swooped toward the sergeant who had just spoken; the look of keen intelligence and superiority was still on his face as his head rolled past his chest and hit the floor. The subsequent release of blood from his neck sprayed everywhere.

The left side of Lieutenant Phoenix's tan shirt got a direct hit from the spray of blood. The dramatic scene just witnessed showed in the shock on everyone's face. For everyone who questioned their seriousness and intent, there was no notice.

Once again Chief Two-Axes spoke. "What if we wish to stay and join you and fight?"

Lieutenant Phoenix looked at the first sergeant; this was something they hadn't discussed. First Sergeant Amra immediately responded. "Any who choose to follow us, who isn't a soldier, must swear to follow and do whatever we tell them. They must understand that we will not give them any weapons until we have trained them in our way on how to fight and use them. Until then, you must agree to do and follow the orders we tell you from any of the men we tell you to follow them from."

Chief Two-Axes heard the translation, nodded, and smiled. He responded to the translator. The translator turned to First Sergeant Amra. "Chief Two-Axes says he respects the big black man's leadership and the fact that he protected someone that wasn't from his tribe. Chief Two-Axes was ashamed because it was his responsibility to protect his people, and big man hurt him for not doing his job as chief. Chief says he agrees to follow the big man's rule and wants to know the name of his new tribe."

Lieutenant Phoenix responded to the first sergeant. "We are not a tribe. We are just people made up of different tribes. Whoever agrees to go along with us, regardless of their color or culture, will also be part of the people. For you to join, you need to give up any customs that hurt or demean another and learn to live as one. All of us, women included, will have to learn how to fight. We have fought in wars and know how to fight what will come. Learn from us, and we in turn can learn from you."

He looked directly at the Rarámuri chief, Tepor. "As I mentioned, Cajoncito will be a good place for our people to hide out, but now we have to handle the current problem of possibly killing other soldiers seeking to kill us and rescue our commander, at least to give him a chance to get away. I think from this point on, we will have to be responsible for our own destiny, but we do owe him a lot."

All the soldiers nodded. Lieutenant Colonel Vetter was a good man, and he had made them the lethal force by teaching them there was nothing noble or personal about war. They performed a task to accomplish and a desired goal. To do it, they had to plan to be better and more efficient. Improper planning and inefficiencies cost lives, something Lieutenant Colonel Vetter always valued. They would save him because he was part of them, and they were part of him.

FIFTY-EIGHT
The Good Life

NEWLY PROMOTED COLONEL Matthews sat in his tent with a hot cup of coffee and a stiff shot of bourbon, which Brigadier General Sprodel had given him as a promotion present. They had settled down for the night after another long day of travel.

His men had left Fort Concho and had been on the road for four days. Weather permitting, they would see Fort Quitman in another two to three days. There was no rush; Colonel Matthews had made sure all communication with Fort Quitman was cut off pending his arrival. He didn't want them to have a heads-up that he was coming to take over the fort and arrest Lieutenant Phoenix and the men who had helped them. He had never liked Lieutenant Phoenix and definitely didn't like First Sergeant Amra. Colonel Matthews would be glad when First Sergeant Amra was gone; he was the scariest nigger he had ever met.

Colonel Matthews had joined Lieutenant Colonel Vetter's unit after the war, so he had never had an opportunity to witness or lead the unit in any conflict. Everybody talked about how dangerous the unit was because they fought at night, but that didn't seem to hold much water with Colonel Matthews. They were just trained monkeys anyway. Besides, if they were so great, they wouldn't have been so easily taken out by a twisted truth. Twisted because the men had been ordered to save hostages, which was the truth, but the truth had been twisted into saying they had gone to destroy innocent whites. Every white man's fear was of black men opening up their eyes and seeking revenge for all the abuse put on them. So strong was the fear that the words just had to be spoken to start a panic.

He had been sent with two hundred soldiers. A majority of them were former rebel soldiers who had the mental strength to keep their hatred and disdain for black soldiers to themselves. They were committed to the greater goal of seeing the rebellion survive. They had learned that blacks, fed information a certain way, coupled with giving away small appreciations and freedoms, would even kill their own and think they were doing the race a favor. Colonel Matthews smiled inwardly; the small freedoms they had been given were already their God-given rights. They were just too stupid to see it that way. Colonel Matthews didn't understand how anybody had to ask for freedom. How preposterous was that? *Can I have my freedom?*

The blacks didn't readily understand that by not taking the time to educate themselves in their freedom, they had simply given up one form of slavery for another. Because they were ignorant, they had to depend on the whites to translate and explain everything going on around them. This was obviously shaped in the white man's perspective and experience. It was something totally alien to a population of former slaves.

It was these types of in-depth thoughts and considerations he felt validated his short moment of treachery against his former soldiers and unit. His greatness never would have been realized under the old conditions. At least here, it enabled him to evolve to a place where his great thinking would be appreciated.

Unlike Lieutenant Colonel Vetter's unit, his white soldiers made a clear distinction between the blacks and whites. No black soldier was promoted above the rank of private. The few black men who became promoted to sergeant would last about a week before they disappeared. As a result, the men were happy in the lot they had been given. Even the camp was set up to minimize the exposure of whites to blacks, with whites on one end and blacks on the other.

Before their leaving, Mr. Jasso and Brigadier General Sprodel had come out and told the men they would be involved in correcting a great wrong against the people of Texas. The people of Texas were looking to them to be their protectors and get rid of the threat to them and their families. At this, the men seemed to hold their chests out farther and their heads a little higher. Many were eager to establish themselves at Fort Quitman and get away from the oppressive Fort Concho. Many thought to curry favor with Colonel Matthews, the new commander.

After his little speech, the blacks were ordered to depart and get ready, and Mr. Jasso asked all the whites to remain. After all the blacks departed, Mr. Jasso gave a gold coin to each white man going on the expedition and told them there was a lot more where that came from. He told the men their job was not only to go out and get rid of the men responsible for this atrocity; he needed the blacks to slaughter the blacks. He informed them that they were being paid to create the motivation that would make it so. In jest, he also told them he didn't expect the blacks to do all the killing; he expected the red-blooded white Americans to get their tribute just to make sure the blacks got more. Everybody laughed at that but clearly understood his intent.

That was when Mr. Jasso looked directly at Colonel Matthews and said, "A free, controlled nigger is worth twenty enslaved niggers. The controlled nigger will do anything to save his perceived freedom, which we are giving him. An enslaved nigger will always be focused on escaping." At the time, Captain Matthews just nodded. Inwardly he sighed; he cared only about being in charge and being comfortable.

Mr. Jasso also told Matthews he didn't want any black man used to killing whites to ever live to tell about it. He looked at Matthews to make sure he understood what he meant. Colonel Matthews promised Mr. Jasso that no black involved in the attack would live to tell about it. He sipped his tea and drifted off to sleep with the promise of his future on his mind.

FIFTY-NINE

Unleashed

AFTER CORPORAL CHARL alerted them of their impending arrest and the change of leadership at Fort Quitman, they decided that their best course of action was to attack the force coming to arrest them. They wanted to do this while that force was still on the road; First Sergeant Amra didn't believe they would be expecting any sort of direct confrontation from the black soldiers. He went on to say that the force would expect them to hand over their weapons without a fight and go into custody, because that was what they were being ordered to do. Everyone agreed and immediately started preparing for the ride and possible battle.

The hostages were given to Señor Perez and Chief Two-Axes, who had started to put his heart into being part of the team. They would take the soldiers who had wanted to leave and head to Cajoncito. Lieutenant Phoenix told them to avoid Fort Quitman; he would send word ahead to scouts in that area that their team had permission to pass. Corporal Charl was sent to Fort Quitman to make sure no message of their imminent arrest had made it there and, if so, to leave and warn Lieutenant Phoenix.

With the hostages out of the way and Corporal Charl sent to watch Fort Quitman, Second Lieutenant Phoenix and the rest of the men moved out to engage Colonel Matthews. They had traveled almost three days before the scouts pinpointed their location. So comfortable were Colonel Matthews and his troops in their superiority that they didn't have forward scouts to give them a warning. First Sergeant Amra and the scouts watched Colonel Matthews's force from a distance for a full day and a half before they felt comfortable enough to attack.

Colonel Matthews's white leadership didn't trust the black soldiers with weapons at night, so they had all the blacks who weren't on some type of guard duty lock their weapons in a wagon at night. The black soldiers were also separated in the camp from the white soldiers, which lessened some of Lieutenant Phoenix's stress. Everyone was concerned about killing the unknowing black men, who were ignorant of the white soldiers' true intent. Since they were separated and weaponless, Phoenix felt a lot better about not having to kill any of them.

Before the attack, First Sergeant Amra laid out a plan using a little dirt model with rocks to represent wagons and groups of twigs to represent people. This was the same way Lieutenant Colonel Vetter had taught them to plan a battle. It helped everyone get a good visual of what their part in the battle would be. First Sergeant Amra informed them that they would hold the black soldiers only at gunpoint, but if any of them stepped out of line, they should end their resistance quickly.

Most of the men in Lieutenant Phoenix's unit were veterans, who had fought in the war. They knew war wasn't personal but a means to an end. Anyone who got in the way would be eliminated. It wasn't what they looked for, but it was what they were prepared to do without hesitation. They were proud that they had all lived this long to be free men. They hadn't lived by luck; they had survived because they were ruthless and efficient when they had to be. They didn't care about being honorable once an enemy was identified. They tried to be honorable when the situation allowed, like in the instance of the black soldiers, whom they were trying to avoid killing. It wasn't their fault that these black soldiers were pawns for the rebels' plans. The rebels meant to enslave every black man, woman, and child. Every man and woman who supported this cause, according to First Sergeant Amra, couldn't be trusted to live. The rebels had made a bet that their belief was a fact, that the black man was nothing more than a farm animal. They were willing to put their lives on the line to see their way as the American reality. For the white soldiers in the camp, their true intent and purpose were enough to support a decision to provide no quarter to them.

The events of the past couple of weeks had started to give Lieutenant Phoenix some insight into how a new form of slavery would evolve in America; he realized that the war for slavery was far from over. The missive he had intercepted made one thing clear: freedom for the black man in America would come at a painful cost, and he would never be equal. They had to try to find their place in a country where active participants were trying to manipulate the legal system to keep them facedown in the mud while simultaneously trying to expand and standardize their rebel culture to new parts of America.

Most of the black men had no education or skills to build on. A few had skills that would enable them to make a living, but even then, they would only be able to serve their fellow blacks, if allowed at all. Laws were being put in place that made it illegal for a black man to own a business, making him vulnerable to white violence at any time. Many had already started going back to what they knew, which was farming or sharecropping, which was typically harsh and restrictive. It was designed to keep them in a perpetual state of indebtedness they would never get out of, a new form of slavery. Even in the South, they had to defend themselves from the people they were supposed to protect. Those who tried to lift their heads and assume the same dream as the whites would quickly find them in a noose. They would have to face a country still divided on black equality. A herculean effort would be required to establish their place in American society.

These thoughts passed through his mind as he thought about the things he had to do next. The price of their freedom would have a cost on his soul. First Sergeant Amra had said, "These are soldiers left over from the recent Civil War. They surrendered and gave their allegiance to the US and committed not to bear arms against it. Now they have been exposed as rebels in US Army uniforms, and they are committed to undermining the US from the inside. We can no longer afford to let a known enemy live!"

Lieutenant Phoenix wholeheartedly agreed.

In the distance, eyes watched the movements of Lieutenant Phoenix and his men. They had been following Lieutenant Phoenix and his men since they destroyed the slave camp and rescued all the slaves. Some of their people had been rescued, so they stayed back. It had been hard to follow Lieutenant Phoenix and his men; their scouts were really good, but there was none better at stealth in the desert than the Apache warrior. He still wondered why the black soldiers had killed the white men at the slave camp. Other black soldiers had come and did nothing for the slaves. These soldiers had come to destroy and free the slaves, but they didn't fight like the whites. They fought like the Apache and used the dark; they were as deadly as the Apache.

He had sent his warriors to follow the rescued slaves but told them not to do anything and not to try to reach out to their people unless they left the group. He had separated from his men with two others to follow the black soldiers. He was curious about the soldiers and what they were doing. He had never met any soldiers who were nice to Indians, black or white. Victorio, the last chief of the Apache tribe, would find out more about these "Buffalo Soldiers" before he decided to kill them.

SIXTY

A Painful Way

THE CAPTURE OF Colonel Matthews's first command was relatively simple; they had been confident there were no threats to their numbers. Under normal circumstances, they would have been right, but the first sergeant led a silent attack that didn't see anyone get killed and gained total control of the camp.

Lieutenant Phoenix's attacking party used their now-signature attack uniform, the burlap bags, so their identities were secret. Both First Sergeant Amra and Lieutenant Phoenix entered Colonel Matthews's tent to secure him. He was sleeping in a small field chair with a drink on a small table in front of him. Lieutenant Phoenix had actually liked Captain Matthews, even though he thought is uniform and looks could use some work.

One of the voices said, "Captain Matthews, sit back down. You cannot run, and we have some questions." A rag was stuffed in his mouth, and a bag was placed over his head. Everything went dark.

Now that they had successfully captured Colonel Matthews and disarmed his men, First Sergeant Amra hurried the men farther away from the road and erased all evidence of them being there. Some scouts would come when the sun was up to finish cleaning up what they couldn't see. They still had a few hours until dawn.

First Sergeant Amra took the burlap bag off Colonel Matthews and debated taking the rag out of his mouth before finally succumbing and removing it. Immediately the newly promoted Colonel Matthews screamed in anger, "Lieutenant Phoenix, I know that is you. I'm a colonel now, and you will be hanged for what you are doing if you don't let me go!"

The pain generating from Matthews's right foot was what had brought him out of sleep. The pain was so intense that he screamed before he realized he wasn't alone. He tried to get up, but his foot didn't hold his weight, and the pain intensified when he tried to step on it. "Uggghhh!" he screamed; the tendon in his right foot had been cut. He looked around, and there were two men with burlap bags over their heads. Now added to the excruciating pain was total fear. He knew the men under those bags; he had seen them before.

Another flash of pain, and he fell face-first as his left tendon was cut. In pain he started to relieve himself. He screamed for a few seconds before someone kicked him in the face. He was lifted like a bag of flour by someone he knew had to be First Sergeant Amra; he was the only man big enough to lift him like a bag of rice. Yet he didn't say anything, which didn't bode well. With pain now throbbing in both legs, he was dragged back into the chair he had fallen out of. Just lifting him sent a fresh wave of pain from his cut tendons all the way through his body. "Yaaaaaaaaagggghh!" he screamed. It was a sound from the depths of his soul.

One of the hooded figures stood in front of him and simply said, "Tell me everything."

Colonel Matthews's screams unsettled Lieutenant Phoenix, but they had to know everything that was happening, who was involved, and what their next steps were. After he cut his second tendon, simply applying a little pressure to his ankle area would get him to start talking. The torture lasted for just over two hours, but they had all the information they needed from him. He even told them about the background of all the white soldiers with him and that they had been instructed to get the blacks engaged in the killing of the other blacks. If their plan had been executed, the one-hundred-plus blacks would have been responsible for the eradication of their fellow brothers all because they had fallen under leadership that valued only their obedience or destruction.

Lieutenant Phoenix and First Sergeant Amra put Colonel Matthews back in his chair, picked him up, and took him outside his tent. All Fort Concho's men were on their knees outside his tent; Lieutenant Phoenix had his men posted behind the Fort Concho men, weapons drawn. The white soldiers had been divested of their uniforms and were in their underclothes, if they had any. A few were stark naked.

They placed Colonel Matthews down in front of the tent; he groaned loudly at being put down. The pain caused by the slash to his tendons made him scream, "Mwaaaaaah!" He moaned. All the men stared at him. There was one more thing they needed him to do to make things right.

Both Lieutenant Phoenix and First Sergeant Amra felt it was important to read the missive they had found and have Colonel Matthews relate what he knew to the black soldiers. They both felt it was important that the black soldiers understand that they were doing this because they had no choice. The men listened to the missive, and First Sergeant Amra filled them in on what he had witnessed at the slave camp. Finally, Colonel Matthews gave a forced account of everything he knew. When he mentioned that all the white soldiers were former rebels, a lot of the men didn't seem startled by this information; some even nodded. One soldier stood and gave his account of how up to ten former soldiers had been beaten to death for minor infractions that were never proved. What started out as a spark of dismay began to burn bright into rage and anger as more men began to witness some of the atrocities visited on them.

Lieutenant Phoenix raised his voice and yelled, "Listen." Immediately, all the black soldiers who had come with Colonel Matthews quieted. Lieutenant Phoenix told them, "We have done nothing wrong. We followed the orders we were given and got rid of an evil that was trying to plant itself on American soil again. For that we were labeled murderers, and then we were pushed to either turn ourselves in for something we didn't do or release the slaves back into slavery they didn't deserve. As stated in the missive, for men like the former rebels in front of you, our right or wrong is never the concern; you only have to be black. For those who refuse to acknowledge our humanity, we can only be in chains or dead. Their intent was for you, the black soldiers, to kill us when you found us. We weren't going to be taken into custody; we were going to be murdered for doing our job. No judge, no jury. You would have been used to kill and murder your brothers and sisters in the name of your country. These men are ruinous to our survival and our family's survival. They taint the very air men who strive to be free breathe every day!"

Lieutenant Phoenix raised his hands, and fifty soldiers stepped behind the prisoners, both black and white, with various sharp instruments. These were fifty soldiers who had been with Lieutenant Phoenix during the war. They had performed the guerrilla mission of sneaking up on sleeping men and killing them. Killing wasn't personal to them, just something they had to do. It was something the soldiers needed to understand; to survive they would have to kill.

Before the black soldiers from Fort Concho, all fifty soldiers cut throats, bludgeoned, or axed the kneeling ex-rebel soldiers. The air was filled with the thunking and whacking sound of metal weapons beating and cutting into flesh. A few heads rolled, so mighty were the swings. The soft "Ugggh" noises as men fell to their deaths before they had a chance to vocalize their outrage were unforgettable. The rich coppery smell of blood filled the air. The horror and disgust at the sight of the squirting blood and men enacting the violence were etched on every man watching. In less than a minute, it was all over.

When it was all over, the soldiers were still. None moved. First Sergeant Amra walked up to Colonel Matthews from the back. He placed his large left black hand over Captain Matthews's forehead and pulled his head back into the large buck knife in his hand. The large knife plunged deep into the back of his skull; death was instantaneous. A bright red spray of blood from the back of his head was all the response Colonel Matthews could give.

In less than a minute, the execution was over. All the white soldiers involved in their demise were dead. The men from Fort Concho were stunned and now scared. What or who was next?

Lieutenant Phoenix turned back to the men. "We do not rejoice in the death of any man. We didn't kill these men out of revenge, and we will never kill a white man because he is white. Each one of these men has a family, a mother, father, and cousins. They may also have wives and children. They were given the opportunity after the war to go back to their families and focus on living their lives. Their leadership confirmed that they were in league with bringing slavery back. They chose to seek fortune and make their life's work the demise and misery of the black race.

"We have white men in our ranks now who have been with us since we officially became free. They are our brothers. Together we go to rescue a white man we consider part of our family, a brother to some, a father figure to others. He trained and taught us what real freedom is. For him and any other brother who chooses to embrace us and our freedom, regardless of their color, we will fight and die. We chose after the war to serve the country and find a place to raise families in peace. They wouldn't let that happen. We will fight to find our peace and let any man, regardless of color, who tries to take that away do so at his own demise."

Silence followed his speech. Lieutenant Phoenix looked around at the men from Fort Concho, trying to look each in the eye. He broke the silence and said, "First Sergeant."

First Sergeant Amra stood and cleared his voice and began to speak. "I am not a follower of the Christian faith, but I believe each man deserves to be treated according to their religion. I am not sure if all these men are all Christian or even of the Christian faith. The men may not deserve the respect we are about to give them, but like the lieutenant mentioned, they do have families. I believe we should respect the enemy dead for their families." With that, First Sergeant Amra started to read.

> If you say, "The Lord is my refuge," and you make the Most High your dwelling, no harm will overtake you, no disaster will come near your tent.
>
> For he will command his angels concerning you to guard you in all your ways; they will lift you up in their hands, so that you will not strike your foot against a stone.
>
> You will tread on the lion and the cobra; you will trample the great lion and the serpent.
>
> "Because he loves me," says the Lord, "I will rescue him; I will protect him, for he acknowledges my name."

He will call on me, and I will answer him; I will
be with him in trouble,
I will deliver him and honor him.

With long life I will satisfy him and show him my
salvation. Amen.

All the men acknowledged his reading with an amen.
Lieutenant Phoenix had given First Sergeant Amra the verses to
read. First Sergeant Amra was initially reluctant and felt it was a
waste of time. The enemy was dead, and that was the end of it.
But Lieutenant Phoenix had swayed him with his words. He had
told him, "We look to the white man to show us the way in everything, because we know nothing. They see us as worthless and
inhuman. At what point do we start thinking for ourselves and
being human? Surviving is not being human; it is just surviving.
But to show a small kindness to a misguided enemy could help
lessen the upcoming backlash of hate that will be directed at all
black people in America for our actions. As we move forward, we
have to be thoughtful of the impact of our actions."

First Sergeant Amra was actually proud of what the Lieutenant
had told him. He knew the Lieutenant was smart, but he was
starting to learn how to use his education to help his people.

First Sergeant Amra was drawn out of his thoughts by the
tasks he had to accomplish. He asked for the senior person from
the men at Fort Concho. When they responded that they were
all privates, Amra swore inwardly. Eventually, one of the soldiers,
whom most of them respected, was identified and told he was in
control of the group of men until something further was decided.
They were divided into workgroups and started the process of
burying the bodies.

SIXTY-ONE

Two Masters

PADRES GARCIA AND Morales lay in the large carriage they had commissioned for their return to Europe. They had hurriedly moved up their plans to leave the country after finding out the people of Cajoncito were on to their schemes. Front-runners for the recently rescued hostages had come to inform the people of the incoming people and refugees. The padres immediately knew their time was up when Señor Perez had invited the refugees to stay in the town. The old Señor Perez wouldn't have done anything without their consent. The front-runner had told of the rapes and abuse the people had received and that they were at a slave camp, not hostages. The people instantly grew angry to learn this; the padres had told them they had confirmation from the kidnappers that everything would be okay. The padres decided that as the former slaves got closer, the angst against the padres would arise. They already had their silver at the mine ready to go; all they had to do was leave Cajoncito.

They had escaped Cajoncito the same night the front-runners arrived. That was over five days ago. They had parlayed at the city outside the mine, Coyame, for two days. Four of the wealthier mining families who had grown rich off the free slave labor decided they also had enough and wanted to get out of the hellish land. The remaining families were only too happy to gain control of all the mines and the remaining slaves.

Their caravan consisted of about twenty wagons, four of which were filled with the bodies of priests being returned to Spain to be interred. In realty, there were only two former priests to be interred, but because of the amount of silver they had, they had added five additional caskets loaded with silver. The two caskets with the real bodies were up front in case anyone had any questions. The additional coffins were also made of pure silver, and the coffins had been painted to hide their true value. The paint on the silver was so good that it resembled natural rock.

Already the trip was the best time in Padre Garcia's life; this was the first time he and Padre Morales had spent so much alone time together without a lot of scrutiny. They were in no rush but had taken to hours of traveling before stopping. This pace allowed them to be in their lush wagon and spend time with each other. Garcia was happy that soon they would be able to get rid of the padre ruse. Once they were back in Europe, their money would allow them to be anything they wanted to be. Nobody decried rich people for being eccentric or crazy. He had seen plenty of noblemen in love with other men. Even among the higher church members, there was a sort of unwritten rule on the sexual aspects of its members. They would be in Galveston in about six days; from there, their lives would really be their own.

They had a later dinner tonight and had finished eating for the night. The caravan had parked in a circle to provide maximum security at night. They hadn't had time to hire real guards to protect the caravan, so they had offered the guards from the mine one hundred silver coins each to protect them until they got to Galveston. Ten additional slaves who had worked in the mine were told that if they assisted until Galveston by cooking and setting up camp, they would be given freedom and some silver. Overall everybody was happy to get paid, and so far no incidents had happened. The other families had also brought their earnings in silver and had them hidden throughout their belongings in case of bandits. The overall look of the caravan was a guarded religious caravan, something a lot of bandits would leave alone, because most bandits knew the church could pay for the best guards.

Padre Morales had just finished writing in his journal for the night, something he did every night since he had joined the monastery to become a priest. He looked over at Padre Garcia and smiled as he watched him sleep so peacefully. He had also been constant in his life since he joined the monastery. They had come a long way together from Spain to the hellhole in Cajoncito. They had spent a good part of their lives serving the rich of Spain; now it was their turn to be served.

He blew out the remaining candle in the wagon and lay next to Padre Garcia. He was closing his eyes to go to sleep when he heard the lonely howl of a wolf in the distance. He lay next to Padre Garcia and smiled; he would never need to be alone again.

Sergeant Hall let the lone call of the wolf alert everyone that the attack would begin shortly. He had gathered Tip, Chacon, and fifteen other men from Fort Quitman and come back for the priest. The slave who had died when Sergeant Hall first came to the area had described how the priest took the silver they mined and was casting it for travel. The slave had been one of the casters; he informed Sergeant Hall that they planned to leave with all the silver they had mined, and the Mexican government had no clue as to the mine and its output.

Sergeant Hall informed Corporal Charl, who at the time had

just delivered a message from Lieutenant Phoenix to Lieutenant Colonel Vetter, who had departed for Fort Concho. Sergeant Hall informed Corporal Charl that the information was only for Lieutenant Colonel Vetter, Lieutenant Phoenix, or First Sergeant Amra but no one else. Corporal Charl agreed, and they had departed to seek out the padres.

They knew how the caravan would stop, and they knew the formation it would be in once it stopped. They had watched it for two nights after they secured the mining town and let all the slaves free. The slaves didn't know what to make of their rescuers but were happy to get out of the mine. When Sergeant Hall told them they were going after the mining families who had departed with the padres, a lot of the freed slaves wanted to follow along to take revenge. Sergeant Hall informed them they were free to do what they wanted but that they would slow him and his men down. He told him they would come back and make sure everyone was fine. They thanked him and departed.

Everyone was staged and ready to attack. Sergeant Hall had told the men that the only survivors were going to be the slaves, women, and children; no one else would make it. The men had seemed grim about that instruction but understood the task. These men had made money on the blood of countless slaves. There was enough silver in the mines for everyone around to live a nice life. Instead, they had chosen to take all the earnings under bondage and torment. The night would be short and bloody.

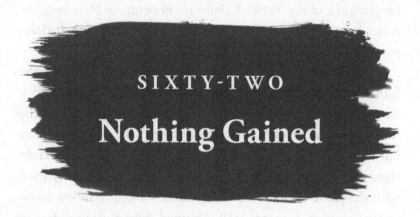

SIXTY-TWO

Nothing Gained

BRIGADIER GENERAL SPODERLY couldn't believe how much of their plan how gotten out of control so fast. It had been two days since the newly promoted Colonel Matthews departed, and both Brigadier General Spoderly and Mr. Jasso had spent time with Lieutenant Colonel Vetter and the men who had come with him. Each had gone through bouts of torture, and they had only the others to thank that they didn't go through more. Between Lieutenant Colonel Vetter and his men, the story unfolded of all they knew.

It was a small relief to find out that Lieutenant Colonel Vetter didn't know anything about the slave camps. He had simply wanted to save people in his zone of concern. He was the only law in the area, and it was for those exact reasons so much time had gone into recruiting him. One of his men had died from the trauma, which helped the others tell what they knew. It was confirmed that Lieutenant Colonel Vetter hadn't known about his lieutenant's attack and destruction of the slave camp. Mr. Jasso found the information about the padres interesting; it would have to be investigated more.

It was a shame that they would have to get rid of Lieutenant Colonel Vetter. Mr. Jasso had had high hopes for him. He had hoped to use him to control Southern Texas. He was a good leader, as witnessed by the effectiveness of his black lieutenant's easy destruction of the slave camp. They had sent riders out to investigate the true damage of the slave camp and found the place totally destroyed, never to be used again. All that remained was the blackened areas where a large fire had been. No sign of the men who had run the slave camp was found.

Yes, Lieutenant Colonel Vetter was a dangerous man and on the wrong side; they would have to get rid of him. The plan was to transfer him to Galveston for a military hearing. En route to Galveston, Indians would attack the caravan carrying Lieutenant Colonel Vetter, and he would assuredly be one of the deceased from the attack. With Lieutenant Colonel Vetter gone, the lieutenant and his band destroyed, and the escaped slaves recaptured, all things would be back on track.

Lieutenant Colonel Vetter coughed a little blood as he lay facedown in the cell he had come to know as home. They had tortured him and his men together, letting each see the others' pain and hear their fellow soldiers' cries. He knew at least three of his ribs were broke from the booted kicks and was too afraid to try to move from his position because of the pain. His left eye was closed and probably out of its socket.

He slowly moved his head and tried to adjust his eye, but the pain flaring from his chest stopped him in his tracks. His breathing became more and more ragged as he tried to exert himself, so he had to stop moving in fear of overburdening his already-ragged heart. He didn't think he could stand another beating before dying. One of his men had already died when the pain as they snapped his arm caused him to have a heart attack. Fortunately, they had decided to save Vetter's legs "for later" if he didn't decide to talk.

His men must have verified the things he told them, because after a few hours, they stopped torturing him and the men. He couldn't believe fellow soldiers could be so brutal to other soldiers, even under orders. These thoughts passed through his head as he passed out once again from the ongoing pain.

SIXTY-THREE

Rescue!

LIEUTENANT PHOENIX DIDN'T waste any time in getting the men ready to move on Fort Concho and rescue Lieutenant Colonel Vetter. Lieutenant Phoenix told First Sergeant Amra that something didn't feel right; he felt the need to hurry and get to Fort Concho.

They had the captured soldiers from Fort Concho; they had individually drawn diagrams of the fort without the other soldiers' knowledge. All the diagrams matched, except for two. The two soldiers who had offered the diagrams that didn't match were pressed on why their drawings were different and why they had lied. First Sergeant Amra acted with certainty that they had lied. The men, not knowing the depth of what the first sergeant already knew, continued with their lie. First Sergeant Amra then showed both men three recent sketches that had been etched in the dirt, drawn by the other men. They were all similar. When pressed on why their drawings were different, the men finally came forth and said they had been trying to protect the people at Fort Concho; they had thought Lieutenant Phoenix and First Sergeant Amra were merely bandits in disguise.

First Sergeant Amra didn't know what to say; he was so surprised by the response. Lieutenant Phoenix had read the missive to the entire group and explained the slave camp they had found. Everything they had experienced they had related to the men for the specific reason of letting them know the facts of the case so they could draw their own conclusions. But they had chosen to ignore the facts and simply call them bandits. He knew the men couldn't read, and like most blacks of the time, they were very distrustful of blacks who had education and could read. These men had comfortable lives, compared to their previous existence, which probably was as a slave.

Now they were at risk of losing it all because some other man was being tracked down by the white man. What had made this their concern? For the first time since they had found out about the treachery and deceit against them, First Sergeant Amra had a trickle of doubt about what the future would hold for them. How could they survive if their own people didn't believe in what they were doing? First Sergeant Amra firmly believed that people who didn't believe in a cause would eventually betray it. It was then that he decided that the only way for men to fight and survive was through shared commitments and struggles. Everyone would have to be equally involved and vested for it to work. The men before him were a small example of the men who would come. They all would have their personal reasons for doing what they had needed to do to survive. First Sergeant Amra would have to make their reasons benefit all and not just themselves.

Once they had figured out the right layout for Fort Concho, they planned their attack for the next night. They would use the uniforms they had taken, and Corporal Charl and the first sergeant would ride in as messengers and subdue anyone in the messengers' quarters. The attack would be multipronged. The information the captured soldiers had provided about Fort Concho was instrumental in helping them put their attack together.

The fort was partially enclosed with stone walls primarily surrounding the hospital and backyards of the officers' quarters. There were about forty permanent structures built of limestone around a large parade ground. Included in the forty structures were stables, blacksmith and carpenter shops, a forage house, an ordnance storehouse, a guardhouse, a powder magazine, a pump house, a bakery, a hospital, an administration building, and a schoolhouse also used as a chapel. There were also several temporary frame buildings for married soldiers' quarters and a telegraph office. A room on top of the post hospital afforded a distant view in every direction.

The scouts would cut the telegraph wires before the attack. Traffic to Fort Concho would be blocked until the operation was over. The arsenal would be secured, and if things went awry, the soldiers were given instructions to explode it to cause a distraction so everyone could retreat to a predetermined location. A lot of their plan depended on quickly securing Brigadier General Sprodel and Mr. Jasso. With the head of the snake taken out, the rest of the body would have no direction, at least for a little while. They needed the white officers to be confused about where to receive initial guidance once they found out they were being attacked. They also needed to be separated and kept from grouping together. The officers were all rebel soldiers, who had moved to the Texas area to support the new rebel movement. Because they all had sidearms, they would pose a certain problem to the success of the plan. The men were told to take them alive if they could but to take them out if they gave too much resistance. The men were definitely told not to hurt any family members who might be residing with the officers.

Lieutenant Phoenix had also learned from the captured black

soldiers that the fighting force with Colonel Matthews was made up of units considered the "fighters" of Fort Concho. They explained that the fighters were the soldiers who were primarily used as escorts for stagecoaches and cattle drives; they generally served as a police force. The remaining soldiers in the camp, who were just as tough, were mainly used as scouts for mapping large portions of West Texas and building roads, telegraph lines, and railroad survey parties. Lieutenant Phoenix hoped their overall lack of battle experience and unfamiliarity with the chaos of battle would make them slow to react and that they could exploit this weakness to their benefit. He wanted his men to secure them as soon as possible and without incident, if possible. He was concerned about killing any black soldiers; he knew they were ignorant of the larger conspiracy to subjugate the whole black race. They would follow orders as dutiful Americans and would fight to defend themselves.

Fort Concho's wall went only a little higher than waist high, so men could easily jump over it. The enlisted black soldiers were required to keep weapons stored in the armory when they weren't on patrol. Fifteen to twenty men would secure the rooms in each barracks. Other groups of up to five men would secure each officers' quarters.

They expected only a small portion of the roving guards to be armed, since a good portion of the men had gone with recently departed Colonel Matthews. Once all the men were set in their positions, a fire would be started right outside by men dressed in the uniforms taken from Colonel Matthews's former men. The drama at the gate should draw all the roving guards, who would then be captured and held outside the gate.

The men in the barracks and the officer housing would be held at gunpoint, pending the capture of Brigadier General Sprodel and Mr. Jasso. First Sergeant Amra told his men to take them quickly and subdue them. "Knock them out if you have to," he said, "but do not kill any of them."

Thus far, the element of surprise had kept them safe and given them an enormous advantage; nobody expected the blacks to fight back. Why would they fight back when they weren't supposed to know they would be killed for doing their duty?

First Sergeant Amra knew this attack would be the largest they had ever attempted. There were multiple moving pieces, and the failure of any of them would lead to death. The black soldiers at Fort Concho were just as tenacious and tough as the men in his unit and wouldn't take to being taken over lightly. He had arrived earlier in the day, along with Corporal Charl. They came in under the guise of messengers. Nobody questioned other black soldiers in uniform on official duty. They even took a few minutes to jest with the men in the room where the messenger met.

First Sergeant Amra was able to get a good layout of the camp, performing the normal functions expected of the messenger. Messengers spent a good part of the day cleaning up and taking care of their horses, something Amra found refreshing considering the circumstances. The men of the camp were very quiet and kept mostly to themselves. They all gave First Sergeant Amra a hard look; he was a big man. He wore the private rank and would be at the mercy of any higher-ranking person who chose to task him with anything. The messengers were normally left alone, but Amra's size was an immediate challenge to a lot of men's egos. Rank could be used as a bullying tool by men who felt inadequate to make them feel bigger. No black wanted to jeopardize the freedom and work they had as soldiers, so bullying by petty men became an excellent tool. He didn't need to be focused on what petty men were thinking or doing. Fortunately, his ruse of bending his back and not looking any man in the eye helped him look lesser than what he really was. Even if he had to take a beating to make some small man feel better, he was prepared to do so. He didn't care; he knew in his heart that the events of tonight would define the rest of their lives. His actions would mean the success or failure of their whole mission and possibly everyone in the unit, including their families.

First Sergeant Amra knew that early warning before the attack would be disastrous for the whole mission. He had taken it upon himself to make sure to secure the room on top of the post hospital, which afforded a distant view in every direction. The security around the area wasn't one that expected an attack; he hoped the place was manned only if there was a known threat. They couldn't take the chance that it wasn't manned. Once he occupied it, he would let the attacking force know by the code they had established. This operation had to happen quickly before things had an opportunity to get out of hand.

The attack started at 0200 in the morning. The horses were left behind with a small follow-up force in case things didn't go as planned. This mission would be on foot, which suited all the men. Horses were great for getting from one place to the next, but these men were trained in guerilla-fighting techniques. The moon wasn't full, but the men had learned how to adjust their eyes, and the limited light didn't pose a problem for them. A flat, treeless, dreary prairie surrounded the fort. There was minimal cover and concealment; the men depended on their stealth and the burlap bags to break up any kind of a man's silhouette. They also had First Sergeant Amra and Corporal Charl inside; they had arrived earlier that morning, and so far no incidents showed them being exposed. So far so good.

Lieutenant Phoenix was in the middle of the attacking force as it warily headed for the front of Fort Concho. There were about fifteen separate columns of men converging at different areas of Fort Concho almost simultaneously. The entire fort was encircled. They all had a point of attack they were responsible for. They knew to wait until they got about two hundred feet out before the final entrance into the fort. They needed to know that First Sergeant Amra had secured his objective before they entered the fort. It was almost as if thought became action. In the distance, slightly to the right of the gate, was the distinct blinking-light signal they had been waiting for. It was First Sergeant Amra in the room on top of the post hospital; he was waving his burlap bag over a lamp and removing it to signal the approaching forces.

On cue, the column began to pick up speed, each man keeping pace with the other. Lieutenant Phoenix also began to pick up his pace into a slow trot, the whole column of men moving as one. Immediately, other columns started to follow suit, all the men outfitted in the burlap bag camouflage. Lieutenant Phoenix briefly looked around; he could barely discern the shifting gray bodies as they moved toward the camp. The moment was surreal, exhilarating, and terrifying all at the same time. He felt alive, he felt in control, he felt free.

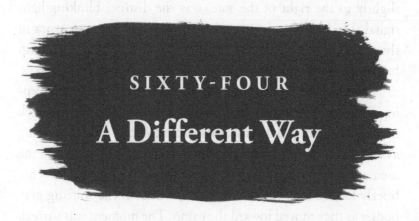

SIXTY-FOUR

A Different Way

IT HAD BEEN five days since his men rescued him. Lieutenant Colonel Vetter had been awakened in his dark cell by Lieutenant Phoenix and could discern in the torchlight that he was surrounded by First Sergeant Amra and a few of the other rescuers. They were smiling and glad to see he was still alive. They had captured Fort Concho with minimal clashes.

Once the soldier from the fort realized the attacking men had no intention of hurting them or causing them harm, the men calmed down to see what was next. They initially thought the attackers were Indians and started to grab furniture or anything that wasn't nailed down to defend themselves. First Sergeant Amra had informed them not to attack or to try to disarm them unless they were attacked; they should simply hold them at gunpoint. They were also told to assure the men that no harm would come to them, and answers would be provided as soon as possible. They were also informed not to provide any other explanation.

Overall, the ploy worked. The men felt comfortable that they weren't being killed and eventually put down the weapons they had picked up. Capturing Brigadier General Sprodel and Mr. Jasso had come at a small price. Their household had more armed men in the area, and a small gunfight ensued. The generals' guards were slain immediately, and two of Lieutenant Phoenix's men were injured; both would survive. Brigadier General Sprodel had initially tried to lock himself in his room but immediately surrendered when he received guarantees that his family wouldn't be hurt. You could imagine both of their surprises when the men took off their hoods and revealed themselves as black men. Lieutenant Phoenix had set up a temporary command center in the main house. Both Brigadier General Sprodel and Mr. Jasso were arrested, gagged, and put in a room in the house under guard. Their families were moved to another location.

Lieutenant Phoenix and First Sergeant Amra had worked out the messaging if they survived. They informed the now-captive soldiers from Fort Concho that both Brigadier General Sprodel and Mr. Jasso had been arrested and that the attacking force was part of the rescue force to save Lieutenant Colonel Vetter. All of which was true.

That had been five days ago, and the men were now waiting for Lieutenant Colonel Vetter to give them a message on what had happened. At least that was what Lieutenant Phoenix had explained that he needed him to do. Lieutenant Phoenix and First Sergeant Amra had put together a plan they hoped would allow them to live in peace without a bounty over their heads. They found out Mr. Jasso had telegraphed the destruction of the "prison" camp to Galveston. Already there were reports of hangings in response to the false news. They had come to an agreement that they would be better served on their own, defending the territory they were now a part of. Before he could further discuss what they had meant by "defending the territory," they gave him the missive and all the documentation they had captured during the takedown of the slave camp. They told him they would talk when he recovered.

Lieutenant Colonel Vetter had just finished going over all the documentation Lieutenant Phoenix had provided two days ago and was extremely troubled by everything he had read. He knew now that true freedom for the black man would be a fight the black man couldn't win, because he couldn't see his enemies. He would never be realized in America as long as powerful forces were always trying to keep his freedom from happening. The implications of the powerful people involved in this endeavor were mind numbing.

Lieutenant Phoenix and First Sergeant Amra had explained their plan to him. They had agreed that no matter what would happen, they would never have a fair opinion in American view. They knew they should be recognized as heroes for destroying the slave camp. But now, because of a lie placed over their names, they would be hunted down by the factions trying to keep the blacks in a slave state. They were now a threat to a hidden disease within the American government, and others didn't wish it to be known.

From the highest pinnacles of power in the American government and citizenry, there was a concerted effort to keep the black man in a perpetual state of second-class citizenry. Their methods had gone from full-out battle during the rebellion to fighting from within. They would always be there and too many to fight. But the lieutenant and first sergeant had a strong feeling about being Americans. They had sacrificed and suffered through countless abuses and believed they had bled and fought for their freedom and were now an integral part of this country, part of its essence. They couldn't leave it and didn't want to live as prisoners for the rest of their lives in a country they were vested in. They also knew a lot of black soldiers wouldn't want to make the same choices they had; they would want to stay in the military and continue to be soldiers. Those men would be forever labeled as threats to whites due to guilt by association. They needed to provide cover for the men who chose not to join them.

That was where they told Lieutenant Colonel Vetter they needed him the most now. They no longer needed him to be their leader or commander; they didn't want to tarnish his name with the choices they felt they had to make. They didn't want him to associate with their cause; they needed him to provide cover for the black men who chose a different path. They didn't want to be known as rebels or soldiers who had turned their backs on their country. They needed someone they trusted and respected to tell their story. They told him that if he wanted to help them, they would have to go separate ways.

Lieutenant Colonel Vetter knew everything they had told him was true. They would never get a fair shake. The system was designed to make it so. Mechanisms were being put in place at the highest levels of government that would never truly make black men free. If they wanted true freedom, they would have to make their own.

Lieutenant Phoenix and First Sergeant Amra had questioned Brigadier General Sprodel and Mr. Jasso in secrecy; they used the same technique they had used on Captain Matthews. Both had been placed in the same cell where Lieutenant Colonel Vetter had been held. Their hands were tied to ropes anchored by metal rungs in the ceiling. Both hands were above their heads, with their toes barely touching the ground. The weight of their bodies was on their arms.

Since Mr. Jasso was the youngest, they started with him and let Brigadier General Sprodel watch. First Sergeant Amra, holding his khopesh out, placed the sharp-bladed weapon on the back of Mr. Jasso's right hamstring and gave it a swift cut. Mr. Jasso, with a loosely placed rag in his mouth, let out a loud, muffled scream; his eyes rolled to the back of his head, so intense was the pain.

They gave him a few seconds to work through his pain before they took the gag off his mouth.

Lieutenant Phoenix said, "I will ask each of you the same question. The one who talks the most will get hurt the least. Tell me everything about the new rebellion. Names, places, plans."

Mr. Jasso, raggedly breathing from the pain pulsating where his tendon used to be, said through clenched teeth, "You niggers will hang for this. You will never get away with this. Release us now!"

Lieutenant Phoenix went to where the rope holding Mr. Jasso was tied off on one of the cell bars. He loosened the rope a little, and Mr. Jasso was lowered slightly, his weight put on the torn tendon. His scream was almost girlish in his agony; a wet spot showed on his pants where he had urinated on himself. Phoenix pulled on the rope a little, and Mr. Jasso was lifted.

Lieutenant Phoenix asked, "Tell me everything about the new rebellion. Names, places, plans."

The questioning of Brigadier General Sprodel and Mr. Jasso lasted about four hours It took minimal effort to get the two men to talk. They told him everything they knew. First Sergeant Amra summed up their interrogation session. "Men in power are used to giving pain, not receiving." Afterward, Lieutenant Phoenix and First Sergeant Amra knew in their hearts that the path before them was theirs to make. The people and powers involved in the new rebellion were too many and too mind numbing. They also knew brute force wouldn't win the war these men and women had chosen to bring on the black man in America.

Lieutenant Colonel Vetter had been asked to listen in on the torture of Brigadier General Sprodel and Mr. Jasso. He told the men that torturing these men was wrong; they had the documentation from the missive, which would be enough to damn them. Lieutenant Phoenix agreed that the missive and the supporting documentation were damning, but no names were mentioned.

They needed to know the people involved and, more importantly, what they were going to face in Texas. As much as Lieutenant Colonel Vetter hated to admit it, the men were right.

Lieutenant Phoenix ended any trepidation Lieutenant Colonel Vetter may have had about what they were doing by saying, "Sir, we didn't start any of this. We will be hunted and slaughtered likes dogs for doing our duty, because we are black. Because we are black, we have people in the government working on separate laws that will try to criminalize and minimize a whole race of people. First, they do it through brutality. Now they do it through legality instead of just recognizing our freedom. When we were slaves, we didn't know anything. They controlled us through fear and ignorance. We are no longer scared and will never be ignorant again! We are not scared, and we now have their tools and knowledge of war. We didn't start this, but if they want to keep pushing without leaving us in peace, we will finish it!"

Lieutenant Colonel Vetter couldn't help but agree that it was what free men did—control their destiny.

BRIGADIER GENERAL SPRODEL and Mr. Jasso had given all the information on the officers in the unit who were collaborating with the "new rebellion." Those officers, along with Brigadier General Sprodel and Mr. Jasso, were seen leaving under much pomp and circumstance to go answer for their crimes. They would never be seen again on this earth.

Lieutenant Colonel Vetter, now in charge of Fort Concho as the senior officer, was getting ready to address the men from Fort Concho to make them all aware of the crimes against their former leadership, Brigadier General Sprodel, and his connection with Southern rebels, who were trying to reinstitute slavery in Texas and the western frontier. He had already telegraphed to Galveston what had happened and that he had taken temporary command of Fort Concho.

The previous day, Lieutenant Phoenix and First Sergeant Amra had called a meeting with Lieutenant Colonel Vetter. He had invited the Indian leaders: Two-Axe, Victorio, and Tepor of the Rarámuri. Also included were Señor Perez of Cajoncito; Jian, the former Chinese diplomat; and the interpreters to help translate the various languages.

The meeting was held in the previous headquarters room where the former Brigadier General Sprodel and Mr. Jasso had arrested Lieutenant Colonel Vetter. They had added a couple of tables together to create one huge table so everyone could sit. A hodgepodge of chairs was brought in to account for the unusual amount of people at the meeting. On top of the table were strewn various maps of the United States, the Texas area, and eastern Mexico.

Everyone was dressed in what little finery they possessed.

Lieutenant Colonel Vetter was dressed in his full blue officer jacket with his military ribbons on display. The large brass buttons shined in the reflected sunlight coming into the room. He now wore a dark-brown leather patch over his left eye. His reddish-brown mustache was neatly trimmed, along with the sideburns coming down to his cheek area. He seemed to be rested but intent.

The Indian council was led by Two-Axe, whom everyone now knew to be a Comanche warrior and chieftain. He had his long Indian hair braided in two large braids, which streamed to the left and right of his chest. A decorative bone hair pipe breastplate was on his chest. Wrapped partially around his shoulders was a very beautiful red-and-black blanket. Victorio represented a large population of loosely strung Apaches, who were spread out all over the Southwest. He wore a large tan headscarf, and a tough leather vest was wrapped around his white homespun clothing. Tepor of the Rarámuri had on a bright maroon shirt and a brightly colored beaded headband. He was cheerful and smiling at everyone at the table.

Señors Perez and Jian were in a silent conversation. Señor

Perez had on a dark-green Spanish-style gentleman's suit with a frilly front white shirt beneath. Mr. Jian wore a rich, dark purple robe of satin or silk finery. He had on an equally fine black short coat over the robe. There had been a lot of talk among the Indians when Jian first walked in. One of the translators asked whether he was a man. When he translated that he was a man back to the Indian leadership, they wanted to know why they had made their enemy wear a dress. After they explained to the Indians who Jian was and where he was from, they were amazed.

Two-Axes asked Jian, "How did you keep the white man from taking your land?" He looked at Lieutenant Colonel Vetter as he asked the question.

Jian responded, "My country has been at war for a very long time and has advanced a lot in the ways of war. We have had foreign aggressors throughout our history. Always the people have had to put away their individual concerns and join together to repel the invaders. It would be costly for any country to attack us since the whole country is armed."

The translator explained to Two-Axes what Jian had said. This time Victorio answered in Indian, and the translator replied, "Yes, all the Indian tribes together could have defeated the white man!"

Now that everyone was seated, Lieutenant Phoenix broke up all small talk by standing up and clearing his voice. Everyone's attention was slowly drawn to him, and the room started to quiet down. He was dressed in one of the light-colored shirts they had converted from some extra canvas to reduce the impact of the desert. He didn't have any emblems or rank on it. His attire was complete with his army-issue pants.

Lieutenant Phoenix surveyed the room and began, "First and foremost, I would once again like to publicly thank the entire congregation of Indians, Señor Perez, and all the others who hurried to support our rescue of Lieutenant Colonel Vetter. Your show of support for our cause showed that there is nothing we cannot do if we are together. Some of you have heard bits and pieces of the story of how we changed from rescuers to criminals overnight based on a lie. We were falsely accused of being criminals because we had inadvertently destroyed a 'new rebellion' effort to establish slave camps throughout Texas. This time they not only tried to enslave blacks but also now aggressively sought out Mexicans and Indians for slavery. Basically, every race that wasn't white was going to be a slave." Lieutenant Phoenix let the translators catch up.

He continued, "I truly believe that if we wouldn't have found out about the efforts to reignite slavery in frontier lands, we would have eventually been marginalized and enslaved or killed. Our knowledge of combat and battle is a threat to every racist white man alive. Are we truly free in the land that set us free? For that matter are any of the races represented in this room that are not white truly free? The Indians are being moved from one reservation to the next as more white people move west. We black people don't own any land and had only the uniforms of our country to protect us. Each of you has been witness to how easily that protection could be so easily taken away simply by another white, who chose to make an accusation against us. A death squad was sent to destroy us on that accusation. There was no judge or jury to see if we were right or wrong. Is that really freedom?"

The translators were explaining, and Lieutenant Phoenix could see the impact of his words on the Indians, who were nodding.

He continued, "This land is unlike anything most of us blacks have ever seen. It is dry, hot, wild, rough, and dangerous. Right now, we make the rules on how to survive in this land. I want to keep it that way, but I don't want to look like this is an uprising of the blacks now that the war is over. This country is still mending from a Civil War, and I don't want to start another. I don't want my actions or yours to be the reason countless blacks, primarily in the South and even here in Texas, are murdered. This land is American land. With your help, I think I have come up with a plan that hopefully will satisfy all interested parties and could help all of us achieve the happiness and balance we want. Either way, we will fight to find our peace and let any man, regardless of color, who tries to take that away do so at their own demise!"

Lieutenant Phoenix drew the team's focus to the maps on the table. He stated, "This is my plan, but first I want to tell you a story about a place called Sparta."

Lieutenant Colonel Vetter listened while amazed, terrified, and happy all at the same time.

EPILOGUE

LIEUTENANT COLONEL VETTER sat outside the office of the president of the United States. It had been almost three months since he met with the group at Fort Concho. He had left Fort Concho a few days after the meeting and headed to Galveston, leading a large contingent of troops, both black and white. The troops he led to Galveston were the ones who had decided not to join Lieutenant Phoenix and First Sergeant Amra's group. They didn't believe that whatever they were doing would end up well. Going against the US government hadn't ended well for the British, the Indians, or the rebels. Now a group of black men, joined with a bunch of Indians and former slaves, was going to do exactly that. Lieutenant Colonel Vetter hoped it wouldn't come to that and had told Lieutenant Phoenix exactly that. Hopefully, his emergency meeting with the president would help.

As if on cue, his name was called, and he was on his way to meet the eighteenth president of the United States.

President Ulysses "Sam" Grant was in his second term as the president of the United States. Lieutenant Colonel Vetter, his next appointment, had just come from an assignment on the frontier in Texas with information he claimed was threatening to the United States, but it was so sensitive only the president could hear it.

The recent disappearance of the commanding general, Brigadier General Sprodel, and a prominent civilian had everyone talking about a possible rebellion in Texas, but by whom? The lieutenant colonel had refused to share this information at the risk of being arrested. The president had agreed to see him only because of outside pressures to find out the whereabouts of the aforementioned General Sprodel and Mr. Jasso.

Lieutenant Colonel Vetter entered, surrounded by four White House guards and Lieutenant General Frame. The whole group stopped in front of the president's desk. Lieutenant General Frame saluted the president and said, "Sir, Lieutenant General Frame reporting. Lieutenant Colonel Vetter is here to provide you with an update he considers an emergency of the state." The last part he said in a very patronizing tone.

The president saluted and said, "Be seated."

There were two chairs already set out. Lieutenant General Frame sat on one and pointed to Lieutenant Colonel Vetter to sit on the other. The president looked at Lieutenant Colonel Vetter and simply stated, "Report."

Lieutenant Colonel Vetter immediately responded, "Sir, for the sake of our country, I ask that I am allowed to speak to you in private. If not totally alone, then with a guard in the room, but far enough to where he can't hear us speak."

Automatically, Lieutenant General Frame vehemently responded. "What kind of bullshit is going on here?"

The president, taken aback by the fervor in Lieutenant General Frame's voice, looked at Lieutenant General Frame and said in a soft voice, "Get out."

The general, looking apoplectic, turned bright red and slowly returned to his original color. He nodded, stood up, and saluted.

The president watched him for a brief second, not immediately returning the salute. After a short pause, the president saluted and said, "Dismissed." The general turned around and departed, followed by three of the guards; one remained by the door.

Lieutenant Colonel Vetter reached into his bag and brought out all the information they had gained, including the missive and all the documentation they had found. He went on to tell the president about all the information gathered from Brigadier General Sprodel and Mr. Jasso, who he informed the president were no longer alive. Lieutenant Colonel Vetter told him the whole story of his men, their loyalty to their country, and how they just wanted to have families and a purpose in life. He talked about their concerns about powerful people who were constantly trying to keep them down as second-class citizens. He spoke of Lieutenant Phoenix and First Sergeant Amra like a father talks about his kids.

President Grant watched this young officer as he told the story of his men. He could see the concern for his men written all over his face. As a former commander himself, he knew the bond between a good commander and his men. He automatically liked the man, "a soldier's solider." The fact that he was here, fighting for black men, even increased the president's praise for the man. However, the president also knew that if public knowledge was made of what those men had done to those slavers, every black in the country would be afraid of the backlash.

Reconstruction efforts in the South were moving at a snail's pace. Even though the war was over for white Americans, the war was just starting for black Americans. The letters and information Lieutenant Colonel Vetter had just provided proved there was still a serious threat from the rebellion. The president had to admit the black man in America was being brutalized daily in the South for the smallest infraction and oft time for no reason. The black man was the most hunted animal in America, and the hate driving this was growing. Texas was a hotbed of racial disparity and tension; now he had learned there were slave camps being created in the frontier.

Lieutenant Colonel Vetter finished his conversation with a heartfelt plea to the president. "Sir, I have trained most of these men while they were slaves, free, and now soldiers who have put their lives on the line to serve this country. They have formed a unique relationship with the Native Indians in the area, and they all feel like they haven't been represented in this country. What harm would it do to let them know they are appreciated and that we do wish the best for them by providing them with land and a purpose? They will die to prevent being enslaved again, and they would give their lives to destroy all those who wish to put them in chains. These men have a plan, have a purpose, and can be the light other blacks and whites need to see. We freed the blacks with no plan for their future. Give them a place they can call their own!"

President Grant sat back in his chair, touched by the passion and truth of what Lieutenant Colonel Vetter had just said. He was right, but the president knew the noise and drama he would get with such an outlandish proposition. But yet it would be a large setback for the opposition trying to take over the country.

The idea of a joint reservation was genius, and he was surprised there had never been a proposition to give blacks reservations as a place of their own. Lieutenant Colonel Vetter was also right to say the men believed in their hearts that they were Americans. Slavery had been around for so long that blacks were now so far removed from their African heritage that they could no longer identify with any other place as their home. It touched his heart that after all the pain, persecution, and now betrayal, they still felt in their hearts that they were Americans.

They talked for over five hours; it took that long for Lieutenant Colonel Vetter to get the full story out. The president canceled multiple appointments so they could continue uninterrupted. The president made only one request during the time, which was for the most detailed map of the Texas area.

After the meeting, President Grant called an emergency meeting with his cabinet. He informed him of his decision to create a new type of reservation that housed both Native Americans and black Americans. The reservation land would be located in Texas, and it would be a land for both Native Americans and blacks who wished to stay there.

On June 19, 1876, President Ulysses S. Grant, the eighteenth president of the United States of America, designated the new Sparta Reservation area for both Native Americans and black Americans.

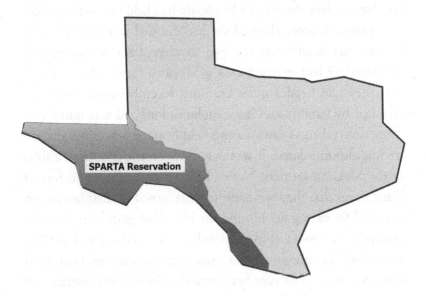

President Profirio Diaz sat in his office, listening to Señorita Gomez and Señor Perez discuss a proposition they wished to express. President Diaz normally didn't meet with just anyone, but Señorita Gomez was a Spanish noblewoman of notable worth. She had resided in Mexico most of her life and was thought to have died. She was one of the original Spanish royalty still remaining in Mexico, a silent but powerful population with worldwide connections. She had asked for a private audience with the president to discuss an issue she felt only the president could help her with. She would be one of the first Spanish nobility he had addressed since his election in May. She had requested an audience as a favor, which President Diaz knew could be cashed in later.

She was speaking on behalf of a confederation of Native American Indians, former black slaves, and local Mexicans who currently occupied the desert area. The area had become a respite for runaway Indians and black slaves from America. There was also a small population of Mexicans and local natives. In elder days, there was a nobleman's retreat near some hot water springs, but that was from long ago when Spain had held rule over Mexico.

Señorita Gomez claimed she had decided to stay in the area because her health was too bad to travel back to Spain, and her daughter had married a local Mexican farmer. She claimed that they had lived a quiet life until recently, when they were attacked by bandits and her daughter's husband was murdered. They were taken as captives and held hostage, where her daughter was also murdered. It was only through the concerted efforts of the Mexican farmers, Native Indians in the area, and former black slaves that they were able to be returned to their homes. As a reward for saving her life and the life of her granddaughter, she wanted to bestow a gift to the people and desired to purchase land from the Mexican government that her rescuers could call their own. She wanted to take her remaining inheritance money and purchase a parcel of land for the people.

President Diaz's interest was piqued by the sound of "purchase" and "inheritance." A good deed for a Spanish noblewoman would go a long way toward establishing fresh relations with Spain, and if he could get paid for selling some desert land, so be it.

On November 24, 1877, President Profirio Diaz, the president of Mexico, signed the Tratado de Reserva de Esparta, which designated the new Sparta Reservation area as a permanent home for indigenous people of the area, escaped slaves, and the Mexican families who lived there. Under this agreement, the people who lived on this land would have sovereignty to govern themselves within the borders of their designated territory.

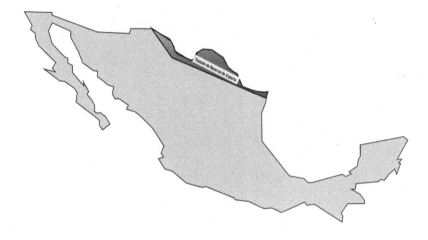